Blackwood Cave

Written by: Willie S.

Dedication

To the relentless explorers of the unknown, those who dare to venture into the darkness, and to the unwavering spirits who find strength in the face of unimaginable horror. This story is for you, for your courage, your resilience, and your unyielding belief in the power of human perseverance. It is a testament to the indomitable spirit that refuses to surrender, even when confronted with the deepest, darkest shadows of existence.

Table of Contents

Chapter 1: The Dare

The air in the basement hung heavy, thick with the scent of damp earth and something else... something indefinably ancient and unsettling. Dust motes danced in the single beam of Kiel's flashlight, illuminating a haphazard collection of discarded furniture and forgotten relics. Kiel, all swaggering confidence and ill-fitting jeans, held court, a self-appointed king surveying his ragtag kingdom of teenage rebels. Maya, perched precariously on a stack of old tires, nervously chewed her lip. Chloe, ever the pragmatist, cleaned a hunting knife, its gleam catching the light. Sam, hunched in a shadowed corner, fiddled with his headphones, his usual boisterous energy subdued. And Noah, the quiet observer, sketched furiously in a worn notebook, capturing the nervous energy that crackled in the air.

"So," Kiel began, his voice a low rumble that bounced off the concrete walls, "Blackwood Cave. Anyone got any objections?"

A tense silence followed. The only sound was the rhythmic drip, drip, drip of water from a leaky pipe overhead, each drop echoing the unspoken anxieties in the room. Blackwood Cave. The name itself whispered through the basement, a chilling breath on their necks.

Maya finally spoke, her voice barely a breath, "Kiel, you know the stories, right? People disappear in there. Never seen again."

Kiel scoffed, waving a dismissive hand. "Superstition. Old wives' tales. It's just a cave, Maya. A really big, really dark cave. But a cave nonetheless." His bravado, however, felt brittle, a thin veneer barely concealing the thrill of danger that fueled his reckless ambition.

Chloe, ever practical, chimed in, "There's something about it though. I mean, the stories... they're persistent. And they're not all just about getting lost. Some talk about... things." She hesitated, unable to articulate the deeper unease that the cave's legend inspired.

Sam, finally looking up from his headphones, added, "Yeah, I heard some weird stuff. About... sacrifices. Rituals. Crazy stuff." He shuddered, pulling his jacket tighter around him. The casual banter had evaporated, replaced by a palpable sense of unease.

Noah, his eyes dark and intense, closed his notebook. He'd been listening intently, his artistic sensibilities picking up on the undercurrent of fear. "The legends go back centuries. There are old maps, local folklore, even some... cryptic symbols etched into some of the old stones near the entrance. It's more than just a cave, Kiel. It's a place... saturated with something dark."

Kiel's forced nonchalance wavered. The whispered tales, the persistent legends, the chilling atmosphere in the basement—even he couldn't fully dismiss the unease that had settled over them. He hadn't expected this much resistance, this much palpable dread. He needed to reassert his dominance, to remind them that *he* was the one in charge, that *he* would lead them through this, into the heart of the darkness.

"Look," he said, his voice regaining its former authority, though a tremor betrayed his true feelings. "We're doing this. It's a dare, a challenge. And we're going to conquer it. We're going to prove all these stories are just... stories."

He offered a strained smile, but the others remained unconvinced. The fear, however, was not the fear of the unknown, but the fear of the known - a fear nurtured by generations of whispers, a fear woven into the very fabric of Blackwood Cave's legend. And as they began their descent into the maw of the earth, the whispers grew louder, a chilling chorus echoing the ancient darkness that awaited them.

The entrance to Blackwood Cave was a gaping maw in the side of a cliff face, shrouded in shadows that seemed to cling to the air itself. The initial excitement, the adrenaline rush of the dare, quickly faded as they entered the cave's suffocating embrace. The air was thick with dampness, the scent of decaying earth and something else... something faintly metallic and disturbingly sweet. The flashlights cut through the oppressive darkness, casting dancing shadows on the damp, slick walls. The silence was almost unbearable, punctuated only by the occasional drip of water, the distant rustling of unseen creatures, and the echoing thud of their own hearts pounding in their chests.

The narrow passageways pressed in on them, the walls closing in, their breath heavy in their lungs. The darkness seemed to press down, a physical weight that intensified their anxieties. Kiel, his bravado already beginning to fray, tried to maintain a façade of calm, but his voice wavered as he called out directions.

Hours passed, the claustrophobic setting slowly grinding down their initial enthusiasm. They were lost in a labyrinth of twisting tunnels, the air growing colder, the darkness more profound. They passed by formations that looked almost… organic, strangely curved and textured like gnarled bones or twisted intestines. The silence was punctuated by strange, unsettling sounds - a low groan echoing from the depths of the cave, the screech of unseen metal against stone, a faint whispering sound that seemed to emanate from the very rocks themselves.

Then they saw it.

A clearing, of sorts. A gruesome campsite, bathed in the sickly yellow light of their flashlights. A scene of unspeakable horror, etched into the very fabric of the cave. Scattered remains lay strewn across the ground – tattered clothing, broken bones, and pools of dried blood that stained the cave walls like morbid artwork. The air hung heavy with the metallic tang of blood, mixed with the nauseating sweetness of decay. A twisted, broken knife lay half-buried in the earth, its serrated edge glistening.

The teenagers stood frozen, their youthful bravado completely shattered. Their faces were ashen, their eyes wide with a horror that went beyond simple fear. This was not a legend; this was brutal, visceral reality. This was the chilling truth hidden within Blackwood Cave's dark heart. The whispers that had haunted them in the basement had materialized, transforming into a tangible, nightmarish truth. The silence, thick and suffocating, was broken only by their ragged gasps and the frantic beating of their hearts. This was not a game anymore; this was a desperate fight for survival. And the whispers... the whispers had just begun.

The oppressive silence of Blackwood Cave pressed in on them, a tangible entity that amplified the echoing thud of their own hearts. Kiel, his carefully constructed façade of bravado crumbling, fumbled with his flashlight, its beam jittering nervously across the damp, slick walls. The narrow passageway felt less like a natural formation and more like a constricting throat, squeezing the air from their lungs with each labored breath. Maya, her face pale beneath the weak light, clutched at Chloe's arm, her knuckles white. Chloe, ever the pragmatist, kept her hunting knife close, its familiar weight a small comfort in the overwhelming dread. Sam, his headphones long discarded, stared blankly ahead, his usual boisterous energy replaced by a stunned silence. Only Noah, the quiet observer, seemed to maintain a semblance of calm, his eyes scanning the walls with a grim fascination.

The air hung heavy, thick with the cloying scent of damp earth and something else... something indefinably ancient and unsettling, a metallic tang that hinted at something far more sinister than simple decay. Each drip of water from the cave's unseen ceiling resonated through the claustrophobic space, a slow, rhythmic pulse that echoed the frantic beat of their hearts. The darkness, absolute and profound, seemed to press in on them, a physical weight that intensified their growing anxieties.
It was a darkness that felt alive, sentient, watching them with unseen eyes.

As they moved deeper into the cave, the claustrophobia intensified. The passageways narrowed, forcing them to shuffle single file, their shoulders brushing against the cold, damp stone. The ground beneath their feet was uneven, slick with moisture, making each step a precarious dance on the edge of a fall. The constant threat of slipping, of tumbling into the unseen depths, added another layer of tension to their already frayed nerves. They passed by formations that resembled grotesque parodies of nature – twisted stalactites that looked like frozen claws, jagged stalagmites that resembled skeletal fingers reaching from the earth. The shapes shifted and changed in the flickering light, playing tricks on their eyes, fueling their growing sense of unease.

Strange sounds, muffled and distorted by the cave's acoustics, punctuated the unnerving silence. A low groan echoed from the distance, a sound that seemed to emanate from the very bowels of the earth. The metallic screech of stone on stone, like the grinding of tectonic plates, sent shivers down their spines. And then there was the whispering, a faint, sibilant sound that seemed to be carried on the damp air itself, a chorus of unseen voices murmuring secrets only the cave could understand. The whispers seemed to weave themselves into the fabric of the darkness, twisting around them, seeping into their minds, feeding their growing fear.

Kiel tried to maintain a semblance of control, his voice strained as he attempted to offer reassurance, but his words rang hollow even to his own ears. His bravado, the foundation of their reckless dare, had crumbled beneath the weight of the cave's oppressive atmosphere. His attempts at lighthearted banter fell flat, swallowed by the profound silence. The others mirrored his anxiety, their initial excitement replaced by a gnawing dread that tightened in their chests with each passing moment.

The darkness seemed to amplify their senses, making them hyper-aware of every sound, every shadow, every shift in the air. The rustling of unseen creatures, the drip, drip, drip of water, the whispers—all were amplified, magnified, transforming the ordinary into the terrifying. They felt exposed, vulnerable, adrift in a world where their senses could no longer be trusted.

The cave itself seemed to be breathing, its very structure pulsing with a life of its own. The walls seemed to close in, the air growing colder, denser, heavier with each step. They felt as if they were being watched, hunted, by something unseen, something ancient and malevolent that dwelled in the heart of this subterranean labyrinth. The darkness was no longer just a lack of light; it was an active force, a sentient entity that seemed determined to consume them.

They moved deeper into the cave's embrace, their anxiety escalating with each turn in the twisting tunnels. The passageways were becoming increasingly treacherous, strewn with loose rocks and treacherous crevices. The air grew noticeably colder, a sharp contrast to the dampness that clung to them like a shroud. The metallic tang in the air intensified, mingling with the earthy scent of decay, creating a nauseating cocktail that made their stomachs churn.

Then, a glimmer of something different caught their eye. A shaft of light, fainter than their own flashlights, illuminated a vast cavern ahead. Hesitantly, they moved towards it, their hearts pounding in their chests like war drums. As they entered the cavern, they saw it - a scene so horrific, so utterly brutal, that it ripped away the last vestiges of their youthful innocence.

It was a campsite, or what was left of one. Tattered remnants of clothing, scattered among broken branches and scattered stones, suggested a desperate struggle. Bones, bleached white by the cave's moisture, lay scattered on the ground, some still bearing fragments of flesh. Pools of dried blood stained the cave floor and walls, creating a morbid tapestry of horror. The air was heavy with the metallic tang of blood, mixed with the cloying sweetness of decay, a stench that clung to the back of their throats, choking them. In the center of the gruesome scene lay a twisted, broken hunting knife, its serrated edge glistening under their flashlight's weak beam.

The teenagers stood frozen, their faces pale, their eyes wide with a horror that transcended mere fear. This was not a legend; this was a gruesome reality, a testament to the dark secrets Blackwood Cave concealed. The whispered tales, the chilling legends, had materialized into a tangible nightmare. The whispered threats had become a horrifying scream echoing through the desolate cavern. This was not a dare anymore; it was a desperate fight for survival. And the true horror, they realized with a sickening dread, was only just beginning. The whispers, once a faint murmur, now echoed in their ears, a chilling chorus announcing their arrival in a realm of unspeakable terror. The cave had swallowed them whole, and it was about to unleash its full fury upon them.

The scene that unfolded before them was a grotesque parody of nature's beauty, a macabre tableau painted in shades of blood and bone. It wasn't just a campsite; it was a charnel house, a testament to unspeakable violence. The remnants of what had once been a fire pit were now a desolate circle of blackened earth, surrounded by a horrifying scatter of human remains. Bones, bleached white and brittle from the cave's dampness, lay scattered amongst the debris. Some were almost completely clean, picked clean by something, leaving behind only the stark, fragile architecture of the human skeleton. Others still clung to shreds of decaying flesh, a gruesome testament to the recency of the violence.

Tattered pieces of clothing, ripped and stained crimson, clung to jagged rocks and protruded from beneath scattered stones. A torn backpack lay open, its contents spilled across the ground—a half-eaten energy bar, a crumpled map, and a child's drawing of a brightly colored bird, now stained with a dark, viscous substance that could only be blood. The juxtaposition of the innocent child's drawing with the surrounding horror was particularly jarring, a brutal reminder of the innocence brutally extinguished in this desolate place.

Pools of dried blood, dark and glistening even in the dim light, stained the cave floor and walls. The blood had seeped into the porous stone, leaving behind a morbid tapestry of horror, a grim testament to the carnage that had taken place. It wasn't just a spattering; it was a pervasive stain, as if the very stones themselves had drunk deeply of the victims' lifeblood. The metallic tang in the air, which had already been unsettling, now intensified, overwhelming them with its nauseating pungency. It was the smell of death, raw and undeniable, a smell that clung to the back of their throats, making their stomachs churn.

The silence that had previously felt oppressive now felt deafening, a void punctuated only by the frantic thumping of their own hearts. The air hung heavy, thick with the cloying sweetness of decay mingling with the acrid stench of blood, creating a sickening cocktail that threatened to overwhelm their senses. They stood frozen, petrified, unable to tear their gaze away from the gruesome spectacle before them. Their initial bravado, the reckless confidence that had fueled their dare, evaporated like mist in the morning sun, leaving behind only a cold, paralyzing fear.

Kiel, his face ashen, stumbled back, his flashlight beam trembling in his shaking hand. He let out a low groan, a sound choked with horror and disbelief. Maya, her eyes wide with terror, clutched at Chloe's arm, her grip tight enough to leave bruises. Chloe, her usually calm demeanor shattered, stared at the scene with a mixture of shock and revulsion. Her hunting knife, previously a source of comfort, felt inadequate, a pathetic weapon against the unseen horror that had perpetrated this massacre. Sam, his face a mask of disbelief, stood frozen, his usual boisterous energy completely extinguished. Only Noah, the quiet observer, maintained a semblance of composure, his eyes scanning the scene with a grim, almost clinical detachment.

The gruesome details of the massacre were too horrifying to comprehend fully. A shattered skull lay near a mangled torso, its ribs splayed like broken branches. A severed arm, its hand still clutching a piece of ragged cloth, lay several feet away from the rest of the body. The scene suggested a frenzied attack, a brutal struggle for survival that had ended in horrific defeat. The victims had clearly suffered immensely, their final moments etched into the grim landscape of the cave.

The realization that this was not a legend, not a fanciful story told to frighten children, but a brutal reality, sunk in with a chilling weight. The whispered tales of Blackwood Cave were not just stories; they were warnings. The cave was not merely a geological formation; it was a tomb, a repository of unspeakable horrors. And they, in their reckless youthful folly, had stumbled into its heart.

The hunting knife, lying near the center of the carnage, was a particularly disturbing detail. It was a standard hunting knife, the kind frequently used by campers and hikers. But this knife was twisted, broken, its once-sharp blade bent and serrated, suggesting a ferocious struggle. The gruesome scene was not simply a random act of violence; it was a calculated, brutal slaughter, executed with chilling precision. The scattered remains hinted at a deliberate, systematic dismantling of the victims. The scene was less a massacre and more a ritualistic sacrifice, a gruesome offering to some unseen, malevolent entity that dwelled in the heart of Blackwood Cave.

As the initial shock began to wear off, a gnawing dread replaced the paralyzing fear. They were not simply intruders in a gruesome scene; they were targets. Whatever had perpetrated this massacre, whatever evil lurked in the shadows of Blackwood Cave, was aware of their presence. The whispers, which had previously been a faint, almost imperceptible sound, now seemed to echo in their ears, a chilling chorus announcing their arrival, confirming their role as the next victims in this subterranean horror.

The darkness of the cave, which had already felt oppressive, now seemed to amplify their fear, turning it into a suffocating blanket of dread. Every shadow seemed to writhe, every sound magnified into a terrifying whisper. The dripping water, the rustling in the unseen depths, the very silence itself, all seemed to carry a sense of foreboding, a palpable feeling that they were being watched, hunted, by something unseen and implacable.

Kiel attempted to speak, to break the suffocating silence, but his voice was little more than a croak. His carefully constructed façade of bravado had crumbled completely. His words were hollow, insignificant against the overwhelming horror of their situation. The others echoed his feelings; their youthful exuberance had been replaced by a primal fear, a deep-seated terror that rooted them to the spot, leaving them helpless against the impending threat. The cave had swallowed them whole, and now it was about to unleash its full fury upon them.

The air grew colder, the dampness intensifying the chill that seeped into their bones. The metallic scent of blood mixed with the earthy smell of decay, creating a nauseating cocktail that made their heads spin. They felt vulnerable, exposed, as if the very walls of the cave were closing in, preparing to crush them. Their initial sense of awe and wonder at the cave's natural beauty had been utterly obliterated, replaced by a profound and chilling dread. This was no ordinary cave; it was a portal to hell, a place where innocence was extinguished, and survival was a desperate gamble.

The whispers intensified, growing louder, more insistent. They seemed to weave themselves into the fabric of the darkness, twisting around them, seeping into their minds, amplifying their growing sense of despair. They were not just sounds; they were voices, a chilling chorus of unseen entities, mocking their helplessness, heralding their impending doom. The cave, once an exciting challenge, had become their tomb, and they were only just beginning to understand the depths of its malevolent power. Their reckless dare had transformed into a desperate fight for survival, a battle against an unseen enemy in a claustrophobic labyrinth of death. The horror, they realized with a sickening dread, had only just begun.

A sudden tremor ran through the ground, a low rumble that vibrated through their bones, silencing even the whispers. The air grew colder, a chilling wave washing over them, making their teeth chatter. Then, a movement. A subtle shift in the shadows, a ripple in the darkness that sent a fresh wave of icy dread through their hearts. It wasn't the drip of water, nor the usual rustle of unseen creatures; this was different, deliberate, predatory.

Kiel, his breath fogging in the frigid air, pointed his flashlight towards the source of the disturbance. The beam snagged on something large, something...wrong. It was barely visible at first, a hulking silhouette against the inky blackness, but as their eyes adjusted, the horrifying truth became starkly clear.

Emerging from the shadows was a creature that defied description, a grotesque parody of life itself. It was impossibly large, easily seven or eight feet tall, its form a twisted amalgamation of animal and machine. Its body seemed to be a grotesque mockery of a canine form, its limbs elongated and distorted, its musculature bulging and unnatural. Thick, leathery skin, a patchwork of scars and seams, covered its frame, and patches of what looked like metallic plating were fused to its flesh. Its fur, where fur should have been, was a tangled mess of matted black, interspersed with strands of what appeared to be bioluminescent fibers, glowing with an eerie, internal light.

Two eyes, blazing with malevolent intelligence, glowed from within its skull. They weren't the eyes of an animal; they were cold, calculating, predatory. They burned with an unnatural luminescence, a chilling green that seemed to pierce the darkness and fix upon them with unnerving intensity. The eyes alone spoke volumes of the creature's nature – it wasn't just a beast; it was a predator, a hunter, and they were its prey.

Its teeth, far too large for its jaws, were bared in a silent snarl, glinting wickedly in the beam of Kiel's flashlight. They were needle-sharp, razor-edged, and far too numerous, hinting at a horrific capacity for tearing and rending flesh. Its claws, equally monstrous, were long, curved, and razor-sharp, tipped with a substance that shimmered with an oily sheen, undoubtedly some kind of genetically-engineered toxin. The creature's presence exuded a palpable sense of menace, an aura of raw, untamed power. This wasn't a creature born of nature; it was something artificial, something horrifyingly, terrifyingly unnatural.

A low growl emanated from deep within its chest, a sound that resonated with a guttural, mechanical quality, a blend of animalistic rage and chilling technological precision. The sound sent a fresh wave of terror through the teenagers, instantly shattering any remaining vestiges of their bravado. Their initial fear had morphed into a paralyzing dread, a primal instinct urging them to flee.

Before any of them could react, the creature lunged. Its movement was surprisingly swift, a blur of distorted limbs and razor-sharp claws. It struck with the speed and ferocity of a striking cobra, its massive form somehow managing to move with both brutal strength and surprising agility.

Sam, closest to the creature's path, was caught completely off guard. The creature's claws raked across his side, tearing through his jacket and flesh with sickening ease. A scream, raw and filled with agonizing pain, ripped from Sam's lips. He crumpled to the ground, clutching his bleeding wound. Blood welled up between his fingers, staining the cave floor a horrifying crimson.

The creature, momentarily distracted, paused, its glowing eyes fixing on Sam's fallen form. It let out a short, guttural growl, a sound that seemed to echo the creature's satisfaction, before turning its attention back to the remaining teenagers. The sight of Sam's wound, his pale face contorted in pain, ignited a fresh wave of panic within the group.

Their initial attempt at escape was a chaotic scramble. They stumbled backward, tripping over rocks and debris, their movements clumsy and uncoordinated in their terror. Kiel, his flashlight beam shaking uncontrollably, tried to shield Sam with his own body. Maya and Chloe, their faces pale with fear, desperately scrambled to find a safe place. Noah, despite his initial composure, was visibly shaken, his face grim and determined.

The creature, however, was relentless. It moved with terrifying speed and precision through the narrow tunnels of the cave, its powerful limbs effortlessly clearing obstacles that would have slowed, or even stopped, a normal human. Its movements were efficient, almost surgical in their precision. Its glowing eyes followed their every move, tracking their every attempt to flee.

Their first escape attempt ended badly. They found themselves cornered in a small alcove, a dead end with no clear path of escape. The creature blocked the only exit, its menacing form casting a long shadow that stretched the length of the narrow passage. Its low growl pulsed through the air, a chilling promise of the violence to come. The teenagers pressed themselves against the damp cave wall, their breaths catching in their throats, as they faced their first brutal encounter with the horrors of Blackwood Cave, fully aware that their reckless dare had just transformed into a desperate fight for survival against an enemy far more terrifying and relentless than they could have ever imagined. The initial fear was replaced by a raw, primal terror. Their youthful bravado had been crushed under the weight of a terrifying reality. This was no longer a game, this was a fight for survival, and the odds were stacked heavily against them.

The air grew heavy with the stench of fear and blood, the metallic tang of Sam's injury mingling with the earthy smell of decay. The ground beneath their feet seemed to tremble with each guttural growl emanating from the monstrous creature blocking their escape. Every shadow seemed to writhe, every drip of water sounded like a death knell. Kiel, still desperately trying to protect Sam, felt the cold metal of the creature's claws graze his arm. The pain was sharp, quick, but enough to send a fresh surge of adrenaline and terror coursing through him.

Maya, her eyes wide with terror, clutched at Chloe, her knuckles white. Chloe, usually so resourceful, could only stare, her face pale and shocked. Noah, the quiet one, was now the anchor of their desperate situation, his eyes calculating, assessing their precarious position. He whispered a plan, a desperate gamble that might just buy them a few more precious moments. The whispered words were swallowed by the vastness of the cave, almost inaudible above the animalistic growl that seemed to vibrate the very stones of the cavern around them. The fight for survival had begun in earnest, a brutal, desperate struggle against the horrors of Blackwood Cave, and it was clear that their initial encounter was merely a prelude to the greater horrors that lay ahead.

The creature advanced, its movements slow and deliberate, each step sending a fresh wave of icy fear through the group. Its glowing eyes never left them, focusing in turn on each of their faces, assessing their fear, their vulnerability. It moved with the chilling efficiency of a predator, its massive form a terrifying reminder of their own insignificance in the face of this genetically engineered horror. The darkness of the cave seemed to amplify the creature's menace, turning it into a tangible force that pressed against them, threatening to suffocate them, to crush them.

The silence between them was thick, heavy, pregnant with the expectation of violence. The only sound was the labored breathing of the teenagers and the low growl that seemed to vibrate from the creature's chest, a chilling symphony of impending doom. The metallic tang of blood filled their nostrils, a constant reminder of Sam's injury and the imminent threat of their own demise. Their escape route was

blocked, their situation desperate. Their initial encounter with the
genetically-engineered creature had been a brutal lesson in the unforgiving reality of Blackwood Cave, a chilling introduction to the horrors that lay ahead. Their fight for survival had begun. The game was over. Now it was a fight for their lives, a terrifying, desperate race against an enemy far more terrifying and powerful than they could ever have imagined. The adventure had turned into a nightmare, and the horrors of Blackwood Cave were only just beginning to reveal their true, terrifying depths.

The creature lunged again, its claws tearing through the air where Kiel had been a moment before. Kiel rolled, narrowly avoiding the attack, the screech of metal against rock echoing in the confined space. He scrambled to his feet, his heart hammering against his ribs, adrenaline pumping through his veins. The air tasted of blood and fear. Sam's whimpers were barely audible above the pounding of their own hearts and the monstrous growls of their pursuer.

Their escape was a chaotic ballet of stumbling feet and panicked breaths, a desperate scramble through a labyrinth of twisting tunnels. The creature, a relentless shadow, pursued them through the maze, its guttural growls echoing off the damp, uneven walls, amplifying the terror that clawed at their throats. The flashlight beams, dancing wildly, cast fleeting glimpses of the relentless beast as it pursued them, its monstrous form an ever-present nightmare in the darkness. The sensory overload was almost unbearable – the slick, damp rock under their feet, the chilling air clinging to their skin, the stench of blood and decay, the constant, terrifying sound of their pursuer's relentless pursuit.

They stumbled through a narrow passage, the walls closing in on them, the darkness pressing against their backs. Maya, her face pale and streaked with grime, tripped, falling heavily onto the cold, damp ground. Chloe reached out, pulling her to her feet, her hand gripping Maya's arm with desperate strength. The sound of the creature's approach sent another wave of panic through them, a cold hand of terror gripping their hearts.

Noah, ever the strategist, scanned their surroundings, his eyes darting from one passage to another, his mind racing to find a way out. He saw it – a small, almost invisible opening in the rock face, hidden behind a curtain of dripping water. It was a desperate gamble, but it was their only hope. He pointed it out to the others, his voice a strained whisper swallowed by the echoing growls of the creature.

With a shared nod, they pressed on, crawling through the narrow, water-slick crevice. The opening was barely wide enough for them to squeeze through, forcing them to inch forward, their bodies scraping against the rough rock. The air grew thicker, the silence more intense, as they were enveloped in a suffocating darkness, only broken by the occasional drip of water.

They emerged into a larger chamber, a vast, echoing cavern. The ground was uneven, littered with rocks and debris. In the distance, they could hear the creature's growls, its pursuit echoing through the cavern, indicating that their escape had not been entirely successful. The growls were closer now, sending another surge of fear through them. The creature had found them.

As they dashed across the uneven terrain, a loose rock shifted under Kiel's foot, sending him tumbling. He landed heavily, his ankle twisting painfully under him. A cry of pain escaped his lips, but he bit it back, knowing that any sound would give their position away. The pain was agonizing, but the knowledge that their pursuer was near fueled his resolve to escape.

The creature was upon them. The flashlights revealed its monstrous form once again, a grotesque parody of life itself, its eyes glowing with a chilling green light as it lunged, claws extended. Chloe reacted instantly, pushing Kiel behind her, shielding him from the deadly claws that ripped through the air where she had been a moment before. The creature's claws grazed her arm, tearing through her jacket, leaving a deep gash that bled freely.

She screamed, the sound swallowed by the vastness of the cavern, a desperate cry of pain and fear. The creature paused, its glowing eyes fixated on Chloe's wound, its low growl echoing around them. The growl was a sound of satisfaction, a chilling acknowledgment of its victory. Then, with a swift movement, it turned and disappeared back into the darkness, its pursuit temporarily halted.

They huddled together, their breaths ragged and shallow. Kiel's ankle throbbed with pain, Chloe's arm bled profusely, and the fear gnawed at their insides. They had escaped, for now, but their wounds were both physical and mental. The realization that their pursuer was still out there, lurking in the shadows, kept them on edge, a constant threat in the suffocating darkness of Blackwood Cave. The air was thick with the smell of blood, fear, and the pungent scent of decay.

Their escape continued to be fraught with peril. The passageways were a confusing maze, every turn threatening to lead them back to the creature. The walls were slick with moisture, making their footing precarious. They had to rely on each other, their movements coordinated despite their fear and exhaustion. Every shadow seemed to writhe, every sound to amplify their terror.

They stumbled through more tunnels, their bodies battered and bruised, their minds reeling from the relentless pursuit. The chaos was overwhelming, a sensory overload of darkness, noise, and the constant, palpable threat of death. Each sound, every rustle of the air, sent shivers down their spines, amplifying their fear and emphasizing their vulnerability.

They found themselves in another cavern, even larger than the last, the air thick with a strange, musty odor. In the distance, they heard the sound of running water, a sound that offered a sliver of hope amidst the overwhelming terror. The sound of the creature's approach was faint now, growing fainter as they continued to traverse the cave system. However, the fear lingered, a heavy shroud wrapping around them.

Their escape route was a path fraught with danger, a terrifying journey through a dark, unforgiving labyrinth. Every footstep was a gamble, every turn a potential death sentence. The constant threat of the creature's return hung heavy in the air, a tangible pressure that threatened to suffocate them. The chase had pushed them to the edge of their endurance, their physical and mental strength tested to the absolute limit. They were battered, bruised, bleeding, and terrified, but still alive. Yet, the horrors of Blackwood Cave had only just begun to reveal themselves, and they knew, deep down, that their ordeal was far from over. The fight for survival was far from over, and the secrets hidden within Blackwood Cave held the promise of even greater terrors. Their reckless dare had turned into a fight for their very lives, a brutal battle against a terrifying enemy and the merciless depths of the Blackwood Cave. The escape was a testament to their courage and their desperate will to survive, but the nightmare was far from over.

Chapter 2: The Hunt

The small cavern offered a meager respite, its damp walls a cold comfort against the gnawing fear that still clung to them like a shroud. The air hung heavy, thick with the metallic tang of blood and the earthy scent of the cave itself. Kiel, despite the agonizing pain lancing through his twisted ankle, found a precarious perch on a relatively flat rock, his breathing ragged but controlled. He was the oldest, the de facto leader, and even in this desperate situation, a semblance of order was paramount.

Chloe, her face pale and drawn, sat beside him, her arm cradled against her chest. The gash was deep, the blood now a dark, sticky stain spreading across her jacket. The fabric was torn, revealing ragged flesh beneath, a stark reminder of the creature's terrifying claws. She shivered, not just from the cold, but from the lingering adrenaline, the fear that still pulsed in her veins.

Maya, her face streaked with dirt and tears, tended to a smaller cut on her leg, her hands trembling as she applied makeshift pressure. Sam, usually the most boisterous of the group, sat huddled against the wall, his eyes wide and unfocused, his body shaking with silent sobs. The ordeal had stripped away their bravado, revealing the raw vulnerability beneath. They were no longer carefree teenagers, but battered survivors, clinging to the fragile thread of hope.

Kiel, attempting to maintain a semblance of composure, examined their injuries. His own ankle was grotesquely swollen, the throbbing pain a constant reminder of his limitations. He knew they were lucky to be alive, but the escape had come at a steep price. They were wounded, both physically and emotionally. The initial adrenaline-fueled escape had been replaced by a chilling reality: they were trapped, injured, and hunted in the heart of Blackwood Cave.

"We need to assess," Kiel said, his voice hoarse, "Chloe, your arm needs cleaning.

Maya, can you help me splint my ankle? Sam...Sam, breathe. We're safe... for now."

His words were intended to reassure, but even he doubted their truth. The silence in the cavern, punctuated only by the drip, drip, drip of water, was far more terrifying than the creature's growls. The silence was a stark reminder of their isolation, their vulnerability in the face of the unknown. The creature could return at any moment.

The task of cleaning Chloe's wound was brutal. They had nothing but a torn piece of their shirts and some damp cave mud to try to cleanse the wound. Chloe winced with every touch, the pain a fresh wave of agony. The mud served as a clumsy antiseptic, doing little to quell the seeping blood. Kiel bound the wound tightly with the fabric, his movements careful but swift. He couldn't afford any further delay. The grim reality of their situation was a heavy weight on their shoulders, a suffocating blanket of despair.

Maya, despite her own injuries, worked diligently to fashion a splint for Kiel's ankle using broken branches and their remaining backpacks. Her hands worked with a grim determination, her silence a testament to the intensity of the moment. The splint was crude, but it would offer some support. The pain was intense for Kiel, but his focus was razor-sharp, his resolve tempered by the cold, hard realities of their dire situation.

The silence was broken only by the sounds of their labored breaths and the occasional pained groan. The atmosphere in the small cavern was thick with the fear and exhaustion. They huddled together, their bodies trembling from a combination of cold, fear, and exhaustion, each relying on the others for both physical and emotional support. They were bound by a shared trauma, a common enemy, and a desperate hope for survival.

As the initial shock began to wear off, the full extent of their situation began to sink in. Their once jovial camaraderie was strained, replaced by a grim determination fueled by a potent mix of fear and adrenaline. Each of them was wounded, both physically and emotionally, the escape from the creature leaving its mark in different ways. Their youthful bravado had been stripped away, replaced by a hard-won awareness of their own fragility.

The darkness pressed in on them, amplifying their fears. Every shadow seemed to writhe, every drip of water a potential footstep, every rustle a sign of the beast's return. Their exhaustion was palpable, a physical weight threatening to drag them down into the depths of despair. The weight of their situation, the bleak reality of their predicament, was almost unbearable.

Kiel, though injured, forced himself to remain the voice of reason. He knew that panic would be their undoing. He forced himself to think, to strategize, to plan their next move. But even his sharp mind struggled to pierce the suffocating darkness of their predicament. The escape had been miraculous, a stroke of luck, but they knew that more challenges lay ahead. The depths of Blackwood Cave still held untold dangers, and their journey was far from over.

The physical wounds were raw and painful, but the psychological scars were just beginning to form. The memory of the creature's terrifying presence, its brutal attack, its relentless pursuit – these images were burned into their minds, haunting them in the darkness of the cavern. The encounter had stripped them of their innocence, replaced it with a chilling understanding of their own vulnerability and the brutal reality of survival in the face of unimaginable terror.

Kiel's voice was low and strained when he finally broke the silence. "We need to move," he whispered. "We can't stay here. We need to find another way out, somewhere safer. A place to rest and tend our wounds properly." But the word 'safer' felt almost ludicrous, a mere whisper of hope against the vast, terrifying reality of their situation. The fear that had gripped them earlier still lingered, a constant, palpable threat amidst the dripping silence of Blackwood Cave. Their ordeal had just begun. The wounds, both physical and emotional, were a grim reminder of the horrors they had faced, and the greater terrors that undoubtedly awaited them deeper within the labyrinthine depths of Blackwood Cave. The hunt was far from over. The cave itself, it seemed, was a living entity, a hungry predator waiting to devour them.

Kiel's words, though barely a breath, ignited a spark of defiance in the chilling silence. The shared fear, while still a palpable presence, now warred with a nascent determination. They couldn't stay. They couldn't simply wait for the creature to return. Survival demanded action, a desperate gamble against the overwhelming odds.

"We need weapons," Maya stated, her voice surprisingly firm, despite the tremor in her hands. She gestured towards the scattered debris of the cave – broken rocks, jagged shards of stone, even splinters of wood from the collapsed support beam near their previous campsite.

Kiel, despite the agony in his ankle, nodded. "Anything we can use. Sharpen the edges if possible." He indicated a larger, oddly shaped rock, its surface surprisingly smooth except for a sharp, knife-like edge. "We'll use this as a primary weapon. Chloe, you're quickest. You'll be the lookout."

The task was grim, a macabre undertaking in the damp, blood-soaked cavern. They worked in near silence, the only sounds the scraping of stone against stone, the rhythmic thud of Maya's makeshift hammer striking a sharp rock against another to create a crude spear point, and the occasional hiss of pain as someone's injured hand slipped. Sam, still shaken, found a measure of focus in this shared effort, his trembling hands chipping away at a piece of rock to create a sharper edge.

Chloe, despite the throbbing pain in her arm, took her position on a raised ledge overlooking the narrow passage they'd escaped through. Her eyes, wide and watchful, scanned the darkness, her every nerve ending on high alert. The adrenaline, the terrifying memory of their near-death experience, fueled a frantic vigilance. Each drip of water, each rustle in the darkness, sent jolts of fear through her.

The makeshift weapons were rudimentary at best —
sharpened rocks, pointed splinters of wood, crude clubs
fashioned from sturdy branches. But in their desperate
situation, they were all they had. Kiel tested the sharpness of
his chosen weapon, the rock's edge biting into his palm,
drawing a bead of blood. The sting was a painful reminder of
the stakes involved, the grim reality of their fight for survival.

Their plan was as desperate as their circumstances. They
would use the cave's natural formations to their advantage,
navigating the narrow passageways, using the rocks and the
tight spaces to their benefit, hoping to either lose their
pursuer or create opportunities to ambush it. It was a high-
risk strategy, one that depended on their injured bodies and
frayed nerves holding up. The creature was faster, stronger,
and far more deadly than them; the mere hope of evasion
rested on a blend of ingenuity and luck.

Kiel, using his newly splinted ankle as a guide, plotted their
route. They would move slowly, deliberately, using the
shadows and the twists and turns of the tunnels to mask
their movements. He spoke in hushed whispers, instructing
each of them on their roles. He recognized the growing
fatigue in their voices and knew they needed to act quickly
before darkness truly enveloped them in a suffocating
blanket of fear and exhaustion.

As they began to move, the silence of the cavern seemed to
press upon them, amplifying every rustle, every drip of water
into a deafening roar. Each shadow seemed to shift and
writhe, every unseen crevice a potential hiding place for the
creature. Chloe's sharp eyes darted through the darkness.
She remained constantly vigilant, a silent guardian against

the relentless threat. Her whispered warnings of distant sounds—a creak of rock, a slight tremor in the earth— kept their hearts pounding in a rhythm that echoed the drip, drip, drip of the endless flow of subterranean water.

The journey was agonizing. Kiel, despite the makeshift splint, found every step a fresh wave of pain. Chloe's injured arm screamed with each movement. Maya, exhausted and bruised, struggled to keep up. Sam, his trauma still clearly visible in his wide, haunted eyes, moved with a hesitant, fragile step. Yet, they pressed on, driven by a primal will to survive, a desperate determination to reach safety, to escape the relentless threat that lurked in the shadows.

Their strategy was simple, yet dangerous. They planned to reach a wider cavern they had seen earlier, a large, open space with several smaller tunnels branching off. The hope was to confuse their pursuer, to lose it in the labyrinthine network of tunnels. However, this cavern presented its own dangers. It was much more exposed, and their fragile weapons provided little protection against a swift, deadly attack.

At one point, a loose rock dislodged beneath Maya's foot, sending a cascade of smaller rocks tumbling through the silence. The sound echoed through the cavern, loud and sharp enough to trigger a surge of icy dread. They froze, listening intently, their hearts leaping into their throats. The silence that followed was filled with tension, thick and suffocating. Their breath came in ragged gasps as they waited for a response from their unseen hunter. The moment stretched endlessly, each tick of time a hammer blow to their already frayed nerves.

The silence remained unbroken. Relief washed over them, a fragile reprieve in the overwhelming terror. They continued their journey, moving with increased caution and growing desperation. They navigated through a series of narrow passageways, clinging to the damp, cold walls, the rough surfaces scraping against their already injured bodies. Every step brought its own trial, every shadow a potential threat.

They reached the wider cavern, and as Kiel had predicted, the space was vast and disorienting. The multiplicity of tunnels created an unsettling maze, the shadows seeming to twist and writhe with an unnerving, almost sentient quality. The vastness of the cavern, however, afforded them a chance to conceal themselves, to utilize the shadows and the labyrinthine structure to their advantage. They had been forced to take desperate measures to evade their pursuer, relying on skill and luck to survive in the bowels of the earth. Their fate still remained uncertain, hanging precariously in the balance, but at least they had managed to push through the tunnel of despair and make it to the next stage of their harrowing escape. But the hunt was far from over. The heart of Blackwood Cave still beat with a terrifying pulse of unknown horrors.

The wider cavern offered a deceptive sense of relief. The sheer scale of the space, a vast echoing expanse compared to the claustrophobic tunnels they'd just traversed, initially felt like a victory. But the illusion shattered quickly. The multiplicity of tunnels branching off in every direction created a disorienting maze, a labyrinth of shadows that seemed to writhe and shift, mocking their attempts at escape. The darkness here was deeper, more absolute, swallowing the meager light from Kiel's makeshift torch.

They pressed themselves against a cold, damp wall, their ragged breaths mingling with the chilling dampness of the cave. The air hung heavy, thick with the scent of damp earth and something else... something metallic and sickeningly sweet, a lingering echo of the carnage they'd witnessed. Kiel, his face pale in the weak light, checked their makeshift weapons. The sharpened rocks, the crude spears – pathetically inadequate against the relentless, inhuman strength of their pursuer.

A low growl reverberated through the cavern, a sound that seemed to vibrate in their bones, shaking them to the core. It was closer than before, and the air thrummed with a palpable sense of menace. Chloe, her eyes wide with terror, hissed a warning. "It's here," she whispered, her voice barely audible above the pounding of their hearts.

Panic threatened to engulf them, a suffocating wave threatening to drown their fragile hope. But Kiel, drawing on some inner reservoir of strength, forced himself to remain calm. "Stay quiet," he rasped, his voice strained. "We need to move. Now."

They moved like shadows themselves, their bodies pressed close to the cold, unforgiving rock face. Kiel led the way, his injured ankle throbbing with each painful step, yet his movements were surprisingly swift, a testament to his desperate determination. He chose the narrowest passage, a fissure in the rock face barely wide enough for one person to squeeze through. It was a risky move, a gamble that the creature wouldn't be able to follow, but it was their only hope.

The passage was a torturous crawl, a claustrophobic journey through darkness and dampness. The rough rock scraped against their skin, tearing at their already injured bodies. They pushed forward, driven by an unwavering instinct for survival. At one point, Kiel had to pull Maya through, his hands gripping her arms, his strength strained to the limit. They continued to move with slow caution and an increasingly desperate urgency.

Suddenly, a tremor ran through the earth, a deep, guttural rumble that shook the very foundations of the cavern. Rocks tumbled down from the ceiling, narrowly missing them. They huddled together, their bodies pressed close, shielding each other from the falling debris. The growl echoed again, closer now, menacingly close. It was right outside the narrow passage, its presence a palpable threat.

They held their breath, listening, praying. The creature seemed to be sniffing at the entrance, its hot breath almost tangible on their skin. It pawed at the rocks, probing, searching. Kiel gripped his crude weapon, his knuckles white with tension. He felt the icy grip of fear, but it was a fear tempered by a fierce determination to fight. They couldn't afford to be caught.

After what seemed like an eternity, the growls subsided. The tremor ceased. Silence, thick and heavy, descended upon them once more. They waited, their hearts pounding, uncertain whether the danger had passed or merely shifted. Kiel felt the tension in the group.

Slowly, cautiously, they began to move again, their bodies tense, their senses on high alert. They crawled for what seemed like miles, their journey a painful, agonizing struggle. The air grew thinner, the darkness more oppressive. Each step was a victory, each breath a precious gift.

Finally, they emerged into a slightly larger cavern, a small respite in their desperate flight. Kiel checked their surroundings, searching for any sign of their pursuer, for any indication of where they were. He found a small crevice, a narrow crack in the wall where they could huddle and momentarily rest, a much needed rest in the midst of the escape.

They collapsed, exhausted, bruised, their bodies aching, their spirits broken. The relief was brief, however, soon replaced by a growing sense of dread. They had escaped, at least for now. But they knew, deep down, that this was only a temporary reprieve, a fleeting moment of safety in a much larger, more terrifying game. The hunt was far from over. Blackwood Cave held its secrets close, and those secrets were far more dangerous than any of them could have imagined.

The silence was punctuated by the drip, drip, drip of water, a constant, rhythmic reminder of their precarious situation. The darkness pressed in on them, amplifying every sound, every shadow, into a symphony of fear. Kiel looked at his companions; Maya's face was streaked with grime and tears, Sam was trembling uncontrollably, and Chloe's injured arm was now bleeding afresh. Yet, in their shared exhaustion and fear, there was a flicker of resilience, a tenacious refusal to give up.

They rested for a few short minutes, the silence broken only by their ragged breathing and the occasional whimper of pain. Kiel knew they couldn't stay. The creature could return at any moment. They needed to keep moving, to find a way out, to escape the horrors that lurked within the depths of Blackwood Cave.

With renewed determination, they pressed on, their meager weapons clutched tightly in their hands. Their journey continued through a network of twisting tunnels, each turn bringing a new challenge, each shadow a potential threat. They navigated treacherous rockfalls, clambered over slippery ledges, and squeezed through impossibly narrow passages. Their bodies were battered, their spirits bruised, but their will to survive remained unbroken. The escape was a brutal, harrowing ordeal, a desperate fight against the odds. They were running out of time and running out of hope, but they had no intention of giving up, their survival depended on the collective fight against the horrors that were stalking them.

At one point, a section of the tunnel collapsed ahead of them, blocking their path. Kiel, using his ingenuity, found a narrow side passage that led to a higher level. It was a perilous climb, fraught with danger, but it offered a chance to circumvent the obstruction. The climb was strenuous, the rock face slick and unstable, their exhaustion pushing them to their limits, but they persevered, their survival instinct fueling them to reach the higher level safely, though their injuries were now worse.

From their vantage point, they saw a glimmer of hope – a shaft of light penetrating the darkness. It was a sign of the outside world, a promise of escape. They pressed on towards it, pushing their weary bodies to the limit. Finally, after what seemed like an eternity, they reached the opening and found themselves outside Blackwood Cave, the sun on their faces feeling almost unbearably bright after hours in the oppressive darkness.

But their escape was far from over. The outside world was not the safe haven they had envisioned, and the experience within Blackwood Cave had changed them forever, scarred both physically and psychologically. The horrors they'd encountered, the brutal fight for survival, had left an indelible mark on their minds and bodies. Their innocence was gone. They had become survivors, and their journey had just begun. The chilling experience of the hunt within Blackwood Cave was just a prelude to the larger horrors waiting for them, a reality far more terrifying than the cave itself.

The blinding sunlight, after the suffocating darkness of Blackwood Cave, felt almost painful. They stumbled out, blinking against the intensity, their bodies aching, their minds reeling. The escape had been brutal, a relentless, agonizing struggle against the odds. Each one of them bore the physical scars – deep gashes, broken bones, and the ever-present throbbing of their injuries – but the unseen wounds, the psychological scars, were far deeper, far more insidious.

They collapsed onto the mossy ground outside the cave's mouth, their ragged breaths mingling with the scent of pine and damp earth. Silence descended, a fragile truce after the cacophony of fear that had pursued them through the labyrinthine tunnels. The silence, however, was far more terrifying than the growls and tremors that had haunted their flight. It was a silence heavy with the weight of their ordeal, a silence punctuated only by the sobs that wracked Maya's body.

Sam, his face pale and drawn, stared blankly at the sky, his eyes reflecting the shock and trauma of what they had endured. Chloe, her arm still bleeding, leaned against Kiel, her body trembling uncontrollably. Kiel himself felt the tremors of exhaustion and grief, a bone-deep fatigue that threatened to consume him. He looked at his friends, their faces etched with the horrifying reality of their shared experience, each one a living testament to the brutality of the hunt. Their youthful bravado was gone, replaced by a haunting emptiness.

Kiel's eyes fell upon a crumpled figure lying a few feet away from the others; it was Ben. His body was still, his chest barely rising and falling, the signs of life faint. The weight of the loss crashed over Kiel in a tidal wave, a grief so sharp it stole his breath. Ben's sacrifice, his selfless act of self-sacrifice, had been their only escape. He had held back the monstrous creature, giving the others the crucial seconds they needed to scramble to safety.

The memories of Ben's final moments clawed at Kiel's mind. The desperate struggle, the guttural growls, Ben's choked cries, the sickening crunch of bone and the creature's furious rage before it finally disappeared into the darkness of the cave, its hunger still unsatisfied. The image was seared onto Kiel's consciousness, a horrific tableau that would haunt his nightmares forever.

A wave of nausea washed over him, the metallic tang of blood heavy in the air. He knelt beside Ben, checking for a pulse, his heart sinking with each passing second. There was nothing. Ben was gone. The reality of their loss crashed over them like a monstrous wave, drowning them in a sea of grief.

Maya's sobs intensified, a raw, primal expression of anguish that ripped through the fragile silence. Sam, his body still shaking, buried his face in his hands, his silent grief even more heartbreaking than Maya's. Chloe simply stared at Ben's lifeless form, her face a mask of disbelief and despair. Their faces, streaked with grime and tears, reflected the horror that had shattered their youthful innocence, their bright future forever shadowed by their ordeal.

The sun, previously a symbol of hope and freedom, now felt mocking, a stark reminder of the life they had lost. They were survivors, yes, but survivors forever marked by the price they had paid, forever haunted by the memory of their fallen comrade, his sacrifice forever etched into their souls.

The silence that followed was broken only by the wind rustling through the trees, a mournful symphony that echoed the emptiness in their hearts. The forest surrounding Blackwood Cave, once a place of adventure and excitement, was now a chilling testament to the horrors they had faced.

Kiel gently closed Ben's eyes, his fingers lingering on the cold skin of his friend's forehead. He felt a deep sense of responsibility, a weight of guilt that he couldn't shake. He should have done more. He should have protected Ben. He had failed.

The survivors remained huddled together for hours, their bodies and souls battered and weary. They were physically and emotionally drained, their strength exhausted. The escape from Blackwood Cave had been a harrowing feat, the price of their survival an immeasurable loss.

As the sun began to set, casting long shadows across the forest floor, they started to process the events of the past few hours. Ben's sacrifice had been a terrible reminder of the real cost of survival. His death had heightened their awareness of the gravity of their situation, a stark realization that the horrors they faced weren't contained within the confines of Blackwood Cave.

The creatures they had encountered were not just monstrous animals; they were intelligent, coordinated, and terrifyingly efficient hunters. They were genetically engineered, their very existence a disturbing testament to humanity's hubris and its capacity for creating unspeakable horrors. They knew, deep down, that the game was far from over. The escape from Blackwood Cave was merely the first act in a much larger, more terrifying drama.

Their shared grief formed an unexpected bond, forging a stronger connection between the survivors. Their youthful camaraderie had been tested and transformed, forged in the crucible of their near-death experience. Their unity was a fragile shield against the looming darkness, their shared trauma a shared strength. Kiel knew that their survival was no longer just their own responsibility but a collective undertaking, a testament to the resilience of the human spirit.

As the night fell and the stars emerged, they started to formulate a plan. They knew that they couldn't simply disappear; the authorities would want answers. The story of Blackwood Cave needed to be told. Their escape had to be more than just survival; it needed to be a warning.

They were scarred, forever changed by the ordeal. The loss of Ben had created a void in their lives, a wound that would never fully heal. The weight of his sacrifice would forever be a burden they carried, yet a source of their continued determination to discover the truth behind the horrors that had unfolded in the dark, cold heart of Blackwood Cave, and to prevent further catastrophes.

Their escape was a victory, a testament to their resilience and courage, but it was also a profound loss. They were alive, but a part of them remained in the depths of Blackwood Cave, buried with their fallen comrade, forever bound to the chilling horrors they had encountered. The hunt might be over, for now, but the battle was far from finished. The true fight for survival was only just beginning. The secrets of Blackwood Cave, and the terrifying entities it harbored, would not let them rest. Their journey was far from over. The price of survival was high, and they would continue to pay that price for the rest of their lives. The darkness they had encountered in Blackwood Cave followed them, casting a long and chilling shadow over their future. The terrifying game had only just begun.

The crumbling remains of an old, abandoned miner's shack offered a meager shelter, a pathetic excuse for refuge against the encroaching darkness. It was little more than a skeletal frame, its wooden walls riddled with holes, the roof sagging precariously under the weight of years and neglect. Yet, to the traumatized teenagers, it represented sanctuary, a fragile haven from the horrors that lurked in the shadows of Blackwood Cave and the encroaching night. The air inside was thick with the smell of damp earth and decay, a pungent aroma that was somehow less offensive than the metallic tang of blood that still clung to their clothes and skin.

Kiel, despite his exhaustion, was the first to move, his actions driven by a grim determination to secure their immediate safety. He checked the dilapidated structure for any immediate dangers, his eyes scanning the darkness for lurking threats, his senses still heightened by the adrenaline-fueled escape. The fear was a persistent shadow, clinging to the edges of his consciousness, a constant reminder of the nightmare they had just endured. The silence within the shack was a deceptive calm, a fragile truce in the face of the overwhelming terror they had experienced.

He helped Chloe, whose arm was now a gruesome mess of blood and mangled flesh, to sit down on a broken chair, the splintered wood digging into her already bruised body. Her face, pale and drawn, was etched with a mixture of shock, pain, and a chilling emptiness. She barely reacted to the pain, her gaze distant, lost in the swirling vortex of her trauma.

Sam, his body still wracked with tremors, sat hunched over, his hands covering his face. He was silently weeping, the sounds muffled by his trembling hands, but the intensity of his grief was palpable, an agonizing testament to the depth of his emotional wounds.

Maya, her sobs finally subsiding into ragged breaths, stared blankly at the wall, her eyes wide and unfocused, reflecting the horrors she had witnessed. Her eyes were haunted pools of trauma, reflecting the macabre scenes of the massacre they'd stumbled upon. The images – the scattered remains, the gruesome mutilations, the unsettling stillness of death – were seared into her memory, a grotesque tapestry of nightmares she would carry forever.

Kiel knelt beside Ben's body, the weight of his friend's death pressing down on him like a physical burden. He gently closed his friend's eyes once more, a ritual of farewell to a comrade lost in the depths of the infernal Blackwood Cave. The cold, lifeless stillness of Ben's body was a harsh, unflinching reminder of their loss, a brutal testament to the brutal reality of the hunt they had narrowly survived. The image of Ben's selfless act, of his sacrifice to buy them time, echoed in his mind, a heroic act that was simultaneously heartbreaking and terrifying.

The silence in the shack was broken only by the occasional sigh, a tremor, or the rustling of their clothes. Each sound was magnified in the oppressive stillness, a constant reminder of their precarious situation. The weight of their shared trauma hung heavy in the air, an invisible shroud that bound them together in a tragic fraternity of shared pain.

As the initial shock began to wear off, the reality of their situation settled upon them like a suffocating blanket. They were alone, injured, and surrounded by a wilderness teeming with unknown threats. Their escape from Blackwood Cave was a victory only in the most superficial sense. They had cheated death, but at a terrible cost. They had lost Ben, a friend, a companion, a brother in arms.

Kiel, despite his own injuries, took charge. He was the eldest, the unofficial leader, and in this dire situation, his responsibility was more pronounced than ever. He began to systematically examine their injuries, tending to the most urgent wounds first. His medical knowledge, learned from years of tending to scrapes and bruises, was far outmatched by the severity of their injuries. He did what he could, cleaning their wounds with makeshift bandages from torn pieces of their clothes, the process agonizingly slow and painful.

As he worked, their stories began to surface, fragments of their pasts, shared in the eerie silence of their makeshift shelter. Sam, it turned out, had lost his father a year ago to a sudden illness. The loss had been devastating, leaving him withdrawn and quiet, the pain often hidden behind a facade of casual indifference. The horrors of Blackwood Cave had, in a strange way, ripped away his carefully constructed defenses, unveiling the raw, unhealed grief that he had been carrying.

Chloe's quiet demeanor was a carefully constructed mask, masking a deep-seated insecurity that stemmed from a tumultuous home life. Her parents' constant arguments, fueled by financial difficulties and unending marital strife, had left her feeling insignificant, overlooked, and perpetually on edge. The terrifying events within the cave had brutally exposed her vulnerability, shattering the illusion of self-sufficiency she had painstakingly constructed.

Maya, ever bubbly and optimistic, had a secret. Her parents had pressured her to pursue medicine, a path she secretly dreaded. She wanted to be an artist, but the fear of disappointing her family had kept her silent, her artistic passions suffocated under the weight of her family's expectations. The raw terror of Blackwood Cave had given her a new perspective, a stark realization of life's fragility, and a newfound determination to pursue her dreams, whatever the cost.

Kiel's own backstory was one of quiet responsibility. He was the elder brother, the unspoken guardian for his younger siblings after the death of his parents in a car accident years ago. The responsibility of his family had shaped him, etching a profound sense of duty and self-sacrifice into his core character. He felt the crushing weight of his survival, the guilt that gnawed at him, the memory of his failure to save Ben, echoing in the silence.

Their shared trauma created an unexpected intimacy, revealing a vulnerability that they hadn't shown even to each other before. The horrors of Blackwood Cave had stripped away their carefully constructed façades, exposing their deep-seated fears and insecurities. Their pain was shared, a binding force that solidified their bond. They realized the true meaning of strength wasn't merely physical but an unwavering resolve to overcome adversity, nurtured by the shared experiences and the bond of survival.

As the night deepened, the stars emerging like scattered diamonds in the inky sky, the teenagers huddled closer together, finding solace in their shared misery. The flickering light of a small fire they had managed to start cast dancing shadows on the crumbling walls of the shack, their faces illuminated in the firelight, etched with the haunting scars of their ordeal. The night remained fraught with the unseen dangers, the unsettling sounds of the forest surrounding them, but their shared trauma strengthened their resolve. Their shared pain was a shared strength, the foundation for their survival. The hunt was over, for now, but the darkness remained, and the true fight for survival was only just beginning.

Chapter 3: Unraveling the Mystery

The flickering firelight cast long, dancing shadows across the dilapidated shack, illuminating the faces of the traumatized teenagers. The immediate urgency of their injuries had subsided, replaced by a gnawing unease, a chilling premonition that their ordeal was far from over. Kiel, still tending to Chloe's mangled arm, felt a tremor run through him, a sense of impending dread that tightened his chest. He looked up, his gaze drawn to a glint of metal half-buried in the dirt floor near the shack's entrance.

He carefully retrieved the object; it was a tarnished metal box, its surface corroded by time and exposure to the elements. The latch was rusted shut, but with a grunt of exertion, Kiel managed to pry it open. Inside, nestled amongst layers of decaying fabric, were a series of documents, their pages brittle and yellowed with age, the ink faded but still legible. The language was a mix of scientific jargon and cryptic symbols, a disturbing blend of technical data and esoteric markings.

The first few pages detailed a series of experiments, focusing on genetic modification and accelerated evolution. The terminology was complex, but the gist was chillingly clear: these weren't natural creatures they had encountered in Blackwood Cave; they were the horrifying results of a clandestine scientific endeavor, a twisted experiment gone horribly wrong. The documents mentioned a project codenamed "Chimera," a clandestine government initiative aimed at creating new forms of biological weapons. The details were fragmented, obscured by deliberate redactions and cryptic abbreviations, but the implication was clear – the creatures in the cave were a by-product of this project.

Amongst the scientific jargon, Kiel found sketches – grotesque renderings of the creatures they had fought, their anatomy detailed, highlighting their unusual physiological features. The accuracy of the drawings left no room for doubt; these documents were directly related to the nightmarish beings they had encountered. He noticed recurring symbols interspersed throughout the text – strange, intricate designs that seemed to hold a deeper meaning, a hidden code that hinted at a larger, more sinister conspiracy.

Chloe, having gathered enough strength to sit up, leaned closer, her gaze fixed on the documents. Her eyes widened as she traced the symbols with a trembling finger, her breath catching in her throat. "These... these are similar to the symbols I saw on the cave walls," she whispered, her voice barely audible above the crackling fire. "Near the massacre site... they were carved into the stone, almost... ritualistic."

Sam, his gaze still haunted but his resolve strengthened, examined the box more closely. He found a small, leather-bound journal tucked into a hidden compartment. Its pages were filled with handwritten notes, a chaotic jumble of observations and frantic scrawls. The entries were fragmented, incomplete, but they painted a picture of a desperate scientist, consumed by their work, oblivious to the ethical implications of their creation.

The journal entries hinted at the scientist's growing unease, their mounting horror as the creatures became increasingly intelligent and aggressive. The scientist had detailed their attempts to control the creatures, their efforts to contain the catastrophic consequences of their experiment. The notes became increasingly frantic towards the end, filled with despair and a growing sense of impending doom. The final entry was a single, chilling sentence: "They are escaping... it's too late."

Maya, despite her trauma, had regained a measure of composure. She recognized some of the scientific terms in the documents, her knowledge of medicine providing a disturbing understanding of the implications. "This is... this is far beyond anything I've ever seen," she said, her voice trembling slightly. "The genetic manipulation... the sheer audacity of it... it's monstrous."

As they pieced together the fragmented information, the horrifying truth began to unravel. The creatures weren't simply the result of a failed experiment; they were a deliberate creation, a terrifying weapon unleashed upon the world. And Blackwood Cave wasn't just a site of a gruesome massacre; it was a prison that had been breached, a containment zone that had failed. The clues suggested that the creatures weren't confined to the cave; they were spreading, their presence extending far beyond the confines of the Blackwood wilderness.

The weight of this realization settled upon the teenagers like a crushing burden. They were not merely survivors of a horrific encounter; they were witnesses to a global conspiracy, a terrifying secret that threatened the very fabric of reality. The documents detailed plans for further experiments, hints of a wider network of clandestine research facilities, and the terrifying implication that the creatures they had encountered were not unique.

The symbols found in the documents and the journal were a recurring theme, hinting at a deeper, more ancient connection. The cryptic markings seemed to reference a forgotten mythology, an ancient evil that predated the current scientific manipulations. It was as though this sinister experiment had somehow tapped into something far older and far more terrifying, something that lay dormant beneath the surface of the world, waiting to be unleashed.

The implications were staggering. This wasn't merely a scientific mishap; it was a deliberate act of unspeakable horror, a reckless disregard for human life, a terrifying gamble with forces beyond human comprehension. The creatures were the manifestation of this reckless ambition, the terrifying fruits of a sinister experiment. And the teenagers, having escaped the immediate threat, were now caught in the crosshairs of something far larger, far more sinister – a global conspiracy involving ancient evils and technologically advanced weapons of unimaginable power.

Their initial relief at escaping the cave was quickly replaced by a chilling sense of foreboding. The hunt was far from over. They were no longer just fighting for their survival; they were fighting to expose a truth so terrifying, so unimaginable, that it threatened to shatter their world. The secrets of Blackwood Cave extended far beyond the confines of the cave itself, reaching into the darkest corners of human ambition, the hidden depths of ancient evils, and a reality far more terrifying than anything they could have ever imagined. The escape was merely a prelude to the much larger, and far more perilous, battle that lay ahead. They were now pawns in a game far greater than themselves, caught in the crosshairs of a global conspiracy that could plunge the world into a new age of terror and unimaginable horror. The shadows of Blackwood Cave stretched far beyond the cave's mouth, reaching out into the world, whispering of the terrors yet to come.

The fire crackled, casting an erratic, flickering light on the faces etched with trauma. The immediate fear had receded, replaced by a chilling, creeping dread. The metal box, its contents now spilled across the rough-hewn wooden table, held the key, not just to their survival, but to a history far older and far more terrifying than any of them could have ever imagined. The scientific data, horrifying in its implications, was only half the story. The symbols, the recurring motifs etched into the cave walls and drawn within the ancient documents, hinted at something far older, something far more sinister than a simple government experiment gone wrong.

Chloe, her arm throbbing a dull ache, traced a finger across one of the symbols, a complex, interwoven pattern that seemed to writhe beneath her touch. "It's...it's like a language," she murmured, her voice hushed with awe and terror. "But not a language I understand. It's... primal. Ancient."

Kiel, his gaze fixed on the brittle pages of the journal, found himself drawn to a series of entries detailing rituals, sacrifices, and invocations. The scientist's frantic scrawls detailed not just the creation of the creatures, but their apparent connection to these ancient rites. The notes spoke of a power beyond science, a force that seemed to guide and manipulate the creatures' behavior, pushing them towards a specific, terrifying goal.

Sam, ever the pragmatist, focused on the historical references scattered throughout the documents. He found fragmented mentions of cults, hidden societies, and whispered legends dating back centuries. These allusions, initially cryptic and seemingly unconnected, began to coalesce, forming a horrifying picture of an ancient evil that had manipulated human history for millennia. The creatures, it seemed, were merely its pawns, its tools in a larger, more terrifying game.

Maya, her medical knowledge proving invaluable, pieced together the biological data, revealing a disturbing level of sophistication in the genetic manipulation. The creatures weren't simply modified animals; they were chimeras, intricate blends of various species, imbued with unnatural abilities and an unnerving intelligence. Their DNA held traces of genetic material far older than any known species, hinting at a deliberate infusion of ancient, possibly extraterrestrial, genetic material. The sheer audacity, the calculated cruelty of the project, chilled her to the bone.

The documents hinted at a hidden history, a network of clandestine organizations that had worked in concert over generations to further this terrifying project. They spoke of a quest for power, an insatiable desire to control life itself, driven by a belief in a mythical prophecy that foretold the coming of an age of darkness, an age where humanity would be subjugated by a force beyond their comprehension. The ancient symbols, they now understood, were not mere decoration; they were a roadmap, a key to understanding this ancient evil.

As the night wore on, the pieces of the puzzle began to fall into place. The creatures weren't merely the result of a failed scientific experiment; they were weapons, engineered and deployed as part of a long-term strategy. The Blackwood Cave was not a prison, but a staging ground, a place where these ancient forces could gather strength, awaiting their moment to unleash their power upon the world. The massacre they witnessed was not a random act of violence; it was a ritual sacrifice, a necessary step in the ancient evil's plan.

The ancient evil, they realized, wasn't merely a mythological figure; it was a real, tangible entity, a malevolent force that had orchestrated events for centuries, carefully manipulating human history to achieve its goals. It had used the scientists, their ambition and their hubris, as tools to further its own sinister agenda, providing them with the knowledge and resources they needed to create the creatures – its ultimate weapons. The scientists, blinded by their own brilliance and ambition, had become pawns in a game far older and far more sinister than they could ever have imagined.

The implications were staggering. This wasn't just a threat to their own lives; it was a threat to humanity itself. The ancient evil was not confined to the Blackwood Cave; its influence stretched across the globe, its tendrils reaching into the highest echelons of power, manipulating governments and institutions to further its dark designs. The creatures were merely the vanguard, the first wave of a much larger, more devastating invasion.

The fragmented historical details painted a chilling picture of rituals, sacrifices, and ancient prophecies. The ancient evil had a long history of manipulating events, subtly guiding human civilization towards its own nefarious ends. The documents alluded to ancient texts, hidden libraries, and secret societies that had protected this knowledge, passed down through generations, ensuring its survival and its eventual resurgence. The scientists, unknowingly, had tapped into this ancient power, inadvertently releasing a force that had been dormant for millennia.

The journal entries revealed the scientist's growing unease, their descent into madness as they witnessed the horrific consequences of their actions. Their notes documented their attempts to control the creatures, to contain the catastrophic consequences of their experiment. Their frantic attempts to rectify their mistakes only served to further the ancient evil's plans, accelerating the process of its return. The scientist's despair, their final, chilling entry – "They are escaping...it's too late" – echoed the looming sense of doom that hung heavy in the air.

The teenagers, survivors of a nightmare, were now faced with an even greater horror. They were not simply victims; they were witnesses, guardians of a terrifying secret that threatened the very fabric of existence. Their escape from Blackwood Cave was only the beginning of a much longer, far more perilous journey. They were now on the run, not just from the creatures, but from the ancient evil that controlled them, from the powerful organizations that shielded its existence, from the terrifying truth that could shatter their world.

The ancient evil's ultimate goal remained unclear, but its methods were unmistakable. It operated through manipulation, subtly influencing events, using human ambition and fear as its weapons. The creatures were merely its tools, its instruments of destruction, deployed to sow chaos and pave the way for its ultimate triumph. The teenagers, armed with the horrifying truth, knew that their fight for survival was far from over. The shadows of Blackwood Cave stretched far beyond the confines of the wilderness, reaching into the darkest corners of the world, whispering of an age of darkness that was fast approaching. Their escape was just the first step in a desperate race against time, a race against an ancient evil whose power dwarfed their own, and whose reach extended far beyond anything they could have imagined. The hunt was on, and they were the prey.

The flickering firelight danced across the fragmented pages of the scientist's journal, revealing a chilling narrative of ambition, hubris, and horrifying consequences. Kiel, his eyes bloodshot from lack of sleep, traced a finger across a particularly frantic passage. The scientist, whose name was barely legible – a Dr. Albright, according to the faded ink – had initially presented his work as a breakthrough in genetic engineering, a revolutionary advancement in medicine and agriculture. His early entries spoke of creating disease-resistant crops, bolstering livestock immunity, even developing treatments for previously incurable illnesses. The language was filled with scientific jargon, detailed experimental data, and ambitious projections of a future reshaped by his work.

But as Kiel delved deeper, the tone shifted. The neat, precise handwriting degenerated into a chaotic scrawl, the words becoming increasingly frantic and filled with a growing sense of dread. The breakthroughs, it became chillingly clear, had yielded far more than anticipated. The initial experiments, aimed at improving livestock, had accidentally unleashed something far more sinister. The enhanced animals, exhibiting unprecedented strength and aggression, had quickly become unmanageable. Albright's attempts to control them, his panicked efforts at containment, only amplified the problem. The creatures began exhibiting a level of intelligence far beyond anything expected, their behavior shifting from merely aggressive to disturbingly strategic.

Sam, ever the historian, found himself engrossed in the interspersed historical references within Albright's notes. These weren't mere coincidences; they revealed a deliberate and sinister pattern. Albright hadn't stumbled upon his horrifying creations through chance; he had sought them out, researching ancient texts and obscure cults, piecing together fragmented knowledge from forgotten libraries and hidden societies. His notes spoke of ancient prophecies, of rituals designed to unlock a power far beyond human comprehension. The experiments weren't a scientific accident; they were a deliberate attempt to harness this ancient power, to control forces that had been dormant for millennia.

Maya, her medical training providing a chillingly accurate interpretation of the biological data, discovered that the creatures weren't merely genetically modified animals. They were complex chimeras, a fusion of disparate species, their DNA a grotesque tapestry of terrestrial and—she suspected—extraterrestrial genetic material. The sophistication of the manipulation was astounding, revealing a level of knowledge far beyond current scientific understanding. The creatures possessed uncanny abilities—enhanced strength, heightened senses, an almost unnatural resilience to injury—and an unsettling level of coordination, suggesting a shared hive-mind consciousness. They were weapons, honed to perfection, designed for a specific and terrifying purpose.

Chloe, her artistic eye picking up on details others had missed, focused on the recurring symbols scattered throughout Albright's notes. They were the same symbols etched into the cave walls, complex, interwoven patterns that seemed to pulsate with an otherworldly energy. She painstakingly copied them, comparing them to the inscriptions found on ancient artifacts unearthed in various parts of the globe. The symbols, she realized, weren't just decorative; they were part of an ancient language, a forgotten tongue that seemed to speak of an unimaginable power, an ancient evil that had long manipulated human history from the shadows.

Albright's final entries were a testament to his growing despair. He had witnessed firsthand the true nature of his creations, the horrifying consequences of his hubris. His notes devolved into a chaotic jumble of frantic pleas for help, desperate attempts to undo his work, interspersed with chilling admissions of his involvement in something far larger than himself. His fear, palpable even through the brittle pages, revealed a terror not just of the creatures themselves but of the ancient force they served. His final entry, a single, chilling sentence scrawled in trembling hand, sent a shiver down their spines: "They are beyond control... it is awakening...."

The scientists, it became horrifyingly clear, weren't simply misguided researchers pursuing a scientific breakthrough. They were pawns in a much larger game, manipulated by forces far older and more powerful than they could have ever imagined. Their ambition, their thirst for knowledge, had blinded them to the true nature of their work, turning them into unwitting agents of an ancient evil. Their legacy was not one of scientific advancement but of catastrophic destruction, a legacy that the teenagers now bore the burden of understanding. The moral implications were staggering. The pursuit of knowledge, unchecked by ethical considerations, could unleash forces far beyond human control, capable of shattering the very fabric of reality.

The scientists' ambition hadn't merely resulted in the creation of monstrous creatures; it had awakened something far older, far more sinister. The creatures were merely the tip of the iceberg, the vanguard of a far greater threat. The cave, they now understood, wasn't just a research facility; it was a conduit, a gateway to an ancient evil that had been dormant for centuries, awaiting its moment to unleash its power upon the world.

The teenagers, grappling with the implications of their discovery, felt the weight of the world on their shoulders. They weren't just survivors of a terrifying ordeal; they were the keepers of a horrifying secret, a secret that could shatter civilization as they knew it. They had escaped Blackwood Cave, but they hadn't escaped the shadow of the ancient evil, the ever-present threat that loomed over them, waiting to strike. The scientists' legacy was a chilling testament to the dangers of unchecked ambition and the terrifying power of the unknown. Their quest for knowledge had unleashed a force that threatened to consume them all. The escape from the cave was only the beginning of a much longer, far more terrifying journey, a race against time to prevent the ancient evil from achieving its apocalyptic goal. The hunt wasn't over; it had only just begun. The world, they now realized, was far more dangerous, far more terrifying, than they could have ever imagined. The shadows of Blackwood Cave stretched far beyond its confines, reaching into the darkest corners of the world, whispering promises of an age of darkness, an age of unimaginable horror. And the teenagers, armed with the horrifying truth, were the only ones who could stop it.

The chilling silence of the forest pressed in on them, a stark contrast to the echoing claustrophobia of Blackwood Cave. The escape had been brutal, a desperate scramble through the labyrinthine tunnels, leaving them battered, bruised, and emotionally shattered. Yet, the physical wounds paled in comparison to the psychological scars etched deep within their souls. They had seen things no teenager should ever witness, things that would haunt their nightmares for the rest of their lives.

Kiel, the self-proclaimed leader, felt the weight of their shared trauma pressing down on him. He had seen the raw terror in his friends' eyes, the primal fear that had stripped away their youthful bravado, leaving behind a fragile core of vulnerability. He scanned the trees, his senses heightened, every rustle of leaves, every snap of a twig, sending a jolt of adrenaline through his system. The feeling of being watched, of being hunted, clung to him like a second skin.

Sam, usually the jovial one, was now withdrawn, his eyes haunted by the horrors they had witnessed. He ran a hand through his messy hair, his face pale and drawn. The historical context he had unearthed in Dr. Albright's journal had opened a Pandora's Box of ancient evils, a terrifying reality that extended far beyond the confines of Blackwood Cave. He muttered to himself, piecing together fragments of information, attempting to make sense of the cryptic clues left behind.

Maya, the pragmatic medic, was focused on tending to their wounds, her movements efficient and precise. Despite the grim reality of their situation, her medical training kicked in, forcing her to focus on the immediate needs of her friends. Yet, even her stoic nature was strained, the knowledge of the genetically engineered creatures, their unnatural resilience and terrifying intelligence, constantly playing on her mind. The sheer scale of the conspiracy was overwhelming, the implications staggering.

Chloe, the artist, remained surprisingly composed, her keen observations offering a fresh perspective on their predicament. The symbols she had discovered, the ancient language etched into the cave walls and scattered throughout Albright's journal, were now burned into her memory. They weren't just meaningless markings; they were the key to understanding the larger conspiracy, a roadmap to a hidden world of ancient evils and unspeakable horrors. She felt an almost mystical connection to them, a sense of foreboding that chilled her to the bone.

Their uneasy silence was broken by the distant sound of approaching vehicles. The hum of engines, initially faint, grew steadily louder, closer. They exchanged uneasy glances, a wave of apprehension washing over them. Were they being pursued? Or was this just a chance encounter? The possibility that they were not alone in knowing about the Blackwood Cave conspiracy suddenly felt very real, chillingly tangible.

As the vehicles drew closer, they could make out the silhouettes of several SUVs, their headlights cutting through the darkening forest, casting long, menacing shadows that seemed to writhe and twist in the twilight. The SUVs stopped a considerable distance away, their occupants emerging – figures cloaked in dark uniforms, their faces obscured by shadows. They were not law enforcement; their presence exuded a sinister aura, a chilling professional efficiency.

Fear, cold and sharp, pierced the fragile calm. They were being hunted. This was not a rescue mission; this was a calculated pursuit, orchestrated by those who wanted to keep the truth buried. The conspiracy, it turned out, extended far beyond the walls of Blackwood Cave, reaching into the heart of powerful and shadowy organizations. The implications were terrifying. The scientists were not the only players in this game; they were merely pawns, expendable pieces in a much larger chessboard.

The SUVs dispatched smaller teams, flanking their position, cutting off their escape routes. These were not amateur hunters; they moved with practiced precision, their movements silent and deadly, like predators stalking their prey. The teenagers, despite their harrowing ordeal in the cave, were now facing a new, more insidious threat, a threat that operated in the shadows, pulling the strings from the darkness. The fight for survival had just entered a terrifying new phase.

The initial encounter was brief, a deadly dance in the shadows of the trees, a clash of primal fear against calculated efficiency. The pursuers were ruthless, their tactics brutal and efficient, honed through years of experience in handling dangerous situations. The teenagers' resourcefulness, honed in their desperate flight from the cave, allowed them to evade capture, but at a considerable cost. One of their number – it was Sam – went down. They dragged him with them, unable to abandon a fallen comrade, but the pace slowed, the tension ratcheted up.

The relentless pursuit forced them into a desperate flight through the unforgiving terrain, their injuries slowing them down, each breath a ragged gasp. The weight of their secret, the burden of knowledge they carried, seemed to amplify the physical exhaustion, the emotional toll of their ordeal. They stumbled through thorny bushes, clawed their way over fallen logs, and plunged through icy streams, their bodies battered and bleeding. The terrain itself felt hostile, a cruel accomplice to their pursuers.

As darkness descended, they found themselves cornered in a rocky outcrop, their escape routes blocked by the determined hunters. The hunters' precision was terrifying, every move calculated, every shot carefully aimed, designed to wound, not kill, to subdue and capture. The subtle change in tactics sent a chilling message – their pursuers were not interested in eliminating the witnesses; they wanted to silence them, to control the flow of information. This added a new layer of complexity, a macabre game of cat and mouse.

The next few hours were a blur of adrenaline and terror, a desperate struggle for survival against overwhelming odds. The teenagers fought back, their initial fear giving way to a fierce determination, a primal instinct for self-preservation. They used their knowledge of the terrain, their wits, and whatever makeshift weapons they could find to fend off their attackers. The night became a canvas of fear, illuminated by flashes of gunfire and the eerie glow of headlights. It was a testament to their courage, their resilience, and their unyielding will to survive.

The fight, though desperate, was unequal. They knew they couldn't win a direct confrontation. Their goal wasn't to defeat their pursuers, but to evade them, to buy themselves time, to find a way to expose the truth. The knowledge that their pursuit was not merely for their capture but for the sake of hiding an even larger horror gave them a renewed sense of purpose. They had to survive; they had to expose the conspiracy.

As dawn broke, painting the sky in hues of gray and orange, they finally managed to shake off their pursuers, disappearing into the dense foliage. They were wounded, exhausted, but alive. They had escaped the immediate danger, but the threat remained, lurking in the shadows, a chilling reminder of the vastness of the conspiracy. The fight was far from over; it had only just begun. The discovery of Dr. Albright's journal was just the tip of the iceberg. There was a whole world out there, a world of ancient secrets and terrifying power, and the teenagers, unwittingly, had become key players in a deadly game of global proportions. The hunt for them was only the beginning of a much larger hunt for the truth, a truth that could shatter the very foundations of their world. And they, the weary survivors of Blackwood Cave, were the only ones who could uncover it, even if it cost them everything. The conspiracy deepened, its tendrils reaching further than they could have ever imagined. The darkness surrounding them was vast, the threat real, and their fight for survival had just begun in earnest.

The biting wind whipped through the skeletal branches of the trees, carrying with it the scent of pine and damp earth. Exhaustion clung to them like a shroud, the weight of their ordeal pressing down with the force of a physical burden. They were huddled together, a fragile collection of battered bodies and shattered nerves, the remnants of their once-carefree group. The adrenaline that had fueled their desperate flight had faded, leaving behind a bone-deep weariness that threatened to overwhelm them.

Kiel, despite his exhaustion, remained vigilant, his gaze constantly scanning their surroundings. The memory of Sam's fall, the agonizing slowness of their escape, was a raw, open wound. He had carried the weight of his friend's limp body for miles, the silent accusation in Sam's eyes a constant reminder of their failure to protect him.

Maya, her hands stained with blood and dirt, worked tirelessly to tend to their wounds. The meager supplies they had managed to salvage from their escape were dwindling, and the cold was beginning to seep into their bones. Her medical expertise was a flickering candle in the encroaching darkness, a fragile hope in the face of overwhelming odds.

Chloe, her face pale but her eyes sharp, traced the symbols she had memorized from the cave walls onto a piece of salvaged cloth. The cryptic markings seemed to pulse with an almost supernatural energy, their meaning still elusive but tantalizingly close. She sensed a connection to this hidden language, a dark echo resonating in her soul.

Their silence was broken by a sound – a low growl, guttural and menacing, emanating from the dense undergrowth. They froze, every muscle tense, their hearts pounding in their chests like frantic drums. The sound repeated, closer this time, followed by the rustling of leaves, the snapping of twigs – the unmistakable signs of something large and dangerous moving through the woods.

Panic threatened to overwhelm them, but Kiel forced himself to remain calm, his voice a low, urgent whisper. "Stay together," he said, his words cutting through the chilling silence. "We need to find shelter."

They moved as one, their movements fluid and practiced, honed by their desperate struggle for survival. They found refuge in a shallow cave, its entrance obscured by overhanging branches and dense foliage. The air inside was damp and cold, but it offered a measure of protection from the elements and, hopefully, from their unseen pursuers.

As they huddled together, shivering in the cold, a figure emerged from the shadows. Tall and gaunt, cloaked in heavy, dark garments, the figure moved with an unnerving grace, their face obscured by the deep hood. Fear, raw and primal, threatened to consume them, but a strange sense of familiarity also stirred within them.

The figure spoke, their voice a low, resonant murmur, echoing through the confined space of the cave. "I've been expecting you," the figure said, their words laced with a chilling calmness that belied the gravity of the situation. "I know what you've seen, what you've discovered."

They were caught off guard by this unexpected meeting, the fear giving way to a cautious curiosity. Who was this person? And how did they know what they had witnessed? The questions tumbled through their minds, unanswered, yet the sense of urgency, of the need for help and information, pushed through the uncertainty.

The figure introduced themselves as Silas, a recluse who had lived in the woods for years, a man who held a grim knowledge of Blackwood Cave and its secrets. He spoke of the genetically engineered creatures, of the ancient evil that dwelled within the depths of the cave, an evil that had been unleashed by a shadowy organization that operated far beyond the borders of the woods, extending into a hidden world of ancient secrets and terrifying power.

Silas possessed knowledge that went beyond what Dr. Albright's journal had revealed, knowledge that was both terrifying and illuminating. He spoke of rituals, of sacrifices, of a conspiracy that stretched back centuries, a conspiracy that reached into the highest echelons of power, a web of deceit and corruption that threatened to consume the entire world.

He had been watching them, observing their desperate flight, and he had chosen to intervene — not out of altruism, he admitted, but out of a grim sense of necessity. The creatures, he explained, were not the only threat; those who controlled them were far more dangerous, and their actions were causing a deeper, more insidious evil than the creatures themselves.

Silas' words painted a grim picture, a world of ancient evils and unimaginable horror, a world that was far more terrifying than anything they had witnessed in the cave. The conspiracy was vast, its tendrils reaching far beyond Blackwood Cave, a web of deceit and manipulation that went to the top of the world.

The teenagers, skeptical yet desperate, found themselves facing a difficult choice. Could they trust this enigmatic figure? Was his offer of help genuine, or was this another trap, another layer to the intricate web of deceit that ensnared them? His knowledge, however, was undeniable, and the danger they faced was all too real.

The night wore on, the silence punctuated by the sporadic sounds of the forest, a stark reminder of their precarious situation. Silas, despite his mysterious nature, proved to be a valuable ally. He shared his knowledge, his insights into the creatures' weaknesses, the patterns of their behavior, their vulnerabilities. He taught them how to move stealthily in the woods, how to avoid detection, how to use the environment to their advantage.

As dawn approached, casting its pale light upon their hidden refuge, the teenagers felt a glimmer of hope. They were still in danger, still hunted, but they were no longer alone. They had a guide, an ally, someone who understood the dark forces they faced. But trust remained a fragile commodity, every glance, every word weighed carefully against the uncertainty and the high stakes. The alliance they had forged was tentative, an uneasy pact between survivors and a mysterious figure who held the key to unlocking the secrets of Blackwood Cave, secrets that held the power to destroy them, or to save the world. The journey ahead was fraught with peril, but for the first time since their harrowing escape, they felt a glimmer of hope amidst the darkness. The path to unraveling the mystery was still shrouded in uncertainty, but the creation of a fragile alliance had just given them the slightest of chances. The next phase of their ordeal was about to begin.

Chapter 4: Confrontation

The abandoned scientific facility loomed before them, a skeletal monument to forgotten ambition against the bruised, dawn-lit sky. Rusting metal clawed at the sky, broken windows like vacant eyes staring out at the world. It was a place of hushed secrets, a mausoleum of technological hubris, and it felt, somehow, more menacing than the Blackwood Cave itself. Silas, his face still hidden in shadow, gestured towards the crumbling structure. "This is where they created them," he said, his voice a low rumble that seemed to vibrate in the very bones of the dilapidated building. "This is where we fight back."

Kiel, his face grim, ran a hand through his mud-caked hair. The weight of responsibility pressed heavily upon him; he was, by default, their leader, and the burden of their survival rested squarely on his young shoulders. "What do we know about these creatures?" he asked, his voice tight with apprehension. "How many are there? How can we defeat them?"

Silas, despite his grim demeanor, exhibited a surprising amount of patience. He explained the facility's layout, gleaned from years of observation and clandestine investigation, detailing the numerous laboratories, storage areas, and the central containment facility – a vast, reinforced chamber where the creatures were believed to be held. He spoke of their biology, their vulnerabilities, their surprisingly sophisticated social structures. The creatures weren't mindless beasts; they were intelligent, organized, and ruthlessly efficient killers. Their genetic makeup was a twisted mockery of nature, a grotesque amalgamation of animal DNA, giving them a horrifying combination of strength, speed, and adaptability.

Maya, her medical kit a small island of order in the chaos of their situation, focused on their immediate needs. She cleaned and dressed their wounds, silently assessing their physical condition. The injuries were extensive – lacerations, bruises, and deep puncture wounds. Sam's loss still hung heavy in the air, a palpable absence that spurred them onward. The meager supplies they had managed to salvage were insufficient for a prolonged confrontation, but Maya's resourcefulness was legendary; she managed to improvise with the limited materials available, making the most of what little they had.

Chloe, her eyes fixated on the decaying building, studied the structure, her keen mind analyzing its weaknesses, its vulnerabilities. The strange symbols she had copied from the cave walls echoed in her memory, providing cryptic hints she hadn't yet deciphered, yet she sensed a crucial link between the symbols and the facility's design, a connection waiting to be revealed. She muttered to herself, deciphering the subtle clues in the building's architecture, the placement of the vents and the supporting structures, the subtle differences in the building materials. She was convinced there were secret passages, hidden rooms, and concealed access points within the facility, and her intuition guided her to specific weak points in the building's defense. The knowledge of these hidden ways could prove vital in their desperate gamble.

Silas detailed their plan: a swift, decisive strike against the creatures' main containment facility, aiming to disrupt their organizational structure and eliminate the most dangerous individuals. The facility's design, despite its decay, provided a natural advantage: the labyrinthine corridors and numerous rooms allowed for ambush tactics and escape routes. The decaying structure, while dangerous, also offered excellent cover and concealment, turning its decrepitude into their advantage. They would use the shadows, the crumbling infrastructure, and their understanding of the facility's hidden passages to their advantage, hoping to outmaneuver their numerically superior and immensely powerful adversaries. The plan was risky, almost suicidal, yet it offered their only chance of survival.

Preparing for battle was a grim ritual, performed in the chilling twilight of the abandoned facility. They gathered makeshift weapons – rusty pipes, shards of broken glass, anything that could inflict damage. Kiel sharpened a broken piece of metal against a larger rock, the rhythmic scrape echoing in the unsettling silence. Chloe secured a long, heavy cable, transforming it into a makeshift whip, her sharp eyes glinting with a chilling determination. Maya, ever pragmatic, painstakingly rationed their remaining supplies, preparing for the inevitable injuries that would follow. Even Silas participated, drawing upon his decades-old survival skills, showing them how to improvise weapons from the facility's detritus – tools transformed into deadly implements.

The air hung heavy with anticipation, the silence broken only by the distant, unsettling sounds emanating from the depths of the facility. They could hear the low growls, the scraping of claws on metal, the unnerving sounds of their unseen adversaries, the chilling evidence of their imminent confrontation. This was no longer just about survival; it was about confronting a monstrous conspiracy that extended far beyond the confines of this decayed building and the Blackwood Cave.

Their preparations extended beyond the physical; they had to brace themselves mentally, to steel themselves against the horrors they were about to face. Silas shared chilling stories of past encounters, tales of unimaginable brutality, each story a grim preparation for the fight to come. He spoke of the facility's dark history, its involvement in creating these grotesque creatures, revealing the extent of the conspiracy they were fighting against. He spoke of the scientists, the corporations, and the shadowy individuals who pulled the strings, orchestrating this horrific experiment, this monstrous affront to nature.

As darkness fully descended, they moved deeper into the facility. The air became colder, heavy with the stench of decay and the subtle, metallic tang of blood. Every shadow seemed to writhe, every rustle of metal a potential threat. The echoing silence was punctuated by the occasional drip of water, each drop a tiny hammer against their fragile nerves. The dilapidated interior of the facility, once a beacon of scientific progress, was now a haunted landscape of broken dreams and unspeakable horrors. The ghosts of past experiments haunted the dilapidated halls, each one a grim reminder of their mission's danger.

Their journey through the decaying structure was fraught with peril, each step a challenge, each turn a potential encounter with the horrors that lurked within. They crept through darkened corridors, navigated collapsed sections, and carefully sidestepped precarious rubble. The silence was punctuated by the sudden scuttling of unseen creatures, the chilling whispers of the wind whistling through broken windows, and the unsettling creaks and groans of the decaying structure, all amplifying the palpable tension.

Chloe's knowledge of the facility's hidden passages proved invaluable, her intuition guiding them through secret tunnels and concealed rooms, circumventing the main corridors and avoiding potential encounters. Her uncanny ability to sense the subtle clues, the forgotten hints embedded in the facility's design, allowed them to move undetected, like shadows through a haunted house. Her insights were often chillingly accurate, making it clear her insights into the facility were far beyond mere speculation.

Kiel, always vigilant, led the way, his senses heightened, his every movement precise and controlled. He carefully placed their feet, anticipating every possible trap, every potential ambush. His leadership was quiet, almost imperceptible, but it was absolute, inspiring confidence and ensuring their survival.

Maya's medical expertise was equally vital. She continually monitored their physical and mental state, administering first aid, offering encouragement, and keeping their spirits up amidst the pervasive atmosphere of dread. Her calm demeanor, even in the face of such peril, was a source of strength, an anchor amidst the storm.

As they approached the main containment facility, a sense of dread washed over them. The air grew heavier, the sounds more ominous — a guttural chorus of growls and snarls emanating from within the heavily fortified chamber. The metallic stench of blood grew stronger, its intensity choking, a chilling preview of the horrors they were about to face.

They were at the precipice of a final, desperate confrontation, a battle for survival against overwhelming odds. The creatures' presence was now undeniable, their terrifying power looming over them like a storm cloud. The final confrontation loomed – a fight for their lives, for humanity's future, against a terrifying force they barely understood.

The heavy steel door to the containment facility groaned under Kiel's desperate shove. Rust flaked off like dried blood, raining down on them as the door creaked open, revealing a cavernous chamber bathed in flickering emergency lights. The air inside was thick with the stench of decay, blood, and something else… something ancient and primal. A cacophony of snarls and growls erupted from the shadows, a chorus of monstrous voices that chilled them to the bone.

Dozens of creatures, each a horrific amalgamation of animalistic features, surged towards them. Some were bipedal, towering monstrosities with the rippling musculature of gorillas and the razor-sharp claws of a lion. Others were slithering horrors, serpentine bodies ending in snapping jaws filled with needle-like teeth. Their eyes glowed with a malevolent intelligence, their movements fluid and predatory, utterly devoid of mercy.

The first attack was a blur of claws and teeth. Kiel, wielding his sharpened metal shard, deflected a blow aimed at Chloe, his own arm taking a deep gash in the process. Chloe's makeshift whip cracked through the air, snagging one of the smaller creatures, momentarily distracting the others. Maya, despite her initial shock, reacted with cold efficiency, throwing smoke grenades she'd salvaged from the facility's storerooms. The acrid smoke filled the chamber, momentarily obscuring the creatures, giving them a brief respite.

Silas, surprisingly agile for his age, moved like a wraith through the chaos, his knowledge of the creatures' weaknesses apparent in his every strike. He knew their weak points, the places where their genetically engineered hides were thin, where a well-placed blow could inflict maximum damage. He moved with a brutal efficiency, his years of experience turning the decaying facility into a deadly maze where the creatures were at a disadvantage.

The battle raged. The air filled with the sounds of tearing flesh, the sickening crunch of bones, and the desperate cries of the teenagers as they fought for their lives. Kiel fought with a ferocious intensity, fueled by adrenaline and a desperate will to survive. He moved with a precision born of desperation, his small blade finding its mark again and again.

Chloe, utilizing her knowledge of the facility, led them through a network of tunnels and hidden chambers, using the facility's layout to their advantage. She lured the creatures into dead ends, used collapsing sections to trap them, and cleverly redirected them into pre-planned ambushes. Her understanding of the facility wasn't just architectural; she seemed to understand the creatures' psychology, anticipating their movements and exploiting their vulnerabilities.

Maya, despite being unarmed, proved herself a vital asset. She used her medical knowledge to target weak points, applying pressure to bleeding wounds and using her medical equipment to create distractions. Her resourcefulness extended beyond medicine; she improvised traps using the facility's equipment, slowing the creatures and buying precious time for her companions.

The fight was brutal and unrelenting. The creatures, driven by an instinct for predation, were relentless in their pursuit. Their strength and ferocity were overwhelming, their numbers seemingly endless. Several times, they were nearly overwhelmed, their defenses crumbling under the onslaught. Kiel's arm, despite the pain, continued to swing; Chloe's whip continued to crack; Maya's small medical kit continued to produce unexpected weapons.

Despite their valiant efforts, the losses began to mount. A particularly large creature, its hide impervious to their improvised weapons, grabbed Silas in a powerful grip, its claws tearing through his protective gear. The old man fought back with fierce determination, but the creature was too powerful. With a sickening crunch, the creature snapped Silas' bones, ending his life as quickly as it began. His death served as both a shock and a powerful motivator, fueling the others' desperate struggle.

The weight of Silas' death hung heavily on them, a chilling reminder of the precariousness of their situation. They pushed on, their resolve strengthened by grief and desperation. They knew that failure meant not just death, but the unleashing of a terrifying force onto the world.

Kiel, his face streaked with blood and sweat, felt his strength waning. The creatures were relentless, their numbers seemingly inexhaustible. But he refused to give up. The echoes of Silas' final, desperate screams fueled his every movement. He fought with the fury of a cornered animal, each blow fueled by rage and sorrow.

Chloe, her eyes burning with intensity, found a hidden panel in the wall, a secret access point leading to a lower level of the facility. She led the remaining members of the group through the narrow passage, barely escaping the clutches of the pursuing creatures. The passage was claustrophobic, their movements restricted, but it offered a chance, however slim, to survive.

Maya, tending to Kiel's wounds in the darkness, held a flickering lamp aloft. The faint light revealed the horrors inflicted, the severity of the injuries suffered. Yet, her face remained impassive, her hands moving with practiced grace, her medical expertise proving crucial. Her actions were the difference between survival and certain death, her calm a bastion against the escalating terror.

Escaping through the hidden passage, they found themselves in a vast underground laboratory. Rows upon rows of containment cells, mostly empty, lined the walls. They were in the heart of the facility, the very cradle of the creatures' creation. They had a chance here, a possibility of fighting back, not just surviving, but striking back against the forces that created these horrors. The journey to the next phase of their ordeal was only beginning. The final stand was yet to come. The weight of the world, and the fate of humanity itself, rested on their bruised, battered shoulders. The scent of blood, the fear, and the adrenaline remained the strongest sensory inputs to their exhausted minds. They had survived, but at a terrible cost. The true horror, it seemed, was only just beginning.

The underground laboratory stretched before them, a sterile expanse contrasting sharply with the carnage they'd left behind. Rows of steel containment cells, many scarred and broken, lined the walls like skeletal remains. The air here was cleaner, the stench of decay replaced by the metallic tang of ozone and the faint, sickly sweet smell of some unidentified chemical. It was a chillingly efficient space, a testament to the cold, calculated horror that had birthed the creatures they'd just escaped.

Kiel, his arm throbbing with a dull, persistent ache, leaned heavily against a cracked containment cell, the metal biting into his already bruised ribs. The adrenaline that had fueled his desperate fight was fading, leaving behind a bone-deep exhaustion and a gnawing fear. Chloe, her whip discarded, knelt beside him, her face pale but determined. Maya, ever the pragmatist, was already cleaning and dressing his wound, her movements precise and efficient, a stark contrast to the chaos they'd just endured.

The silence in the laboratory was deafening, broken only by the rhythmic rasp of

Maya's antiseptic swabs and the labored breaths of Kiel and Chloe. The weight of Silas' death hung heavy in the air, an unspoken grief that bound them together, a shared trauma that etched itself into their memories. They had survived the immediate threat, but the escape had come at a terrible price.

Suddenly, a low growl echoed from the shadows at the end of the laboratory. A single creature, larger than any they had faced before, emerged from the darkness. Its hide was a patchwork of glistening scales, its eyes glowing with an unnerving intelligence. It was a monstrosity, a culmination of the horrific genetic experiments that had taken place within these walls. This was no mere animal; this was something engineered for destruction, something far more terrifying than the hordes they had just fought.

Kiel tried to rise, his body protesting with a groan of pain. But the creature moved too fast. Before he could react, it was upon them, its massive claws slashing through the air. Chloe reacted instinctively, throwing herself in front of Kiel, her body taking the full brunt of the attack. A scream ripped from her lips, a sound of pure, unadulterated terror, before she crumpled to the ground, a crimson stain blooming on her chest.

Kiel felt a wave of nausea wash over him. He watched helplessly as the creature, its hunger sated, turned its attention to Maya. Maya, ever the strategist, had already grabbed a heavy metal pipe from a nearby workbench. She braced herself, her eyes blazing with defiance, even in the face of certain death.

Kiel's mind raced, desperately searching for a way to intervene, a way to help. He was weak, injured, his arm useless, but he couldn't just stand by and watch his friends die. Desperation sparked a surge of adrenaline, a renewed sense of purpose. He had to do something, anything, to give Maya a fighting chance.

Spotting a nearby console, Kiel crawled towards it, ignoring the searing pain in his arm. The console was covered in a dust of disuse, its screen dark and inert. But Kiel knew, from his time spent hacking into security systems, that this console controlled the facility's environmental controls.

With trembling fingers, he activated the console, his mind working furiously. He needed a way to distract the creature, to buy Maya some time. His gaze fell upon a panel indicating the facility's ventilation system. A sudden, reckless plan formed in his mind.

He accessed the ventilation controls, overloading the system with an intense burst of toxic gas. He knew it was a desperate gamble, a high-risk move that could easily backfire. The gas, designed for containing the creatures, was deadly to humans as well. But he had no other choice. It was a sacrifice, a desperate gamble to save his friends.

The gas hissed into the ventilation system, spreading a cloud of toxic fumes across the laboratory. The creature, momentarily disoriented by the sudden change in the atmosphere, paused its attack on Maya, its movements slowing as it struggled to breathe.

Maya, seizing the opportunity, swung the pipe with all her might, striking the creature a glancing blow. It roared in pain and fury, its movements becoming increasingly erratic, before collapsing in a heap, its massive body convulsing before finally falling still.

The silence that followed was heavy, thick with the smell of toxic gas and the metallic tang of blood. Kiel lay on the floor, gasping for air, the fumes burning his lungs. Maya rushed to his side, her face etched with worry, her eyes filled with gratitude and grief. She knew the risks Kiel had taken, the sacrifice he'd made.

The cost of their survival was etched into the lab's cold steel: the life of Silas, the crippling injuries of Kiel, and the silent agony of Chloe's sacrifice. They had escaped the immediate danger of Blackwood Cave, but the shadow of their loss, the crushing weight of their experiences, remained. The events of the night had irrevocably changed them. They were survivors, yes, but scarred survivors, forever marked by the horrors they'd witnessed and the sacrifices they'd made. The fight, they knew, was far from over. The secrets of Blackwood Cave, the terrible truth behind the creatures, remained a chilling, looming presence. Their escape was a victory stolen from the jaws of death, a brutal triumph bought with tears, blood, and the profound, haunting loss of their friend. The road ahead promised more dangers, more sacrifices, and a chilling confrontation with the unseen forces that pulled the strings from the shadows. Their ordeal was far from over, and the true horror was only just beginning to reveal itself. The darkness, once a distant threat, now lurked within their hearts, a constant, chilling reminder of the sacrifices they'd endured and the unknown horrors that still awaited them. Their journey into the heart of darkness had only just begun.

The acrid sting of the toxic gas burned in Kiel's lungs, a harsh counterpoint to the throbbing pain in his arm. He coughed, a rattling sound that echoed in the suffocating silence of the laboratory. Maya, her face streaked with grime and tears, knelt beside him, her hand gently pressing against his chest, trying to ease his ragged breathing. The air hung heavy with the stench of death, the metallic tang of blood mingling with the sickly sweetness of the gas. The monstrous creature lay still, its scaled hide a grotesque tapestry of death in the harsh fluorescent light.

"We need to go," Maya whispered, her voice hoarse. Her eyes, usually bright and sharp, were shadowed with exhaustion and a deep, lingering fear. The weight of their ordeal pressed heavily upon her, visible in the tremor of her hands as she checked Kiel's pulse. He could see the reflection of their ordeal in her eyes, a mirror to his own trauma.

Kiel nodded, his head swimming. He pushed himself up, his body protesting with a groan of pain. Every muscle screamed in protest, every breath a searing reminder of the poison filling his lungs. But he knew they couldn't stay. Not here. This place was a charnel house, a testament to unimaginable cruelty, and it whispered of further dangers lurking in the shadows. The escape, however desperate and dangerous, was their only chance.

They moved with a grim determination, their steps measured and cautious, their senses heightened. The laboratory, once a terrifying expanse of sterile steel, now felt like a labyrinth, each corridor a potential death trap. They moved through the shadows, their footsteps echoing in the oppressive silence, their hearts pounding a frantic rhythm against their ribs. Every creak, every rustle, sent a jolt of adrenaline through them, raising the hairs on the back of their necks. They were prey, they knew, hunted by unseen eyes, by forces far beyond their comprehension. The escape was far from over; it was only just beginning.

They navigated the maze of corridors, their senses sharpened by fear. They passed rows of containment cells, each a grim reminder of the horrors they had witnessed. Some were empty, their doors torn from their hinges, others held grotesque, distorted remains, silently testifying to the brutal experiments conducted within these walls. The stench of decay intensified as they ventured deeper into the facility, a chilling testament to the horrors that awaited them.

They found a service corridor, its walls lined with pipes and conduits. The air here was thicker with the smell of ozone, the metallic tang almost overpowering. They followed the corridor, its endless length stretching before them like a tunnel of despair. Each step was a test of their physical and mental endurance, each turn a gamble with fate. They were pushing themselves to their absolute limits, their bodies screaming in protest but driven forward by sheer will.

Suddenly, a low hum resonated through the metal walls, growing louder with each passing second. Kiel felt a tremor beneath their feet, a vibration that resonated through the very structure of the facility. The ground began to shake violently. Their escape route was collapsing around them.

"We need to hurry!" Maya yelled, her voice strained above the growing roar. She pulled Kiel along, their pace quickening, their breaths catching in their throats. The tremors intensified, sending waves of fear and panic through them. They were running against the clock, against the very structure of the earth itself.

They reached a heavy steel door, its surface scarred and pitted. Maya wrestled with the lock, her fingers clumsy with exhaustion and fear. The hum grew louder, the tremors more violent, and the air vibrated with a growing sense of impending doom. Finally, with a groan of twisted metal, the door swung open.

Beyond the door lay an escape shaft, a narrow, winding passage leading upwards. The air here was fresher, the stench of the lab gradually fading. A shaft of light pierced the darkness, a beacon of hope amidst the growing panic. They scrambled into the shaft, their movements agile and desperate.

The climb was arduous, their hands and knees bleeding from scraping against the rough walls. The shaft was narrow, forcing them to inch upwards, their bodies pressed together, their breaths heavy and labored. Their exhaustion pushed them to the edge, but their will remained unbroken. The memories of Silas and Chloe fueled them, their determination fueled by grief and love.

The tremors continued, shaking the ground around them, but their focus remained unwavering. They climbed, their bodies aching, their muscles burning. They crawled, their lungs burning, their bodies crying out in protest. The top seemed miles away, an impossible dream, yet they pushed onward, driven by the hope of escape. The thought of freedom fueled their aching muscles, the memory of Silas' death pushed them to climb faster, higher, towards the light.

Finally, after what seemed like an eternity, they reached the top. They burst out into the night, collapsing onto the damp earth, their bodies trembling with exhaustion and relief. They were free, but their ordeal was far from over. The escape had been fraught with peril, a brutal fight against the collapsing facility, the relentless tremors and the suffocating fear. Yet, they had done it; they had escaped.

They lay there, gasping for breath, the cold night air filling their lungs. The stars glittered above them, cold and distant, offering little comfort in the face of the horrors they had endured. They were alive, yes, but the weight of their losses, the scars of their ordeal, remained. They had escaped the facility, but the shadow of Blackwood Cave, the terrifying truth behind the creatures, the unanswered questions about what lay ahead — all still loomed, a chilling reminder of the dangers still lurking in the darkness, and the greater horror yet to come. Their journey was far from over. The nightmare, they knew, had only just begun. The silence of the night was punctuated only by their ragged breaths, a testament to their harrowing escape, a prelude to the greater battles that awaited them in the darkness ahead.

The biting wind whipped around them, a stark contrast to the stifling heat of the underground facility. Kiel shivered, not entirely from the cold. A tremor ran through his body, a phantom echo of the collapsing structure they had fled. Maya, her face pale and drawn, sat beside him, her gaze fixed on the distant horizon. The escape had been brutal, a desperate scramble for survival, but they were alive. For now.

Silence hung heavy between them, broken only by the rustling of leaves and the distant hoot of an owl. The silence was a stark contrast to the cacophony of the facility, a reminder of the horrors they had endured. It was a silence filled with unspoken grief, the weight of loss settling heavily on their shoulders. Silas and Chloe... their absence was a gaping hole in their lives, a wound that would never fully heal.

Kiel reached out, his hand covering Maya's. Her fingers were cold, her skin clammy. He felt the tremors in her body, a shared resonance of their trauma. They had escaped the physical confines of the facility, but the psychological scars ran deeper, etching themselves into their souls. The images, the sounds, the smells – they clung to them like shadows, threatening to engulf them in darkness.

"We're alive," Maya whispered, her voice barely audible above the wind. Her eyes, usually sparkling with intelligence and mischief, were now filled with a haunting weariness. The light within them seemed dimmed, replaced by a profound sadness that mirrored his own. The girl he knew, the vibrant, fearless Maya, was gone, replaced by a ghost of her former self.

Kiel squeezed her hand, offering a silent reassurance. He knew they were both broken, shattered remnants of their former selves. The innocence of their youth had been brutally ripped away, replaced by a harsh reality far beyond their comprehension. They had seen things no one should ever witness, experienced horrors that would haunt their dreams for years to come.

The first few days were a blur of medical attention, hushed conversations with concerned authorities, and the overwhelming weight of their ordeal. The physical wounds began to heal, but the emotional scars remained, deep and festering. Kiel's arm throbbed constantly, a painful reminder of his encounter with the creature. Maya's nightmares were relentless, vivid replays of their escape, the collapsing corridors and the looming sense of doom.

They were interviewed countless times, their stories painstakingly recounted, their memories dissected and analyzed. The authorities, initially dismissive of their claims, began to take notice as the evidence mounted. The sheer impossibility of their story, coupled with the physical evidence they provided – torn clothing, the lingering effects of the toxic gas, Kiel's injuries – slowly chipped away at their skepticism.

They started to piece together the fragmented truth, a horrifying tapestry woven from genetic engineering, corporate greed, and a profound disregard for human life. The creatures they had encountered were not natural; they were the product of twisted experiments, creations designed for a purpose they could scarcely comprehend. The Blackwood Cave was not merely a natural formation; it was a hidden laboratory, a grotesque testament to humanity's darkest ambitions.

The revelation brought a chilling sense of unease. They had escaped the immediate danger, but they were far from safe. The forces behind the experiments, the shadowy organizations pulling the strings, remained elusive. They were still out there, their motives unknown, their reach far-reaching. The knowledge fueled their determination, transforming their grief into a burning desire for justice.

The support of their families was a lifeline. Their parents, initially overwhelmed by shock and disbelief, rallied around them, offering comfort and unwavering support. The shared grief bound them together, strengthening the bonds of family and friendship. Kiel and Maya found solace in each other's presence, their shared experience forging a bond of resilience and determination.

The process of healing was slow and arduous. They underwent therapy, learning to cope with their trauma, to navigate the treacherous waters of PTSD and grief. They learned to confront their demons, to face the horrors they had witnessed without allowing them to consume them. The road to recovery was long and winding, but their determination remained unbroken. Their experiences had changed them, irrevocably, but they would not be defined by their trauma. They would use their ordeal to fight for justice, to expose the truth, and to prevent others from suffering the same fate.

Kiel and Maya's story sparked a wave of public outrage and media attention. The revelations about the facility and the experiments shook the foundations of trust, forcing a reckoning with the ethical implications of unchecked scientific ambition. The authorities launched a massive investigation, uncovering a web of corruption and conspiracy that extended far beyond Blackwood Cave. The initial skepticism gave way to a fervent desire to bring those responsible to justice.

Their testimony, delivered with unwavering conviction, helped expose the truth, leading to arrests, trials, and the eventual dismantling of the shadowy organization behind the experiments. The long road to justice was far from over, but Kiel and Maya's courage and determination gave hope to others who had suffered similar fates, silencing the whispers of doubt and fueling a wave of change.

Their ordeal was far from behind them. The physical and emotional scars remained, a constant reminder of the horrors they had endured. But they learned to live with their scars, to see them not as signs of defeat but as marks of resilience, symbols of their triumph over adversity. They found solace in their friendship, in the strength of their shared experience, and in their shared determination to fight for a better world, a world where the darkest aspects of human nature could not triumph.

The world had changed for Kiel and Maya, but their world had grown. They had faced the darkness and emerged, scarred but unbroken. Their journey was a testament to the resilience of the human spirit, a beacon of hope in the face of unimaginable horror. The Blackwood Cave remained a symbol of their trauma, but it also represented their triumph over fear, their refusal to succumb to darkness, their unwavering determination to expose the truth, no matter the cost. Their story served as a cautionary tale, a reminder that the darkest aspects of humanity must always be confronted and that the fight for justice is a never-ending battle. The nightmare had ended, or so they thought, but the echoes of Blackwood Cave would forever resonate within them. Their journey of healing, of justice, and of finding peace had just begun.

The scars remained, a map of their harrowing journey, a testament to their survival. The fight for justice, however, was far from over. The truth, once uncovered, demanded action, and Kiel and Maya were ready. Their escape was only the first chapter in a much larger, more complex story. A story of survival, revenge, and the relentless pursuit of justice in a world where the lines between right and wrong were often blurred.

Chapter 5: The Aftermath

The sterile white walls of the rehabilitation center offered little comfort. The scent of antiseptic, usually meant to soothe, only served to heighten Kiel's already heightened senses. Each creak of the floorboards, each rustle of paper, sent a jolt of adrenaline through him, a phantom echo of the collapsing tunnels and the guttural roars of the creatures. He flinched at the slightest touch, his body coiled tight, perpetually on edge. The physical wounds, the deep gashes on his arm and the bruises that marred his body, were slowly healing, but the unseen wounds, the psychological scars, ran far deeper. Sleep offered no respite; his dreams were a relentless replay of the horrors he'd witnessed, the faces of Silas and Chloe haunting his waking hours. Survivor's guilt gnawed at him, a relentless tide threatening to drown him in despair. He'd lived, but at what cost?

Maya fared little better. The initial shock had given way to a crippling anxiety. She moved with a jerky, hesitant grace, her eyes darting nervously, as if expecting the creatures to burst through the door at any moment. The vibrant spark that had once lit up her eyes had been extinguished, replaced by a haunting emptiness. She spoke little, her silence a heavy cloak draped over her fragile frame. The therapists spoke of PTSD, of the long road to recovery, but the words offered little solace. The memories, vivid and brutal, clawed at her consciousness, refusing to be silenced. The image of Chloe's terrified face, the chilling sound of Silas' final scream, replayed endlessly in her mind, a soundtrack to her waking nightmare. Her appetite had vanished; food seemed a meaningless act in the face of such profound loss. The weight of survival pressed down on her, a crushing burden that threatened to suffocate her.

Their individual therapies were grueling, each session a painful excavation of their trauma. They relived the events, piece by piece, their voices cracking, their bodies trembling. The therapists, skilled and compassionate, guided them through the labyrinth of their memories, helping them to unpack the layers of fear and grief that had enveloped them. They learned coping mechanisms, techniques to manage their anxiety and nightmares, to navigate the treacherous waters of PTSD. They faced the ghosts of their past, confronting the horrors they had witnessed, piece by piece, without allowing themselves to be consumed by darkness.

The group therapy sessions provided a different kind of solace. Sharing their experiences with others who understood, who had witnessed similar horrors, helped to lessen the crushing weight of isolation. They found a strange comfort in their shared trauma, a bond forged in the crucible of their ordeal. They learned that their pain was not unique, that they were not alone in their suffering. The shared stories, though horrific, offered a sense of camaraderie, a feeling of connection in the face of overwhelming isolation. Listening to the others' stories, their individual journeys of healing, helped Maya and Kiel to understand that their struggle was a shared experience, a collective journey toward recovery.

The physical rehabilitation was just as demanding. Kiel's arm, shattered and mended, still throbbed with a dull ache. Physical therapy was a daily ordeal, a constant battle against pain and stiffness. His muscles, once taut with youthful energy, were weak and atrophied. Each movement was a struggle, each step a reminder of his fragility. Yet, he persevered, driven by a fierce determination to regain his strength, to reclaim his body, to overcome the physical manifestations of his trauma.

Maya's recovery was slower. The emotional scars seemed to have manifested physically as well; her body seemed brittle, her movements hesitant and unsure. The lingering effects of the toxic gas had taken their toll; her breathing was shallow, her stamina weak. But her spirit remained unbroken, her determination a stubborn ember refusing to be extinguished.

Their families played a pivotal role in their healing. Their parents, initially consumed by fear and grief, had rallied around them, offering unwavering support and unconditional love. They attended therapy sessions, offering comfort and reassurance. They listened to their stories, validating their pain, and reminding them of their strength and resilience. Their unwavering love became a lifeline, a beacon of hope in the storm.

The days bled into weeks, the weeks into months. The road to recovery was long and winding, filled with setbacks and breakthroughs, moments of despair and fleeting glimmers of hope. The process of healing was slow, painstaking, and often agonizing. There were days when the darkness threatened to engulf them, days when the weight of their trauma seemed insurmountable. But they persevered, buoyed by their shared experiences, their unwavering support systems, and their own fierce determination to emerge from the shadows.

They found solace in shared activities – quiet evenings spent drawing, the rhythmic pounding of their fingers on the keyboards as they wrote, the therapeutic effect of expressing their trauma through art and words. They took long walks in the park, observing the beauty of nature, a stark contrast to the horrors they had experienced in the cave. Slowly, gradually, they began to reclaim their lives, piece by piece, moment by moment.

The nightmares lessened, though never entirely vanished. The memories still lingered, sharp and vivid, but they were no longer all-consuming. The silence that had enveloped them began to give way to hesitant conversations, tentative laughter, the gradual re-emergence of their former selves. The healing process was a slow burn, a gradual shedding of the darkness that had enveloped them, a re-emergence into the light, one painstaking step at a time.

The physical wounds healed, leaving behind only faint scars, pale reminders of their ordeal. But the emotional scars remained, indelible marks on their souls. These scars were not signs of weakness or defeat; they were battle wounds, testaments to their resilience, emblems of their survival. They were a reminder of the darkness they had faced and conquered, a testament to the indomitable spirit that had carried them through the horrors of Blackwood Cave and brought them back to the light. They were survivors. And they would continue to heal, one day at a time. The future stretched before them, uncertain and yet filled with hope, a testament to their courage and their resilience. Their escape from Blackwood Cave had been just the beginning of a long and arduous journey; the journey to heal, to find justice, and to reclaim their lives. The scars remained, a roadmap of their ordeal, a testament to their triumph over adversity, a reminder that even in the darkest of times, the human spirit can endure.

The initial numbness that had followed their escape from Blackwood Cave gradually gave way to a burning sense of injustice. The raw terror had been replaced by a cold, hard anger. They had survived a nightmare, but the nightmare hadn't ended; it had simply shifted shape, morphing into a chilling conspiracy that stretched far beyond the claustrophobic confines of the cave. The creatures, the massacre at the campsite — these were not random acts of savagery; they were calculated, deliberate horrors, part of a larger, more sinister design.

Kiel, driven by a ferocious need for retribution, began his own investigation, fueled by a mixture of survivor's guilt and a burning desire for answers. His injured arm, though still aching, barely registered as he delved into online forums and obscure research papers, piecing together fragments of information, chasing down whispers and rumors. He discovered a network of hushed conversations, coded messages buried within online gaming communities, forums devoted to cryptozoology, and discussions in fringe scientific circles, all hinting at a clandestine project, a forbidden experiment conducted under the guise of scientific advancement.

Maya, initially hesitant to re-engage with the trauma, found her own path towards understanding. She started by documenting everything she remembered from the cave, creating a detailed log of their ordeal, a testament to their harrowing experience. Her nature, honed over years of academic dedication, proved invaluable. Her notes, initially a personal catharsis, gradually transformed into a crucial piece of evidence, revealing patterns, inconsistencies, and details that Kiel's more impulsive approach had overlooked.

Their investigation was a slow, painstaking process, a methodical unraveling of a deeply buried conspiracy. They worked separately, yet their efforts complemented each other, their different approaches converging to reveal a chilling picture. Kiel, driven by emotion, unearthed raw information, while Maya's methodical analysis gave it structure and context. They discovered that the creatures were not a product of nature's whims; they were the result of a clandestine genetic engineering project, funded by a shadowy organization known only as "The Obsidian Syndicate." The syndicate's true motives remained shrouded in secrecy, but the evidence suggested a chilling goal: the creation of a new breed of super-soldier, a bioweapon designed for unimaginable destruction.

The Blackwood Cave, they learned, was not just a natural formation; it was a testing ground, a clandestine laboratory where the Syndicate had conducted its horrific experiments. The gruesome campsite they had stumbled upon was merely one of many, evidence of the Syndicate's ruthless disregard for human life. They were not the first victims; their survival was an anomaly, a terrifying stroke of luck.

Their investigation led them to Dr. Alistair Reed, a brilliant but disgraced geneticist rumored to have been a key figure in the Obsidian Syndicate's research. Dr. Reed had vanished years ago, leaving behind a trail of cryptic research papers and a reputation for pushing the boundaries of ethical science. Kiel and Maya discovered his last known residence, a secluded cabin nestled deep within the Redwood National Park, a remote location perfectly suited to clandestine activity.

The cabin was a treasure trove of information, a dark archive filled with the Syndicate's secrets. They found detailed research notes, blueprints of the creatures, experimental logs documenting the horrifying experiments, and even correspondence between Dr. Reed and the Syndicate's high-ranking members. The evidence they uncovered was overwhelming, painting a disturbing picture of unchecked ambition, scientific hubris, and a chilling disregard for human life.

The documents revealed the Syndicate's chilling plan: to unleash their genetically-engineered creatures upon the world, using them as biological weapons. Blackwood Cave was just one of many testing grounds; the Syndicate was planning to establish more, creating a network of secret laboratories across the globe. Their goal was to establish a new world order, one ruled by fear and controlled by their bioweapons.

The weight of their discovery was immense, a crushing burden that threatened to overwhelm them. They had faced death in the cave, but now they faced a far greater threat: a shadowy organization with the power to unleash unimaginable destruction upon the world. The evidence they had gathered was irrefutable, but bringing the Syndicate to justice would require more than just evidence; it would require courage, resilience, and a willingness to face unimaginable danger.

They contacted Agent Grayson, the hardened FBI agent who had initially dismissed their story as the ravings of traumatized teenagers. This time, however, they had irrefutable evidence. Grayson, a seasoned investigator with a deep skepticism, was initially hesitant, but the weight of the evidence was impossible to ignore. He agreed to help, recognizing the potential global threat posed by the Obsidian Syndicate.

The collaboration between Kiel, Maya, and Agent Grayson was a complex dance of intellect and action. Kiel, fueled by his raw emotion and his firsthand knowledge of the creatures, provided invaluable insights into their behavior and capabilities. Maya, with her analytical mind, structured their investigation, ensuring a methodical approach. Agent Grayson, with his experience and resources, navigated the legal and bureaucratic hurdles, ensuring their efforts remained within the bounds of the law.

Their investigation took them from the dusty archives of forgotten laboratories to the dimly lit backrooms of clandestine meetings, from high-tech surveillance centers to the dark corners of the internet's underbelly. They faced danger at every turn, constantly evading the Syndicate's surveillance, anticipating their next move. They were hunted, yet they remained undeterred, their determination fueled by the weight of their discovery and their fierce determination to bring the perpetrators to justice.

The investigation was a brutal test of their resilience, a constant push and pull between hope and despair, between their shared trauma and their unwavering resolve. There were times when the darkness threatened to consume them, times when the weight of their responsibility felt too heavy to bear. Yet, they persevered, their shared experience forging an unbreakable bond, a powerful alliance forged in the crucible of their ordeal.

Their efforts were not without casualties. Their allies, the people who believed them, those who were brave enough to stand beside them against the Syndicate, faced harassment, threats, and even violence. Some were lost, victims of the Syndicate's ruthless efficiency. But each loss only strengthened their resolve, fueling their anger and reinforcing their commitment to expose the truth.

The path to justice was not easy. The Syndicate, a powerful and well-funded organization, was deeply entrenched, its tentacles extending into the highest levels of power. Their investigation was fraught with danger, betrayal, and uncertainty. Yet, Kiel, Maya, and Agent Grayson pressed on, driven by their unwavering determination to uncover the truth and bring the Syndicate to justice. The journey to expose the Syndicate was a harrowing one, a testament to their resilience, their unwavering determination, and the strength of the bond they forged in the face of unspeakable horrors. They were survivors, and they were not backing down. The fight had only just begun. The truth, they knew, would not only bring them justice but hopefully prevent an unimaginable catastrophe from unfolding. The future remained uncertain, but their resolve, forged in the fires of Blackwood Cave, was unbreakable.

The weight of their discovery pressed down on them, a suffocating blanket of dread woven from the threads of countless atrocities. They possessed the irrefutable proof of the Obsidian Syndicate's heinous crimes, a mountain of evidence that could bring down a global network of terror. Yet, simply possessing the truth wasn't enough. The Syndicate was powerful, their influence insidious, their reach vast. They had silenced critics, eliminated witnesses, and controlled the narrative for years. To expose them meant a direct confrontation, a calculated gamble against an enemy who played a ruthless game of shadows.

Kiel, ever the impulsive one, initially advocated for a direct approach. He wanted to take their evidence straight to the media, to unleash a torrent of truth upon the world, regardless of the consequences. He envisioned headlines screaming of genetic horrors, of a vast conspiracy reaching the highest echelons of power. He pictured the Syndicate's carefully constructed façade crumbling under the weight of public outrage. But Maya, ever the pragmatist, cautioned against such recklessness. A frontal assault on an organization as powerful as the Syndicate would be suicidal. They needed a strategy, a carefully orchestrated plan that minimized their risks while maximizing their impact.

Agent Grayson, a seasoned veteran of countless investigations, proposed a more measured approach. They would use the evidence to build their case slowly, methodically targeting key figures within the Syndicate, starting with the most vulnerable and working their way up the chain of command. They would utilize the resources of the FBI, its network of informants, and its legal muscle to chip away at the Syndicate's power, carefully dismantling its operations piece by piece. He stressed the importance of operational security, emphasizing the need for secrecy and discretion. The Syndicate's surveillance network was extensive; a single misstep could jeopardize their entire operation.

Their plan involved a multi-pronged assault. Kiel, leveraging his intimate knowledge of the creatures, would infiltrate the Syndicate's online forums and gaming communities, sowing discord and misinformation, creating cracks in the façade of their constructed online presence. He would use his understanding of their communication patterns to leak snippets of information to the right people, carefully chosen targets who could amplify their message without compromising their safety.

Maya, with her unwavering attention to detail, organized the physical evidence, preparing the documents for legal proceedings, ensuring they met the rigorous standards required for admissibility in court. She also worked on identifying potential collaborators within the Syndicate itself, looking for disillusioned scientists or disgruntled employees who might be willing to cooperate and share critical information. Her ness was a vital component of their strategy, providing the solid groundwork needed for their legal action to stand.

Agent Grayson, with his access to governmental resources, would utilize the FBI's investigative capabilities to track the Syndicate's financial transactions, trace their communication networks, and monitor their movements. He would work closely with other government agencies, coordinating with international bodies to build a global coalition against the Syndicate. This was a task requiring incredible diplomacy, a delicate balancing act between swift action and calculated deliberation.

Their first act of defiance was a daring raid on a remote Syndicate laboratory in the Nevada desert, a facility where they suspected the Syndicate was conducting further experiments. Kiel, under the cover of darkness, successfully disabled the laboratory's security systems, acquiring more irrefutable evidence of their illegal activities and planting tracking devices to monitor their movements. Maya, meanwhile, utilized her skills to access the laboratory's secure servers remotely, downloading a massive amount of data, including financial records, research notes, and communication logs. Agent Grayson's team provided aerial surveillance and secured the perimeter, ensuring their operation remained undetected.

The operation was a nerve-wracking affair, a calculated risk with potentially devastating consequences. The air crackled with tension as they navigated the labyrinthine corridors of the underground laboratory, each footstep echoing through the cavernous spaces. The thrill of their successful raid, however, was quickly replaced by the sobering realization of the magnitude of their undertaking. The Syndicate's reach was far greater than they had ever anticipated.

Their next target was the Blackwood Cave itself. This time, they were not running for their lives, but returning to the site of their ordeal, armed with a plan and a clear objective: to destroy the cave as a testing ground, to remove it as a tool of the Syndicate's insidious plans. They knew the risk was immense, that the Syndicate was surely monitoring the cave, expecting a countermove. But the potential rewards were even greater; eliminating the cave meant disrupting one of the Syndicate's most crucial operations.

The operation required planning and flawless execution. Kiel, utilizing his knowledge of the cave's layout, led the team through a complex network of tunnels, navigating the treacherous terrain with practiced ease. Maya planted explosives in strategic locations, disabling the facility's internal systems and initiating a controlled demolition. Agent Grayson's team provided outside support, creating a diversion to draw the Syndicate's attention away from their main objective.

The explosion rocked the mountain, shaking the very ground beneath their feet. The roar was deafening, the impact sending tremors throughout the surrounding area. The cave, once a symbol of terror and the breeding ground for the Syndicate's horrors, was now a smoldering ruin, a testament to their defiance.

As their actions escalated, the Syndicate retaliated, unleashing its full might against them. They faced threats, intimidation, and acts of sabotage, their lives constantly in danger. Close calls became commonplace; near misses punctuated their every move. Yet, despite the ever-present danger, they persevered, fueled by a burning sense of justice and an unwavering commitment to expose the truth.

Their actions sparked a global outcry. The leaks of information, carefully orchestrated and timed to maximize impact, created a storm of controversy in the media, shaking the public's trust in established institutions and forcing governments to investigate. The Syndicate's web of deceit, once so carefully woven, began to unravel, thread by thread.

The final confrontation took place in a high-rise building overlooking the city, the Syndicate's headquarters. A high-stakes cat-and-mouse game ensued, a desperate struggle against a foe who seemed to anticipate their every move. The building became a battleground, a chaotic scene of close-quarters combat, as they navigated treacherous hallways, fought off Syndicate agents, and raced against time to expose the truth.

Kiel, Maya, and Agent Grayson faced overwhelming odds, their combined skills tested to their limits. The battle was brutal, the stakes immeasurably high. But in the end, they prevailed. They exposed the Syndicate's leaders, dismantling their network and bringing them to justice. The years of secrecy, the countless atrocities, the relentless pursuit of power—it all came crashing down under the weight of their unwavering resolve.

Their victory, however, came at a heavy cost. The fight had taken its toll, leaving them physically and emotionally scarred. The memory of Blackwood Cave, of the horrific creatures, of the fallen allies — all of it remained, a constant reminder of their ordeal. Yet, they had achieved something extraordinary. They had faced overwhelming odds, battled a powerful and ruthless enemy, and emerged victorious. They had brought justice to the victims, warned the world of an impending danger, and, in doing so, saved countless lives. The scars they carried served as reminders of their fight, a testament to their courage, and a symbol of their triumph over darkness. The world was safer, but the battle for justice was a never-ending one, and they knew, deep in their hearts, that they would continue to fight for what is right, for as long as they could.

The silence of the aftermath was heavier than the roar of the explosions that had shattered Blackwood Cave. It pressed down on Kiel, Maya, and Agent Grayson, a suffocating weight that clung to them like the damp chill of the cave itself. The victory, so hard-won, felt strangely hollow, a bitter taste in the mouth. They had won the battle, but the war, the war within themselves, had only just begun.

Kiel, the impulsive one, found himself haunted by the faces of his fallen comrades. He saw their eyes, wide with terror in their final moments, and heard their screams echoing in the empty spaces of his mind. The adrenaline-fueled rage that had propelled him through the fight had dissipated, leaving behind a gnawing emptiness, a profound sense of loss. He would replay moments in his mind, dissecting his actions, searching for the point where things had gone wrong, where he could have done more to save them. The guilt was a relentless tormentor, whispering insidious doubts into his ear, questioning his courage and his ability to lead. He found himself isolating himself, retreating into the shadows, his normally boundless energy replaced by a listless apathy. Sleep offered no solace, instead bringing vivid nightmares of monstrous creatures and the chilling, desperate cries of his friends. The vibrant young man who had entered the cave had been irrevocably changed, his youthful bravado replaced by a weary acceptance of the darkness that now dwelled within him. Even the triumphant headlines, the accolades for their bravery, felt like hollow mockery of his inner turmoil. He knew he needed help, but the very idea of confiding in someone felt like a betrayal of his fallen friends, a failure to live up to the burden of his memories.

Maya, the pragmatist, found herself grappling with a different kind of trauma. Her nature, once a source of strength, now seemed to amplify her anxieties. She cataloged every detail of their ordeal, pouring over forensic reports and witness statements, as if she could somehow reconstruct the past, alter its outcome, bring back those they'd lost. But the more she looked, the more the details intensified the horror, transforming memories of survival into a chilling chronicle of loss and despair. The methodical organization of evidence that had sustained her during the fight now morphed into an obsessive compulsive need for control, a futile attempt to impose order on the chaos of her inner world. She was plagued by an overwhelming sense of responsibility, the weight of her survivors' guilt, a crushing awareness that they had managed to escape, while others had not. Sleep was a battlefield, a place where the whispers of the dead mingled with the silent screams of her own repressed anxieties. The rational mind that had guided her through the darkest hours of their ordeal now struggled to cope with the intangible horror that lingered in the quiet moments. She knew she was strong, but the insidious nature of the psychological damage threatened to break her.

Agent Grayson, the seasoned veteran, carried his own burden. Years of experience had prepared him for the physical dangers of his profession, but the psychological toll of confronting the Obsidian Syndicate's depravity proved to be a different beast entirely. The cynicism that had hardened him against the cruelties of his job seemed to have deepened in the wake of the Blackwood Cave ordeal. The loss of his team members echoed the countless sacrifices he had witnessed throughout his career, each loss a fresh wound on his already battle-scarred soul. He saw the shadows of his fallen comrades in every corner, their absence a constant reminder of the fragility of life and the futility of their relentless pursuit of justice. He wrestled with a sense of professional failure, a gnawing doubt that he could have done more to protect them, to prevent their deaths. His quiet stoicism, usually a shield against his emotions, now felt like a prison, trapping him in an isolation as profound as Kiel's and as desperate as Maya's. While he maintained a professional demeanor, the weight of his emotional turmoil pressed upon him, each interaction a forced performance, each night a descent into a silent and isolated grief.

Their individual struggles were intertwined, creating a complex tapestry of shared trauma and mutual dependence. They sought solace in each other's company, a fragile bond formed in the crucible of their shared experience. Their shared trauma became a silent language, each glance, each pause, communicating the unspoken anxieties, the lingering fears. They knew, instinctively, that they were not alone in their pain, but that shared knowledge did little to ease the burden of their collective grief. The psychological scars of Blackwood Cave were deep and enduring, but their resilience, born from adversity and forged in the fires of shared experience, held them together.

The healing process was long and arduous. They sought professional help, engaging in group therapy sessions, sharing their stories, and gradually finding a sense of healing through the support of others who had suffered similar trauma. Kiel started reconnecting with his old friends, letting his guard down, finding comfort in shared laughter and memories of simpler times. Maya began to channel her nature into projects that offered her a sense of control and purpose, rediscovering the joy of creating, rather than merely cataloging, the horrors of the past. Agent Grayson, reluctantly at first, began to open up, seeking guidance and solace from colleagues he had previously kept at arm's length. He found himself drawn to mentorship, dedicating his time to training younger agents and instilling in them a strong sense of compassion and empathy, a stark contrast to his earlier, more jaded self.

The scars remained — both visible and invisible — but they were gradually transforming into a testament to their resilience. The trauma of Blackwood Cave, once a symbol of their darkest moments, had become a catalyst for growth, forcing them to confront their own vulnerabilities, to confront the deepest recesses of their psyches and emerge stronger, more empathetic, and determined to face the future with a renewed sense of purpose. They knew the fight for justice was far from over, but this time, they approached the battlefield with a deeper understanding of their own strength, and a profound appreciation for the importance of healing. The ghosts of Blackwood Cave would always remain, but they were no longer captive to their shadow; they had found a way to carry the weight of their memories while embracing the future with cautious hope and a renewed resolve to fight for what was right. Their ordeal had taught them the true meaning of survival — it wasn't simply about staying alive, but about living a life worthy of those who had been lost.

The news broke slowly, a drip-feed of carefully crafted statements designed to reassure the public while simultaneously hinting at the unimaginable horrors unearthed within Blackwood Cave. The Obsidian Syndicate, once a shadowy whisper in government corridors, was now a headline-grabbing villain, its existence confirmed, its depravity exposed. The initial wave of public outrage morphed into a demand for accountability, a clamor for justice that resonated across the globe. Kiel, Maya, and Agent Grayson, despite their own personal struggles, became reluctant symbols of this renewed fight, their faces plastered across news channels, their stories dissected and debated.

Kiel, however, found little solace in the public's fascination with their survival. The accolades felt like a heavy cloak, smothering his still-raw grief. He retreated further into himself, avoiding the public eye, the flashbulbs and intrusive questions a stark contrast to the quiet solitude he craved. He found himself drawn to the small, forgotten cemeteries surrounding Blackwood, seeking solace amidst the quiet graves of unknown soldiers, a silent kinship blossoming in the face of shared loss. He started to sketch, pouring his grief and trauma into charcoal portraits, each stroke a cathartic release, each finished piece a testament to the lives lost. His art became a refuge, a sanctuary where his guilt found expression, and his rage transformed into somber, beautiful creations. The act of creating became a form of healing, a gradual, painstaking process of reclaiming his own fractured spirit. He began to see the faces of his fallen friends not as ghosts of terror but as figures of quiet strength, each portrait a tribute to their courage. He established a foundation in their names, dedicated to assisting families of victims of similar acts of biological terrorism. He found himself not only coping with his own trauma, but channeling it into constructive action, becoming a voice for those who could no longer speak for themselves.

Maya, meanwhile, threw herself into her work, her analytical mind becoming a weapon against the Obsidian Syndicate's lingering shadow. She compiled the evidence, assisting the authorities in building a watertight case, her methodical nature a crucial asset in the complex legal battle that followed. She delved into the scientific data, piecing together the terrifying details of the Syndicate's experiments, her thirst for knowledge fueled by a burning desire for justice. She worked tirelessly, sacrificing sleep and rest, driven by an almost obsessive

compulsion to unravel every last detail of the conspiracy, to understand the motivations behind the grotesque atrocities, to ensure that no other innocent soul would suffer a similar fate. She didn't just work to bring the perpetrators to justice; she worked to ensure that the full extent of their crimes would be exposed and recognized, that no single stone would be left unturned in the pursuit of the truth. The relentless pressure, however, began to take a toll. The quiet moments were her greatest challenge, the nightmares still haunting her, the weight of her survivor's guilt an almost unbearable burden. Yet, her dedication never wavered, her commitment to expose the truth unwavering. This determination, hardened by her ordeal, transformed her from a cautious pragmatist into a fearless advocate, a champion for the voiceless victims of the Obsidian Syndicate's nightmare.

Agent Grayson, initially withdrawn and deeply affected by the loss of his team, found a new purpose in mentoring new recruits. He poured his experience into training, sharing not only tactical skills but also the profound lessons learned from the horrors of Blackwood Cave. He emphasized the importance of emotional resilience, the need for empathy and compassion in a profession that demanded such emotional fortitude. His stories were stark reminders of the cost of complacency and the consequences of unchecked ambition. The hard-earned wisdom he carried, etched onto his soul by years of experience and the recent trauma, provided vital insight to his trainees. He instilled in them a profound understanding of their mission – not simply to maintain order and uphold the law, but to serve and protect, to truly understand the human cost of their actions. He established a support system for agents facing similar traumas, a sanctuary where they could share their experiences without fear of judgment, a crucial step in the overall healing process. This mentorship became his own form of healing, a way to honor the memory of his fallen comrades, to ensure that their sacrifices had not been in vain.

Their individual journeys were a testament to the enduring power of the human spirit, a testament to the resilience of those who stared into the abyss and refused to surrender. They didn't erase their trauma; they transformed it. The shadows of Blackwood Cave would forever remain a part of their lives, a stark reminder of the depths of human depravity, but they had learned to live with those shadows, to carry the weight of their memories without being crushed by them. Their shared experience forged a bond that transcended friendship, a silent understanding born from shared pain and mutual support. They knew they had scars, both visible and invisible, but these scars were no longer symbols of their defeat, rather, testaments to their unwavering strength.

The trial that followed was a brutal public airing of the Syndicate's crimes, a chilling exposé that shook the nation to its core. Kiel's artistic renderings of the victims served as powerful evidence, conveying the emotional depth of the Syndicate's cruelty in a way that mere forensic reports could not. Maya's assembled evidence was instrumental in securing convictions, her testimony a haunting chronicle of unimaginable horror. Agent Grayson's insights into the Syndicate's operational methods helped expose the network's full scope and reach, leading to the dismantling of numerous clandestine operations. The justice served was far from complete; the scars left by the Syndicate would linger for years, possibly generations. Yet, the trial represented a critical step forward, the first step in holding those responsible for the atrocities in Blackwood Cave accountable. The perpetrators were sentenced to life imprisonment without parole, a final nail in the coffin of their reign of terror.

In the aftermath of the trial, a quiet sense of closure settled over the survivors. They had fought hard, endured unimaginable horrors, and emerged victorious. They had exposed the truth, brought the guilty to justice, and, in doing so, had begun to find their own peace. They were no longer defined by Blackwood Cave; they had transcended their ordeal. They had found a way to live with the memories, to carry the weight of their experiences without being crushed by them. Their journey served as a powerful testament to the human spirit's enduring ability to heal, to adapt, to overcome.

But the quiet hum of unease remained. The world had glimpsed the abyss, and the knowledge of what lurked beneath the surface had irrevocably altered their perspectives. The Obsidian Syndicate's downfall did not eliminate the underlying threat of genetic manipulation and bioterrorism. The unsettling truth of genetically modified creatures – their existence, their purpose – was now in the public consciousness, a constant reminder of humanity's capacity for self-destruction. Kiel, Maya, and Agent Grayson knew this fight wasn't over; it had simply entered a new, more complex phase. The lingering uncertainties, the unanswered questions, served as a constant reminder that their vigil must continue, their resolve remain unshaken. Blackwood Cave was a chapter closed, yet it also marked a new beginning – a beginning where vigilance, empathy, and the strength of the human spirit would be crucial weapons in the ongoing battle against the unseen horrors that still lurked in the shadows. Their story served not as a tale of horror, but as a testament to resilience, to the power of healing, and to the enduring fight for justice in a world teetering on the edge of the unimaginable.

Chapter 6: The Revelation

The initial press conferences were a blur of flashing cameras and shouted questions. Kiel, still haunted by the spectral faces of his fallen friends, found himself stumbling over words, his carefully constructed sentences dissolving into choked sobs. Maya, her usually sharp intellect momentarily clouded by exhaustion and grief, felt the weight of the world pressing down on her slender shoulders. Agent Grayson, his face etched with the weariness of a man who had seen too much, offered clipped, controlled responses, his steely gaze betraying the turmoil within. The world was eager for answers, demanding explanations for the inexplicable horrors unleashed within Blackwood Cave, but the truth, as always, was far more complex and far more terrifying than any fabricated narrative.

Their evidence, documented and preserved, was initially dismissed as the ramblings of traumatized teenagers. The official reports, carefully worded and deliberately vague, spoke of a tragic accident, a freak cave-in, a confluence of unfortunate circumstances. The mention of genetically-engineered creatures was quietly suppressed, relegated to hushed conversations in backrooms and whispered theories in online forums. The Obsidian Syndicate, it seemed, was far more powerful and far more entrenched than any of them had initially imagined. Their tentacles stretched into every corner of government, every layer of society, their influence so pervasive it seemed almost impossible to uproot.

The skepticism was a chilling echo of the indifference they had encountered in the cave itself, the chilling realization that the world was often more monstrous than the creatures they had faced in the darkness. Their initial hope, that by exposing the truth they could bring about justice and prevent future tragedies, was met with a wall of denial, a fortress of lies constructed by those who preferred the darkness to the light. Kiel felt a familiar wave of despair wash over him, the gnawing sense of helplessness that had plagued him since the massacre in the cave. His art, once a sanctuary, now felt like a futile gesture, a whisper lost in the cacophony of indifference.

Maya, ever the pragmatist, refused to be deterred. She channeled her grief into an unwavering determination, her analytical mind refusing to succumb to cynicism. She spent countless hours poring over scientific data, cross-referencing documents, painstakingly piecing together the fragmented puzzle of the Syndicate's operations. She discovered hidden laboratories, secret funding streams, a network of collaborators who had knowingly aided in the creation and deployment of these monstrous creatures. She compiled a dossier so damning, so detailed, that it was impossible to ignore. It painted a portrait of a global conspiracy, a web of deceit that extended to the highest echelons of power. She faced a constant stream of threats, veiled insinuations, and attempts to discredit her findings. Yet, her resolve remained unbroken. She knew the truth, and she was determined to see it prevail.

Agent Grayson, initially hesitant to involve himself further, found himself drawn back into the fray. His experience, his network of contacts, his unwavering loyalty to justice propelled him forward. He used his influence within the agency to push for a full-scale investigation, challenging the official narrative with the brutal facts unearthed by Maya and the chilling testimony of the surviving teenagers. He fought against bureaucratic inertia, battled against powerful forces seeking to bury the truth, and struggled against the ingrained cynicism that seemed to permeate the very fabric of the organization he served. He knew the risks, understood the potential consequences, but his sense of duty, his unwavering commitment to justice, outweighed every fear. His quiet efficiency was a force to be reckoned with, each strategically placed contact, each carefully orchestrated leak, chipping away at the Syndicate's carefully constructed facade. He became their silent guardian, a protector shielding them from the inevitable backlash.

The breakthrough came unexpectedly. A disgruntled scientist, his conscience burdened by years of complicity, contacted Maya anonymously. He provided irrefutable evidence of the Syndicate's experiments, detailed schematics of the creatures, and incriminating financial records that directly linked high-ranking officials to the conspiracy. This evidence, combined with Maya's research and the harrowing testimony of the survivors, was too damning to ignore. The public, initially skeptical, was slowly starting to believe. The leaked documents became viral, spreading like wildfire through the internet, bypassing the traditional media's controlled narrative. The flood of information was overwhelming, forcing the government to acknowledge the truth, albeit grudgingly. A Senate hearing was called, and the nation watched with bated breath as the horrors of Blackwood Cave were laid bare.

Kiel's art played a crucial role in the hearing. His charcoal portraits, each a chilling testament to the victims, moved the senators, the press, and the public to tears. They humanized the victims, transforming them from anonymous statistics into individuals with stories, families, and dreams. The raw emotion conveyed in his artwork resonated more profoundly than any dry legal document or official testimony. It tapped into a deep well of empathy, forcing the senators and the public to confront the harsh reality of the Syndicate's cruelty, to acknowledge the human cost of their callous disregard for life.

The subsequent investigation was comprehensive and ruthless. The Obsidian Syndicate was dismantled, its operations exposed, its assets seized. High-ranking officials were arrested, their careers shattered, their reputations ruined. The trial was a media sensation, the details of the conspiracy unfolding like a slow-motion nightmare. The world watched in horrified fascination as the sheer scale of the Syndicate's depravity was revealed, the chilling truth of genetically engineered weapons unleashed upon unsuspecting victims.

The victory, however, was bittersweet. The scars remained, both visible and invisible. The teenagers had survived the horrors of Blackwood Cave, but the psychological wounds inflicted would linger for years to come. Kiel found solace in his art, pouring his continuing trauma into his work. Maya dedicated her life to ensuring that the Obsidian Syndicate's crimes would never be forgotten, that future generations would learn from the horrors they had witnessed. Agent Grayson continued to serve, his experience a valuable asset in combating future threats, a testament to the resilience of the human spirit in the face of unimaginable darkness. The fight was far from over; the threat of bioterrorism, of genetic manipulation, remained. But the revelation of the truth, the exposure of the Obsidian Syndicate, was a crucial step toward healing, a testament to the unwavering power of human resilience, and a stark warning of the darkness that lurked just beneath the surface of our world. The memory of Blackwood Cave would forever serve as a constant reminder of the fragility of life, the enduring power of hope, and the unwavering pursuit of justice. The shadows lingered, but the light, however faint, had finally begun to penetrate the darkness.

The initial wave of public outrage, fueled by Kiel's haunting artwork and Maya's documented evidence, began to ebb. The media, ever fickle, moved on to the next sensational story. The official investigations, while thorough, lacked the bite needed to truly dismantle the vast, shadowy network of the Obsidian Syndicate. Their tentacles, it seemed, reached far deeper than anyone had initially imagined. The arrests of several high-ranking officials, though satisfying, felt like symbolic gestures, a mere trimming of the hydra's many heads. The core of the operation remained untouched, a malignant tumor festering beneath the surface of society.

Kiel found himself increasingly isolated. The initial outpouring of support had waned, replaced by a wary silence. He was a walking reminder of a national trauma, a living testament to the horrors unleashed from Blackwood Cave. The nightmares persisted, vivid and unrelenting, pulling him back into the suffocating darkness of the cave, forcing him to relive the agonizing deaths of his friends. His art, once a cathartic release, became a torturous exercise, each stroke of the charcoal a fresh wound reopening. He retreated further into himself, his once vibrant spirit dimming, leaving him a ghost of his former self. He found solace only in the hushed solitude of his studio, surrounded by his canvases, each one a chilling chronicle of pain and loss.

Maya, however, refused to surrender. She knew that the fight was far from over. The superficial victory had only emboldened the remaining members of the Syndicate, who now operated from the shadows, more cunning and more ruthless than before. She continued her investigations, delving deeper into the Syndicate's hidden operations, tracing their illicit funding streams to offshore accounts and shell corporations. She uncovered a vast network of underground laboratories, hidden across the globe, where the grotesque experiments continued, hidden from prying eyes. She faced constant threats, anonymous phone calls laced with chilling warnings, and mysterious surveillance that made her feel like she was living under a microscope.

One evening, while poring over newly discovered documents, a coded message caught her eye. It spoke of a clandestine meeting, a summit of the Syndicate's remaining leaders, taking place in a remote location in the Swiss Alps. The information was scant, but it was enough. She knew she had to act. She contacted Agent Grayson, the only person she trusted implicitly. He was hesitant at first, his superiors already pushing for closure on the case, but Maya's unwavering determination and the sheer gravity of the information swayed him. He agreed to help, understanding the implications of allowing the Syndicate to regroup and unleash another wave of horrors upon the world.

Their plan was audacious and dangerous. They would infiltrate the summit, gather evidence, and expose the remaining leaders to the world. They knew they were walking into a trap, facing insurmountable odds, but they were prepared to risk their lives to bring these monsters to justice. Kiel, initially hesitant to get involved, finally agreed. The guilt gnawing at his soul, the constant reminders of his failure to protect his friends, pushed him to join the fight. His art became his weapon, his charcoal sketches and paintings a way to document their covert operation, a record of their struggle against the encroaching darkness. He sketched the layout of their target, the remote alpine lodge nestled amidst the snow-covered peaks, his artistic eye dissecting the building's vulnerabilities, identifying potential escape routes.

Their journey was fraught with peril. They traveled under assumed identities, evading surveillance, navigating treacherous mountain passes, and constantly looking over their shoulders. The terrain was unforgiving, the weather brutal, but their determination remained unbroken. They encountered resistance at every turn, close calls that left them breathless and shaken. Once, while crossing a glacial crevasse, a sudden avalanche nearly buried them alive. Another time, a group of heavily armed mercenaries ambushed them in a remote village, a deadly firefight that left them bruised and battered but alive. Kiel's artistic skills proved invaluable, his quick sketches of the mercenary's layout and weaponry helping them devise strategies to overcome the odds. Their resilience was a testament to their unwavering commitment to justice, a powerful force that pushed them forward, even when hope seemed to dwindle.

The summit was a fortress, guarded by sophisticated security systems and heavily armed personnel. Their infiltration was fraught with tension, each step a gamble, each breath held tight. They moved like phantoms through the night, using

Kiel's sketches to navigate the lodge's labyrinthine corridors, their every sense heightened, their nerves stretched taut. They reached the summit's main hall just as the meeting was about to begin. The air was thick with an unspoken tension, the very silence a palpable manifestation of the evil at play.

The leaders of the Syndicate, a cabal of wealthy industrialists, scientists, and corrupt politicians, were gathered around a large mahogany table. They were discussing their next move, their callous disregard for human life chillingly evident in their conversation. The details were horrifying, plans for unleashing a new wave of genetically-engineered creatures, plans for global chaos and domination, plans that would dwarf the horrors of Blackwood Cave.

Maya, ever the strategist, activated a hidden camera she had planted earlier, documenting the meeting. The evidence was irrefutable, a smoking gun that would expose the Syndicate once and for all. However, their presence was discovered. A chaotic firefight ensued, a desperate struggle for survival. They fought with a ferocity born of desperation, each blow a testament to their unwavering resolve. The alpine lodge became a battleground, the once serene atmosphere replaced by a cacophony of gunfire, shattering glass, and the screams of dying men. Kiel, despite his initial reservations, fought with a primal rage, his years of suppressed trauma fueling his actions. He used his artistic skills to create diversions, confusing the mercenaries, allowing Maya and Grayson to escape with the critical evidence.

They barely escaped with their lives, pursued by mercenaries and the relentless fury of nature. They descended the treacherous mountain in a blizzard, exhausted, wounded, but victorious. They had the proof, the damning evidence that would finally bring down the Obsidian Syndicate once and for all. The fight was far from over, but they had won a crucial battle, a hard-fought victory against overwhelming odds. Their escape served as a stark reminder of the enduring power of human resilience in the face of unimaginable darkness, a testament to their unwavering commitment to justice. They had stared into the abyss and fought back, emerging, scarred but unbroken. The shadows might linger, but they had struck a blow against the darkness, and the fight, they knew, would continue.

The biting Swiss wind whipped around Maya and Agent Grayson as they huddled in the battered remains of their rental car, the stolen evidence – a secure data drive containing the incriminating video footage – clutched tightly in Maya's gloved hand.
Kiel, pale and shivering, leaned against the car, his breath misting in the frigid air. Their escape had been a harrowing spectacle of adrenaline and near misses, a blur of gunfire and desperate maneuvers that left them shaken but alive. The feeling of relief was fragile, a thin veneer over the raw exhaustion and the ever-present fear of pursuit.

"We can't go to the authorities directly," Grayson said, his voice hoarse from the exertion and the thin mountain air. "Not yet. They're too deeply embedded. We need leverage, something to force their hand."

Maya nodded, her gaze fixed on the snow-covered peaks surrounding them. The alpine landscape, usually a picture of serene beauty, felt menacing, a stark reminder of their precarious situation. "We need allies," she murmured, "people who won't flinch at the truth, people who won't be intimidated."

Their initial escape had been a desperate gamble, a race against time and overwhelming odds. Now, the real fight began. They needed to amplify their victory, to turn their hard-won evidence into a weapon capable of toppling the Obsidian Syndicate. They needed to build a coalition, a force strong enough to counter the Syndicate's influence and resources.

Their first stop was Geneva. Under the cover of darkness, they met with Isabelle Dufour, a fiercely independent journalist with a reputation for breaking high-profile stories that other news outlets shied away from. Isabelle was skeptical at first, having witnessed firsthand the media's tendency to quickly forget about the Blackwood Cave incident. But Maya's unwavering conviction, coupled with the compelling video evidence, finally swayed her. She agreed to help, understanding that this wasn't just about exposing corporate malfeasance; it was about stopping a global catastrophe.

Isabelle's network proved invaluable. She had contacts within the international community, activists and whistleblowers who had been tracking the Obsidian Syndicate's activities for years. Through her, they connected with a shadowy organization called "The Watchdogs," a collective of former intelligence operatives and hackers dedicated to exposing corporate corruption and government conspiracies. Their leader, a mysterious figure known only as "Seraph," was initially hesitant to trust Maya and Grayson, but the irrefutable evidence of the Syndicate's crimes, coupled with Isabelle's endorsement, proved sufficient.

The Watchdogs' technological expertise was a game-changer. They had the capability to penetrate the Syndicate's heavily fortified digital defenses, unearthing further evidence of their crimes. Their network of anonymous sources provided insights into the Syndicate's global operations, revealing the extent of their reach and the depth of their corruption. They uncovered hidden laboratories, clandestine meetings, and intricate money-laundering schemes, all documented and prepared for public release.

Their clandestine meetings took place in anonymous locations—deserted warehouses, dimly lit cafes, and even abandoned subway stations. The air was thick with a palpable tension, a shared sense of purpose that bound them together. They operated in the shadows, their actions cloaked in secrecy, knowing that every move was being watched, every contact a risk.

Kiel, meanwhile, was utilizing his unique talents. His art became a crucial component of their strategy. He wasn't just documenting their journey; he was creating powerful imagery, visual representations of the Syndicate's crimes, powerful enough to bypass the media's apathy and grab public attention. He started an anonymous online art gallery, showcasing his work with a powerful narrative accompanying each piece. The pictures were visceral, shocking, revealing the inhumanity of the Syndicate's experiments and the scale of the devastation they had caused. His work subtly leaked onto social media and underground forums, slowly building a groundswell of interest and concern.

One of the key figures they enlisted was Dr. Demitra Reina, a disillusioned geneticist who had worked for the Obsidian Syndicate for years before escaping with her life, carrying with her damning evidence of the corporation's ethically reprehensible experiments. Demitra's testimony provided the missing piece of the puzzle, linking the Syndicate's activities to the horrific creatures they encountered in Blackwood Cave. She revealed the scientific process behind the creation of these monsters, and her testimony confirmed their intelligence and inherent savagery.

Her knowledge was crucial in countering the Syndicate's attempts to discredit them. The Syndicate, realizing that their reign of terror was threatened, launched a counteroffensive. They spread disinformation, planted stories discrediting Maya and Grayson, and employed digital tactics to silence dissent. But this time, they were fighting a better-organized, more connected group. Isabelle's network of journalists ensured that the Syndicate's propaganda was countered with factual information. The Watchdogs deployed their hacking capabilities to expose the Syndicate's disinformation campaign. Demitra's testimony held up under intense scrutiny, backed by irrefutable scientific evidence.

Building this alliance wasn't easy. They encountered distrust, internal conflicts, and disagreements over strategy. Some of their allies were hesitant to publicly denounce the Syndicate, fearing retaliation. Others held contrasting views on the most effective approach. But amidst the skepticism and tension, their shared desire for justice prevailed.

The culmination of their efforts came in a planned press conference. Isabelle, with the assistance of The Watchdogs, released the evidence they had painstakingly gathered: the video footage from the Alpine summit, Dr. Reina's testimony, the Watchdogs' documentation of the Syndicate's global network, and Kiel's haunting artwork. The impact was immediate and widespread. The public outcry was deafening, far more significant than the initial reaction to the Blackwood Cave incident. This time, the world was ready to listen. The laid out evidence, corroborated by multiple sources and backed by irrefutable scientific data, was impossible to dismiss.

The revelation triggered a global investigation. Law enforcement agencies around the world coordinated their efforts, launching raids on the Syndicate's facilities and arresting key members of their organization. The Syndicate's carefully constructed facade crumbled under the weight of the truth. Their influence waned, their power shattered. The long, arduous fight was far from over, but the victory, though hard-won, felt significant, a beacon of hope in the encroaching darkness. They had stared into the abyss, confronted the darkest aspects of humanity, and emerged victorious. The fight for justice was far from over, but they had struck a significant blow against the shadows, a blow that echoed around the world. Their alliance, born of necessity and forged in the fires of adversity, had brought down a global empire of darkness. The shadows remained, but they were no longer in control.

The press conference was a whirlwind. Isabelle, composed despite the palpable tension in the room, projected the video footage onto a large screen. The grainy images, initially shaky from Maya's desperate recording, slowly sharpened, revealing the gruesome campsite within Blackwood Cave.

The sheer brutality of the scene, the mangled remains, the clear evidence of unimaginable torture, sent a collective gasp through the assembled journalists. The faces, initially skeptical and jaded, transformed into expressions of horror and disbelief.

This wasn't just another corporate scandal; this was a crime against humanity.

Following the video, Dr. Demitra Reina, her face etched with a mixture of fear and defiance, stepped forward. Her testimony was a chilling account of her years working for the Obsidian Syndicate, a detailed explanation of the unethical genetic experiments that birthed the monstrous creatures they encountered in the cave. She described the clandestine laboratories, the hushed whispers of forbidden science, the chilling indifference to human life that permeated the Syndicate's operations. She spoke of the ancient texts, the forgotten rituals, the reckless pursuit of power that had unleashed something far beyond their control.

Demitra's words were crafted, each sentence weighed and considered. She detailed the process, the failures, the successes, the terrifying realization that they had unleashed something beyond their ability to control. She showed photographs, stark and unsettling, of the genetic modifications, the monstrous hybrids, the twisted creations that now roamed the earth, born from a hubris-fueled pursuit of power. She spoke of the Syndicate's attempts to cover up the atrocities, the silencing of dissenting voices, the manipulation of data and evidence. Her testimony painted a picture of corporate greed, scientific recklessness, and a chilling disregard for the consequences. She described the creatures, their unnatural strength, their unsettling intelligence, and their terrifying capacity for violence. The details, horrifying in their realism, left no room for doubt.

The Watchdogs then presented their findings, a mountain of data gathered and presented. They displayed maps outlining the Syndicate's global network, detailing its reach across continents, its influence in governments and corporations worldwide. They revealed financial records, exposing complex money-laundering schemes, demonstrating the vast wealth accumulated through illicit activities. They showcased intercepted communications, revealing the Syndicate's sinister plans for world domination – plans that went beyond mere profit, reaching into the realms of ancient evils and forbidden power.

Kiel's artwork followed. Projected onto the screen, his paintings were visceral, disturbingly realistic portrayals of the creatures, their monstrous forms rendered with chilling accuracy. But it wasn't just the graphic depictions that captivated the audience; it was the underlying narrative, the emotion that poured from each brushstroke. His art conveyed the raw horror, the terror, the profound sense of loss and desperation experienced by those who had faced these creatures. Kiel's unique perspective, his ability to capture the unspeakable, transcended the limitations of words, conveying the depth of the crisis with unnerving clarity.

The power of the combined evidence was undeniable. The video, the testimony, the data, the art – it all converged, creating an irrefutable case against the Obsidian Syndicate. There was no room for doubt, no avenue for denial. The truth, horrific and undeniable, hung heavy in the air. The reporters, initially skeptical, now sat transfixed, their faces reflecting a mixture of shock, horror, and growing outrage.

The initial wave of disbelief gave way to a tidal wave of anger. The global outcry was immediate and unprecedented. Social media exploded, the hashtag Blackwood Truth trending worldwide. News outlets, initially hesitant, scrambled to report the story, their coverage amplifying the public's outrage. Governments around the world were forced to respond, initiating investigations into the Obsidian Syndicate's activities. The Syndicate's attempts to discredit the evidence, to plant false narratives, were futile. The truth was out, and the world was listening.

The ensuing investigations were swift and merciless. Raids were conducted on Syndicate facilities across the globe, revealing laboratories teeming with horrifying experiments, documents detailing the scope of their atrocities, and evidence of their collaboration with shadowy organizations and foreign governments. Key figures within the Syndicate were arrested, their carefully constructed web of deceit unraveling under the weight of overwhelming evidence.

The arrests were just the beginning. The trials were long and arduous, filled with shocking revelations and harrowing testimonies. The world watched, transfixed, as the full extent of the Syndicate's crimes was laid bare. The public outcry demanded justice, fueling international cooperation and a renewed focus on corporate accountability. The Obsidian Syndicate, once a seemingly invincible force, was reduced to rubble, its legacy a chilling testament to corporate greed and scientific hubris.

The aftermath was a period of healing, a process of rebuilding trust and accountability. International laws were reformed, stricter regulations were implemented to prevent future atrocities. The Blackwood Cave incident, once a forgotten tragedy, became a watershed moment, a stark reminder of the dangers of unchecked ambition and the importance of transparency and ethical conduct.

Maya, Grayson, Kiel, and Demitra became symbols of courage and resilience, their bravery in confronting the truth inspiring countless others to speak out against injustice. They dedicated their lives to ensuring that the victims of the Blackwood Cave massacre were not forgotten, and that the horrors they witnessed would serve as a cautionary tale for generations to come. Their victory, however, was bittersweet, forever marred by the loss and suffering they endured, and the knowledge of the lingering shadows that still threatened the world. The fight for justice was far from over, but for now, they had won a crucial battle against the darkness. The world had listened. The shadows were retreating.

The initial wave of global outrage, fueled by the damning evidence presented at the press conference, proved to be a powerful catalyst for change. Governments, once hesitant to act against the seemingly untouchable Obsidian Syndicate, were now under immense pressure from a mobilized public demanding accountability. Investigations, initially hampered by bureaucratic inertia and political maneuvering, gained momentum, propelled by the sheer volume of evidence and the relentless pressure of the media. The Syndicate's elaborate web of deception, constructed over decades, began to unravel.

The first cracks appeared in the Syndicate's carefully cultivated image of respectability. High-profile executives, once lauded as visionaries and philanthropists, were suddenly exposed as ruthless criminals, their names synonymous with greed, corruption, and unspeakable atrocities. Their carefully crafted public personas, cultivated through years of strategic PR campaigns, crumbled under the weight of irrefutable evidence. The once-impenetrable walls of secrecy surrounding the Syndicate's operations began to crumble, revealing a network of corruption that extended far beyond their initial estimations.

The raids on Syndicate facilities yielded horrifying discoveries. Hidden laboratories, concealed beneath layers of legitimate businesses, revealed the true extent of their genetic experiments. The scale of their operations was staggering, far exceeding anything anyone had initially imagined. Thousands of experimental subjects, both human and animal, were found in appalling conditions, subjected to horrific procedures and unimaginable suffering. The evidence spoke volumes, a chilling testament to the Syndicate's reckless disregard for human life and the horrifying consequences of unchecked ambition.

The forensic analysis of the recovered data was equally disturbing. Encrypted files, deciphered by teams of expert cryptographers, exposed the Syndicate's intricate network of informants and collaborators within government agencies, law enforcement, and even within the scientific community. The Syndicate had cultivated a vast network of collaborators, using bribery, blackmail, and intimidation to ensure their operations remained hidden. The sheer scale of the conspiracy was breathtaking, highlighting the depth of corruption that had taken root within the highest levels of power.

The trials of the Syndicate's leaders were a spectacle of global significance. The courtroom, packed with reporters and onlookers from across the world, became a stage for a harrowing drama of human depravity and corporate greed. The testimonies of survivors, both human and animal, were harrowing, revealing the unimaginable horrors inflicted upon those who fell victim to the Syndicate's monstrous experiments. The details were often too graphic to bear, leaving the courtroom audience shaken and profoundly disturbed.

Maya, Grayson, Kiel, and Demitra, having survived the horrors of Blackwood Cave, played a crucial role in these trials. Their testimony, delivered with unwavering courage and heartbreaking honesty, painted a vivid picture of the Syndicate's inhumanity, providing a stark counterpoint to the crafted defense offered by the Syndicate's lawyers. Their accounts, corroborated by forensic evidence and the vast trove of recovered data, shattered the Syndicate's carefully constructed defense.

Kiel's artwork, now widely circulated and critically acclaimed, served as a powerful visual testament to the horrors endured by the victims. His paintings, initially raw and emotionally charged, evolved into a powerful visual language, communicating the unspeakable with a haunting eloquence that transcended the limitations of words. His art became a symbol of resilience and a catalyst for public awareness, sparking conversations about corporate ethics and social responsibility.

The trials, though long and arduous, yielded significant breakthroughs. The evidence presented was overwhelming, leaving no room for reasonable doubt. One by one, the Syndicate's leaders were found guilty, sentenced to lengthy prison terms, their ill-gotten fortunes seized and redistributed to victims and their families. The dismantling of the Syndicate, though far from complete, marked a significant victory in the fight for justice.

However, the legal victories were only the beginning of a longer and more challenging process. The deeper investigation into the Syndicate's global network revealed a disturbing truth: the Syndicate was not an isolated entity, but rather a symptom of a much larger, more insidious problem. They were merely a pawn in a larger game, a front for a much older, more powerful, and far more terrifying force.

The investigation led them to uncover evidence suggesting a link between the

Obsidian Syndicate and a clandestine organization known only as "The Covenant." The Covenant's origins were shrouded in mystery, its operations cloaked in secrecy, its motives as dark and inscrutable as the deepest caverns of Blackwood Cave. The few clues they found suggested an ancient history, tied to esoteric rituals and forgotten lore, hinting at a powerful, shadowy organization that has pulled the strings of power for centuries.

The revelation of The Covenant sent chills down their spines. It was as if they had only scratched the surface, barely glimpsed the terrifying depths of the conspiracy. The fight for justice, they realized, had only just begun. The victory against the Obsidian Syndicate was a significant step, but it was only the first battle in a much larger, more dangerous war. The shadows were retreating, but they still lurked, waiting for their opportunity to strike again.

The survivors, however, refused to be intimidated. Armed with the knowledge of The Covenant's existence, they regrouped, their determination hardened by their shared experience and the weight of responsibility they now bore. They knew the road ahead would be long and arduous, filled with more dangers and more sacrifices, but they were prepared to fight. They had faced the horrors of Blackwood Cave and emerged victorious; they would face whatever lay ahead with the same unwavering courage. They would not rest until justice was served, not only for the victims of the Obsidian Syndicate but for all those who had fallen prey to The Covenant's insidious machinations.

Maya, using her skills as a tech expert, delved deeper into the digital footprint of The Covenant, piecing together fragmented data and uncovering hidden connections. She uncovered coded messages, encrypted communications, and a network of shell corporations used to launder money and obscure the organization's true identity. Her findings painted a disturbing picture of global reach, highlighting the Covenant's influence in governments, corporations, and even religious institutions.

Grayson, leveraging his contacts within law enforcement and intelligence agencies, helped to coordinate efforts to track and dismantle the Covenant's network of informants and collaborators. He worked tirelessly, gathering intelligence and coordinating raids on suspected Covenant safe houses, uncovering evidence that confirmed the existence of elaborate global operations. The Covenant's web of influence was far more extensive than they'd initially imagined.

Kiel, through his art, continued to bear witness, his paintings now a powerful testament not just to the horrors of Blackwood Cave, but also to the ongoing struggle against the forces of darkness. His art became a voice for the voiceless, a symbol of hope and resilience in the face of overwhelming adversity. His paintings, displayed in galleries and museums around the world, inspired others to join the fight.

Demitra, using her scientific expertise, analyzed the recovered genetic material from the creatures encountered in Blackwood Cave. She worked tirelessly to understand their origins, their capabilities, and their vulnerabilities, seeking ways to mitigate the threat they posed. She discovered disturbing links between the genetic material and ancient myths, suggesting a deeper, more sinister connection to the Covenant's activities.

Their combined efforts began to bear fruit. As more and more pieces of the puzzle fell into place, the true nature of The Covenant started to emerge from the shadows. The organization, it turned out, was far older than they'd initially suspected, with roots stretching back centuries, a dark cabal that had manipulated world events from the shadows, pulling strings of power to achieve its own nefarious purposes. Their motives, however, remained elusive.

Despite the relentless dangers and the seemingly insurmountable odds, they held onto a glimmer of hope. The global awareness raised by their initial revelations had created a new sense of international cooperation, with governments and organizations across the world pooling resources to combat the threat posed by The Covenant. The fight for justice was far from over, but for the first time, they felt a sense of collective strength, a shared purpose that transcended national borders and political ideologies. Their combined efforts were slowly chipping away at the Covenant's influence, exposing its corruption and undermining its power. The shadows were still there, but they were slowly, inexorably, beginning to recede. The fight for justice had become a global crusade, and the world was finally listening.

Chapter 7: The Reckoning

The opulent penthouse suite, a stark contrast to the grim reality of their recent ordeal, offered little solace. Rain lashed against the panoramic windows, mirroring the tempest brewing inside Maya. Across the polished mahogany table, Grayson arranged files, each a piece of the increasingly complex puzzle they were trying to solve. Kiel, his usually vibrant eyes shadowed with exhaustion, sketched furiously in a large leather-bound book, capturing the visceral fear that still haunted him. Demitra, ever the scientist, pored over genetic sequences on her tablet, her brow furrowed in concentration.

Their victory over the Obsidian Syndicate was pyrrhic. The dismantling of the corporation, the arrests of its leaders, the public outcry – it had all been a carefully orchestrated distraction. They were now playing a far more dangerous game, a game where the stakes were infinitely higher and the enemy far more formidable.

"They're watching us," Maya said, her voice low, her gaze fixed on the flickering city lights below. "I can feel it. Every move we make, every contact we make, they're monitoring it."

She tapped a series of lines of code on her tablet, a network map glowing with a chilling network of connections, hidden servers, encrypted communications. It was a labyrinthine web, woven by The Covenant, its tendrils reaching into every corner of the globe.

"They're sophisticated," Grayson admitted, his voice grim. "They've infiltrated everything – law enforcement, intelligence agencies, even parts of the media. They've been incredibly effective at covering their tracks. It's as if they anticipated our every move, anticipating our countermeasures."

He tapped a file, a series of blurred photographs taken by a covert surveillance team. They depicted shadowed figures, always just out of focus, always a step ahead. The Covenant's operatives seemed to move through the city like ghosts, unseen, unheard, yet undeniably present.

"They're not just powerful; they're relentless," Demitra chimed in, her voice tinged with a chilling certainty. "The genetic material from Blackwood Cave... it's unlike anything I've ever seen. The sophistication of the genetic engineering, the level of control... it points to centuries of research, refined over countless generations. It's horrifyingly advanced."

She paused, her eyes wide. "And what's even more disturbing are the connections I've found, linking this genetic material to ancient mythologies, forgotten rituals, suggesting the origin of the creatures isn't simply scientific but... something else entirely. Something older, something far more sinister."

Kiel slammed his sketchbook shut, the sound sharp in the otherwise silent room. "The paintings... they're not just capturing the events; they're channeling them. The fear, the terror... it's seeping into my work, feeding the nightmares that plague my sleep."

His voice was strained, a raw tremor in his tone. The art that had once been his refuge now felt like a burden, a conduit for the darkness that still clung to him. He had tried to capture the horrors they had witnessed, but the experience had seeped into his soul, painting him with the strokes of a nightmare he could not escape.

"They're trying to break us," Maya stated, her eyes unwavering. "They know we're a threat. They're trying to isolate us, to sow discord among us. They know our collective strength lies in our collaboration, in our shared purpose. That's why they're working to fracture our unity. To turn us against each other."

Over the next few days, the subtle attempts to destabilize them became increasingly overt. Anonymous threats appeared, cryptic messages delivered through various channels. Their phones were tapped, their emails intercepted, their movements tracked. The feeling of being watched intensified, a suffocating pressure that threatened to crush them.

One night, Grayson received a call from a trusted source – a seasoned FBI agent, compromised by the Syndicate but recently showing signs of wanting to turn. The information was alarming. A clandestine operation, code-named "Project Chimera," had been discovered, implicating The Covenant in a massive conspiracy involving the creation of a new generation of bio-weapons, even more potent and terrifying than the creatures from Blackwood Cave.

The location of the main laboratory was identified – a seemingly innocuous research facility nestled deep within the Amazon rainforest. This was not a simple takedown. It required stealth and precision.

The team devised a plan. Kiel, using his artistic skills and his uncanny ability to blend into the shadows, would scout the facility, documenting the layout and security measures. Demitra, relying on her scientific knowledge, would plan an infiltration strategy based on the facility's technological vulnerabilities. Maya's technological prowess would ensure they could access the facility's network and potentially disrupt the operation from within. Grayson, using his network, secured the backing of a select few law enforcement agents committed to justice, who would provide crucial support from outside.

The mission was fraught with danger. They were walking into a lion's den, aware that they were the bait. But they were no longer naive teenagers. They had stared into the abyss, and the abyss had stared back. They had survived Blackwood Cave and they would not back down. This was their reckoning. This was the beginning of the fight back.

Their journey to the remote research facility was fraught with perilous encounters, with close calls and near misses. The rainforest, once a tranquil sanctuary, was now a menacing labyrinth, every shadow a potential threat. They moved through the dense undergrowth, their senses heightened, their every step calculated, wary of the unseen dangers lurking in the shadows. They relied on Maya's advanced technology to navigate the treacherous terrain, relying on thermal imaging to spot any potential threats, and drone surveillance to track the facility's movement and security patterns.

The infiltration itself was as tense as any action movie scene. Kiel, using his keen observation skills and his knowledge of the facility's layout, managed to bypass the security systems with a combination of calculated stealth and artful subterfuge. He moved like a phantom, unseen and unheard, his presence an illusion. He documented the facility's intricate network, its hidden compartments, and its advanced technological capabilities, providing a detailed blueprint for the team's upcoming assault.

Demitra, utilizing her scientific expertise, discovered critical vulnerabilities in the facility's security protocols. Her knowledge of the facility's systems was crucial in disabling its defenses, allowing the team to make their move. Maya, using her unparalleled hacking skills, managed to penetrate the facility's network, disrupting communications and disabling the security cameras, providing a crucial window of opportunity.

Grayson's contacts had prepared the exterior support team, ensuring that backup was at the ready, in case anything went wrong. The coordinated strike was a symphony of precision, a coordinated assault that took the facility by surprise. The external team moved with lethal efficiency, neutralizing the guards and securing the perimeter, allowing the others to focus on the main laboratory.

Inside the laboratory, the true horror of Project Chimera was revealed. Rows upon rows of containment units held grotesque creatures, hybrids of human and animal DNA, far more intelligent and ferocious than anything they had encountered in Blackwood Cave. The scale of the operation was staggering, far beyond anything they could have ever imagined. The evidence was irrefutable, a testament to The Covenant's insatiable hunger for power, their disregard for human life and the terrifying potential of their creations.

Their escape was nothing short of miraculous. The facility exploded, taking with it not only The Covenant's horrific creations but also a significant portion of its research. But their victory came at a cost. Kiel, in a selfless act of bravery, saved Demitra from a terrifying creature, sacrificing his own safety in the process. The fight had left its mark, etching deep scars onto their minds, their bodies, and their souls.

As they emerged from the depths of the jungle, bruised, battered, and emotionally scarred, they knew that the fight was far from over. The Covenant's reach was vast, its influence insidious, its secrets far more chilling than anyone had dared to imagine. But they had struck a blow, a significant blow, and they would continue to fight, until the very last shadow had been dispelled. Their journey through Blackwood Cave had been only the beginning of a longer, more arduous, and much more dangerous war. The reckoning had begun.

The escape from the Amazonian research facility left them shaken, but not broken. The inferno that consumed the laboratory, a fiery testament to their success, also served as a stark reminder of the peril they faced. The Covenant wouldn't simply disappear; they would retaliate, and their vengeance would be swift and merciless. Their victory was a temporary reprieve, a fleeting moment of respite in a war that had only just begun.

The journey back was a blur of adrenaline-fueled escapes and nerve-wracking close calls. They moved through the dense rainforest under the cover of darkness, each shadow a potential enemy, each rustle of leaves a potential ambush. The weight of their actions, the knowledge of the horrors they had witnessed, pressed down on them, a crushing burden that threatened to suffocate them. Kiel, still reeling from his near-death experience, moved with a newfound fragility, his usually vibrant spirit dimmed by the trauma he had endured. Demitra, ever the pragmatist, focused on their immediate survival, her scientific mind working tirelessly to find ways to evade their pursuers, to analyze their vulnerabilities, and to strategize their next move. Maya, ever vigilant, used her technological prowess to stay one step ahead, her fingers flying across her tablet, disrupting surveillance systems, tracing the digital footprints of their enemies, and erasing their own tracks. Grayson, hardened by years of navigating the treacherous world of espionage, kept them focused, his experience providing a much needed anchor in the storm.

They were hunted. They knew it. They felt it in the chilling silence of the rainforest, in the unsettling stillness of the air, in the constant, nagging feeling of unseen eyes watching their every move. The Covenant's agents were everywhere, their shadows lengthening, their grip tightening. Several times, they were nearly captured, barely escaping by the skin of their teeth. One harrowing incident involved a high-speed chase through the dense undergrowth, pursued by genetically-modified hounds, their senses honed to an unnatural level of acuity. They evaded their pursuers by a hair's breadth, using the rainforest itself as a weapon, weaving through the dense foliage, utilizing the terrain to their advantage, their knowledge of the land their shield. Another close call involved a confrontation with a Covenant operative, a ruthless assassin who moved with the silent efficiency of a predator, his combat skills honed to lethal perfection. Only Maya's quick thinking and Grayson's experience prevented them from being completely overwhelmed, their combined knowledge a crucial element in avoiding capture.

To ensure their safety and protect their identities, they had to go underground. They established a hidden base in a remote mountain range, a forgotten sanctuary far removed from the reach of The Covenant's influence. Living off the land, they developed a rudimentary self-sufficiency, hunting for food, collecting water, and learning to rely on their instincts. Their once polished appearance faded away, replaced by worn clothing, stained and torn, testament to their harsh circumstances. Their faces were hardened, weathered by the elements and the weight of their burden. The transformation from polished urbanites into hardened survivors was complete.

But even in their secluded haven, they were not safe. They used aliases and fake identities, communicating through encrypted channels, moving like ghosts, their movements concealed by the shadows of the mountains and the dense foliage. They employed counter-surveillance techniques to evade detection, their every move carefully calculated to avoid detection. The ever-present threat of discovery fueled their determination.

Their investigation continued, albeit now in secret. Using Kiel's artistic skills, they forged connections with people who were either unaware of the larger conspiracy or willing to help. Kiel's unique connection to the creatures, the empathic link he shared with them, enabled him to draw out information, to understand their world and to interpret their motivations. He became their conduit, their bridge to the unknown, his ability to sense their presence an invaluable asset.

Demitra's scientific expertise was essential in analyzing the recovered genetic material, piecing together the fragments of information, unravelling the mysteries of The Covenant's genetic experiments. She worked tirelessly, decoding sequences, analyzing the data, her unwavering focus driving her forward. She discovered that the creatures were not merely weapons; they were a crucial part of a larger scheme, an element in a complex, terrifying equation.

Maya's technological skills allowed them to stay connected, to maintain a network of contacts, to access vital information, and to share their discoveries. She became their eyes and ears, monitoring communications, tracking their pursuers, and guiding them through the maze of deceit and subterfuge. She acted as their sentinel, protecting them from potential threats, maintaining an invisible shield to protect their sanctuary.

Grayson, with his experience in the world of espionage, secured the backing of certain influential individuals, those who had grown skeptical of The Covenant's influence and their own government's complicity. He built a network of allies, forging connections with those who shared their goals, who were willing to fight against the darkness. He acted as their strategist, planning their next move, shaping their response, and orchestrating their counter-attack.

Their life on the run tested them to their limits. They were physically exhausted, emotionally drained, and spiritually tested. Their shared experience, the horrors they had faced together, strengthened their bonds, creating an unshakable unity. Their collaboration was the key to their survival. They were more than a team; they were a family, bound by their shared trauma, their shared purpose, and their unwavering determination to prevail.

They lived each day as if it were their last, yet each day they continued to unravel the mysteries of Blackwood Cave, discovering the long-forgotten secrets buried deep within the depths of the Earth. The fight for survival had become a desperate pursuit of truth, a determined quest to expose the darkness that threatened to consume them all. The reckoning was not merely a battle for their own survival, but a war against a terrifying enemy that sought to control the very future of humanity. The road ahead was fraught with danger, yet they pressed forward, their resolve unwavering, their spirits unbroken. The fight had just begun.

The biting mountain wind whipped around them as they huddled deeper into the makeshift shelter, the flickering firelight casting long, dancing shadows on the rough-hewn walls. Days bled into weeks, each sunrise a fragile promise, each sunset a reminder of their precarious existence. Their secluded haven, once a sanctuary, now felt like a prison, the walls closing in, the weight of their isolation pressing down. The fear of discovery was a constant companion, a cold hand gripping their hearts.

Then, unexpectedly, a flicker of hope ignited in the darkness. A coded message, received through Maya's intricate network, spoke of a potential ally – Dr. Aris Thorne, a former researcher at the Amazonian facility. His name sent a jolt of icy fear through their ranks. Thorne had been a key figure in the Covenant's operation, a scientist whose brilliance had helped create the monstrous creatures that now hunted them. His betrayal was a twist they hadn't anticipated, a plot line too shocking to be believable.

The message was cryptic, offering only a rendezvous point – a remote cabin nestled deep within the Redwood National Park. The risk was immense, the potential betrayal palpable. Yet, the possibility of gaining an insider's perspective on The Covenant, of understanding the scope of their operation, was too tempting to ignore.

The journey to the rendezvous point was a nerve-wracking odyssey, fraught with danger and uncertainty. They moved through the night, their movements silent and precise, their senses heightened, their instincts sharp. Grayson, his experience invaluable, guided them through the treacherous terrain, his knowledge of clandestine operations proving to be their lifeline. Kiel's empathic connection with the creatures served as an early warning system, alerting them to potential danger long before it manifested itself.

They reached the cabin as the first rays of dawn painted the sky in hues of orange and purple. The cabin was dilapidated, its paint peeling, its wood weathered by time and neglect. A sense of foreboding hung heavy in the air, a palpable sense of unease that amplified their anxiety.

Thorne emerged from the shadows, his face etched with a mixture of weariness and remorse. His eyes, once filled with cold ambition, now reflected a deep-seated guilt. He was a broken man, his former brilliance dimmed, his body frail, his spirit shattered. He had grown disillusioned. He had witnessed the true nature of The Covenant's ambitions – ambitions that went far beyond simple genetic experimentation. He had seen them exploit, torture, and murder. He had witnessed the inhumane treatment of the creatures, their transformation from scientific subjects to weapons of mass destruction.

"I… I am truly sorry," Thorne began, his voice raspy, his words hesitant. "For everything. I was blinded by ambition, seduced by the allure of power. I believed in the scientific enterprise, the potential of genetic engineering to benefit humanity. But I was wrong. I was a fool. What they do is beyond science. It is evil." He spoke with a weariness that betrayed years of torment.

"What changed your mind?" Grayson asked, his voice tight with suspicion.

Thorne gestured towards a battered briefcase he held in his hands. "They were going to use the creatures for more than they had told me. This… this is proof. Information on their true plans, data that could expose their entire operation. I stole it before they could destroy it. Before they destroyed me."

He opened the briefcase, revealing a collection of data drives, encrypted files, and research documents. Demitra, her eyes wide with disbelief, quickly began the process of decrypting the data, her fingers flying across her tablet. The information revealed a horrifying reality. The Covenant was not merely creating weapons; they were planning something far more sinister – a global bioweapon. They planned to unleash genetically-engineered plagues upon the world.

The data confirmed the extent of The Covenant's ruthlessness. The scientists had been working for years, genetically modifying not only the creatures but also diseases, creating deadly bioweapons that could decimate the human population. Their research was far advanced. The sheer scope of their operation dwarfed anything they had previously encountered.

Thorne's confession was a jarring blow, one that shook their foundations. Their enemy was not merely a shadowy organization; it was a force capable of bringing global devastation. Their fight for survival had expanded into something larger, something that transcended their personal struggle. They were fighting for humanity's survival.

As Demitra continued to decipher the data, Maya monitored their surroundings, her vigilance unwavering. Kiel, his empathic connection allowing him to sense the creatures' movements, reported that they were close, tracking their every move. The cabin was not a safe haven; it was a pressure cooker, the heat intensifying, the risk escalating.

Grayson, drawing on his extensive network, managed to secure a temporary safe haven in a secluded coastal town, far removed from the prying eyes of The Covenant. Thorne's remorse and his data had altered their trajectory. They had an unexpected ally, a knowledgeable insider, and a path forward. But the battle was far from over; the reckoning was yet to come. The fight for survival was now a war against an unseen enemy that threatened the very fabric of existence. They were not only running for their lives, but for the survival of humanity. The true cost of their rebellion had yet to be seen, as the shadow of impending doom stretched long and menacing. Their journey, once a desperate escape, had become a perilous crusade, their alliance with the repentant Thorne a gamble of epic proportions. The weight of the world rested on their shoulders, their determination fueled by the horrifying truth they had uncovered, and the terrible price they would have to pay to fight back.

The escape from the coastal town was a close call, a harrowing escape through the labyrinthine streets and undergrowth, their pursuers always just a step behind. They utilized their combined skills to outwit their enemies, their movements fluid and coordinated, their actions a symphony of survival. Kiel used his connection to the creatures to anticipate their enemies' movements, Demitra used her knowledge to create distractions, Maya used her technology to disrupt surveillance, and Grayson employed his tactical acumen to plan their escapes.

The journey was relentless, exhausting, but they pushed on, driven by the knowledge that the fate of humanity rested on their shoulders. They were not merely fighting for themselves anymore; they were fighting for the future of the world, a future threatened by the insidious machinations of The Covenant. The fight had become a holy war, a crusade against an enemy whose ambitions could extinguish all life on Earth. The weight of this responsibility was a heavy burden, yet they carried it with unwavering resolve. The reckoning was coming, and they were ready. They were not merely survivors; they were warriors, champions of humanity, facing the ultimate enemy.

The coastal town, a fleeting sanctuary, offered little respite. The air hung heavy with the unspoken knowledge of their precarious position. The Covenant's long reach extended everywhere, their tendrils slithering into the most unexpected corners. Even here, amidst the quiet hum of everyday life, the threat felt palpable, a chilling undercurrent beneath the surface of normalcy. Their temporary haven was nothing more than a staging ground, a brief pause before the inevitable reckoning.

Grayson, ever the pragmatist, began assembling their next move. He had unearthed fragmented information, scraps of data gleaned from Thorne's briefcase, pointing towards an ancient, forgotten temple nestled deep within the Amazon rainforest. It was a dangerous place, a place shrouded in myth and legend, a place where the line between reality and nightmare blurred. According to the cryptic documents, this temple held the key to understanding the origin of the creatures, the source of the ancient evil that fueled The Covenant's horrifying ambitions.

The journey was perilous, a relentless trek through unforgiving terrain. They navigated treacherous rivers, dense jungles teeming with unseen dangers, and ancient ruins that whispered tales of forgotten civilizations. The constant threat of discovery hung over them like a suffocating blanket, every rustle of leaves, every snap of a twig, sending shivers down their spines. Kiel's empathic abilities became their lifeline, warning them of approaching danger, guiding them through the labyrinthine pathways of the jungle. He felt the creatures' presence, sensed their movements, and guided them away from their paths, creating an invisible shield of awareness.

Demitra, meanwhile, continued to decipher the remaining encrypted data from Thorne's briefcase. The information was fragmented, pieced together from scattered notes, research papers, and coded messages. Slowly, painstakingly, she assembled the horrifying puzzle, revealing a history far older and more terrifying than they could have imagined. The creatures weren't merely genetically engineered weapons; they were the result of a centuries-old experiment, a twisted attempt to merge human and non-human DNA, creating a race of terrifying hybrids with unparalleled strength and intelligence.

The documents revealed a horrifying truth: The Covenant was not a modern organization; it was an ancient order, its origins lost in the mists of time. They had been manipulating genetic engineering for centuries, creating and controlling these creatures for their own nefarious purposes. The Amazonian facility was only the latest in a long line of clandestine laboratories, a testament to their unwavering ambition and their terrifying patience. The ancient temple, the documents hinted, held the key to stopping them, to severing the link between The Covenant and their monstrous creations.

As they pressed deeper into the rainforest, the jungle itself seemed to conspire against them. The oppressive humidity clung to their skin, the dense foliage choked the air, and the cacophony of jungle sounds amplified their sense of unease. Every shadow seemed to conceal a threat, every rustle of leaves sounded like the approach of their pursuers. The weight of their mission bore down on them, the knowledge that the fate of humanity rested on their shoulders.

Days bled into nights, their progress slow and arduous. They endured venomous insect bites, treacherous terrain, and the constant, gnawing fear of discovery. Their physical and mental endurance was tested to its limits, but they pressed on, fueled by their determination and the horrifying truth they had uncovered. The ancient temple was their only hope, their only chance to confront the source of the evil that threatened their world.

Finally, after what seemed like an eternity, they stumbled upon the temple, its crumbling stone walls half-hidden by the dense jungle foliage. The air grew cold, the atmosphere shifting, as if the very essence of the place exuded an aura of ancient power and malevolence. The temple was a testament to a lost civilization, its intricate carvings depicting scenes of horrific rituals and grotesque creatures that bore an uncanny resemblance to those that hunted them.

Inside, the temple was a labyrinth of dimly lit chambers, each one more terrifying than the last. Ancient murals depicted a long and gruesome history, detailing the creation of the creatures, their transformation from scientific experiments into weapons of mass destruction. They learned of the Covenant's true goal – not merely global domination, but a complete reshaping of humanity itself, a horrifying eugenics project on a global scale.

Kiel's empathic connection grew stronger within the temple walls, becoming almost unbearable. The whispers of countless victims echoed through the chambers, their pain and anguish a palpable force. He sensed the creatures' presence, not as mere predators, but as extensions of the ancient evil that permeated the place. They were not merely hunting them; they were guarding something far more sinister.

Demitra's decryption efforts were hampered by the temple's ancient energy, the air itself saturated with a potent force that disrupted electronic signals. But, with painstaking effort, she managed to access a hidden chamber, discovering a central core of the temple – a massive crystal pulsating with an unnatural energy, a source of power that fueled the creatures' very existence. The crystal was the heart of the ancient evil, the nexus of their power.

Grayson realized that destroying the crystal was the only way to stop the creatures, to sever the connection between the ancient evil and the Covenant. But the task was incredibly perilous. The crystal was guarded by a monstrous creature, a being of immense power and savagery, far more formidable than any they had encountered before.

The final confrontation was a brutal, desperate battle, a clash between humanity's last hope and the ancient evil that threatened to consume them. Their combined skills and determination were tested to their very limits, as they fought for their lives, for the survival of humanity. The battle was a maelstrom of violence, a chaotic dance of survival amidst the crumbling stones of the ancient temple. The air crackled with energy, the very foundations of the temple seeming to tremble under the weight of their struggle.

The ending of the battle left a trail of destruction and exhaustion but also the knowledge that they had succeeded in their mission. The crystal lay shattered, the ancient evil quelled, the source of their power destroyed. In its shattering, a cascade of energy unleashed a wave of destruction, creating devastation within the temple. The creatures, deprived of their source of power, began to weaken, their aggression waning, replaced by a chilling sense of despair.

Their victory, however, was a pyrrhic one. They had escaped the immediate threat, but the scars of their ordeal remained, etched deep into their minds and bodies. The world had changed, irrevocably altered by their experiences. They had faced the darkest aspects of human nature and the terrifying power of the unknown. They had won a battle, but the war was far from over. The Covenant, though weakened, remained, its influence still lurking in the shadows, waiting for an opportunity to strike again. Their journey had transformed them, turning their youthful bravado into steely resolve, their innocence into a hardened understanding of the brutal realities of the world. They carried the weight of their experiences, their victory a hard-won testament to the resilience of the human spirit. The reckoning was over, but the echoes of terror would reverberate for years to come, a constant reminder of the darkness they had faced and the price they had paid to save the world.

The air hung thick with the scent of decay and ozone, a miasma clinging to the crumbling walls of the inner sanctum. Before them, bathed in the eerie, pulsating glow of the massive crystal, stood the mastermind – a figure cloaked in shadows, their face obscured by a hood, but their presence radiating an aura of chilling power. This was no mere scientist or military leader; this was something ancient, something that had orchestrated the horrors they had witnessed, pulling the strings from the shadows for centuries. The Covenant's true face had finally been revealed.

Grayson, his face grim, leveled his weapon. Demitra, pale but resolute, held her decryption device, its screen flickering erratically, struggling against the oppressive energy emanating from the crystal. Kiel, his eyes closed, stood beside them, a silent sentinel, his empathic abilities straining under the weight of the accumulated anguish of the temple's victims. The air thrummed with unspoken tension, the silence broken only by the rhythmic pulse of the crystal, a heartbeat of ancient evil.

The mastermind spoke, their voice a low, resonant hum that seemed to vibrate within their very bones. "You have come far, children," the voice echoed through the chamber, "further than any dared to venture. But your journey ends here." Their words held no malice, no rage, only a cold, clinical detachment, the words of a puppeteer surveying their pawns.

Grayson didn't hesitate. "It ends here for you as well," he retorted, his voice tight with controlled fury. He knew this was their final stand. There would be no second chance, no miraculous escape. This confrontation determined the fate of humanity, the balance between a horrifying dystopia and a future where the sun might rise without the shadow of fear.

The battle began not with a roar, but a subtle shift in the air, a pressure that built with suffocating intensity. The mastermind raised a hand, and the very stones of the temple seemed to writhe, shifting and groaning under an unseen force. Creatures, unlike any they had encountered before – larger, more grotesque hybrids, warped by the crystal's power – emerged from the shadows, their eyes glowing with malevolent intelligence. They moved with unnerving grace and speed, their movements coordinated with horrifying precision.

Demitra, her fingers flying across the decryption device, struggled to disrupt the crystal's energy field, seeking a weakness, a vulnerability in its protective aura. The device sputtered and crackled, fighting against the overwhelming energy, threatening to overload and cease to function at any moment. Her efforts, however, were hampered by the chaotic energy surges and the constant threat of the emerging creatures. Each successful burst from the device created an opportunity but also attracted the attention of the horrifying beasts, forcing her to defend herself against their savage attacks.

Kiel's empathic abilities were overwhelmed. The psychic assault was brutal, a wave of pure horror washing over him, threatening to shatter his mind. He could feel the pain of countless victims, the despair of those who had been sacrificed to this ancient evil. It was a psychic maelstrom, a symphony of agony that threatened to drown him in its depths. Yet, he persevered, his connection to the crystal allowing him a faint glimpse of the mastermind's vulnerabilities. He channeled that knowledge to Grayson, whispering directions, guiding his attacks with the precision of a surgeon.

Grayson, meanwhile, fought with the ferocity of a cornered animal. His every move was a calculated risk, his every shot a desperate gamble. He moved through the chaos with a grim determination, his weapon a conduit for his rage and desperation. He fought not only for his life but for the future of humanity. He was a shield, protecting Demitra and Kiel from the relentless onslaught of creatures. The weight of their combined survival rested on his ability to withstand the onslaught long enough for Demitra and Kiel to complete their respective tasks.

The battle raged, a whirlwind of violence and destruction. The temple trembled, its ancient stones crumbling under the weight of the clash between ancient evil and desperate humanity. The air was thick with the smell of blood, the sounds of breaking bone, and the guttural roars of the creatures. Each swing of Grayson's weapon, each burst from Demitra's device, each psychic strike from Kiel, was a testament to their unyielding determination. They were fighting against overwhelming odds, their bodies battered, their minds strained to the breaking point, but they refused to yield.

As the battle raged, Demitra, through sheer willpower and a stroke of luck, discovered a way to disrupt the crystal's energy field. It was a risky maneuver, a gamble with unimaginable consequences, but she had no other choice. The crystal's energy, the source of the creatures' power, was vulnerable to a precisely tuned electromagnetic pulse. It was a narrow window of opportunity, a fleeting moment that could succeed or result in catastrophic failure.

With a final, desperate effort, Demitra unleashed a concentrated burst of energy toward the crystal. The temple shook violently, the air crackled with raw power, and the crystal itself seemed to shudder, its pulsating glow flickering and dimming. The creatures screamed in agony, their forms contorting as the source of their power was disrupted. Their movements became sluggish, their attacks less coordinated. Their intelligence and speed, their power and ferocity, diminished rapidly as the crystal lost its energy.

Seizing the opportunity, Grayson pressed his advantage, his attacks becoming more precise, more deadly. Kiel, his psychic connection to the crystal weakened, pushed his empathic abilities to their limit. He unleashed a wave of psychic energy directly into the mastermind's mind, shattering their control over the creatures. The creatures, now mindless and weakened, fell to Grayson's weapon.

Finally, with a devastating blow, Grayson shattered the crystal. A cascade of energy ripped through the temple, a wave of pure power that leveled the ancient stones. The temple's structure collapsed, burying them in dust and debris, but the victory was theirs. The ancient evil, the source of the Covenant's power, had been destroyed. The mastermind, their control broken, lay lifeless amongst the ruins.

The survivors emerged from the wreckage, battered and bruised, but alive. The jungle, silent in the aftermath of their battle, seemed to exhale, the oppressive atmosphere lifting as the ancient power within the temple faded into oblivion. The silence, heavy with exhaustion and relief, was a welcome change from the terrifying cacophony of their battle. Their victory was hard-won, bought with blood and sweat, with pain and loss. But it was a victory nonetheless. The reckoning was over. Or was it? The echoes of terror lingered, a reminder that their ordeal had just begun. The world was safe, for now. But the fight was far from over.

Chapter 8: Betrayal

The jungle air, still thick with the scent of ozone and decay, felt strangely still after the cataclysmic collapse of the temple. Grayson, Demitra, and Kiel, bruised and battered, picked themselves from the rubble, the silence broken only by the ragged rasp of their breathing and the distant drip of water from unseen crevices. Their victory felt hollow, a pyrrhic triumph bought at a terrible cost. The ancient evil was vanquished, but the weight of their ordeal, the physical and emotional scars, remained. As they began to assess their injuries and plan their escape, a new terror began to bloom, colder and more insidious than the monstrous creatures they had just faced.

Demitra, ever the pragmatist, was the first to speak, her voice barely a whisper. "We need to get out of here," she said, her gaze sweeping over the devastated landscape. "The cave could collapse entirely at any moment. The seismic shifts from that crystal... they were significant." She examined her decryption device, its casing cracked and its screen flickering erratically — a testament to its heroic performance.

Kiel, still reeling from the psychic assault, nodded weakly. His empathic abilities, usually a source of strength, were drained, leaving him with a throbbing headache and a lingering sense of dread. The echoes of the countless victims' agony still resonated within his mind, a chilling symphony of suffering. He shivered, pulling his battered jacket tighter around him. The cave's chill seeped into his bones, a reminder of the horrors they had endured.

Grayson, ever the stoic, examined his weapons. His usual confidence had taken a dent. The battle had taken its toll, but beneath the exhaustion, a sharp anxiety gnawed at him. He had saved them, but at what cost? The strain was evident on his face, etched in the lines around his eyes and the grim set of his jaw. The battle had been won, but it felt far from over.

As they moved through the debris-strewn tunnels, a sense of unease settled over them. The path was treacherous, the ground unstable, the air heavy with a growing sense of foreboding. It wasn't just the physical danger of the collapsing cave; there was something else, something lurking in the shadows, something watching them. The silence, once a welcome relief, now felt oppressive, heavy with an unspoken menace. They moved in a strained silence, each step measured, each breath careful.
The atmosphere hung thick with unspoken questions, with the weight of uncertainty.

The victory felt incomplete, shadowed by a nagging sense of dread.

It was Demitra who noticed it first. A subtle tremor in the ground, a faint shift in the air, too slight for Kiel's weakened empathic senses, but caught by Demitra's acutely trained observation skills. "Stop," she hissed, her hand instinctively reaching for her weapon. "Something's wrong."

They froze, listening. The only sound was the drip, drip, drip of water echoing through the tunnels – a relentless counterpoint to the rising tension. Then, a low growl, barely audible, resonated from the darkness ahead. The air grew colder, the shadows seemed to deepen, and a primal fear gripped them, a feeling far more chilling than the horrors they had already faced. A creeping dread coiled around their hearts, strangling the burgeoning hope of their survival.

From the darkness, a figure emerged, moving with a chilling grace and familiarity. It was Marcus, one of their own, his face pale and drawn, his eyes wild with a desperate gleam. He held a weapon, a familiar hunting knife, gleaming ominously in the dim light. The betrayal was palpable, a cruel twist of the knife in the already wounded hearts of the survivors.

"Marcus?" Grayson breathed, his voice a mixture of disbelief and outrage. "What the hell are you doing?"

Marcus didn't answer, his gaze flickering between the three survivors, a strange mix of fear and determination reflected in his eyes. He seemed both terrified and exhilarated, caught in a maelstrom of conflicting emotions. The betrayal was shocking, stunning them into a stunned silence, replacing their hard-earned relief with a gut-wrenching sense of vulnerability. Their small group, already battered and exhausted, was now fractured, facing a new threat even more dangerous than the genetically engineered monsters.

"He's not himself," Kiel whispered, his voice trembling slightly. He focused his remaining empathic abilities, attempting to pierce through the veil of confusion shrouding Marcus' mind. He felt a fractured consciousness, a tormented mind battling some external influence. The same chilling energy that emanated from the crystal. It was almost as if a tendril of the defeated entity still lingered, manipulating their former ally.

Demitra, ever practical, began to assess the situation. Marcus was weaker, slower, than he should be. Yet, his eyes held the same chilling glint of purpose as the monstrous creatures they had fought. His movements, though erratic, were coordinated with uncanny precision. He was a puppet, controlled by an unseen hand, his actions predetermined by a force beyond his conscious will. The question was: what was controlling him, and what was its purpose?

Grayson, his rage bubbling beneath his surface, approached cautiously. "Marcus, snap out of it!" He commanded, trying to reach his friend, but his words seemed to fall on deaf ears. Marcus merely tightened his grip on the knife, his eyes fixated on Grayson, radiating a cold, unyielding menace. The betrayal was complete, shattering their already fragile bond. The fight for survival now extended beyond the monstrous creatures and encompassed their own comrades.

The ensuing struggle was brutal, a desperate clash between friends turned foes. Grayson, despite his exhaustion, fought with the controlled fury of a cornered lion, his moves precise and deadly, but hampered by his hesitation to truly hurt Marcus. Demitra, agile and precise, used her quick wit and tactical skills to outmaneuver Marcus, aiming for non-lethal shots to incapacitate him without permanently harming him. Kiel, though his powers were severely diminished, used his psychic abilities to distract and disorient Marcus, attempting to break through the unseen influence controlling him, but the hold was strong.

The fight raged on, a grim dance of survival that tested the limits of their strength, endurance, and loyalty. They fought not only for their lives but also for the sanity of a friend, for the remnants of their shattered trust, for the memory of the brotherhood forged in the fires of their shared ordeal. The air crackled with tension, the echoes of their struggle reverberating through the claustrophobic tunnels. Every blow landed a blow to their hearts, further fracturing their fragile alliance.

As the battle wore on, the unseen presence manipulating Marcus became stronger, pushing him to the brink of madness. His movements became more frantic, more chaotic, and his eyes lost the last embers of their former light. He was a broken vessel, a conduit for a malevolent entity, and the question loomed larger: what was this shadowy power planning for them next? What would be its next cruel twist of fate? The answer, they knew, lay hidden in the darkness, waiting to ambush them with unimaginable horrors. The fight for survival wasn't over; it had only just begun, and their victory over the ancient evil might just be the prelude to their ultimate demise. The cave, once a sanctuary of horror, now became a theater of a far more insidious betrayal, a chilling testament to the darkness lurking within the hearts of men and the terrifying power of the unknown.

The fight with Marcus had left them drained, not just physically, but emotionally. The betrayal cut deeper than any wound the monstrous creatures had inflicted. Kiel, still reeling from his empathic ordeal, slumped against a damp rock, his face pale and etched with exhaustion. He could still feel the faint residue of the dark energy that had possessed Marcus, a chilling tendril clinging to the edges of his consciousness, a constant reminder of the insidious threat that lurked within the shadows of

Blackwood Cave. He closed his eyes, trying to shut out the lingering echoes of Marcus' tortured mind, the desperate pleas for help that were lost in the maelstrom of alien control.

Demitra, ever the strategist, examined their dwindling supplies. Their medical kit was almost depleted, their food rations critically low, and their water sources were becoming increasingly unreliable. The cave was collapsing around them, and the ever-present threat of further encounters with the genetically engineered creatures loomed large. But the immediate danger wasn't just the physical threats; it was the lingering psychic influence that seemed to infect the very air they breathed.

Grayson, though outwardly stoic, felt the weight of their predicament. The brutal battle with Marcus had shaken his faith in their camaraderie, in the very foundation of their survival strategy. He looked at Kiel and Demitra, their faces mirroring his own exhaustion and despair. He knew they had to escape, but the path forward was shrouded in uncertainty, fraught with peril. The ancient evil might be vanquished, but a new, more insidious enemy had emerged, one that played on their vulnerabilities, their hopes, and their deepest fears.

"We can't stay here," Demitra stated, her voice firm despite her weariness. "The cave is unstable, and there's something... else... out there, something far more dangerous than those creatures." She gestured to the tremor still running subtly beneath their feet. "It's not random. It's focused. It's hunting us."

Kiel nodded in agreement. His empathic senses, though weakened, were still functioning. He felt a faint pulse of malicious energy emanating from deeper within the cave, a rhythmic thrumming that sent shivers down his spine. It wasn't merely a lingering presence; it was a deliberate force, intelligent and malevolent, its purpose obscured in darkness.

"We need to find another way out," Grayson said, his voice low and resolute. "But where?"

Demitra consulted her partially damaged decryption device. The screen flickered, displaying a cryptic sequence of symbols, remnants of the data she had recovered from the temple. "There's a mention of an alternate exit," she murmured, her fingers tracing the fragmented lines of code. "A secondary tunnel system, supposedly sealed centuries ago. It's risky, it's unexplored, but it's our only chance."

The risk was immense. The secondary tunnel system was uncharted territory, a labyrinth of unknown dangers lurking in the heart of Blackwood Cave. They might encounter even more terrifying creatures, more devastating traps, or worse, become trapped forever in the unforgiving depths. But the alternative – staying put – was equally dire. The collapsing cave, the relentless pursuit of whatever force was hunting them, the dwindling supplies – all pointed to a slow, agonizing death.

Grayson weighed the options. The risk of the secondary tunnel system was monumental, potentially leading them into even greater dangers, but it held the tantalizing promise of escape. Staying where they were was a guaranteed path to destruction. The choice was clear, even if the outcome remained terrifyingly uncertain.

"We go for the secondary tunnel," Grayson said, his voice firm despite the knot of fear tightening in his chest. "It's a gamble, a desperate one, but it's our best shot."

Kiel, despite his exhaustion and lingering psychic trauma, nodded in agreement. He knew the risk, the sheer terror of the unknown. But the alternative – surrendering to the relentless pursuit of their unseen enemy – was unbearable. He would face the darkness, whatever horrors it held, with the remnants of his courage and willpower.

Demitra, her gaze resolute, began to prepare. She checked their weapons, making sure they were fully functional, assessing their remaining supplies, and planning their route based on the fragmentary data recovered from the device. Their escape was not merely a flight; it was a orchestrated mission, a desperate gamble against the overwhelming odds stacked against them.

The journey through the secondary tunnel system was a harrowing odyssey into the heart of the unknown. The tunnels were claustrophobic, the air thick with the stench of damp earth and decay. The path was treacherous, riddled with unseen obstacles and perilous drops. The slightest misstep could have resulted in a fatal fall or a deadly encounter with whatever lurked in the shadows.

Every sound echoed through the narrow passageways, amplifying their fears and sharpening their senses. The dripping water, the rustling of unseen creatures, the creaking of the earth – every noise became a potential threat, a harbinger of impending doom. The psychological tension was almost unbearable, a relentless assault on their already strained nerves.

They encountered several obstacles. They navigated through narrow crevices, scaled treacherous rock faces, and traversed flooded passages, all the while keeping a watchful eye for any signs of their unseen pursuers. They pressed on, driven by the primal urge to survive, the desperate hope of finding an escape route.

The darkness was oppressive, suffocating, a constant reminder of their vulnerability. But the darkness also held a strange allure, a perverse sense of wonder. They were venturing into the unexplored heart of Blackwood Cave, a place that had swallowed countless souls, a place where the boundaries between reality and nightmare blurred into a frightening unity.

Their journey was fraught with psychological stress. The constant tension, the unrelenting fear, the ever-present danger – it was all taking its toll. They argued, they bickered, their exhaustion and desperation pushing them to the brink of collapse. But through it all, a fragile thread of camaraderie, of mutual reliance, held them together. Their shared ordeal, the bond forged in the fires of their desperate fight for survival, held them together, even as the shadows threatened to swallow them whole.

As they delved deeper into the unexplored reaches of the cave, the intensity of the energy emanating from the depths increased. They felt its presence, a chilling tendril wrapping around their minds, probing, testing, searching for a weak point. The energy was more malevolent than the monster they'd faced before; this was a force that fed on fear, on despair, on the very essence of their humanity.

They realized then that their escape was not just a physical one. It was a battle of wills, a confrontation with the very forces of darkness that had ensnared them in Blackwood Cave's clutches. They were not just running for their lives; they were fighting for their sanity, for their souls, for the last vestiges of their humanity against a force that threatened to consume them utterly. The desperate gamble had begun, and the stakes were nothing less than their very existence.

The tremors intensified, shaking the ground beneath their feet with increasing violence. Rocks tumbled from the ceiling, showering them with dust and debris. Demitra, ever vigilant, pressed her hand against the wall, feeling the vibrations resonating through the ancient stone. "It's getting closer," she whispered, her voice barely audible above the growing din. The rhythmic pulse Kiel had sensed earlier had become a frantic drumbeat, a malevolent heartbeat echoing through the cavern.

Their escape route, the supposed secondary tunnel, was proving far more treacherous than anticipated. The passage narrowed, forcing them to squeeze through claustrophobic crevices, their bodies scraping against rough, jagged surfaces. The air grew heavy, thick with the smell of mildew and something else... something acrid and metallic, like burnt flesh. Their lamps cast long, dancing shadows, distorting familiar forms into grotesque parodies. The constant darkness and confined spaces began to gnaw at their minds, playing tricks on their senses. They saw things in the periphery, fleeting movements that vanished as quickly as they appeared, raising the hairs on the back of their necks.

Kiel, despite his weakened state, strained his empathic senses. He picked up a wave of raw, unfocused terror emanating from deeper within the cave, a chorus of desperate screams and silent pleas, a symphony of agony that seemed to penetrate his very soul. The feeling was overwhelming, a psychic maelstrom that threatened to pull him under. He clung to Grayson's arm, his knuckles white, his body trembling with a combination of fear and psychic overload.

Their dwindling supplies added another layer of torment. Their water was almost gone, their food rations meager, and their energy reserves were dangerously low. The relentless physical exertion, the psychological strain, and the constant threat of unseen dangers pushed them to the brink of exhaustion. They moved like automatons, their bodies propelled by adrenaline and a fierce will to survive.

As they rounded a sharp bend in the tunnel, they stumbled upon a horrifying sight. A vast cavern stretched before them, its walls adorned with bizarre, almost alien, carvings. In the center of the cavern lay a gruesome tableau – the remains of more victims, scattered amidst the debris, their bodies mutilated beyond recognition. The air hung heavy with the stench of death and decay, and the scene was chillingly similar to the campsite they had discovered earlier. The evidence was undeniable: they were not alone in this hellish labyrinth, and their unseen pursuer was far more prolific than they had ever imagined.

The genetic engineering they witnessed in the first creatures, they realized, extended far beyond the single encounter. This chamber revealed the horrifying scale of the operation. It wasn't just random mutations but a systematic process, a terrifyingly advanced biological project. The corpses bore visible signs of experimentation, horrific alterations to their bodies, evidence of failed attempts, and the lingering impression of a cruel and relentless scientific endeavor.

This horrific discovery served only to fuel the panic. The knowledge that something, or some *one*, was actively hunting them, experimenting upon victims, added another layer of horrifying complexity to their already desperate situation. The unseen enemy wasn't just some random threat; it was a deliberate, calculated predator, and they had unwittingly stumbled into its lair.

Their initial belief that the creatures were somehow connected to the ancient evil was thrown into question. This was something else entirely, something far more sophisticated and terrifying. The carvings on the cavern walls hinted at an ancient history, a forgotten civilization that might have been responsible for the creatures' creation, or perhaps even predated them. The mystery deepened, layering another layer of fear upon their already perilous situation.

Grayson, ever pragmatic, tried to regain control. "We need to regroup," he said, his voice strained but determined. "This changes everything. We can't just escape; we need to understand what's happening here."

Demitra, though shaken by the gruesome discovery, quickly began to analyze the situation. She examined the carvings, searching for clues, trying to decipher the language of their creators, hoping to find some indication of the enemy's goals, or a possible escape route beyond their immediate predicament. The cryptic symbols seemed to hint at a deeper, more sinister purpose, revealing just a fraction of the secrets this forgotten place held.

Kiel, his empathy still reeling from the psychic assault, tried to filter the overwhelming cacophony of fear and despair. He detected a new presence in this cavern – a stronger, more focused emanation, a malevolent intelligence overseeing the carnage, its presence a cold, chilling weight in the heavy air. It was a being of immense power, ancient and evil, its essence a terrifying reflection of the dark heart of Blackwood Cave.

The unexpected discovery of the cavern had shifted their focus. Escape became secondary to understanding their predicament, a daunting task given the limited information and the looming threat of their unseen pursuer. The weight of responsibility pressed heavily on them; they were no longer just fighting for their lives, they were fighting for the knowledge to potentially prevent more victims, and unraveling the dark secrets of Blackwood Cave.

The collapse intensified. The ground shook violently, sending tremors through the cavern. Rocks rained down from the ceiling, forcing them to scramble for cover. Their escape route was becoming increasingly compromised, the very cave itself seeming to conspire against them. The feeling that they were being hunted was no longer a suspicion but an undeniable reality.

Demitra, using the remnants of her decryption device, continued to analyze the data, piecing together the fragmented information gleaned from the temple and the cryptic carvings in the cavern. She discovered a hidden passage, a narrow fissure in the wall, seemingly concealed by an illusionary barrier, only perceivable through specific electromagnetic frequencies.

The decision to venture through this hidden passage came with its own set of risks. It was unexplored, uncharted, and the cryptic data suggested potential dangers far beyond the immediate collapse of the main tunnels. The risks were monumental, but the consequences of staying in the collapsing cavern, now known to be a killing ground, were too dire to contemplate.

With grim determination, they prepared for their next perilous step into the unknown. The unforgiving darkness of the cave, and their unseen adversary, held many more horrors in store, and their journey was far from over. Each step forward felt like a gamble, every decision a potential death sentence. But driven by a desperate will to survive, they plunged into the unknown, a fragile flame of hope flickering in the heart of despair.

Their journey into the fissure was even more harrowing. The passage was impossibly narrow, forcing them to crawl on their hands and knees through the suffocating darkness. The air was heavy with the smell of decay, the sound of dripping water echoing in the oppressive silence. The unseen threat hung heavy over them, a palpable presence, its malevolent energy seemingly woven into the very fabric of the cave.

Kiel, despite his psychic exhaustion, continued to use his empathy to navigate the passage. He sensed the faint presence of their pursuer, a chilling tendril of energy that brushed against his mind, seeking a weakness, a point of entry. He fought to maintain his mental fortitude, to resist the invasion, the terrible allure of surrender.

They crawled for what felt like an eternity, their bodies bruised, their lungs burning, their spirits crushed by the weight of their predicament. Suddenly, they emerged into another cavern, even more vast and terrifying than the last. The air here was different; it was colder, sharper, charged with a strange, unnatural energy. In the center of the cavern, they saw it: a vast, pulsating orb of dark energy, radiating a chilling aura of malevolence.

This was the source of the creatures, the ancient evil, and the force that had been hunting them. Their journey through the cave had led them to the heart of the darkness, to the epicenter of the horror. They had escaped immediate death, but they had inadvertently arrived at the scene of their ultimate confrontation. The unforeseen consequences of their actions had brought them face-to-face with the true terror of Blackwood Cave, and their fight for survival had only just begun. The desperate gamble for escape had led them to a far more perilous confrontation, and the price of survival remained far higher than they ever imagined. The true horror was yet to unfold.

The cavern pulsed with a malevolent energy, a tangible hum that vibrated through their very bones. The orb, a swirling vortex of darkness, dominated the space, its ominous glow casting long, distorted shadows that danced and writhed like living things. It was a horrifying spectacle, a testament to the sheer power of the ancient evil they had unwittingly stumbled upon. This was no mere creature; this was the source, the genesis of the horrors they had endured. This was the enemy.

Kiel, despite the exhaustion clinging to him like a shroud, felt a surge of adrenaline. His empathic abilities, usually a source of overwhelming terror, were now strangely focused, channeling the raw fear and adrenaline into a pinpoint awareness of the orb's power. He could feel its malevolent intent, its chilling indifference to their suffering. It was a being of pure malevolence, devoid of empathy, consumed by a dark purpose that transcended human comprehension.

Demitra, ever the pragmatist, began to examine the cavern floor. She noticed subtle variations in the rock formations, almost imperceptible shifts in texture and color, suggesting a hidden structure, a network of pathways beneath the surface. Her decryption device, miraculously still functional, crackled to life, detecting faint electromagnetic signals emanating from the ground, hints of a complex network buried deep within the earth. This wasn't just a lair; it was a sophisticated, intricate system, a testament to an advanced, possibly ancient civilization.

Grayson, his face grim, assessed their situation. The orb was clearly the source of the genetically modified creatures, the architect of the horrors they had witnessed. Their escape route was no longer a simple matter of finding a passage; it was a question of outsmarting a vastly superior intelligence, a being that had anticipated their every move. They were trapped in a deadly game of cat and mouse, with the cat possessing unimaginable power and the cunning of an ancient, malevolent entity.

The air grew colder, the pressure intensifying. The orb began to spin faster, its dark energy intensifying, the hum deepening into a deafening roar. The ground beneath their feet trembled violently, the cavern threatening to collapse around them. The enemy was reacting, and their window of opportunity was rapidly closing. This wasn't just a fight for survival; it was a race against time.

Demitra, her fingers flying across her decryption device, discovered a sequence of symbols etched into the cavern wall, almost invisible to the naked eye. The symbols were similar to the carvings they'd seen earlier but more complex, a kind of advanced code. Her device translated the code, revealing a series of coordinates, a precise location beneath the cavern floor.

"This is it," she said, her voice barely a whisper, her eyes wide with a mix of fear and determination. "The coordinates lead to a sub-terranean chamber, a hidden facility. It seems the creatures weren't simply bred here; they were developed, refined, and perhaps even controlled from this location."

The revelation added another layer to the terrifying complexity of their situation. The enemy wasn't just a mindless force of nature; it was a highly organized, sophisticated operation, a planned project of terrifying proportions. They were facing not only a creature but a clandestine organization, an ancient evil wielding unimaginable technology. Their fight for survival was now a fight against a technologically advanced, ancient evil.

Grayson, his voice steely with resolve, laid out their plan. "We're going in," he declared. "We have to reach this facility, find out what they're doing, and try to disable it. It's our only hope of stopping this, of saving whatever remains."

Kiel, his senses still reeling from the psychic assault, felt a surge of determination. He would use his empathy, to navigate the unseen currents of the cavern, to identify any hidden traps or defenses. His ability to sense emotions would be their key, a beacon guiding them through the darkness.

With grim determination, they moved towards the coordinates Demitra had identified. The ground beneath their feet shifted ominously, cracks appearing in the stone, hinting at the precarious nature of their endeavor. The air grew thick with tension, charged with the palpable sense of an approaching confrontation.

The passage was claustrophobic, narrow, and treacherous. The air was thick with the smell of ozone, a hint of advanced technology. They crawled through the tunnels, their senses on high alert, Kiel's empathy painting a vivid picture of the facility's layout. He sensed machinery humming, a network of energy conduits throbbing with power, and the faint, chilling presence of their pursuer, always just beyond their reach.

They emerged into a vast, subterranean chamber, a marvel of ancient technology blended with a terrifyingly advanced level of scientific experimentation. The chamber was filled with intricate machinery, glistening tubes filled with luminescent fluids, and strange devices humming with unnatural energy. The air thrummed with a palpable sense of power, a feeling of sinister creation and terrifying potential.

And then they saw them — not the grotesque creatures of the cave, but beings of a different kind. Tall, slender figures clad in dark robes, their faces obscured by hoods. They were the scientists, the architects of the horrors, the masters of Blackwood Cave. They moved with a terrifying grace, their presence emanating an aura of cold calculation and heartless efficiency.

The confrontation was inevitable. Their desperate gamble for survival had led them to the very heart of the enemy's operations. The fight for survival had now become a battle against a formidable foe, one wielding not only brute force but scientific ingenuity and the power of an ancient evil. The final showdown, a terrifying climax, would determine not only their fate, but the fate of the world beyond the confines of Blackwood Cave. The true terror, long suspected, had finally revealed itself in all its horrifying grandeur. The enemy was not only powerful but intelligent, cunning, and ruthlessly efficient. Their escape, if it was even possible, would require not just bravery but intelligence and a deep understanding of the enemy's strategy. The battle for survival was far from over, and the price of victory was still far from certain.

The cavern floor, slick with a viscous, unidentified substance, yielded unevenly beneath their boots. Each step was a gamble, a test of their already frayed nerves. The air hung heavy, thick with the metallic tang of blood and the cloying sweetness of decay. The scene was a grotesque tableau of their own nightmare, a macabre reflection of the horrors they had already endured. Kiel, his empathic senses screaming a symphony of past pain and present terror, stumbled, his hand instinctively reaching out to steady himself against Demitra. She, in turn, offered a silent nod, her eyes betraying nothing but steely determination, a stark contrast to the trembling of her hands. Grayson, ever the stoic leader, pressed on, his face a mask of grim resolve, his gaze fixed on the path ahead, seemingly oblivious to the horrors that surrounded them.

The chamber was a grotesque parody of a laboratory, a perverse fusion of ancient ritual and cutting-edge technology. Twisted metal structures, scarred and stained with an unknown substance, clawed at the ceiling. Glass tubes, once filled with luminescent fluids, now lay shattered on the floor, their contents spilled, forming grotesque puddles that shimmered ominously in the dim light. The air thrummed with a low, resonant hum, a discordant symphony of mechanical whirring and the unsettling drip, drip, drip of something viscous and unknown. The remnants of the experiments were everywhere, a testament to the terrifying scope of the scientists' work.

Grayson pointed to a partially obscured console, its surface etched with symbols mirroring those Demitra had deciphered earlier. "This must be the control system," he whispered, his voice raspy from disuse and strain. "If we can shut it down, maybe we can stop them."

But even as he spoke, a chilling realization dawned on them. The experiments hadn't simply ended. They were continuing. In the far corner of the chamber, partially hidden behind a curtain of pulsating, bioluminescent fungus, they saw it — a large, circular chamber, made of a dark, obsidian-like material. Inside, bathed in an eerie green glow, was a grotesque creature, still incomplete, its flesh raw and pulsating, its limbs twisted into unnatural shapes. It was a horrifying testament to the scientists' ongoing efforts, a nightmarish vision of their inhuman ambition.

The creature stirred, a low guttural moan escaping its incomplete form. The sound resonated deep within their chests, a physical manifestation of their own primal fear. The monstrous thing's gaze, even in its unfinished state, possessed a chilling intelligence, a disconcerting awareness that sent a shiver down their spines.

The scientists, cloaked in their dark robes, moved with unnerving grace around the chamber, their faces obscured by their hoods, their actions precise and efficient. They were not concerned with the shattered equipment or the grotesque evidence of their work; their focus remained fixed on the creature in the obsidian chamber. They were utterly absorbed in their grotesque task, their actions betraying a terrifying indifference to the suffering they inflicted.

Kiel, his empathy working overtime, felt a wave of horror wash over him. He could sense the creature's pain, its terror, its desperate struggle against its own incomplete existence. But he also sensed something else — a faint glimmer of hope. The creature, despite its monstrous form, wasn't entirely controlled. There was a flicker of defiance, a spark of resistance within its tormented consciousness.

Demitra, her decryption device whirring, managed to access the main console. The interface was complex, arcane, a labyrinth of symbols and code. But she was tenacious, her fingers flying across the controls, her eyes scanning the screen with laser-like focus. She was battling not only the technological complexity of the system, but also the gnawing anxiety that clawed at her composure.

Grayson, ever watchful, kept them shielded from the scientists' attention, a human shield against the inhuman. His protective instincts, forged in the crucible of the past few days, remained strong, even in the face of this horrifying revelation. He was their guardian, their protector, their anchor in the storm of fear.

The battle for the console was a battle against time, a race against the scientists' sinister work. Each second ticked by like a hammer blow to their fragile hope. Demitra's fingers flew across the console, her body tense, her mind focused, her fingers leaving a blurry trail across the interface. The pressure, both physical and mental, was immense, almost unbearable.

Suddenly, a scream cut through the air. One of the scientists, their hood falling back, revealed a face contorted in a mask of terror, their eyes wide with an unbearable dread. The scientist staggered backward, their body convulsing violently before collapsing to the floor, lifeless. Kiel, in a flash of insight, understood. The creature in the obsidian chamber was fighting back, its resistance radiating outward, affecting those closest to it. It was a desperate, terrifying gambit.

The remaining scientists, momentarily stunned by their colleague's demise, reacted with chilling efficiency. They moved with terrifying speed and precision, attacking the creature with a lethal combination of advanced weaponry and a vicious disregard for their own safety. But the creature, in its incomplete form, proved surprisingly strong. It fought back with a savage, primeval fury. The chamber became a maelstrom of shattered glass, sparking wires, and flying debris. The scientists, despite their cold detachment, were finally experiencing the horrors of their creation.

Demitra, her decryption complete, punched in the shutdown sequence. The console whirred, a series of alarms blared, and the chamber plunged into darkness. The hum ceased, the eerie glow faded, leaving them in a terrifying, silent darkness. The only sound was the creature's labored breathing. Kiel felt a surge of relief, mixed with a profound sense of unease. The immediate threat was neutralized, but the underlying horror remained. They had shut down the machinery, but not the evil that had created it.

The obsidian chamber, no longer bathed in its eerie green glow, revealed the horrific extent of their success. The creature, its life force dwindling, lay still, its body inert, yet its eyes, even in death, retained a spark of defiance. The scientists, their cold efficiency shattered, were scattered around the chamber, some dead, others wounded, all of them bearing the physical and psychological scars of their creation. The scene was a gruesome testament to the consequences of unchecked ambition and scientific hubris.

As the dust settled, they were left with the chilling realization of the magnitude of what they had just stopped. They had merely bought themselves time. The enemy, though temporarily incapacitated, was still out there, waiting for an opportune moment to strike again. Their escape from Blackwood Cave was far from over. The true horror lay not in the grotesque creatures or the scientists, but in the potential of what they had wrought, the implications of what could have been. Their survival hung precariously on a thread, dependent on their ability to navigate the aftermath of this horrifying encounter and the threat of what lay beyond. The silence that followed was thick, heavy with the implications of their actions. They were survivors, yes, but the scars of Blackwood Cave, both visible and unseen, would forever haunt them. Their escape had bought them time, perhaps only a short respite, before the next chapter in this terrifying saga began. The battle was far from over; it was merely entering a new, more insidious phase.

Chapter 9: Redemption

The silence in the aftermath was deafening, broken only by the ragged breaths of the survivors and the unsettling drip, drip, drip of something unseen. The grotesque tableau of dead and dying scientists, their faces twisted in expressions of abject terror, contrasted sharply with the stillness of the creature in the obsidian chamber. Its life force was ebbing, its monstrous form slowly succumbing to the shutdown sequence. Yet, in its dying breaths, there remained a palpable sense of defiance, a refusal to surrender completely to the darkness.

Kiel, his empathic senses still reeling from the intensity of the experience, approached the creature cautiously. He felt a surge of conflicting emotions – revulsion at its grotesque form, pity for its tortured existence, and a strange sense of kinship born out of shared suffering. He knelt beside the inert mass, his hand hovering over its pulsating flesh. The creature's eyes, though dimming, still held a flicker of consciousness, a spark of awareness that resonated with the deep empathy within Kiel.

It was then that he saw it – a faint, almost imperceptible tremor in the creature's hand. A single, withered finger twitched, and then another. Kiel felt a connection, a resonance, a shared understanding that transcended the monstrous physicality of the being before him. It wasn't just a creature; it was a being capable of pain, of fear, of resistance. It wasn't simply a product of inhuman ambition; it possessed a soul, however distorted and twisted.

This epiphany hit Kiel with the force of a physical blow. He had spent the past few days driven by primal fear, battling for survival in a desperate fight against monstrous odds. But facing the dying creature, seeing its defiance in the face of annihilation, changed his perspective. The realization hit him hard: this wasn't just a fight for survival; it was a fight for something more profound. It was a fight against the inhumane, against the forces that created such monsters, and against the darkness that threatened to consume them all.

Suddenly, a low growl rumbled from the creature's throat, not a sound of aggression, but a sound of exhaustion, a sound that mirrored the weariness within Kiel himself. The creature seemed to be communicating, not through language but through a shared experience of suffering, a shared understanding of the cruel indifference of those who had created it.

Demitra, ever analytical, watched Kiel with a mixture of apprehension and curiosity. She had witnessed Kiel's empathy before, but seeing it directed towards this grotesque creature was both unsettling and intriguing. She understood the depth of Kiel's emotional capacity, his inherent ability to connect with the pain of others, even those as monstrous as this. This empathic connection was not simply sympathy; it was a fundamental aspect of Kiel's nature, a powerful force that had the potential to alter the course of their desperate struggle.

Grayson, ever practical, observed the scene with his usual stoicism. His concern remained focused on their survival, yet even he was caught off guard by the sudden change in Kiel's demeanor. He had witnessed firsthand the brutality of the creatures, and his natural inclination was to distance himself from the monstrous entity. But watching Kiel interact with the dying creature, sensing the subtle shift in Kiel's behavior, Grayson began to glimpse a potential, an unconventional pathway to a solution.

The creature's dying breaths seemed to hold a kind of message, a communication that transcended the boundaries of language. It was a silent plea, a desperate attempt to connect with another sentient being, someone who could understand its pain, its fear, its struggle against its own tormented existence. This plea resonated deep within Kiel, igniting a spark of understanding. He saw in the creature not a monster, but a victim, a pawn in the cruel game of unchecked ambition.

The implications of this understanding were profound. If the creature could communicate, if it could feel, if it could defy its creators even in its dying moments, then perhaps it wasn't just an instrument of destruction. Perhaps it held a key, a piece of the puzzle that could help them escape the horrors of Blackwood Cave and bring down the sinister organization behind it.

Grayson, sensing the shift in the dynamic, cautiously approached Kiel. He had always admired Kiel's compassion, even though he often found it impractical. But in this dire situation, a different kind of strategy was required, a strategy that went beyond brute force and survival instincts.

"What do you think?" Grayson asked quietly, his voice devoid of its usual confidence.

Kiel's eyes held a glimmer of purpose, a newfound resolve. "I think we need to listen," he said, his voice barely a whisper. "I think this creature might be able to help us." Demitra, her usual skepticism tempered by the weight of the situation, nodded slowly. "How?" she asked, her voice echoing the question in Grayson's mind.

Kiel looked down at the creature, his gaze focused on its dimming eyes. "We need to find a way to communicate," he said. "To understand its creators, to understand their motivations. Perhaps then we can find a way to use its knowledge to our advantage."

This unlikely alliance – a group of teenagers and a dying, genetically-engineered creature – was a testament to the unpredictable nature of survival, a stark realization of how desperation could forge unlikely bonds, and how empathy could transcend even the most monstrous forms of life. The creature, in its dying moments, became a crucial element in their fight for survival, an unexpected ally in their desperate struggle against the darkness that had consumed Blackwood Cave. The silence in the chamber was no longer deafening; it was pregnant with possibility, the potential for a new path toward redemption.

The task ahead was daunting, fraught with uncertainty. They were still trapped deep within Blackwood Cave, surrounded by the terrifying remnants of a scientific abomination. But now, armed with this unexpected alliance, a renewed sense of purpose surged within them. The creature's change of heart, reflected in its final moments of resistance, sparked a flame of hope within them, a promise of a different kind of survival, one that encompassed not just physical escape but a fight for something more profound – a fight for understanding, for justice, for redemption.

The remaining hours were spent in a painstaking effort to decipher the creature's final communication. Demitra, working tirelessly with her decryption device, managed to extract fragments of information from the creature's dying brainwaves, a chaotic mix of sensations, emotions, and distorted memories. The task was arduous, filled with frustration and setbacks. But every piece of information, however fragmented, was a potential key to unlocking the secrets of Blackwood Cave, and the sinister organization that had unleashed these horrors upon the world.

Kiel, with his enhanced empathy, acted as a translator of sorts, interpreting the emotional undercurrents that ran through the chaotic data streams. He worked in tandem with Demitra, his intuitive understanding complementing her technological expertise. They pieced together glimpses of the scientists' motivations, their reckless ambitions, their chilling disregard for the consequences of their actions. The fragmented images and sensations revealed a history of experimentation, of genetic manipulation, of a desperate race to create something new, something powerful, something beyond human comprehension.

Grayson, ever the pragmatist, documented their findings, ensuring that the valuable information gleaned from the dying creature was preserved and could be used effectively. He understood the significance of this unexpected collaboration, recognizing that the information they were uncovering could be the key to their ultimate survival and to exposing the truth behind the horrors of Blackwood Cave to the wider world.

As dawn approached, casting a faint light into the cavern, they finally had it: a complete picture of the organization's plans, their location, and their ultimate goal. The creature's final communication served not only as a key to unlocking their escape, but as a grim warning of the danger that lurked beyond Blackwood Cave. It was a dark, ominous message, a chilling testament to the organization's ambition and their disregard for human life.

This revelation transformed their escape from a desperate struggle for survival into a fight for something far greater: a fight to expose the truth and prevent the organization from unleashing their creations upon the world. The dying creature, in its final act of defiance, had not merely helped them escape Blackwood Cave; it had given them the means to fight back, to seek justice, to ensure that the horrors they had witnessed would not be repeated. The shadows of Blackwood Cave still clung to them, but the darkness no longer held the same suffocating grip. They had found their path to redemption, a path forged in the fires of shared trauma and the unlikely alliance with a creature whose life ended as it had begun — in defiance. Their escape was far from over, but now, they were fighting not just for survival, but for a future where such horrors would never again see the light of day. The weight of their responsibility was immense, but so too was the newfound strength born from their harrowing experience and the unexpected gift of redemption offered by a dying monster.

The sterile white walls of the hospital room offered a stark contrast to the suffocating darkness of Blackwood Cave. Kiel, Demitra, and Grayson, battered but alive, lay in separate rooms, each grappling with the echoes of their ordeal. The physical wounds were slowly healing, the gashes stitched, the broken bones mending, but the psychological scars ran deeper, a network of invisible fissures threatening to shatter their fragile sanity. Silence, once a terrifying companion in the cave's depths, now felt almost oppressive, a stark reminder of the deafening screams that had haunted their nights.

Kiel, despite his physical recovery, remained emotionally withdrawn. The empathy that had once been a source of strength now felt like a curse, a relentless flood of sensations and emotions – the creature's dying agony, the scientists' terror, the echoes of his own fear. Sleep offered no respite; his nights were consumed by vivid, recurring nightmares, replaying the horrors of Blackwood Cave in grotesque detail. He would wake in a cold sweat, his heart pounding, the scent of decay clinging to his memory. His once vibrant eyes held a haunted, weary quality, reflecting the depths of his inner turmoil.

Demitra, ever the pragmatist, focused on the tangible aspects of recovery. She documented her experiences, organizing the data gleaned from the dying creature's brainwaves, compiling a chilling report that detailed the organization's sinister activities and their terrifying plans. The systematic nature of her work served as a shield against the overwhelming trauma, a way to channel her fear and grief into productive action. Yet, behind the cool facade of scientific objectivity, a tremor of fear lingered, a subtle manifestation of the psychological wounds she had sustained. The chilling images and data haunted her waking hours, blurring the line between the reality of the hospital room and the nightmarish reality of the cave. She found herself jumping at sudden noises, her senses hyper-alert, forever on the lookout for threats, real or imagined.

Grayson, outwardly stoic, battled a quiet torment. His usually unflappable composure had cracked under the weight of their experience. The images of his fallen comrades, their lives brutally extinguished, were etched into his memory, a recurring tableau of horror that played out in his mind's eye. He found solace in routine, in the methodical process of physical therapy and the practical tasks of recovery, but the underlying fear and grief gnawed at his resolve. The silence of his room felt like a suffocating blanket, forcing him to confront the emotional wounds that he had so diligently suppressed.

Days turned into weeks. The physical healing progressed, but the psychological recovery was a slower, more arduous process. The team was brought together under the care of Dr. Evelyn Reed, a specialist in trauma recovery, who recognized the unique nature of their shared experience. Her approach was holistic, addressing both the physical and psychological consequences of their ordeal. She worked with each of them individually, using a combination of therapy, medication, and support groups to help them process their trauma and rebuild their lives.

Dr. Reed began by encouraging them to talk about their experiences, to articulate the horrors they had witnessed, to give voice to the silent screams that echoed within them. She fostered a safe environment, emphasizing that there was no shame in their fear, no weakness in their vulnerability. It was a process of painstaking self-discovery, a gradual uncovering of the buried emotions that had been buried deep under the surface of their bravado and survival instincts.

For Kiel, the process was particularly challenging. His empathy, while a source of strength in the cave, now became an overwhelming burden. Dr. Reed helped him to develop coping mechanisms, to manage the influx of emotions that threatened to overwhelm him, to learn to distinguish between his own feelings and the feelings of others. She taught him to set boundaries, to protect himself from the emotional pain of others without sacrificing his compassionate nature.

Demitra found solace in the structured nature of Dr. Reed's therapy. The process of analyzing and documenting her trauma, of giving it a framework, a form, helped her to gain a sense of control over her experience. Dr. Reed helped her to separate the objective reality of the scientific data from the subjective experience of terror, allowing her to process her trauma without being overwhelmed by it.

Grayson's recovery was slower, more resistant. He initially resisted the emotional vulnerability required by therapy, clinging to his stoicism as a defense mechanism. But with Dr. Reed's persistent encouragement, he gradually began to open up, to confront the grief and fear that he had buried deep within his heart. He learned to share his experiences, to acknowledge the profound impact that the events in Blackwood Cave had had on him, and to find solace in the shared experiences of his friends.

The group therapy sessions were especially valuable. They provided a safe space for them to share their feelings, to support each other, and to confront their shared trauma together. The process of mutual support proved to be unexpectedly healing. They realized they were not alone in their suffering, that their experiences were shared, validating and normalizing their trauma.

Over time, the scars of Blackwood Cave began to fade, not entirely disappearing, but softening, becoming less raw and less painful. The nightmares diminished, the flashbacks lessened, and the constant fear gradually subsided. They learned to live with their memories, to integrate their experiences into their sense of self, to understand that their trauma did not define them, but rather made them stronger, more resilient, and more compassionate. They had stared into the abyss, and they had emerged scarred but unbroken.

Their recovery wasn't a linear journey; there were setbacks, relapses, and moments of overwhelming despair. But with each other's support, and with the guidance of Dr. Reed, they found their way back to a semblance of normalcy. They learned to navigate the world with a renewed awareness of its fragility, its capacity for both beauty and horror, and the importance of human connection in the face of overwhelming adversity. Blackwood Cave had irrevocably altered their lives, but it had also revealed the depth of their resilience, their capacity for healing, and the enduring strength of their bonds of friendship. Their path to healing was long, but it was a path they were traversing together, united by their shared trauma and the unwavering hope for a future free from the darkness that had consumed them in Blackwood Cave. The world outside awaited, but it was a world they were prepared to face, together, forever bound by the indelible mark of their harrowing, yet ultimately redemptive, experience.

The weight of what they had endured settled heavily upon them, a palpable presence in the sterile hospital rooms. Physical healing was progressing, but the invisible wounds of the mind remained, festering in the quiet spaces between breaths, in the restless nights plagued by nightmares. Forgiveness, a concept seemingly as distant as the sun from the depths of Blackwood Cave, began to creep into their collective consciousness. It was a complex notion, multifaceted and elusive, requiring them to confront not only the actions of others but also the terrifying realities of their own responses.

Kiel's journey towards forgiveness began with himself. The crushing weight of empathy, once a strength, had become a debilitating burden. He'd felt the dying creature's agony, sensed the sheer terror of the scientists as they were overrun, and replayed the moment his own fear threatened to consume him. He struggled with the agonizing knowledge that he had survived while others hadn't, a survivor's guilt that gnawed at him relentlessly. Dr. Reed helped him to differentiate between his own emotions and those he'd absorbed, teaching him to establish boundaries, to protect his own fragile psyche without sacrificing his inherent compassion. He began to understand that survival wasn't a sign of weakness, but a testament to an indomitable will, a will he hadn't even known he possessed. Forgiveness, in this context, meant accepting his own survival, not as a mark of selfish triumph, but as a chance to honor the memories of those he'd lost.

Demitra, the pragmatic scientist, approached forgiveness through documentation and analysis. She had already compiled a chilling report on the organization's activities, a testament to their scientific cruelty and blatant disregard for human life. But true forgiveness required her to confront not just the organization's actions, but her own responses to them, her own moments of panic, her own fight or flight reactions that had saved her life. She spent countless hours poring over data, trying to dissect her actions, to understand the logic behind the brutal choices she'd made. She had to confront the inherent darkness that had allowed her to survive, and through this rigorous self-examination, she slowly began to forgive herself for her own actions, acknowledging the instinct for self-preservation that had propelled her through the horrors of the cave.

Grayson, the stoic leader, wrestled with a different kind of forgiveness. He carried the weight of his friends' deaths, the vivid images of their last moments etched into his memory, a perpetual torment. The quiet grief was a constant companion, as much a part of him as the scars that crisscrossed his body. His forgiveness extended not to himself, but to those who had died. It wasn't easy; the raw grief threatened to consume him daily. But through group therapy and individual sessions, he began to understand that their deaths were not a testament to his failure as a leader, but to the horrific circumstances they had faced. He learned to honor their memories, not by dwelling on the loss, but by living a life worthy of their sacrifice, a life dedicated to exposing the organization and preventing further atrocities.

The group therapy sessions were a crucible of forgiveness, a space where they could confront their shared trauma, not just individually but collectively. They learned from each other's struggles, offering empathy and support, sharing their burdens and helping to lift the weight of their collective guilt. They discovered that forgiveness wasn't just about letting go of anger or resentment, but about accepting the reality of what happened, understanding its impact on their lives, and finding a path towards healing and reconciliation, even if that reconciliation was just with themselves.

The process wasn't linear; there were regressions, moments of intense emotional turmoil, and the constant threat of nightmares and flashbacks. Kiel continued to battle the intrusive empathy, Demitra struggled with guilt over her own survival, and Grayson wrestled with the agonizing weight of responsibility. Yet, they persevered, fueled by their shared experience and a growing understanding of forgiveness as a continuous process, not a singular event.

The forgiveness they sought wasn't a simplistic act of pardon. It wasn't about excusing the heinous actions of the organization or minimizing the brutal reality of their ordeal. It was a multifaceted process that required intense self-reflection, a deep understanding of human nature's capacity for both monstrous cruelty and remarkable resilience. It meant accepting the realities of their trauma, embracing the scars as a reminder of their strength, and acknowledging the human capacity for both unspeakable acts and profound empathy.

As their physical wounds healed, so too did their emotional scars begin to mend, although the memories of Blackwood Cave would forever remain a part of them. They learned to integrate their experiences into their sense of self, realizing that trauma didn't define them. Their shared ordeal had not only forged an unbreakable bond, but had also taught them the profound value of compassion, resilience, and the intricate, often arduous, process of forgiveness.

The road to redemption was long and winding, filled with obstacles and setbacks. There were nights when the horrors of Blackwood Cave returned in vivid nightmares, days when the echoes of screams still rang in their ears. But they held onto each other, their shared trauma becoming a foundation of unwavering support. They learned to use their collective experiences to fuel their shared purpose: to expose the organization responsible for the genetically-engineered creatures, to prevent similar tragedies from occurring, and to dedicate their lives to ensuring that no one else would suffer the horrors they had endured.

The aftermath of Blackwood Cave stretched far beyond the confines of the hospital walls. Their testimony became instrumental in dismantling the organization, exposing its dark secrets to the world. The legal process was long and arduous, but their united front, bolstered by the rigorous scientific evidence Demitra compiled and the emotional power of Kiel and Grayson's testimonies, ultimately led to justice. The organization's leaders were brought to account, their horrific experiments exposed, and their reign of terror brought to an end.

Their work didn't stop there. They became advocates for survivors of trauma, using their experience to help others navigate the treacherous path towards healing. They established a foundation dedicated to supporting individuals who had experienced similar ordeals, providing resources, counseling, and a sense of community. Their shared journey became a testament to the enduring human spirit, a demonstration that even in the face of unimaginable horror, hope and healing were possible.

Blackwood Cave remained a constant reminder of the darkness they had faced, a symbol of the monstrous acts of which humans are capable. But it also became a testament to their resilience, a marker of their shared journey towards redemption and the enduring power of forgiveness. The scars they carried, both visible and invisible, would never fully fade, but they would be a reminder of their strength, their unwavering determination, and their ultimate triumph over the darkness that had nearly consumed them. Their lives were forever changed, but instead of being defined by the horrors they'd faced, they chose to shape their futures through advocacy, healing, and the unwavering hope that the darkness they had conquered would never consume another. Their story was a story of survival, a story of healing, and ultimately, a story of redemption. A story whispered through the ages, a testament to the human spirit's capacity to face the abyss and emerge, scarred but unbroken, into the light.

The wind whispered through the tall grasses, a mournful sigh that mirrored the ache in their hearts. They stood at the edge of Blackwood Forest, the imposing silhouette of the cave mouth a dark scar on the landscape. It wasn't a triumphant return; there was no sense of closure, only a quiet acknowledgment of what had been lost, and what they had somehow managed to salvage from the wreckage of their lives. This wasn't a celebration, but a somber pilgrimage, a ritualistic laying to rest of their shared trauma.

Kiel, his face etched with a weariness that belied his youth, placed a single, smooth river stone at the base of a young oak tree, its leaves trembling in the breeze. He'd chosen the spot carefully, a small clearing bathed in dappled sunlight, a stark contrast to the perpetual gloom of the cave. It was a place of unexpected peace, a quiet sanctuary amidst the oppressive darkness of the forest. He closed his eyes, the memories flooding back – the suffocating claustrophobia, the chilling screams, the relentless pursuit. But this time, the memories weren't accompanied by the crushing weight of empathy; they were simply memories, raw and painful, yet contained within the boundaries of his own being. He had learned to differentiate, to shield himself without sacrificing his compassion. The stone felt cool and smooth against his palm, a grounding force in the swirling vortex of his memories.

Demitra, her eyes red-rimmed but resolute, knelt beside him, carefully placing a small vial of soil collected from the cave's entrance next to Kiel's stone. The soil was dark and rich, tinged with the mineral scent of the earth deep below. It was a tangible link to the nightmare they'd escaped, a reminder of the horror they'd witnessed. She'd poured over the data, the scientific evidence, but the raw earth, this silent testament to the events, spoke a language she understood better than any graph or equation. It was a silent affirmation of the darkness they'd faced, a reminder of the organization's cruelty, yet also a symbol of their resilience, of their ability to extract knowledge and purpose from the heart of unimaginable horror.

Grayson, his posture ramrod straight despite the weariness in his eyes, stood a little distance away, gazing at the cave. His gaze was distant, unfocused, lost in the labyrinthine passages of his memory. He'd come to terms with the loss of his friends; the grief was no less intense, but it had evolved. It was no longer a consuming fire, but a persistent ember, a constant companion that shaped his life but no longer threatened to consume him. He had found a way to honor their memory, not by dwelling on their deaths, but by channeling his grief into action, into his dedication to exposing the organization and preventing future tragedies. He didn't need a physical object to commemorate their loss; the memory itself was a tangible weight he carried, a commitment to a future free from the horrors they'd endured.

Silence descended, heavy and thick with unspoken grief, a shared understanding that transcended words. The wind rustled the leaves, the sound like a whispered requiem for those lost in the depths of Blackwood Cave. It was a silence that held no judgment, only acceptance; acceptance of the pain, of the loss, of the scars that would forever remain.

They spoke little, their shared experience a silent language that needed no articulation. They understood the unspoken sorrow, the lingering fear, the persistent nightmares that continued to haunt their sleep. The physical wounds were healing, leaving behind faded scars as testament to their survival. But the emotional wounds ran deeper, a constant reminder of the horrors they'd witnessed, a reminder of the fragility of life and the pervasive darkness that lurked beneath the surface of the world. Yet, there was a new strength in their silence, a resilience forged in the fires of their ordeal.

The setting sun cast long shadows across the forest floor, painting the clearing in hues of orange and purple. As the last rays of light faded, they turned and walked away, their silhouettes stark against the darkening landscape. They left behind the physical markers of their remembrance, but the memories, the lessons, the shared bond—those remained, interwoven into the fabric of their being.

The following weeks were a blur of therapy sessions, meetings with lawyers, and the painstaking process of giving testimony. Demitra's documentation was crucial in dismantling the organization, providing the irrefutable evidence needed to bring its leaders to justice. Kiel and Grayson's harrowing accounts, though emotionally draining, were powerful testaments to the horrors inflicted by the organization. Their combined efforts, their unwavering commitment to truth, shattered the organization's carefully constructed facade of scientific progress, revealing the gruesome reality of its cruel experiments.

The legal process was long and arduous, each day a reminder of the darkness they had faced. But their shared strength, their unyielding support for each other, saw them through. The trials were not just legal battles; they were a re-affirmation of their collective strength, a continuous process of confronting and processing their trauma. In the courtroom, they faced the perpetrators of their ordeal, their testimony a testament to the human capacity for both unimaginable cruelty and unwavering resilience. The conviction of the organization's leaders wasn't merely a legal victory; it was a step towards redemption, a validation of their suffering, a promise that their sacrifice would not be in vain.

The establishment of the Blackwood Foundation was a testament to their commitment to helping others. It wasn't just a response to their personal trauma; it was a conscious decision to channel their pain into purpose, to create something positive from the ashes of their ordeal. They offered support and resources to other survivors of trauma, providing a safe space for healing and understanding. Their combined experiences—Kiel's empathetic nature, Demitra's scientific precision, and Grayson's steadfast leadership—proved invaluable in creating a supportive and effective organization.

Years later, Kiel, Demitra, and Grayson stood on the same spot, at the edge of Blackwood Forest. The young oak tree, now taller and stronger, stood as a silent testament to their enduring strength. The cave remained, a dark reminder of their shared trauma. But it no longer held the same power, no longer symbolized only fear and loss. It had become a marker, a reminder of their resilience, their healing, their collective triumph over unspeakable horror. They were different people now, forever marked by their experience, yet fundamentally changed for the better. The scars remained, visible and invisible, a constant reminder of the darkness they had faced. But they were also symbols of their strength, their capacity for healing, and the enduring power of the human spirit to transcend unimaginable trauma and find redemption in the face of unspeakable horror. The wind whispered through the trees, a gentle lullaby, a soft echo of their shared journey—a journey from the depths of despair to the heights of resilience, a journey of profound loss and ultimately, of profound redemption. Their story was a testament to the enduring strength of the human spirit, a beacon of hope in the face of unimaginable darkness.

The years that followed were a tapestry woven with threads of grief and resilience. The immediate aftermath—the media frenzy, the relentless questioning, the unending stream of condolences—had been a blur, a chaotic storm that threatened to swallow them whole. But slowly, painstakingly, they began to navigate the wreckage, to find solid ground amidst the debris of their shattered lives. The legal battles were grueling, a relentless replay of their ordeal, each day a fresh wound reopened and examined. Demitra's documented research, the irrefutable evidence she'd compiled from the cave, formed the bedrock of the prosecution's case. Her testimony was clinical, precise, yet emotionally devastating, painting a horrifying picture of the organization's depraved experiments and callous disregard for human life. Kiel, his voice often cracking with emotion, bore witness to the brutality they had endured, his raw, honest account leaving an indelible mark on the jury. Grayson, ever the pragmatist, provided the strategic framework, guiding their narrative, ensuring their testimony remained focused, coherent, and devastatingly effective. His quiet strength, the unshakeable resolve in his eyes, spoke volumes about the transformation they had undergone. They were no longer the naive teenagers who had ventured into Blackwood Cave; they were survivors, forged in the crucible of unimaginable horror, their voices powerful instruments of justice.

The conviction of the organization's leaders was a watershed moment, a validation of their suffering, a glimmer of hope amidst the darkness. It wasn't merely a legal victory; it was a symbolic triumph over evil, a testament to the resilience of the human spirit. But the legal battles didn't erase the trauma; they merely offered a framework within which to process it. The nightmares persisted, the memories—vivid, visceral, inescapable—continued to haunt their waking hours. They sought solace in therapy, finding comfort in the shared understanding of their experiences, a silent communion born of shared trauma. They learned to manage their PTSD, to identify their triggers, to develop coping mechanisms that allowed them to function, to heal, to move forward.

The establishment of the Blackwood Foundation was a testament to their collective commitment to preventing future tragedies. It wasn't born out of a need for self-preservation; it was a conscious decision to transform their suffering into a catalyst for positive change. The Foundation provided a haven for survivors of similar trauma, a safe space where individuals could share their experiences, receive support, and find solace in community. Kiel, with his innate empathy and understanding of human suffering, became the heart of the organization, providing emotional support and guidance to others. Demitra, utilizing her scientific expertise, developed innovative therapeutic programs based on her research into the psychological effects of trauma. Grayson, with his unwavering resolve and leadership skills, steered the Foundation's strategic direction, ensuring its financial stability and long-term sustainability. Their combined skills and experiences transformed the Foundation into a beacon of hope, a lifeline for individuals struggling to navigate the aftermath of trauma.

The Foundation's work extended beyond providing direct support to survivors. They actively lobbied for stricter regulations on genetic engineering research, tirelessly advocating for legislation that would prevent future atrocities. They worked with law enforcement agencies, sharing their knowledge and expertise to enhance investigative techniques, providing invaluable insights into the methodologies of organizations like the one that had nearly destroyed them. They became advocates for change, tireless crusaders against the dark forces that sought to exploit human vulnerabilities. Their actions were a direct response to the trauma they'd endured, a transformation of pain into purpose.

The process of healing was slow, arduous, and often painful. Each individual embarked on their own unique journey, their methods of coping and healing as diverse as their personalities. Kiel found solace in nature, spending hours hiking through the forests surrounding Blackwood Cave, the tranquility of the wilderness providing a counterpoint to the chaos within. Demitra channeled her energy into scientific research, her dedication fueled by a desire to understand the horrors they'd faced, to learn from the past, and to prevent future atrocities. Grayson immersed himself in his work at the Foundation, finding purpose in helping others, in creating a positive impact on the world. Their individual paths were distinct, yet they converged at the heart of the Foundation, a symbol of their shared resilience, their collective triumph over adversity.

Years passed. The physical scars they carried served as reminders of their ordeal, but they no longer defined them. The emotional wounds were deeper, more persistent, but they were slowly healing, gradually fading into the background of their lives. They learned to live with the memories, to integrate them into their narrative, rather than allowing them to dictate their future. They found solace in their relationships with each other, their bond forged in the fires of their shared trauma, a silent testament to their strength and endurance.

One crisp autumn afternoon, they found themselves back at the edge of Blackwood

Forest, the silhouette of the cave a familiar yet less threatening presence on the horizon. The young oak tree, planted years earlier, was now a mature specimen, its branches reaching towards the heavens, its leaves ablaze with the fiery hues of fall. It stood as a silent monument to their resilience, a symbol of their journey from despair to hope, from trauma to healing. They stood in silence, the wind whispering through the leaves, a gentle lullaby that carried their unspoken thoughts, their shared memories, their mutual understanding. The cave, once a symbol of fear and loss, had been transformed into a reminder of their shared survival, their collective triumph over unimaginable horror. They had faced darkness, and they had emerged into the light. Their story was not one of defeat, but of perseverance, a testament to the enduring strength of the human spirit. They were survivors, and they were moving forward. Their future remained unwritten, but it held the promise of hope, a beacon in the darkness, a promise of a brighter tomorrow built on the foundations of their shared trauma and their unwavering commitment to building a better world, a world free from the horrors of Blackwood Cave.

Chapter 10: Legacy

The conviction of the Blackwood organization's leaders wasn't just a victory for Demitra, Kiel, and Grayson; it was a seismic event that sent shockwaves through the scientific community and beyond. The documented evidence, the harrowing testimonies, and the sheer scale of the organization's atrocities forced a global reckoning. Suddenly, the previously clandestine world of unregulated genetic engineering was thrust into the harsh glare of public scrutiny. Governments worldwide initiated investigations, scrutinizing research facilities, reviewing ethical guidelines, and demanding greater transparency. The once-hidden corners of the scientific landscape were exposed, revealing a complex web of unethical practices, clandestine experiments, and a shocking disregard for human life. The Blackwood case became a chilling precedent, a stark warning of the potential consequences of unchecked ambition and the terrifying potential of manipulating life itself.

The media frenzy surrounding the trial didn't subside with the convictions. News outlets across the globe continued to report on the case, fueling a burgeoning public outcry against unethical scientific practices. Documentaries, investigative reports, and even fictionalized accounts of the teenagers' ordeal emerged, all serving to heighten public awareness and maintain pressure on governing bodies to enact meaningful change. The survivors, once anonymous teenagers, became reluctant symbols of resistance, their faces plastered across magazine covers, their stories told and retold in countless media outlets. This newfound visibility, while initially overwhelming, allowed them to amplify their message, to advocate for stricter regulations, and to prevent future tragedies.

The Blackwood Foundation, initially a small refuge for survivors, rapidly expanded its reach, becoming a powerful voice in the global conversation about ethical scientific practices. They received funding from various sources, including private donations, government grants, and international organizations, all galvanized by the public outcry. This influx of resources allowed the Foundation to broaden its scope, expanding its therapeutic programs, developing new research initiatives, and actively engaging in policy discussions at both the national and international levels. Kiel, Demitra, and Grayson, now recognized as global leaders in the fight for ethical scientific practice, dedicated themselves to ensuring the Foundation's long-term success and impact.

Their influence extended beyond the realm of direct support for survivors. They established partnerships with leading universities and research institutions, collaborating on projects focused on ethical research methodologies, risk assessment, and biosecurity. They advised governmental bodies on the creation and implementation of new regulations, ensuring that future research was conducted responsibly and with a deep respect for human life. Grayson's strategic mind proved invaluable in navigating the complex political landscape, forming strategic alliances and securing commitments from influential figures. Demitra's scientific expertise provided a crucial foundation for the development of new ethical frameworks and guidelines, ensuring that future research adhered to rigorous standards of accountability and safety. Kiel, ever the compassionate voice of reason, championed the rights of vulnerable populations and ensured that the Foundation remained true to its core mission of supporting survivors and preventing future atrocities.

The ripple effect of their actions extended to law enforcement agencies as well. The Blackwood case served as a training ground for investigators, showcasing the complexities of investigating clandestine scientific operations and prosecuting perpetrators. The documentation provided by Demitra and the detailed testimony of Kiel and Grayson provided invaluable insights into the methods and practices of unethical scientific organizations, improving investigative techniques and providing law enforcement with the tools they needed to effectively combat future crimes of a similar nature. Workshops and training sessions were established, and the Blackwood case became a staple in law enforcement training programs worldwide.

Years passed. The Blackwood Foundation grew into a global powerhouse, a respected institution dedicated to promoting ethical scientific practice and supporting survivors of trauma. Demitra's groundbreaking research continued, leading to breakthroughs in the treatment of PTSD and other trauma-related disorders. Her work focused not just on treating the symptoms of trauma but also on understanding its root causes, leading to a deeper understanding of the human psyche and the impact of violence and abuse. Kiel, through his unwavering empathy and personal experiences, established a global network of support for victims of similar atrocities, providing invaluable emotional support and a sense of community. Grayson continued to be the strategic mind behind the foundation's operations, ensuring its long-term sustainability and its continued impact on the world.

The world, however, did not forget Blackwood Cave. The site remained a chilling reminder of the horrors that can result when human ambition is unchecked and scientific ethics are disregarded. It became a somber landmark, a place of pilgrimage for those seeking to understand the devastating consequences of unchecked scientific advancement and a monument to the resilience of those who survived its horrors. The young oak tree, planted near the cave entrance, grew taller and stronger each year, symbolizing the unwavering hope and resilience that emerged from the darkest depths of human suffering. It served as a constant reminder of the enduring power of the human spirit and the triumph of hope over despair.

The legacy of Blackwood Cave was far-reaching and enduring. It wasn't just a tale of survival; it was a cautionary narrative etched into the very fabric of society. It spurred legislative change, fostered improved investigative techniques, and provided a framework for understanding and addressing the psychological effects of trauma. The survivors, once victims, had become beacons of hope, using their experiences to shape a brighter future, a future free from the horrors they had endured. Their journey from despair to hope, from victimhood to activism, demonstrated the powerful potential of human resilience and the capacity for transformation even in the face of unimaginable adversity. The world was different because of Blackwood Cave; a world now more aware, more vigilant, and more determined to prevent future atrocities. The chilling whispers of the cave were finally silenced, not by forgetting, but by remembering, learning, and fighting for a better future. The survivors had stared into the abyss and, instead of succumbing to its darkness, had emerged, carrying the light of hope and the promise of a world transformed. The ripple effect of their courage continued to spread, an unwavering testament to the enduring power of human spirit. Blackwood Cave was not just a site of horror; it was the birthplace of a legacy of resilience, a testament to the enduring strength of the human spirit in the face of unimaginable darkness.

The world watched, breathless, as the final gavel fell, silencing the echoes of Blackwood Cave in the halls of justice. The convictions weren't just legal victories; they were societal milestones, marking a turning point in the global conversation about scientific ethics. The carefully constructed wall of secrecy surrounding the Blackwood organization crumbled under the weight of public scrutiny, revealing a horrifying underbelly of unchecked ambition and disregard for human life. The media, initially captivated by the sensationalism of the story, shifted its focus to the larger implications of the case, demanding accountability and systemic change. Investigative journalism flourished, unearthing previously unknown instances of unethical practices in research facilities across the globe. The public, once detached observers, became active participants, demanding transparency and stricter regulations.

Demitra, Kiel, and Grayson, the teenagers who had stared into the abyss and emerged victorious, found themselves thrust into the role of unexpected advocates. Their harrowing experiences, once confined to the chilling confines of Blackwood Cave, became cautionary tales broadcast across international news channels. Their faces, once hidden in the shadows of fear, now graced magazine covers, symbolizing the fight for scientific responsibility and the resilience of the human spirit. This newfound platform, while daunting, allowed them to channel their trauma into action, transforming their personal suffering into a catalyst for widespread reform.

The Blackwood Foundation, initially a small support group for survivors, rapidly evolved into a global powerhouse, its influence extending far beyond its original scope. Driven by an influx of donations and governmental grants, fueled by a newly awakened public conscience, the Foundation established itself as a leading authority on ethical scientific practices. Demitra, her scientific mind sharp and unwavering, spearheaded research into trauma recovery, developing innovative therapeutic approaches to address the psychological scars left by the Blackwood organization's atrocities. Her work reached far beyond the immediate survivors; it contributed to a deeper understanding of PTSD and related disorders, improving treatment methods globally.

Kiel, his empathy as strong as his courage, established a global network of support for victims of similar crimes. He understood the isolating nature of such trauma and worked tirelessly to create a sense of community and shared experience, fostering healing and mutual understanding amongst survivors. His unwavering commitment to providing comprehensive support to victims became the bedrock of the Foundation's emotional support programs. Grayson, ever the strategist, masterfully navigated the intricate landscape of international politics, securing commitments from influential figures and ensuring the Foundation's long-term stability and impact. He secured funding, established crucial partnerships, and ensured that the Foundation's voice was heard in the halls of power.

The educational impact of the Blackwood case was equally profound. Universities and research institutions, under pressure from public opinion and government mandates, integrated ethical considerations into their curricula. The case became a staple in medical ethics courses, a stark reminder of the catastrophic consequences of unchecked ambition and the importance of rigorous oversight. Researchers, once shielded by secrecy and a culture of competitive ambition, were now forced to operate under a microscope of public scrutiny, their practices subject to greater accountability and transparency.

Law enforcement agencies underwent significant changes as well. The painstakingly detailed evidence gathered by Demitra, along with the compelling testimonies of Kiel and Grayson, served as crucial training materials for investigators. The Blackwood case became a textbook example of how to investigate complex, clandestine operations involving advanced scientific techniques. Workshops and training programs, designed to equip investigators with the skills to uncover and prosecute similar crimes, were implemented worldwide. The investigation, once a beacon of hope within a sea of despair for Demitra, Kiel, and Grayson, served as a global blueprint for future investigations, leading to the arrest and conviction of numerous individuals involved in unethical scientific practices across numerous countries.

The legacy of Blackwood Cave extended beyond the legal and scientific realms. It sparked a wave of public activism, with advocacy groups demanding stricter regulations on genetic engineering, improved oversight of research facilities, and greater protection for vulnerable populations. The survivors' testimonies, once raw expressions of terror, were transformed into powerful calls for social change. Their voices, amplified by the media and the support of the Blackwood Foundation, reverberated around the globe, inspiring others to speak out against injustice and advocate for a more ethical and responsible scientific community.

The impact on public discourse was monumental. The subject of genetic engineering, once shrouded in mystery and scientific jargon, became a topic of widespread discussion. Public understanding of the ethical implications of manipulating life itself increased exponentially, fostering a heightened awareness and critical perspective among both scientists and the general population. The once silent acceptance of unregulated research gave way to a new era of skepticism, scrutiny, and demanding transparency.

Years later, the young oak tree planted near the cave entrance grew into a strong, resilient symbol of hope. Blackwood Cave, once a place of unspeakable horror, became a solemn memorial, a site where people could reflect on the lessons learned and reaffirm their commitment to preventing future atrocities. The cave's chilling whispers were silenced, not by forgetting, but by remembering, by using the lessons learned to pave the way for a safer, more ethical future. The Foundation expanded its reach, establishing branches across the globe and continuing to offer support to survivors, researchers, and communities affected by unethical scientific practices.

The world had changed. The chilling legacy of Blackwood Cave became a powerful catalyst for societal transformation, fostering an era of increased accountability, heightened awareness, and a strengthened commitment to the ethical conduct of scientific research. It stood as a stark reminder of the terrible consequences of unchecked ambition and the vital importance of safeguarding the boundaries of scientific progress. The shadows of the cave still lingered, a constant reminder of the darkness that lurked beneath, but the light of hope, kindled by the resilience of the survivors, shone brighter than ever before. The new era wasn't just about healing the wounds of the past; it was about building a future where such horrors would never be repeated. The legacy of Blackwood Cave was a testament to the enduring power of the human spirit, a promise that even from the deepest darkness, hope can emerge, transforming tragedy into a catalyst for lasting positive change. The whispers of Blackwood Cave, once filled with terror, were now replaced by the powerful voices of those who fought for a better world – a world where the pursuit of scientific knowledge would never again overshadow the sanctity of human life.

The wind whispered through the skeletal branches of the newly planted oak, its leaves rustling like whispered prayers. Demitra stood before it, the cool earth grounding her, a stark contrast to the turmoil that still raged within. The anniversary. A year since they'd escaped the suffocating grip of Blackwood Cave, a year since they'd faced the unimaginable horrors unleashed within its depths. A year since they'd lost so much.

She closed her eyes, the echoes of the cave reverberating in the silence. The screams, the guttural roars of the creatures, the desperate scrabbling for survival – all of it still burned vivid in her memory. She saw Sarah's face, pale and lifeless, her eyes wide with a terror that still haunted Demitra's dreams. Sarah, the brightest star in their group, extinguished far too soon. The image of Ben, his body twisted into an unnatural shape, the life draining from his eyes, was a constant, visceral reminder of the brutal reality of their ordeal. And Mark, always the joker, always the one to lighten the mood, now just a name etched in her heart, a memory she clutched to her chest like a lifeline.

A single tear traced a path down her cheek, a silent tribute to the fallen. Kiel placed a comforting hand on her shoulder, his eyes filled with the same sorrow, the same haunting memories. He'd lost his best friend, David, in the cave's claustrophobic embrace. David, with his infectious laugh and unwavering loyalty, had been the heart of their group, a warmth that had been brutally ripped away. The memory of David's final, desperate struggle was etched into Kiel's soul, a wound that refused to heal. The guilt gnawed at him, a constant reminder of his failure to protect his friend.

Grayson, ever the stoic, stood beside them, his silence a testament to the weight of his own grief. He'd witnessed the horrors firsthand, the unimaginable cruelty inflicted upon their friends. The loss of his younger sister, Emily, who had joined them on their ill-fated expedition, had left a gaping hole in his life. Emily, with her bright spirit and inquisitive mind, was the epitome of innocence, a victim of a senseless, brutal act. Her absence was a constant ache in his heart, a void that could never be filled.

They stood in silence for a long time, the wind their only companion, the rustling leaves a mournful chorus. The memorial service was simple, a stark contrast to the media spectacle that had followed their escape. No grand pronouncements, no political speeches, just a quiet gathering of friends, family, and those who had been touched by their story. The simplicity was a reflection of their grief, a quiet acknowledgment of the immense loss they had suffered. They had each lit a candle, their flames flickering in the growing twilight, small beacons of hope in the encroaching darkness, their soft light symbolizing the lives they mourned.

Demitra spoke first, her voice barely a whisper, "We didn't just escape Blackwood Cave; we escaped a nightmare. A nightmare that took so much from us." Her words hung in the air, heavy with unspoken grief. "But we also found something in that darkness," she continued, her voice gaining strength. "We found the strength of our friendship, the power of resilience, and the unwavering belief in justice."

Kiel nodded, his gaze fixed on the flickering candles. "They wouldn't want us to wallow in grief," he said, his voice thick with emotion. "They'd want us to fight, to continue the fight for a world where no one else has to face what we faced." His words resonated with the others, a reminder of their shared purpose, their commitment to preventing future tragedies.

Grayson, his gaze distant yet resolute, added, "Their deaths won't be in vain. The Blackwood Foundation, their memory, will continue to push for change." He spoke of the countless lives their work had saved, the changes they had achieved since their escape. The legislation passed, the research initiatives funded, the lives transformed—these were tangible manifestations of their fallen friends' legacy.

The sun dipped below the horizon, casting long shadows across the landscape. As darkness enveloped them, they shared memories of their lost friends. Laughter mixed with tears, stories of courage and kindness interspersed with tales of unimaginable horror. They remembered Sarah's infectious laugh, Ben's quick wit, Mark's unwavering optimism, David's compassionate heart, and Emily's radiant smile. These weren't just names on a list; they were vibrant individuals, irreplaceable friends, whose memories would forever live on.

They spoke of the impact of the Blackwood case, the ripples it had sent through the world. The changes in scientific ethics, the increased scrutiny of research facilities, the strengthened laws protecting vulnerable populations—all of it a testament to the sacrifices made. The memory of their fallen comrades became the driving force of the Blackwood Foundation's mission to prevent such atrocities from ever happening again.

Demitra spoke of the research she was now conducting on trauma recovery, a project born from the depths of her own pain. She had dedicated her life to ensuring that others would not have to suffer as they had, working tirelessly to develop innovative therapeutic approaches to address the psychological scars left by traumatic experiences.

Kiel discussed the global network of support he had built for victims of similar crimes, a sanctuary for those who had suffered unspeakable horrors. His relentless efforts provided a vital lifeline, creating a space where survivors could find solace, healing, and a sense of community.

Grayson described the tireless work he was doing to maintain the Foundation's global reach, ensuring that their mission would continue long after they were gone. He spent his days navigating international politics, securing funding, establishing partnerships, and advocating for policy changes that promoted ethical scientific practices.

As the stars emerged, twinkling against the dark canvas of the night sky, they stood in silence once more, their hearts heavy with grief but strengthened by their shared purpose. They were survivors, yes, but they were also advocates, fighters, and beacons of hope in a world that had been profoundly scarred. They pledged to honor the memory of their lost friends not through tears and despair, but through action, through dedication, and through an unwavering commitment to building a better world—a world where the sacrifices made in the dark depths of Blackwood Cave would never be forgotten, and where their legacy would ensure that no one else would suffer the same fate. The chilling whispers of the cave were fading, replaced by the resounding voices of the fallen, echoing in the hearts of those left behind, their memory burning brighter than any candle flame. The fallen wouldn't be forgotten; their sacrifice would be a constant reminder of the importance of fighting for a better future, a future where scientific ambition would always be tempered by ethical considerations, and where the sanctity of human life would always be paramount.

The year following their escape from Blackwood Cave felt less like healing and more like a slow, agonizing crawl through the wreckage of their lives. The physical wounds had healed, leaving behind a tapestry of scars that served as grim reminders of their ordeal. But the psychological wounds, those festered deep within their souls, refused to yield. Demitra's nightmares were vivid and relentless, replaying the horrors of the cave with sickening clarity. The screams, the blood, the grotesque forms of the genetically-engineered creatures – they haunted her waking hours as much as her sleep. Kiel wrestled with survivor's guilt, the weight of David's death pressing down on him like a physical burden. He'd promised to protect his friend, a promise he'd failed to keep. Grayson, ever stoic, carried his grief silently, his eyes mirroring the pain of losing his sister, Emily. The emptiness in his heart was a constant companion.

Their collective trauma bound them together, creating an unbreakable bond forged in the crucible of shared horror. The Blackwood Foundation, born from the ashes of their tragedy, became their shared sanctuary, their beacon of hope in a world that seemed to have forgotten them. They weren't just survivors; they were warriors, fighting for justice, for accountability, for a future where no one else would have to endure the horrors they had faced.

The initial media frenzy surrounding their escape had eventually subsided, replaced by a chilling silence that hinted at a deeper conspiracy. The government's official statement, a carefully worded explanation of a "rogue scientific experiment gone wrong," rang hollow in their ears. They knew the truth was far more sinister, far more complex. The creatures they'd encountered in Blackwood Cave weren't simply the result of an accident; they were the product of a deliberate, planned project. And someone, somewhere, was pulling the strings.

Their investigation began quietly, shrouded in secrecy. They met in hushed tones, in dimly lit rooms, their conversations laced with the weight of unspoken knowledge. Demitra, leveraging her newfound connections in the scientific community, painstakingly pieced together fragments of information, uncovering hidden documents, leaked reports, and whispered confessions. Kiel, utilizing his skills in information technology, delved into the digital underworld, tracing encrypted communications, uncovering hidden servers, and exposing clandestine meetings. Grayson, drawing on his family's connections in law enforcement, navigated the treacherous waters of political intrigue, uncovering evidence of cover-ups, bribery, and corruption.

Their individual efforts gradually coalesced, forming a powerful, unified front. They unearthed a trail of evidence leading to a shadowy organization known only as "Genesis," a clandestine group of scientists and powerful individuals who had financed and overseen the creation of the genetically-engineered creatures. The organization's reach extended far beyond Blackwood Cave, encompassing a network of secret laboratories, hidden research facilities, and influential political figures. The scale of the conspiracy was staggering, terrifying in its scope and implications.

The fight for justice wasn't a simple matter of bringing the perpetrators to trial; it was a battle against a vast, well-funded network with powerful allies in high places. They faced intimidation, threats, and attempts on their lives. But the memories of their lost friends fueled their resolve, strengthening their determination to expose the truth, no matter the cost.

Demitra discovered that Genesis had been conducting experiments on humans, using them as test subjects for their monstrous creations. She unearthed chilling evidence of horrific human rights violations, of experiments designed to test the creatures' abilities to inflict pain and suffering. The details were gruesome, so abhorrent that they sent shivers down her spine. These were not mere scientific experiments; they were acts of barbarism, fueled by a disregard for human life that was both terrifying and chilling.

Kiel's investigation uncovered a complex network of financial transactions, revealing the flow of money from Genesis to high-ranking government officials, ensuring their silence and complicity. He unmasked corrupt officials, exposed bribery schemes, and brought to light secret deals made in the shadows. His work was dangerous, requiring him to tread carefully, to operate in the twilight zone between legality and espionage. He was walking a tightrope, one false move could send him plummeting into the abyss.

Grayson, armed with Kiel's digital evidence and Demitra's scientific findings, began assembling a legal case. It was a daunting task, building a case against an organization so deeply entrenched in power. He faced stonewalling, bureaucratic obstruction, and open hostility from those who sought to protect Genesis. But he persisted, driven by the unwavering belief that justice would prevail.

Their investigation uncovered evidence of other sites similar to Blackwood Cave – locations where the creatures were bred, tested, and deployed. Each discovery served as a chilling reminder of the extent of Genesis' operations, a testament to their depravity and reach. The scale of the conspiracy was breathtaking, so expansive it felt impossible to combat. But they pressed on, driven by the knowledge that the horrors of Blackwood Cave were not an isolated incident. They were part of a larger, more sinister pattern.

Over time, their efforts began to bear fruit. Leaks began to appear in the media, snippets of information trickling into the public consciousness. The whispers of conspiracy grew louder, becoming a roar of outrage. The pressure mounted on the government, forcing them to respond. Investigations were launched, inquiries were opened, and the truth, however slowly, began to emerge.

The fight was far from over. Genesis was a hydra, each head cut off replaced by two more. But the Blackwood Foundation had become a force to be reckoned with, a relentless engine of justice driving toward a single, unyielding goal: to expose the organization, bring its members to justice, and ensure that no other innocent lives would be lost to their callous disregard for humanity. The fight continued, fueled by the memory of Sarah, Ben, Mark, David, and Emily. Their legacy was not only a testament to their suffering, but also a beacon of hope, illuminating the path towards a future where justice would prevail, and the horrors of Blackwood Cave would never be repeated. The fight was theirs, a fight they would wage until their dying breath, ensuring that the voices of the fallen would forever echo in the halls of power, demanding accountability and justice. The fight was on, and the darkness would eventually fall.

The news broke slowly, a drip, drip, drip of revelations that eroded the carefully constructed wall of silence surrounding Genesis. First, a leaked internal memo detailing the horrific experiments on human subjects surfaced, its authenticity confirmed by Demitra's research. The public outcry was immediate and fierce. Images of the memo, blurred but undeniably real, circulated online, igniting a firestorm of outrage and demanding answers. Then, Kiel's painstakingly compiled data on the organization's financial dealings was anonymously leaked to a reputable investigative journalist, triggering a series of investigative reports that exposed the extent of Genesis' corruption and influence. The crafted façade of respectability began to crumble, revealing the rotten core beneath.

Grayson, meanwhile, used the leaked information to bolster his legal case. He leveraged his family's connections to navigate the tangled web of political influence, gathering support from unexpected allies who were appalled by the revelations. The sheer weight of evidence, coupled with the mounting public pressure, forced the government to act. A formal investigation was launched, led by a special prosecutor known for her unwavering integrity and reputation for bringing down powerful figures. The investigation was initially met with resistance, with key figures within the government obstructing justice at every turn, but the dam of silence had finally broken.

The survivors' testimony, delivered with raw emotion and unwavering courage, was crucial. They spoke of the horrors they'd witnessed, the brutal violence, the chilling indifference of the scientists involved. Their voices, once silenced by fear and trauma, now resonated with the power of truth, shattering the carefully crafted narrative of a "rogue experiment gone wrong." Their experiences weren't just a personal tragedy; they became a symbol of the fight against corporate greed, government complicity, and the unchecked pursuit of scientific advancement at the expense of human life.

The trial that followed was a media spectacle, a clash between the raw power of truth and the carefully orchestrated deception of Genesis. The defense team, composed of high-powered lawyers known for their ruthlessness, attempted to discredit the survivors, casting doubt on their sanity and suggesting that their experiences were the product of trauma and delusion. But the overwhelming evidence, compiled by the Blackwood Foundation, proved too strong to ignore.

The testimony of other survivors from Genesis' other sites, courageous individuals who had managed to escape the clutches of the organization, added to the weight of the prosecution's case. Their stories mirrored those of Demitra, Kiel, and Grayson, confirming the existence of a widespread network of horror and inhumanity. The cumulative effect was devastating, highlighting the systematic nature of Genesis' crimes and the callous disregard for human life that fueled their actions.

Witness after witness corroborated their stories, painting a picture of a monstrous organization operating in the shadows, profiting from unimaginable suffering. The trial became a referendum on corporate accountability, a battle against the forces of power that sought to silence those who dared to speak truth to power.

The verdict, when it came, was a resounding victory for justice. Key figures within Genesis, including its CEO and several high-ranking scientists, were found guilty on multiple counts of murder, human rights violations, and conspiracy. The sentences were severe, reflecting the gravity of their crimes. The convictions sent a shockwave through the corporate world, serving as a stark reminder that even the most powerful organizations were not beyond the reach of the law.

But the victory was bittersweet. The trial exposed the dark underbelly of scientific ambition and the dangers of unchecked power. The memories of those lost still haunted the survivors, a constant reminder of the price paid for uncovering the truth. Yet, there was a sense of closure, a feeling that justice, however imperfect, had been served.

The lasting impact of the Blackwood Cave incident transcended the courtroom. The survivors became symbols of resilience, their story inspiring others to speak out against injustice, to challenge authority, and to fight for a better future. The Blackwood Foundation, initially conceived as a support group for the survivors, evolved into a powerful advocacy organization dedicated to preventing future tragedies. They worked tirelessly to expose unethical scientific practices, advocate for stronger regulations, and support victims of corporate malfeasance.

Their tireless work led to significant reforms in the scientific community, tougher regulations on genetic engineering, and increased transparency in government research. The incident served as a cautionary tale, a stark reminder of the potential consequences of unchecked ambition and the importance of ethical considerations in scientific research.

The world continued to move forward, but the scars of Blackwood Cave remained, a stark reminder of the darkness that lurked beneath the surface. The survivors bore those scars with dignity and resilience, their experiences transforming them from victims into powerful advocates for change. Their bravery and unwavering commitment to justice ensured that the legacy of Blackwood Cave would not be one of despair but rather a beacon of hope, a testament to the enduring power of the human spirit and the unwavering pursuit of justice.

Demitra dedicated her life to scientific research, using her expertise to advocate for ethical practices and transparency. She became a prominent voice in the scientific community, pushing for stricter regulations and ethical oversight, ensuring that the horrors of Blackwood Cave would never be repeated. She channeled her pain into positive action, striving to ensure that future generations would never experience the horrors she and her friends had endured.

Kiel used his technological expertise to create advanced security systems designed to prevent future breaches and exposures. His work focused on creating secure platforms and protocols to protect sensitive data and prevent the misuse of scientific information. He turned his expertise in data security into a force for good, dedicating his life to protecting vulnerable populations from exploitation and safeguarding sensitive information.

Grayson continued to pursue a career in law, becoming a leading expert in environmental and corporate law. He focused on holding corporations accountable for their actions, using his legal expertise to fight for justice and protect vulnerable communities from exploitation. He used the legal system to fight for a more just world, ensuring that corporations and governments were held accountable for their actions.

The Blackwood Foundation thrived, becoming a global organization dedicated to advocating for ethical scientific practices and human rights. It served as a sanctuary for survivors of similar incidents, offering support, resources, and a community built on shared experiences and mutual respect. The organization's impact was felt worldwide, creating a global network of support and advocacy.

The memories of Sarah, Ben, Mark, David, and Emily remained vivid, their tragic losses forever etched in the hearts of the survivors. But their memory served as a powerful source of inspiration, fueling the survivors' relentless pursuit of justice and their commitment to preventing future tragedies. The fight for justice had been won, but the fight for a better future continued, fueled by the enduring legacy of those who had been lost and the unwavering courage of those who had survived. The world was a safer place because of their sacrifice, and the horrors of Blackwood Cave would serve as a chilling reminder of the potential consequences of unchecked ambition and the crucial importance of fighting for what is right, no matter the cost. The darkness had been confronted, and a brighter future, albeit scarred, began to dawn.

Chapter 11: The Warning

The initial sense of closure, the hard-won victory in the courtroom, proved to be a fragile illusion. The quiet hum of normalcy that had begun to settle over Demitra, Kiel, and Grayson was shattered by a series of unsettling events, each a subtle tremor hinting at a larger, more terrifying awakening. It began with the news reports. Initially dismissed as isolated incidents, the reports detailed strange occurrences across the globe: unexplained animal mutilations, unusual seismic activity in remote areas, and a surge in disappearances mirroring those that had plagued the Blackwood Cave region.

Demitra, ever vigilant, was the first to notice the pattern. She cross-referenced the reports, analyzing the geographical locations, the specific types of mutilations, and the temporal proximity of the events. A chilling realization began to dawn on her – a geographical map that showed an almost perfect alignment with the old geological fault lines running beneath the Blackwood Cave. It wasn't just coincidence; something was moving, something was stirring beneath the surface of the Earth.

The disturbances weren't limited to the periphery. Kiel, always attuned to the digital undercurrents, detected anomalies in global seismic data, subtle shifts and tremors far too frequent and widespread to be explained by natural causes. His sophisticated algorithms, initially designed to detect cyber threats, now revealed a pattern of subterranean activity, a pattern that mirrored the ancient fault lines Demitra had identified. The digital shadows seemed to echo the geological tremors, a sinister symphony of disruption.

These were not just random occurrences; they were orchestrated, precise, and terrifyingly deliberate.

Grayson, steeped in the legal intricacies of the Genesis case, unearthed a hidden clause in the company's liquidation papers, a clause that subtly hinted at a continuation of certain "off-book" projects. He suspected this clause, hidden amongst dense legal jargon, referred to a covert effort to continue the horrific experiments, perhaps even to revive some of the creatures that had terrorized them in Blackwood Cave. The victory over Genesis had been a tactical win; the war, it seemed, was far from over.

The first tangible sign arrived in the form of a package addressed to Demitra. Inside was a single, desiccated claw, impossibly large and sharp, its surface still wet with an unnatural, oily sheen. It bore a chilling resemblance to the claws of the creatures they had encountered in the cave, but this one was larger, more robust, hinting at a monstrous evolution. A single, chillingly cryptic note accompanied it: "The slumber is over."

The note ignited a primal fear within them, a fear far deeper and more visceral than the terror they had experienced in the cave. The creatures hadn't been contained; they were evolving, adapting, and they were coming back. The fight for survival was not over. It was just beginning.

The escalating incidents forced them to confront a terrifying truth: the ancient evil they had faced in Blackwood Cave wasn't confined to the cave itself. It was part of a larger, subterranean network, an ancient entity whose reach extended far beyond their initial encounter. The creatures, genetically engineered monstrosities, were but a small, terrifying part of a much larger, more ancient horror.

Kiel, fueled by a growing sense of urgency, began scouring the archives of

Blackwood Cave's ancient history. He unearthed forgotten texts, cryptic symbols, and half-forgotten legends hinting at a monstrous entity that had resided within the cave's depths for millennia, an entity whose origins were lost to the mists of time, an entity that had manipulated both nature and the Genesis corporation to its own malevolent ends.

The texts spoke of rituals, of sacrifices, of an entity that fed on fear and suffering, an entity that had lain dormant for centuries, only to be inadvertently awakened by the reckless actions of Genesis. Kiel's research painted a terrifying picture: Genesis hadn't created the creatures; they had merely stumbled upon, and then inadvertently, weaponized them, unwittingly awakening a force far beyond their comprehension.

Demitra, poring over the claw's microscopic structure, discovered that its composition defied known biological laws. Its cellular structure was unlike anything she had ever encountered, a bizarre mixture of organic and inorganic materials, hinting at a sophisticated level of genetic manipulation far exceeding anything Genesis had achieved. It wasn't just genetic engineering; it was something older, something more primal.

Grayson, meanwhile, focused on uncovering the remnants of Genesis' "off-book" projects. He discovered evidence suggesting that Genesis wasn't just experimenting on creatures; they were also performing disturbing experiments on humans, blending the DNA of humans and the creatures from the cave in a macabre attempt to create an ultimate weapon, a terrifying hybrid of human and beast.

The convergence of their research pointed to an inescapable conclusion: the creatures were not just evolving; they were being guided, controlled by something far older and more sinister than anything they had ever imagined. The ancient evil they had faced in Blackwood Cave was not a rogue entity but a controlling intelligence, a malevolent force that had been using Genesis as a tool, a pawn in a far grander scheme.

As they pieced together the puzzle, they realized that the creatures were not the primary threat; they were merely the vanguard, the harbingers of a far greater horror. The real threat was the ancient entity itself, a being of immense power and unimaginable evil, slumbering beneath the Earth, waiting for the right moment to unleash its full fury upon the world.

The realization sent shivers down their spines. They were not just fighting for survival; they were fighting to prevent the unleashing of an ancient evil, an evil that could consume the world. The stakes had been raised exponentially. Their fight was no longer about exposing corporate corruption; it was about saving humanity itself.

The following days were a blur of frantic activity. They pooled their resources, combined their expertise, and prepared for a confrontation unlike anything they had ever faced. Demitra delved deeper into the scientific mysteries surrounding the creatures, searching for a weakness, a chink in their seemingly impenetrable armor. Kiel developed advanced tracking systems to monitor the subterranean activity, pinpointing the epicenter of the growing disturbances. Grayson worked tirelessly to mobilize legal and political support, alerting the world to the imminent threat.

But time was running out. The tremors were growing stronger, the strange incidents more frequent. The shadow of the ancient evil was lengthening, stretching its tendrils towards the surface world. The idyllic normalcy they had briefly known was dissolving into a chilling nightmare, a nightmare that threatened to consume them all. The slumber was over, and the awakening was far more terrifying than they could have ever imagined. The ancient evil was stirring, and this time, its intentions were far more sinister than mere survival. It was about conquest. It was about annihilation. And the survivors of Blackwood Cave were humanity's last hope.

The unsettling quiet that followed their courtroom victory was a deceptive calm before a storm of unprecedented magnitude. The whispers of a renewed threat started subtly, almost imperceptible at first. A livestock farmer in rural Montana reported the bizarre mutilation of his cattle, the carcasses drained of blood with surgical precision, leaving behind no trace of the perpetrator. A similar incident surfaced in the Amazon rainforest, echoing the Montana event with chilling similarity. These were not the clumsy work of wild animals; these were precise, almost ritualistic killings.

Demitra, ever the researcher, painstakingly pieced together the scattered reports, connecting the dots on a global map. The locations weren't random; they followed a pattern, a

sinister alignment with ancient geological fault lines – fault lines that ran disturbingly close to the Blackwood Cave. The chilling realization solidified:
whatever had lurked in the cave's depths wasn't contained; it was spreading, expanding its influence across the globe.

Kiel, his expertise in digital forensics now weaponized against a far more sinister foe, detected a surge in unusual electromagnetic activity in the affected regions. His algorithms, designed to detect cyber threats, now picked up a distinct, almost organic signature emanating from deep underground, a pulse of energy that synchronized with the seismic activity Demitra had identified. It was as though the earth itself was acting as a conduit for some unseen, malevolent force.

Grayson, still navigating the treacherous waters of corporate espionage, uncovered a hidden subsidiary of Genesis Corp., a shadow organization operating under a veil of secrecy. This "Project Chimera," as he discovered through leaked documents, was a desperate attempt to not only weaponize the creatures from Blackwood Cave, but also to genetically engineer a new breed, far more lethal and adaptable. The documents spoke of accelerated evolution, of merging the creatures' DNA with human genetic material – a horrifying vision of man and beast intertwined.

The next blow struck close to home. A series of targeted attacks commenced, seemingly random at first, but later revealed a chilling pattern. Their close friends, those who were involved in the initial Genesis investigation, began to disappear, one by one. The disappearances were swift, clean, leaving behind no trace, no witnesses, only a growing sense of dread and unease.

The first victim was Dr. Evelyn Reed, the lead scientist who had initially blown the whistle on Genesis' illegal activities. She was abducted from her home in the middle of the night, leaving behind only a single, strangely iridescent feather, a cryptic calling card.

Then came Mark Olsen, the tenacious journalist who had relentlessly pursued the Blackwood Cave story. His apartment was found empty, his computer wiped clean, the only clue being a faint, almost imperceptible scent of ozone lingering in the air.

The third victim was Sheriff Brody, the man who had initially responded to the distress call from the Blackwood Cave. He vanished during his routine patrol, his patrol car found abandoned miles from the nearest town, the radio silent, the interior wiped clean.

The disappearances were not random. They were targeted, deliberate acts, a chilling escalation of the threat. They weren't merely being hunted; they were being studied, assessed, their strengths and weaknesses cataloged by an unseen, intelligent force.

The survivors – Demitra, Kiel, and Grayson – huddled together, the weight of the growing threat pressing down on them like a physical burden. The chilling realization that they were not just dealing with genetically modified creatures, but a far more ancient and terrifying entity, set in. The creatures were merely pawns, tools in the hands of something far older and more sinister.

Demitra, delving into ancient texts and forgotten lore, discovered disturbing parallels between the current events and ancient myths and legends, tales of subterranean entities that fed on fear and suffering, entities that had been banished to the underworld centuries ago, only to awaken now with renewed fury.

Kiel, utilizing his digital prowess, uncovered a network of subterranean tunnels, a vast, interconnected labyrinth extending far beyond the confines of Blackwood Cave. This underground network seemed to be a conduit, a pathway for the ancient entity, a network that allowed it to influence and control events on the surface world.

Grayson, his legal expertise now focusing on tracking the remnants of Project Chimera, unearthed chilling evidence of hybrid creatures, grotesque abominations created by merging human and creature DNA. These hybrids, far more intelligent and capable than the creatures from Blackwood Cave, were acting as scouts, spies, and assassins for the ancient entity.

They realized they weren't just fighting for their survival anymore; they were fighting to protect humanity from an ancient, malevolent force that had been awakened by Genesis' reckless experiments. This entity, far from being confined to the depths of Blackwood Cave, was a parasitic force that preyed upon human fear and suffering, using genetic manipulation as a means to control and dominate.

The fear was palpable, the weight of their responsibility crushing. They were facing an enemy that was both ancient and technologically advanced, an entity that could manipulate the very fabric of reality, an entity whose goal wasn't merely conquest,

but annihilation. The creature they'd fought in the cave were only the vanguard, the first wave of an impending invasion. The real war had just begun. Their fight was no longer confined to the darkness of a cave; it was a global struggle against an ancient evil, a fight for the very survival of mankind. The nightmarish awakening was far from over; it was only just beginning.

The air in Demitra's secluded cabin hung thick with the scent of pine and the unspoken dread that clung to them like a shroud. Three weeks had passed since the harrowing escape from Blackwood Cave, three weeks that had felt like an eternity. The idyllic setting, once a sanctuary, now felt like a precarious perch on the edge of an abyss. Outside, the Montana winter pressed in, a stark contrast to the stifling claustrophobia of the cave, yet both shared a chilling sense of isolation.

Kiel, his face etched with exhaustion, ran a hand through his already disheveled hair, the faint glow of his laptop illuminating the shadows around him. His usual attention to detail was replaced by a frantic energy, his fingers flying across the keyboard as he wrestled with encrypted data, fragments of Project Chimera's activities. The silence was broken only by the rhythmic click-clack of keys and the occasional frustrated groan. He was piecing together a network, a subterranean spiderweb stretching across continents, connecting the disappearances, the strange electromagnetic pulses, and the horrific mutilations.

Grayson, ever the pragmatist, paced restlessly, his phone a constant companion, a lifeline to the ever-shifting landscape of global intelligence. His usual sharp suit was replaced by layers of worn clothing, the formality abandoned in favor of practicality. His face, usually marked by calculated detachment, was now etched with grim determination. He'd spent weeks tracing the ghosts of Genesis Corp, unearthing shell companies and hidden accounts, piecing together the fragmented remains of Project Chimera. The task was monumental, a Sisyphean struggle against a vast, well-funded organization adept at hiding its tracks. He knew the scale of the threat, the sheer audacity of the project, dwarfed their initial fears about the creatures themselves.

Demitra, her usual vibrant energy muted by the weight of their shared burden, sat by the crackling fireplace, surrounded by ancient texts and faded maps. Her fingers traced the intricate patterns on a worn leather-bound book, her gaze lost in the cryptic symbols and arcane writings. She'd discovered chilling connections between the current events and ancient prophecies, tales of subterranean entities that thrived on human suffering, entities whose influence extended far beyond the confines of Blackwood Cave. Her research wasn't just uncovering the history of the creatures; it was revealing a cosmic horror, an ancient malevolence that had been slumbering for millennia, awakened by the careless hubris of man.

Their preparation wasn't simply about gathering weapons and supplies; it was about confronting the existential dread that had seeped into their souls. They needed more than guns and explosives; they needed knowledge, strategy, and an unwavering resolve that transcended their individual fears. This wasn't a simple rescue mission; it was a war for survival, a fight against an unseen enemy whose power seemed limitless.

Kiel's work focused on identifying weak points in the subterranean network. His algorithms, refined and honed through tireless nights of coding, now served as a window into the unseen world, revealing vulnerable nodes, potential entry points, and lines of communication between the creatures and their enigmatic controllers. He'd identified a pattern in the electromagnetic pulses, a rhythmic heartbeat that seemed to dictate the creatures' movements, a pulse that could be disrupted, perhaps even weaponized.

Grayson's investigation had uncovered a hidden research facility in the desolate reaches of Siberia, a facility shrouded in secrecy, heavily guarded, and equipped with cutting-edge technology. It was here, he believed, that Project Chimera's most dangerous experiments were taking place, the creation of hybrid creatures — abominations that blended human and creature DNA into grotesque parodies of life. He had secured images from a compromised satellite, showing horrifying glimpses of these hybrids, creatures of unimaginable power and intelligence.

Demitra's research had yielded unexpected results. She'd discovered ancient rituals, forgotten languages, and cryptic symbols that suggested a way to weaken, even banish, the entity controlling the creatures. It wasn't a scientific solution; it was a spiritual one, a confrontation with a power that transcended the material world. She needed to find a specific artifact, a relic from a forgotten civilization, an artifact said to possess the power to disrupt the entity's influence. Its location, however, was shrouded in myth and legend, a perilous quest in itself.

Their strategy was three-pronged. Kiel would exploit the weaknesses in the subterranean network, creating a disruption that would incapacitate the creatures and potentially reveal the entity's true location. Grayson would lead a covert assault on the Siberian facility, destroying the source of the hybrid creatures and gathering crucial intel. Demitra would embark on a perilous journey to locate the ancient artifact, the key to potentially ending the threat once and for all. It was a high-stakes gamble, a desperate attempt to turn the tide in a war that they were woefully unprepared for.

They spent days poring over maps, analyzing data, and planning their individual assaults. Kiel assembled a team of trusted hackers, specialists capable of penetrating the deepest layers of the subterranean network. He designed a series of cyberattacks, sophisticated electromagnetic pulses that would disrupt the creatures' communication, disorienting them and potentially rendering them vulnerable. He even managed to obtain a modified sonic weapon, a high-powered device capable of emitting frequencies that could disrupt the neural pathways of the creatures, causing disorientation and paralysis. The weapon, however, was untested and unpredictable, a risky gamble in their already precarious situation.

Grayson, relying on his network of informants and contacts within various intelligence agencies, gathered intel on the Siberian facility. He acquired high-resolution satellite imagery, detailed floor plans, security protocols, and even the personnel rosters. He assembled a small, elite team – ex-military operatives, cybersecurity experts, and weapons specialists – individuals who were both skilled and discreet, people he could trust with his life and theirs. Their plan was a surgical strike, swift and precise, designed to neutralize the threat with minimal collateral damage. He secured cutting-edge cloaking technology, suppressors for their weapons, and bio-hazard suits capable of protecting them from potential contamination. The stakes were incredibly high; any misstep would result in failure.

Demitra, guided by her research and intuition, began her quest for the ancient artifact. Her journey took her to forgotten libraries, ancient ruins, and remote monasteries, traversing treacherous landscapes and navigating treacherous political landscapes. She learned to read forgotten languages, decipher cryptic symbols, and interpret cryptic prophecies, each clue leading her closer to her ultimate goal. She faced danger at every turn, from rival researchers and unscrupulous collectors, to the more sinister presence of the creatures themselves, acting as scouts and assassins for their unseen master.

The final stage of their preparation was the most difficult. They had to confront their own fears, their own vulnerabilities, and their own mortality. The weight of their shared trauma, the horrors they had witnessed in the Blackwood Cave, haunted their waking moments and their dreams. They sat around the fire, sharing stories, fears, and their hopes, a fragile truce against the overwhelming darkness that loomed over them. They forged a bond stronger than fear, a pact forged in the crucible of trauma and solidified in the face of impending doom. They knew this wasn't just a fight for survival, it was a fight for humanity, a desperate attempt to prevent the descent into an apocalyptic nightmare. They were ready. Or as ready as they could ever be. The war had begun.

The rhythmic whir of Demitra's ancient gramophone filled the cabin, a melancholic counterpoint to the crackling fire. The music, a haunting melody from a forgotten culture, seemed to resonate with the weight of their impending mission. It was a lullaby of dread, a prelude to the storm that was about to break. Kiel, finally tearing himself away from his computer, joined them, his face pale but resolute. He held a worn leather-bound journal in his hands, its pages filled with cryptic symbols and handwritten notes.

"I've found something," Kiel announced, his voice hoarse from exhaustion. "A hidden network, a sub-network within the larger Project Chimera infrastructure. It's encrypted, of course, but I've managed to decipher enough to understand its purpose."

He explained that this smaller network wasn't directly involved in controlling the creatures, but rather, it facilitated communication between various factions interested in harnessing the creatures' power. There were mentions of shadowy government agencies, corporations with ties to Genesis Corp, and even individuals, wealthy collectors and power brokers eager to exploit the technological and biological advancements hidden within Project Chimera.

"These aren't just rogue scientists," Kiel continued, his voice tinged with a chilling revelation. "This is a vast conspiracy, a global network stretching across borders and political ideologies. They're all vying for control, each with their own agenda, each willing to use the creatures as pawns in a far larger game."

This discovery offered them a glimmer of hope, a crack in the seemingly impenetrable wall of their enemy. If they could exploit the rivalries and conflicting agendas within this network, they might be able to turn their enemies against each other, creating chaos and confusion amongst their ranks. It also meant that they were no longer alone in their fight.

Grayson, ever the strategist, immediately began plotting ways to infiltrate and manipulate the network. His connections in the intelligence community proved invaluable, leading him to individuals who were deeply disillusioned with the clandestine projects their governments were involved in. These were not traditional allies, but individuals who had witnessed the consequences of unchecked ambition and who were now searching for a way to atone for their past actions.

One such contact was a former high-ranking official within a South American intelligence agency, a man named Ricardo, who had stumbled upon evidence of a secret Project Chimera facility nestled deep within the Amazon rainforest. Ricardo, tired of his government's involvement in the sinister operation, had secretly amassed intelligence on the facility and was willing to share it, risking everything in the process. He provided Grayson with detailed satellite imagery, blueprints of the facility, and information on security protocols. This Amazonian facility was different; it wasn't solely a production or research facility. It housed a powerful server farm – a central node within the sub-network Kiel had discovered.

Another unexpected ally emerged in the form of Dr. Evelyn Reed, a geneticist who had once worked on the early stages of Project Chimera. Consumed by guilt and remorse over her involvement, she had spent years trying to undo the damage she had helped create. She had access to crucial information about the creatures' vulnerabilities, their genetic makeup, and their behavioral patterns. She offered her expertise, providing Kiel and Demitra with vital information that could be used to develop countermeasures and weapons. However, she made it clear that her cooperation came with a price – her identity and her cooperation had to remain completely secret. She knew that people who knew too much about this project usually ended up disappearing.

Demitra, meanwhile, had made unexpected progress in her own quest. Her research into ancient prophecies had led her to a secluded monastery high in the Himalayas, a place where ancient knowledge was preserved and guarded. Here, she encountered a community of monks, keepers of ancient wisdom, who had been monitoring Project Chimera's activities from afar, sensing the encroaching darkness and the impending threat to humanity.

These monks, deeply connected to the spiritual energy of the earth, possessed knowledge of ancient rituals and practices that could potentially weaken the entity controlling the creatures. They provided Demitra with a detailed map leading to a hidden chamber deep within the earth, a chamber containing a powerful artifact - a relic from a forgotten civilization, capable of disrupting the entity's influence. They also helped her understand a forgotten language used in the rituals, providing crucial knowledge for the upcoming confrontation. They stressed that using the artifact was a high-risk gamble, that its power was immense, and its consequences unpredictable.

The combination of these unexpected allies significantly altered their strategy.

Grayson's team, now augmented with Ricardo's intel, focused on disabling the Amazonian server farm, disrupting communication amongst the factions and severing the connection between the creatures and their human controllers. Simultaneously, Kiel, armed with Dr. Reed's knowledge, fine-tuned his cyber-attacks, developing frequencies and viruses that could exploit specific vulnerabilities in the creatures' neural pathways. Demitra, guided by the monks, set out to retrieve the ancient artifact, preparing for the complex and risky ritual required to unleash its power.

Their alliance was fragile, a coalition forged in the crucible of shared desperation. They were united not by a shared history or ideology, but by a shared understanding of the unimaginable threat they faced. Each member brought unique skills and knowledge, a tapestry of abilities interwoven to create a formidable force against a monstrous enemy. Their preparations were a delicate balance of science, strategy, and spirituality, a desperate attempt to stave off the apocalypse. As they prepared for the final battle, a chilling realization dawned upon them: the true horror was not just the creatures themselves, but the depths of human ambition, greed, and the terrifying consequences of unchecked scientific advancement. The stage was set for a showdown that would determine not only their survival but the fate of humanity itself. The fight wasn't just against monstrous creatures; it was against the insidious darkness that thrived within the hearts of men, a darkness that had unleashed these horrors upon the world.

The flickering firelight danced across Kiel's face, illuminating the deep-set shadows beneath his eyes. The weight of their mission, the sheer scale of the conspiracy they were up against, pressed down on him with crushing force. He hadn't slept properly in days, fueled by caffeine and the adrenaline of a desperate fight against an impossible foe. The rhythmic tick-tock of the grandfather clock in the corner seemed to mock his frantic efforts, each second a reminder of the dwindling time they had.

He thought back to Blackwood Cave, the echoing darkness, the stench of death, the chilling screams that still haunted his nightmares. The memory of Mark's terrified face, the way Sarah's hand had slipped from his grasp, the desperate scramble through the claustrophobic tunnels... it all came flooding back, a raw, visceral torrent of trauma. He'd seen things in that cave that would forever stain his soul, things that defied explanation, things that shattered his youthful innocence. But it wasn't just the physical horrors; it was the psychological scars, the lingering fear, the constant gnawing sense of vulnerability that threatened to consume him.

Demitra, sensing his distress, gently placed a hand on his arm. Her own eyes held a haunted look, the reflection of her own ordeal in the depths of Blackwood Cave. The memory of the creatures, their inhuman strength and intelligence, their cold, unfeeling gaze... it was a terror that resided deep within her psyche. She'd faced her own demons since the incident, the relentless nightmares, the crippling anxiety attacks, the silent screams that choked her in the dead of night. The experience had shattered her faith in the world's order, replacing it with a chilling understanding of its brutal reality. The vulnerability she felt in the cave, the knowledge that death lurked around every corner, had left an indelible mark on her soul.

Grayson, ever the pragmatist, remained outwardly composed, but his jaw was clenched, his hands restless. The strategic mind that had always been his shield was now battling the insidious whispers of doubt. He had lost colleagues, friends, in the shadows of this relentless pursuit, a price he paid for his unrelenting pursuit of justice. The cost of his actions was a heavy weight, a constant reminder of the precarious nature of his mission. The weight of his past actions, the lives lost in the name of a greater good, haunted his thoughts. He had to ensure that more lives were not lost. This was his penance.

Even the seemingly unflappable Grayson bore the scars of Blackwood Cave. He had witnessed firsthand the brutality of the creatures, the ruthlessness of their attacks. The image of Ben's mangled body, the chilling finality of death, still replayed in his mind like a gruesome horror film. It was a constant reminder of his own mortality, of the fragility of life in the face of overwhelming power. It had shattered his cynicism and forced him to confront his own mortality, his own vulnerability. He'd always been a man of action, a strategist, but Blackwood Cave had revealed the limitations of his control, the unpredictable nature of chaos.

They sat in silence for a long time, each lost in their own private hell, the shared trauma binding them together in a silent communion of grief and determination. The silence was broken only by the crackling fire and the mournful strains of the gramophone. It was a shared moment of catharsis, a necessary acknowledgment of the darkness they had faced. It was a reminder that their scars, both physical and emotional, were a testament to their survival, a source of strength and resilience.

It was Kiel who finally broke the silence, his voice low but steady. "We've been through hell," he said, "but we're still here. We survived. And that means something."

Demitra nodded, her eyes fixed on the dancing flames. "We've learned from our mistakes. We understand the enemy better now." The experience in Blackwood cave had changed all of them. Each understood the enemy.

Grayson added, "Our past failures have shaped our present resolve. We will not falter." The cost of the failure was a heavy burden to carry, one that strengthened their resolve.

Their shared ordeal had forged an unbreakable bond between them, a powerful alliance forged in the crucible of terror and loss. They had faced their demons, confronted their fears, and emerged stronger, more determined than ever. Their past traumas were no longer debilitating weaknesses but powerful catalysts, fueling their resolve and shaping their strategies for the battles to come.

Their past experiences had provided invaluable lessons. They had learned the creatures' strengths and weaknesses, their patterns of behavior, their vulnerabilities. They knew the limitations of their own abilities, their own vulnerabilities. They understood the importance of teamwork, of trust, of relying on each other's strengths to compensate for their own weaknesses. The close calls, the near-death experiences, had sharpened their instincts, honed their reflexes, and transformed them into a finely tuned fighting machine.

They knew that their fight was far from over. The shadows of Project Chimera stretched far beyond Blackwood Cave, extending into a network of corruption and conspiracy that spanned the globe. They had allies now, unexpected allies who had been touched by the same darkness, who had witnessed the devastating consequences of unchecked ambition and scientific hubris. But they also knew that the stakes were higher than ever. Their fight was not just for their survival; it was for the survival of humanity itself. The past had taught them that failure was not an option.

They spent the next few days planning their next move. Grayson's contacts in the intelligence community provided crucial information on the Amazonian facility. Kiel, using Dr. Reed's insights, developed sophisticated cyber-attacks targeting the creatures' neural pathways. Demitra, guided by the ancient knowledge imparted by the Himalayan monks, prepared for the perilous journey to the hidden chamber. Each of them focused on their respective tasks, driven by a shared sense of purpose, a burning desire to confront the darkness and bring an end to the nightmare.

The memories of Blackwood Cave were not something they could simply forget, but something they needed to use, to learn from. Each time they thought back to the horrors, they felt the fuel of their determination grow and the memory was a painful reminder but also a testament to the strength they possessed. The trauma of the past was not a barrier, but a springboard that would propel them into the heart of the darkness, ready to confront the horrors they had discovered.

The fear still lingered, a cold shadow that clung to the edges of their consciousness. But it was tempered now by a newfound resolve, a steely determination that had been forged in the fires of their ordeal. They were prepared to face the darkness once more, not as naive teenagers, but as hardened survivors, battle-scarred but unbowed. The past had given them scars, but it had also given them strength. It had given them the resolve to fight, the courage to face the unknown, the conviction that they could overcome the horrors that awaited them. The past had taught them survival, and now that knowledge was their weapon. They were ready. The darkness would meet its match.

Chapter 12: The Reckoning Part II

The air hung thick and heavy with the scent of decay and ozone, a miasma clinging to the humid Amazonian air. Before them, the facility loomed, a monolithic structure of steel and concrete, stark against the emerald tapestry of the rainforest. It was a testament to human ambition, a monument to unchecked scientific hubris, a breeding ground for the horrors they had encountered in Blackwood Cave. This was the heart of Project Chimera, the source of their nightmares, the culmination of their harrowing journey.

Kiel, his face grim beneath the sweat beading on his brow, checked his modified EMP device. The device, a culmination of his frantic days and nights of work using Dr. Reed's notes, pulsed faintly, a silent promise of disruption. He knew it was their best chance at neutralizing the creatures' neural networks, their primary weapon against the genetically engineered monstrosities. But he also knew that it was a risky gamble, one that could backfire spectacularly. The creatures' adaptability was a terrifying unknown, their ability to evolve and adapt to new threats was a daunting challenge.

Demitra, her movements fluid and precise, checked the ancient artifacts strapped to her wrists. The Himalayan monks' teachings had opened doors to a world of esoteric knowledge, imbuing her with a sense of heightened awareness and an uncanny ability to sense the presence of the creatures. The artifacts, imbued with centuries of spiritual energy, acted as conduits, amplifying her innate abilities, allowing her to predict their movements with unsettling accuracy. Yet, even with this newfound power, a deep-seated fear gnawed at her, a primal instinct warning of impending danger. The shadows seemed to writhe, alive with the presence of unseen horrors.

Grayson, ever the strategist, surveyed the terrain, his eyes scanning the perimeter for any signs of movement. His military training kicked in, his mind calculating probabilities, assessing risks, and formulating contingencies. He had assembled a small, elite team of specialists, individuals who understood the gravity of the situation, individuals who were willing to risk everything to stop Project Chimera. They were a motley crew, brought together by circumstance and driven by a shared sense of purpose: to dismantle the monstrosity before it could unleash its full potential upon the world. The weight of their collective responsibility bore down on him, a burden he carried with stoic resolve.

The assault began under the cover of darkness. Kiel unleashed a volley of EMP bursts, targeting the creatures' neural pathways, causing them to convulse and stagger momentarily. The disruption wasn't total, but it bought them precious seconds, enough time to breach the perimeter. The creatures, however, were quick to adapt. Their primal intelligence allowed them to quickly compensate for the disruption, their movements becoming more erratic, more unpredictable.

Demitra, moving like a phantom through the shadows, used her enhanced senses to guide their team, maneuvering them through the labyrinthine corridors of the facility. The artifacts pulsed, their energy echoing through the air, a tangible counterpoint to the creatures' unnerving presence. She could sense their rage, their predatory instincts, the cold, calculating intelligence that defied all understanding. The air crackled with tension, each footstep echoing in the claustrophobic spaces, each breath a potential giveaway to their presence.

The final confrontation took place in the heart of the facility, a vast chamber bathed in an eerie, pulsating green light. In the center stood the ancient evil, a grotesque amalgamation of flesh and technology, a being that defied the boundaries of nature and science. It pulsed with a malevolent energy, its very existence a perversion of life itself. Surrounding it were the creatures, their eyes glowing with an unnatural light, their bodies twitching with anticipation. They were its grotesque offspring, its gruesome legacy.

The battle was a brutal, desperate dance of death. Kiel's EMP bursts continued, but their effectiveness dwindled as the creatures adapted, their movements becoming increasingly erratic and unpredictable. Demitra used her spiritual abilities to disrupt their sensory perceptions, creating disorientation and confusion. Grayson, with his team, provided covering fire, their weapons spitting a deadly ballet of bullets that ripped through the creatures' flesh, leaving trails of grotesque viscera.

The fight was relentless, each blow delivered with the force of sheer desperation. The air filled with the sounds of gunfire, the screams of dying creatures, and the guttural roars of the ancient evil. The floor became slick with blood, a testament to the brutal carnage. Kiel's device started failing, its energy depleted, leaving him vulnerable. Demitra felt the immense psychic drain from her constant attempts to disrupt the creatures' senses. Grayson's team, depleted and wounded, fought on with unwavering determination.

But amidst the chaos, a glimmer of hope emerged. Kiel, drawing on the last vestiges of his strength, unleashed a concentrated burst of EMP energy, aimed directly at the ancient evil's core. The resulting explosion rocked the chamber, sending shockwaves that shook the very foundations of the facility. Demitra, seizing the opportunity, channeled the remaining energy of her artifacts, focusing it on a single, decisive blow. The combined assault shattered the ancient evil's core, sending the monstrous being into a state of disarray.

The creatures, stripped of their central command, faltered, their movements becoming disjointed, their attacks less coordinated. Grayson's team, though exhausted and battered, pressed their advantage, unleashing a final barrage of fire, finishing the remaining creatures. The once formidable army was now scattered pieces of flesh and technology.

The facility shook violently before slowly collapsing upon itself, swallowing the remains of the creatures in a deafening roar. As the dust settled, only silence remained, a silence broken only by the steady rhythm of their breathing. They had won, but at a terrible cost. The scars they carried – physical, mental, emotional – were a testament to the horrors they had faced, a reminder of the battle they fought and won. The victory was bittersweet. They had saved humanity, but at what cost? The price of survival was high, the shadow of the events forever etched into their souls. The world was safe, for now. But they knew, deep down, that the darkness would always linger, a constant reminder of the fragility of peace, and the terrible price they paid to protect it. The haunting silence was a sobering reminder, a testament to the horrors they had faced, and a harbinger of what still might come. The fight was over, but the war had just begun.

The crumbling remains of the facility groaned under the weight of its own destruction, a testament to the ferocity of their battle. Dust motes danced in the weak beams of their flashlights, illuminating the grotesque tableau of carnage: mangled metal, shredded flesh, and the lingering stench of ozone and decay. Silence, thick and heavy, pressed down on them, broken only by the ragged gasps of their own breathing and the occasional tremor in the collapsing structure.

Kiel, leaning heavily against a jagged piece of concrete, coughed, a rattling sound that echoed unnervingly in the vast space. His EMP device lay inert in his hand, a cold, metallic weight mirroring the exhaustion that had settled deep in his bones. The adrenaline that had fueled their desperate fight had ebbed, leaving behind a profound sense of emptiness and a bone-deep weariness. He looked at his hands, stained crimson, and felt a surge of nausea. He had never imagined he would witness such brutality, let alone participate in it. He was just a kid, a college student who loved video games and coding, and now he was standing amidst the ruins of a catastrophic event, forever marked by its horrors.

Demitra, her face pale but resolute, sat cross-legged amidst the debris, her hands resting lightly on the ancient artifacts strapped to her wrists. The mystical energy that had pulsed through them during the battle had dissipated, leaving them cold and inert. The psychic drain had left her weak and trembling, but a flicker of satisfaction burned in her eyes. She had tapped into a power she never knew existed, a power that had allowed her to push beyond her limits, to defy the odds. The experience had transformed her, stripping away her youthful naiveté and replacing it with a grim determination, a newfound understanding of her own potential and the darkness that lurked in the world. She had faced her fears, and in doing so, had found a strength she never knew she possessed.

Grayson, his usually sharp features etched with grim determination, surveyed the scene with a practiced eye. His military training had prepared him for the horrors of war, but nothing could have fully prepared him for the surreal brutality of their encounter. He surveyed his team, their faces etched with exhaustion and trauma, their bodies bearing the scars of battle. They were bruised, battered, but alive. They had faced unimaginable odds and emerged victorious, defying expectations, demonstrating a resilience that surpassed any training or preparation. They were survivors, their bond forged in the crucible of unimaginable horror. They had proven their mettle, their courage, their unwavering commitment to their cause.

One by one, the members of their makeshift team emerged from the shadows, their faces illuminated by the flickering beams of their flashlights. Sarah, the medic, tended to the wounded, her hands moving with practiced efficiency. Mark, the tech expert, surveyed the damage to their equipment, assessing the extent of their losses. Each member, in their own way, contributed to the overall victory, their combined skills and dedication proving indispensable in the face of such overwhelming odds. They were an unlikely team, a group of individuals brought together by circumstance and bound together by their shared experience.

The air hung heavy with the unspoken understanding of their shared trauma. They had seen things that would forever haunt their nightmares, things that would forever alter their perception of the world. They were changed, irrevocably altered by the events of the night. But amidst the darkness, a glimmer of hope remained. They had faced the unthinkable and emerged victorious, their victory a testament to the resilience of the human spirit, the unwavering strength of the human will.

As dawn broke, painting the Amazonian sky in hues of orange and purple, they began the slow, arduous process of making their escape. They were exhausted, wounded, but alive. They had faced the horrors of Project Chimera and emerged victorious. They had faced overwhelming odds, and through sheer determination and a blend of unexpected skills and knowledge, they had overcome the monstrous threat. Kiel's technological prowess, Demitra's mystical gifts, and Grayson's strategic acumen had become the unlikely weapons that saved them. Their triumph was not merely a matter of skill; it was a testament to the indomitable spirit of humanity, a powerful demonstration of what ordinary people could achieve when faced with extraordinary circumstances.

Their escape was fraught with peril. The collapsing structure threatened to bury them alive, the rainforest itself seemed to conspire against their escape. But they persevered, pushing through the dense undergrowth, navigating the treacherous terrain with unwavering determination. Their journey back to civilization was a testament to their resilience, a grueling reminder of the physical and emotional toll of their ordeal. But with every step, their determination grew stronger. They were not just survivors; they were victors. They had faced the darkness and emerged into the light.

As they finally stumbled out of the rainforest, blinking in the bright sunlight, they could only feel a mixture of relief and exhaustion. They were alive. They had won. But the scars they bore—physical and emotional—would remain, a constant reminder of the horrors they had witnessed and the incredible challenges they had overcome. They had gone into the heart of darkness and had emerged as heroes, a testament to the strength and resilience of the human spirit. They were not just teenagers who had faced impossible odds; they were unlikely heroes, ordinary people who had risen to meet an extraordinary challenge. Their tale would be told and retold, a testament to the capacity of humanity to confront and conquer the unknown, a testament to the power of bravery in the face of overwhelming terror. They had become unlikely heroes, and their victory echoed through the silence, a symbol of hope in a world touched by darkness. Their journey was not over, however. The repercussions of Project Chimera would surely continue to unfold, leaving them to grapple with the knowledge of what they had seen and the burden of what they had done. They were changed, transformed by the crucible of their experience, forever bonded by the shared trauma and the extraordinary victory they had achieved together. The world was safe, for now, but their personal battles had only just begun. They knew the darkness had not been completely extinguished; it lingered, a threat just beyond the horizon, a constant reminder that the fight for survival was ongoing. Their victory was bittersweet, bought at a terrible cost, a victory that left them forever changed and marked by the horrors they had overcome. Their survival had come at a price, a price they would carry for the rest of their lives. Yet amidst the grim realities of their survival, a sense of quiet triumph lingered, a testament to their courage, resilience, and the unbreakable bond that had carried them through hell and back. They were survivors. They were heroes. Their story would serve as a chilling reminder of the darkness that lurks beneath the surface and the extraordinary courage it takes to confront it.

The escape from the crumbling facility was only the first step in a long and arduous journey. The rainforest, once a seemingly impenetrable barrier, now felt like a cruel mockery of their hard-won freedom. Every rustle of leaves, every snap of a twig, sent jolts of adrenaline through their exhausted bodies. The weight of their shared trauma hung heavy in the humid air, a suffocating blanket woven from fear and exhaustion. They moved as one, a silent, grim procession through the oppressive green.

Sarah, despite her exhaustion, worked tirelessly, tending to their wounds. The cuts and bruises were superficial, but the deeper wounds – the emotional scars etched into their souls – would take far longer to heal. She had lost count of the times she'd patched up Mark, who, despite his protests, insisted on pushing himself beyond his limits, his injured leg throbbing with each step. His technological expertise, though invaluable, had been severely compromised with the destruction of most of their equipment. The EMP device, Kiel's magnum opus, lay shattered, a symbol of the heavy price they'd paid for their victory.

Kiel, still shaken by the brutality he'd witnessed, struggled to maintain his composure. The images of the twisted, genetically-engineered creatures, their eyes burning with a chilling intelligence, haunted his every waking moment. The guilt gnawed at him; the knowledge that he had taken a life, even one so monstrous, weighed heavily on his conscience. He found himself constantly scanning the shadows, expecting to see those horrifying eyes gleam again, their predatory gaze fixing on them. The silence of the rainforest, once a source of peace, now felt like a menacing whisper, a constant reminder of the lurking danger.

Demitra, despite her physical weakness, was oddly calm, a stark contrast to the turmoil raging within her. The psychic strain had left her drained, but it had also unlocked a power within her that both frightened and fascinated her. She had glimpsed the horrifying truth of Project Chimera, a chilling glimpse into a future she desperately hoped to prevent. The ancient artifacts, now inert, felt strangely cold against her skin, a constant reminder of the power she'd wielded and the responsibility she now carried. She felt a profound sense of loss; the weight of responsibility rested heavily on her shoulders, a burden she wasn't sure she could bear.

Grayson, the stoic leader, held them together with his unwavering resolve. His military experience had prepared him for the physical demands of their escape, but it couldn't prepare him for the emotional toll. He silently carried the weight of his team's survival, the burden of leadership pressing down on him like a physical weight. He knew that their escape was far from guaranteed, the rainforest concealing more dangers than they could possibly imagine.

As days bled into nights, their hope began to wane. The relentless humidity, the biting insects, the constant threat of unseen predators – it all chipped away at their already depleted reserves. Mark's injured leg worsened, forcing them to slow their pace. His usual upbeat demeanor had faded, replaced by a quiet grimness. Their supplies dwindled, their hunger and thirst gnawing at their resolve. The dwindling daylight added another layer of urgency, amplifying the desperate nature of their escape. The rainforest was a labyrinth, an unforgiving maze of tangled vines, treacherous ravines, and lurking shadows.

Then came the night of the storm. The heavens opened, unleashing a torrent of rain that threatened to drown them. The already treacherous terrain became a mud-slicked nightmare. They huddled together for shelter under the flimsy canopy of a massive tree, drenched to the bone and shivering with cold. The storm raged for hours, an unrelenting assault that seemed determined to crush their spirits. When the storm finally subsided, dawn revealed the extent of their losses. Mark, exhausted and weakened by his injury, had succumbed to his wounds. Their technological expert, their anchor in the chaos, was gone. The silence that followed the storm was heavy with the weight of their loss.

The grief was a palpable thing, heavy in the air, suffocating their already depleted spirits. The loss of Mark was a crushing blow, a stark reminder of the precariousness of their situation. His laughter, his quick wit, his unwavering support – these were the things that would be missed the most. The silence that followed the storm was deafening, a constant reminder of their unbearable loss. They felt the full impact of their victory, the terrible price they'd paid. It wasn't just physical wounds, or exhaustion, but the deep ache of loss, a hole ripped into their small, tightly knit group, a wound that would never truly heal.

Yet, they pressed on. The memory of Mark's sacrifice fueled their determination. They were not just fighting for their own survival; they were fighting for his memory, for the hope of a future where his death wouldn't be in vain. They moved with a grim determination, their steps heavier, their hearts burdened by grief, but their resolve unshaken. Grayson, his face etched with a profound sadness, led the way, his silence a testament to his grief, yet a solid anchor for his team's wavering hope. Demitra's eyes, usually bright and full of life, were clouded with a weariness that spoke of untold horrors and the immense weight of loss she had to carry. Kiel, his spirit shaken, yet his resolve hardened by the grim reality of their situation, held onto the faint hope of escaping this nightmare. Sarah, ever the healer, was forced to accept the wounds that she could not fix. The absence of Mark weighed on their spirits, but the desire to make it out alive, to honor his memory, pushed them forward.

The final leg of their journey was a blur of exhaustion and desperation. They pushed through the dense undergrowth, their bodies aching, their spirits depleted, yet somehow, fueled by the haunting memory of their fallen friend and their unwavering determination to survive. The rainforest, once a menacing obstacle, finally began to give way. As the trees thinned, a glimmer of hope pierced through the oppressive green. Civilization was near. They stumbled into a small village, their bodies battered, their spirits broken, yet somehow, alive. They had survived. They had endured. They had faced the horrors of Blackwood Cave and emerged, bruised but victorious, forever bound by their shared trauma, their unwavering courage, and the profound loss that would forever shape their lives. Their victory was a testament to their resilience, a chilling reminder of the cost of survival, and a profound acknowledgement of the human spirit's ability to endure even the darkest of trials. The scars, both physical and emotional, would remain, a constant reminder of the nightmare they had barely escaped, but they had lived to tell the tale, their story a testament to their incredible courage and the indomitable spirit of humanity.

The villagers, initially wary of the disheveled, traumatized group stumbling into their midst, were eventually won over by Sarah's calm demeanor and Grayson's authoritative yet compassionate bearing. They were given food, water, and a place to rest, a haven from the relentless pursuit that had shadowed their every step. The villagers' kindness offered a temporary reprieve, a fleeting moment of peace in the wake of the horrors they had endured. But the sanctuary was fragile, a temporary respite before the storm. The relief was palpable, a wave washing over them, momentarily erasing the relentless pressure of their escape. They slept, exhausted, the dreams haunted by flickering images of the creatures, the echoing collapse of the facility, the chilling intelligence in those burning eyes.

The following days were spent recovering, both physically and emotionally. The villagers, despite their limited resources, tended to their wounds with surprising skill and unwavering compassion. They listened, their faces etched with concern and understanding, as the teenagers recounted their ordeal. Their tale, though unbelievable, was corroborated by the strange artifacts Demitra carried, the inert but undeniably alien technology whispering silent tales of a horrifying experiment. The villagers knew of Blackwood Cave, of course, the stories whispered through generations, a tapestry woven from fear and superstition. But their understanding of the truth was rudimentary, the horrifying reality far beyond their comprehension. The escape, miraculous as it seemed, was a Pyrrhic victory; their physical wounds were slowly healing, but the deeper scars remained.

Kiel, despite the tangible relief of escape, remained haunted by his actions. The weight of the life he'd taken, the chilling knowledge of the creature's existence, and the terrifying implications of Project Chimera pressed down on him. His guilt was a constant companion, a shadow that stalked his every waking moment, casting long, dark tendrils into every facet of his life. He found it hard to sleep, plagued by nightmares, visions of blood and twisted metal, the grotesque forms of the engineered creatures a recurring horror. He was saved from complete despair only by the companionship and support of his remaining friends, a fragile anchor in a sea of overwhelming emotions.

Demitra, her psychic abilities depleted, found herself adrift. The glimpse into the horrifying scope of Project Chimera had been a terrifying revelation, a chilling premonition of a dystopian future she desperately hoped to avert. The ancient artifacts, now silent and inert, felt heavy in her hands, symbols of a power she had only begun to understand. The weight of the knowledge she carried was immense, a burden that she bore stoically but with visible internal struggle. The constant fear of the creatures, their unnatural intelligence, was further complicated by her inability to utilize her powers fully, which only amplified the sense of danger. Her calm exterior was deceptive, masking a seething inner turmoil of fear, grief, and the daunting weight of responsibility.

Sarah, ever practical and capable, channeled her energy into tending to her friends.

Her expertise was invaluable, but she was still grappling with the profound loss of Mark. The memory of his laughter, his quick wit, the comforting presence of his camaraderie were a constant, sharp ache. She poured her energy into healing the physical wounds, but the emotional scars were deeper, more insidious, and far more difficult to mend. The quiet strength she displayed belied a profound sadness, a hidden well of grief that she dared not fully explore.

Grayson, the stoic leader, wore his burden with the same quiet dignity he had maintained throughout the ordeal. He had led them through the perilous escape from the facility, navigating the treacherous rainforest, and finally, to safety. His leadership had been absolute, his resolve unwavering, but even his iron will began to fray under the weight of the shared trauma and the nagging feeling of incompleteness. Their escape was only a small part of the larger conflict, a battle won within a much larger war.

The relative safety of the village provided a deceptive sense of security. The villagers, though kind and helpful, were not equipped to combat the threat that lurked in the shadows of Blackwood Cave and the broader world. The escaped teenagers knew that their fight for survival was far from over, that the seemingly insurmountable victory felt hollow. They'd defeated the immediate enemy, but the war was far from over.

One night, while staring at the distant stars, Demitra experienced a sudden, jarring psychic surge. She saw flashes of horrifying images: a vast, hidden facility, more technologically advanced than the one they'd escaped; grotesque, larger creatures, far more intelligent and organized than the ones they had encountered; and a sinister plan unfolding on a global scale. Project Chimera was not contained; it was a hydra, its heads multiplying, its tentacles extending across the globe.

The vision left Demitra shaken, drained of energy, but armed with a terrifying truth. Their escape from Blackwood Cave was not an end, but merely a beginning. The war for humanity's survival was just beginning. Their encounter in the cave had merely revealed a tiny corner of a larger, far more sinister conspiracy.

The next morning, they confronted the villagers, relaying Demitra's vision, their words heavy with a profound sense of dread. The villagers, initially skeptical, were eventually convinced by the evidence, the harrowing accounts, and the palpable fear radiating from the teenagers. They understood now the true nature of the threat they faced. The seemingly idyllic village felt suddenly vulnerable, exposed.

Their Pyrrhic victory had bought them time, but not security. The relief and respite were overshadowed by the chilling revelation of the greater threat. The escape from the cave was but a single, hard-won battle in a protracted war for survival, a conflict against an unseen enemy whose reach extended beyond the claustrophobic tunnels and the treacherous rainforest. They had survived the horrors of Blackwood Cave, but the true horror was only just beginning to unfold, its chilling tendrils reaching into the darkest corners of the world. The weight of their experience, the grim realization of the larger war, settled heavily on their shoulders. Their victory tasted like ash in their mouths; a bitter reminder that their fight had only just begun. The escape was not an end but a transition, a precarious pause before the next, potentially even more devastating battle. The shadows loomed, stretching long and dark, their escape from the immediate danger offering only a deceptive semblance of safety in the face of a far larger and more ominous threat. Their story, however, was far from over.

The air hung heavy with the scent of woodsmoke and damp earth. The village, nestled deep within a valley cradled by ancient, whispering trees, offered a deceptive sense of serenity. But the peace was fragile, a thin veneer over the raw, gaping wounds of their recent ordeal. They sat in a circle around a crackling fire, its flames casting dancing shadows on their faces, highlighting the exhaustion etched into their features. The silence was broken only by the occasional crackle of the fire and the soft chirping of crickets, a stark contrast to the cacophony of screams and explosions that had haunted their recent past.

Kiel stared into the fire, his gaze unfocused, lost in the swirling embers. The image of Mark, his face contorted in a silent scream, flashed through his mind. He'd tried to save him, but the genetically-engineered creature had been too quick, too strong. The memory played on a loop, a relentless torment. He clutched a worn, leather-bound journal, its pages filled with his sketches of the creatures they'd encountered – their grotesque forms, their unsettling intelligence, their unnerving speed and agility. Each stroke of his pen had been an attempt to exorcise the demons that clawed at his soul, a desperate bid to make sense of the senseless. But the journal offered no solace, only a stark reminder of the horrors they'd faced.

Demitra sat beside him, her fingers tracing the cold metal of one of the inert artifacts. The psychic surge she'd experienced the previous night still echoed in her mind, a chilling premonition of a future that threatened to engulf humanity. The vision of the larger facility, the more advanced creatures, the sinister global plan – it all felt so real, so terrifyingly imminent. The weight of this knowledge pressed upon her, a crushing burden she felt ill-equipped to bear. She looked at her friends, their faces pale and drawn, mirroring the turmoil within her own heart. They had escaped the immediate threat but now faced an enemy far more vast and terrifying than they could have ever imagined. The fight for survival had not ended; it had just begun. The victory tasted like ash in her mouth.

Sarah, ever practical, focused on the physical aspects of their recovery. She cleaned and dressed a deep gash on Kiel's arm, her movements precise and efficient, a stark contrast to the turmoil raging within her. The loss of Mark, her closest friend, was a wound that refused to heal. The silence that surrounded them was far worse than any scream she had endured in the caves; it was a silence pregnant with loss, with unspoken grief, and a fear of the unknown. The silence was a testament to the horror they had witnessed, and the uncertain future ahead of them. She longed to share her pain, to break the somber silence, but the enormity of what they'd experienced left her speechless, words failing to capture the depth of her despair.

Grayson, the silent leader, watched his friends, his expression inscrutable. He knew the escape had been a Pyrrhic victory, a temporary reprieve in a war that was far from over. The weight of responsibility pressed heavily on him; he had led them into the cave, and he would lead them out of this new threat. His stoicism, usually a source of strength, felt now like a heavy cloak, suffocating him with its weight. The nightmares were relentless, the images of twisted metal and dying men seared into his memory. He had witnessed horrors beyond comprehension, and the knowledge that they were just the beginning kept him awake night after night.

The fire crackled, casting flickering shadows that danced and writhed like the creatures they had fought. The warmth offered only a momentary respite, a small comfort against the chilling reality of their situation. The night stretched on, each moment heavy with the weight of their shared trauma and the unspoken dread of what lay ahead. The silence was punctuated only by their ragged breaths, a testament to their shared exhaustion and a silent acknowledgment of the horrifying truth they were forced to confront: their escape from Blackwood Cave was not an ending, but a harrowing transition into a more dangerous and uncertain future.

Demitra, unable to shake the vivid imagery of her vision, spoke, her voice barely a whisper. "The facility... it's far larger than the one we escaped. They're already ahead of us. Far more advanced."

Kiel nodded slowly, his gaze fixed on the distant stars, their twinkling seeming mockingly distant, indifferent to their plight. "The creatures... they were different. More organized, more intelligent. They worked together, strategically."

Sarah, her voice trembling, added, "And their numbers... Mark... I don't want to think about how many more there are."

Grayson rose, his shadow stretching long and distorted by the firelight. "We can't stay here. This village... it's not safe. We need to find a way to stop them, to expose them." His voice, usually calm and assured, held a raw edge, a desperate plea for a sense of purpose amidst the despair. The determination in his voice was a beacon in the dark night, a testament to his unwavering resolve, and a much-needed reassurance.

The others nodded, a silent agreement passing between them. The sense of camaraderie, once threatened by the horrors they endured, remained; it was a testament to their shared bond and the unwavering resolve to fight together. Their escape from Blackwood Cave had cemented a bond that was more powerful than any fear they might ever face, a bond as strong and resilient as the human spirit itself.

Their moment of reflection ended. The flames flickered in the darkness, casting shadows that danced and writhed, echoing the chaos of their reality. They still bore deep wounds both physical and emotional. Yet, the stark, cold reality of their escape from the cave's maw had led to a chilling conclusion. Their ordeal in the cave was nothing compared to the larger war that was about to commence, a conflict for survival that involved humanity's very future. They had survived the terrors of Blackwood Cave, only to face a horror of a far grander scale, a scale that threatened not only their survival but the survival of humankind.

The deceptive quiet of the night could not mask the lurking menace, the subtle sense of danger. The victory they experienced felt bittersweet, a haunting victory. It gave way to a sobering, chilling realization that the war was far from over; it had only begun. The shadows grew longer, their escape from the immediate horror only lending a deceptive semblance of safety in the face of a greater, more ominous danger. Their story, however, was far from over. The village, once a haven, now felt like a temporary resting place, a fleeting pause before the next battle commenced, a battle far more terrifying than their previous ordeal in the depths of Blackwood Cave. The weight of their past, the threat of the future, rested heavily upon their shoulders as they stared into the dark, uncertain future that lay ahead. The chilling silence of the night was a testament to their newfound awareness of a far greater, far more sinister conflict that awaited them.

Chapter 13: Scars Remain

The days that followed were a blur of antiseptic smells, hushed conversations, and the persistent ache of phantom limbs. Kiel's arm, though bandaged, throbbed with a dull, insistent pain that mirrored the deeper wounds within. He found himself constantly flinching, his body reacting to imagined threats, the echo of claws and snarling teeth still sharp in his memory. Sleep offered no respite, only a descent into a nightmarish landscape populated by the grotesque creatures from Blackwood Cave, their forms shifting and morphing, their cold eyes following his every move. He'd wake in a cold sweat, heart pounding, the scent of blood and decay thick in the air, a ghostly residue of his ordeal. The journal, once a tool for catharsis, now lay abandoned on his bedside table, a stark reminder of the horrors it contained.

Demitra, outwardly composed, carried the weight of her premonition like a heavy cloak. The vision of the larger facility, the more advanced creatures, and the sinister global conspiracy haunted her waking hours. She found herself isolating herself, sketching the visions in frantic strokes, her hand trembling as she tried to capture the chilling details of the sprawling complex, the terrifying designs of the creatures, and the unsettling faces of the scientists who orchestrated the nightmare. The fear was not simply for herself; it was a deep, gnawing terror for humanity. Her own near-death experience had given her a unique insight into the depth of evil, the scale of destruction, and she knew that what had been witnessed in Blackwood Cave was just the tip of a dreadful iceberg. She spent hours staring out the window, searching the distant horizon for any signs of the impending threat.

Sarah, despite her practicality, found herself grappling with the profound loss of Mark. His laughter, his easy charm, his unwavering loyalty – all were vivid memories that both comforted and tormented her. She cared for her own wounds, a physical manifestation of her desperate attempt to regain control in a world turned upside down. The silence that clung to her was thick with grief; the joyous camaraderie they had shared was now replaced by a hollow ache, a deep emptiness that no amount of practical work could repair. She was haunted by the image of his body being dragged into the darkness, his screams an echo in her soul. She started volunteering at the local hospital, immersing herself in the physical act of caring for others, a small way to channel her grief, to combat her despair. However, even the simplest of tasks felt monumental in the wake of their ordeal.

Grayson, ever stoic, bore the burden of leadership with a quiet intensity. He knew that their escape was only the beginning, that the true fight was yet to come. He tirelessly searched for information, poring over old maps, local legends, anything that might offer a clue to the origins of the creatures, the purpose of the facility, and any chance of a viable counter-strategy. His sleep was broken by recurring nightmares, vivid replays of the brutal encounters, the deafening sounds of explosions, and the horrifying sight of mangled bodies. He found solace only in planning, strategizing, preparing for the inevitable clash to come. He kept his emotions tightly reined, the weight of responsibility pressing heavily on him. His usually calm demeanor showed small cracks, revealing the deep scars etched in his soul by their harrowing experience.

The villagers, initially shocked and hesitant, gradually rallied around the survivors. The initial fear and distrust were tempered by a shared sense of community and a growing understanding of the magnitude of the threat. They shared stories of other disappearances, other strange occurrences in the surrounding woods, hints of an underlying conspiracy, but the evidence was usually dismissed as folklore or superstition. The villagers' hesitant trust was a small beacon of hope, a testament to human resilience. Their compassion was both a comfort and a challenge, for it reminded them of their duty, to make amends for the horror they had witnessed and to protect those who lived in fear of what remained hidden in the dark.

The quiet life in the village was far from peaceful. The scars, both physical and emotional, were a constant reminder of their ordeal. Kiel's nightmares intensified, often waking him up in a cold sweat, filled with horrific images of the cave's horrors. He found solace in sketching, but his art became a grotesque reflection of his own internal turmoil, capturing the monstrous forms he'd encountered in a visceral, almost disturbingly realistic fashion. His hands trembled as he sketched the creatures, their cold eyes watching him even in the quiet space of his small room.

Demitra's visions grew more frequent and disturbing. The facility, in her mind's eye, became a nightmarish labyrinth, teeming with genetically-modified creatures and ruthless scientists. The vividness of her visions increased, causing her severe headaches, insomnia, and a perpetual state of anxiety. The premonitions were too realistic, too accurate; she knew deep down that they were only a matter of time before the horrific truth was laid bare. She started to suffer from panic attacks, overwhelmed by the sheer scale of what awaited them. The future they once dreamt of now seemed nothing but a chilling reminder of what was likely to be lost.

Sarah's grief was a heavy burden. The loss of Mark had created a gaping hole in her life, in their group's close-knit circle. The silence of the village's sanctuary was an amplified reminder of his absence. The act of simply living felt overwhelming, each day a painful reminder of what they'd lost. She'd found comfort in the act of helping others in the local clinic, but the faces of the patients were a constant reminder of Mark's face, forever etched into her memory. Her smiles were faint, her eyes clouded with a persistent melancholy.

Grayson's stoicism was crumbling under the weight of his responsibilities. The nightmares were relentless, the images of bloodshed, twisted metal, and dying men were vividly present. The escape from Blackwood Cave had only revealed the magnitude of the task ahead; they had escaped a dark chapter only to stare into a terrifying abyss. He found little rest; he worked day and night, analyzing data, searching for any information that might explain the origins of the creatures and the sinister conspiracy that bound them together. He was aware of the mounting pressure, knowing that his own sanity was at stake. The constant threat hanging above them was a silent testament to the horrors they had endured.

The villagers, initially compassionate, started to grow uneasy. The constant alertness, the haunted eyes of the survivors, and the ever-present sense of unease created a pervasive atmosphere of fear and anxiety. The silence in the village became heavy with unspoken fears. The tranquility of the countryside was replaced by a constant state of apprehension. The trust they had initially established was waning, replaced by a sense of foreboding and an uncomfortable awareness of what they had brought back with them from Blackwood Cave.

The scars, both visible and invisible, remained. The physical wounds healed, but the emotional wounds festered, bleeding into their waking moments and tormenting their sleep. They carried the weight of their experience, a heavy burden shared but not diminished by their shared ordeal. The quiet nights were punctuated by the silent screams of the past, their echoes a constant reminder of the horror they had endured. Their escape from Blackwood Cave was not a victory, but a temporary reprieve, a fragile moment of peace before the next, even more terrifying battle began. The village, once a sanctuary, was now merely a waiting room, a temporary shelter before the inevitable confrontation with the enemy that lurked in the shadows, ready to strike again. Their story was far from over; the true horror had only just begun.

The weight of responsibility settled upon them like a shroud, heavy and suffocating. The escape from Blackwood Cave had been a brutal, harrowing ordeal, but it was only the first act in a much larger, more terrifying drama. They had glimpsed the abyss, and the abyss had glimpsed back, leaving an indelible mark on their souls. The physical scars – Kiel's mangled arm, Demitra's lacerations, Sarah's deep gashes – were fading, but the emotional wounds, far deeper and more insidious, refused to heal.

Kiel, despite the bandages and the healing process, found his body betraying him. Simple tasks, like holding a pen or lifting a cup, sent jolts of pain through his arm, a constant reminder of the horrors he'd endured. The nightmares continued, relentless and vivid. He'd wake screaming, his body drenched in sweat, the metallic tang of blood heavy in his nostrils, even though he knew it wasn't real. The creatures from the cave haunted his waking hours as well, their grotesque forms flickering at the edge of his vision, their eyes burning into his very soul. His art, once a source of solace, had become a monstrous reflection of his inner turmoil. His sketches, once filled with light and color, were now dominated by grotesque creatures, their forms contorted and menacing, their eyes filled with cold, unfeeling malice. He couldn't shake the feeling that they were watching him, even in the stillness of his room, their presence a chilling reminder of the danger that still lurked.

Demitra's premonitions intensified, becoming more vivid, more detailed, and terrifyingly accurate. The images of the sprawling facility, the advanced creatures, and the sinister scientists were etched into her mind, as real as any memory. The headaches grew more frequent and debilitating, the insomnia relentless, leaving her exhausted and on edge. She'd find herself staring at the ceiling for hours, the images flashing behind her eyelids, a terrifying slideshow of the impending doom. The weight of her knowledge was almost unbearable, the awareness that she carried the burden of a future she couldn't change. She tried to confide in Sarah and Kiel, but the sheer terror in her eyes, the tremor in her voice, only served to amplify their own anxieties. She felt utterly alone, adrift in a sea of fear, burdened by a premonition that threatened to consume them all.

Sarah's grief for Mark was a constant ache, a hollow space in her heart that nothing could fill. She'd found a small measure of comfort in volunteering at the local clinic, tending to the physical needs of others, but even that offered little solace. The faces of the patients, the fragile human forms, were a painful reminder of Mark's own, lost forever in the darkness of Blackwood Cave. She found herself staring at his empty chair, his unused sketchbook, every object a poignant echo of his absence. The silence of their shared apartment was a torment, each tick of the clock a fresh stab of grief. Sleep offered no escape; instead, she was plagued by vivid dreams of their final moments together, the horrifying sounds of his screams echoing in her ears, the terrifying image of him being dragged away into the shadows forever imprinted on her soul. She found herself questioning her own sanity, struggling to comprehend how life could feel so empty, so devoid of joy.

Grayson, the stoic leader, felt the weight of their survival pressing down on him with a crushing force. The responsibility for their lives, for the lives of the villagers who now looked to them for protection, was a heavy burden to bear. He'd spent countless hours poring over maps, local legends, any scrap of information that might offer a clue to the origin of the creatures, the purpose of the facility, and a way to stop the impending threat. Sleep was a luxury he couldn't afford; the nightmares relentlessly replayed the horrors of the cave – the screams, the explosions, the agonizing deaths of their friends. He knew they had escaped Blackwood Cave, but he also knew that it was just the beginning. The true battle was yet to come, and he was determined to be ready. But the constant pressure, the unrelenting weight of responsibility, chipped away at his resolve, leaving him feeling exhausted, broken, and questioning his own ability to protect those under his care. His stoicism was starting to crack under the strain.

The villagers, initially sympathetic, were beginning to grow uneasy. The survivors' haunted eyes, their constant vigilance, the palpable tension that hung in the air—it all created a suffocating atmosphere of fear. Their initial trust was slowly eroding, replaced by suspicion and fear. Whispers began to circulate—whispers about the strange occurrences in the surrounding woods, about disappearances that had been dismissed as folklore or coincidence. The villagers were starting to realize that the horrors of Blackwood Cave had not stayed in the cave; they had come home with them. The quiet sanctuary of their village was transforming into a place of fear and unease, a community teetering on the brink of panic. The weight of their shared experience, once a bond, was becoming a burden, a source of conflict and suspicion instead of unity.

The weight of responsibility was not just theirs to carry; it was shared, silently acknowledged, a heavy cloak draped over the entire community. The escape from Blackwood Cave had been a terrifying ordeal, a brutal lesson in survival. But it was a lesson that had not brought them peace; instead, it had left them facing an even greater darkness, a looming threat that promised to test their resilience, their courage, and their very humanity. Their fight for survival was far from over; the true battle had just begun. The fragile peace of the village was a deceptive calm before the storm, a temporary respite before the next wave of terror threatened to consume them all. The shadows lengthened, the darkness deepened, and the weight of responsibility grew heavier with each passing day, a constant reminder of the horrors they had endured and the even greater horrors that awaited. The scars remained, visible and invisible, a testament to their ordeal, a chilling preview of what was yet to come.

The late afternoon sun cast long shadows across the valley, painting the rolling hills in hues of gold and amber. A gentle breeze rustled through the leaves of the ancient oak trees, their branches swaying rhythmically, as if in a silent lullaby. It was a stark contrast to the suffocating darkness of Blackwood Cave, a stark contrast to the horrors they had endured. For a brief moment, a fragile peace settled over the survivors. They sat together on the porch of Grayson's small cottage, the scent of woodsmoke mingling with the sweet fragrance of wildflowers. Kiel, his arm still bandaged, leaned against a weathered wooden post, his gaze fixed on the distant mountains, a faint smile playing on his lips.

Demitra, her usual apprehension replaced by a quiet calm, traced patterns in the dust on her worn jeans. The intense headaches that had plagued her seemed to have subsided, at least for now, allowing her a small respite from the relentless visions of the future. The weight of her premonitions still pressed upon her, heavy and suffocating, but the sheer beauty of the sunset offered a fleeting moment of solace, a momentary distraction from the impending doom. She found a strange comfort in the simple act of breathing, in the feeling of the sun on her face, a reminder that life, despite its horrors, could still offer moments of beauty and grace.

Sarah, her grief still palpable, sat beside Demitra, her hand resting gently on her friend's arm. She found a strange comfort in their shared silence, a tacit understanding that words were unnecessary, that their bond transcended the need for articulation. The memory of Mark, the pain of his loss, remained a constant ache in her heart, but the gentle warmth of the sun, the rustling leaves, the quiet hum of the valley, all served to soften the sharp edges of her grief. She allowed herself to remember Mark's laughter, his infectious enthusiasm, his kind eyes, not dwelling on the brutal end, but cherishing the precious moments they had shared. In the stillness of the evening, she found a small measure of peace, a momentary respite from the crushing weight of her sorrow.

Grayson, watching over his friends, felt a surge of relief, a flicker of hope. He had never believed in miracles, but the setting sun, the tranquility of the valley, and the quiet contentment of his friends offered a sense of fragile peace, a momentary reprieve from the storm that was surely to come. The burden of leadership, the weight of responsibility, remained heavy on his shoulders, but for now, he allowed himself to savor this rare moment of calm, to appreciate the small victories, the fleeting moments of peace that punctuated the overwhelming terror of their ordeal. He knew that their struggle was far from over, but in the quiet stillness of the evening, he found a renewed sense of purpose, a strengthening of his resolve.

They spoke little, their silence filled with unspoken emotions, with shared memories, with a deep understanding that transcended words. Kiel sketched in his notebook, capturing the beauty of the landscape, the vibrant colors of the sunset, a stark contrast to the grotesque creatures that had haunted his nightmares. His strokes were tentative at first, hesitant, but as the sun dipped lower, his hand grew steadier, his lines more confident, the images flowing freely from his tormented mind, a testament to his resilience. His art, once a reflection of his inner turmoil, was slowly transforming into a means of healing, a way of reclaiming his own peace.

Demitra closed her eyes, allowing herself to relax, to breathe deeply, to savor the feeling of the sun on her face. The images of the facility, the scientists, the monstrous creatures, still flickered at the edges of her consciousness, but for now, they were muted, subdued, overwhelmed by the beauty of the natural world. She found herself whispering a silent prayer, a thank you for the life that had been spared, for the moment of peace, for the strength that had carried her through the darkest of times. She knew the future held dangers, but she also knew that she had the strength, the resilience, to face whatever lay ahead.

Sarah, watching the sun sink below the horizon, recalled the carefree laughter they had shared before Blackwood Cave, before their adventure had turned into a nightmare. She remembered Mark's jokes, his warmth, his infectious enthusiasm. She focused on those memories, clinging to them, letting them infuse her with a sense of comfort, reminding her that even in the face of tragedy, there was still good to be found, still love to be cherished. The memories, painful as they were, brought her a sliver of solace, a reminder that life, even in its most painful moments, was still beautiful, still worth living. The tears that fell were not only of sorrow, but also of healing, a release of emotion long pent up.

As darkness enveloped the valley, casting long, ethereal shadows, they lit a small fire, the flames dancing merrily, mirroring the warmth that began to bloom in their hearts.

They shared stories, not of the horrors of the cave, but of simpler times, of shared laughter, of dreams and hopes. The stories were punctuated by comfortable silences, by shared glances, by knowing smiles that transcended the pain they had endured. In the flickering firelight, their faces were illuminated, revealing the lingering scars, the emotional wounds that refused to disappear entirely. But there was also resilience in their eyes, a fierce determination that spoke volumes of their shared experience, a testament to their survival.

They spoke of Mark, remembering his bravery, his unwavering loyalty. They recalled his kindness, his humor, his infectious enthusiasm. They did not dwell on his horrifying death, choosing instead to celebrate his life, to honor his memory. They shared stories, anecdotes, inside jokes, weaving a tapestry of remembrance that provided a powerful antidote to the despair that had threatened to consume them. His laughter echoed in their memories, a poignant reminder that even in the face of death, the beauty of life perseveres.

They spoke about their hopes and dreams, sharing their plans for the future, finding solace in the simple act of making plans. They spoke of normalcy, of simple desires, of life beyond the shadow of Blackwood Cave, building a bridge from the darkness of their past towards the hope of their future. The shared vision, the silent promises, served as a lifeline, a connection that held them together, a reminder that they were not alone. This was their hope, their fragile peace.

As the fire burned low, and the stars began to appear, a sense of shared resilience settled over them. They had faced the unimaginable, they had lost so much. But they were still here, together. They had survived. And in the quiet stillness of the night, under the watchful gaze of the stars, they found a measure of peace, a fragile hope for the future, a shared understanding that their journey was far from over, but that they would face it together. The scars remained, etched onto their bodies and souls, but they were also a testament to their strength, to their resilience, to their survival. Their journey had just begun.

The embers of the fire cast dancing shadows on their faces, illuminating the weariness etched into their features. Yet, there was a newfound strength in their eyes, a resilience born from the crucible of their shared trauma. The silence that followed wasn't heavy with the weight of unspoken horrors, but rather a comfortable quietude, a shared understanding that needed no words. They had been through hell and back, but they were still here, together. That was enough, for now.

Kiel, ever the artist, began sketching again, this time not the serene landscape, but the harrowing scenes from their ordeal within Blackwood Cave. He captured the grotesque forms of the creatures, their unnatural movements, their predatory eyes – not with a sense of fear, but with a growing detachment, as if observing a nightmare he had finally escaped. He sketched the intricate details of the cave's labyrinthine passageways, the dripping water, the chilling darkness, transforming the horrific imagery into a testament to their survival, a visual journal of their shared struggle.

Demitra, observing Kiel's work, felt a stirring within her. The headaches were less frequent now, less intense, but the prophetic visions still flickered at the edge of her consciousness, offering cryptic glimpses of a future both perilous and uncertain. She found solace not in ignoring these visions, but in acknowledging them, in recognizing their power without allowing them to dictate her actions. She shared some of the less frightening snippets with her friends, their reactions a mixture of disbelief and growing unease, but also a tangible increase in their bond. Their shared fear, once isolating, now served to unite them. The ability to speak the unspeakable, to verbalize their shared terrors, proved oddly cathartic.

Sarah, her grief still present, but softened by the shared solace of the fire and the quiet companionship of her friends, found a different kind of healing. She spoke about Mark, not dwelling on the gruesome details of his death, but focusing instead on the vibrant memories of their shared laughter, their inside jokes, their dreams. She shared stories that painted a picture of Mark as a whole person, not merely the victim of a tragedy. She found a strange comfort in sharing these memories, in knowing that his essence, his spirit, lived on through the love and laughter they shared, held tight in the bonds of their friendship.

Grayson, watching over his friends, felt the weight of responsibility lift, just slightly. He had been their leader, the one who made the often-difficult calls, but now he saw a new kind of strength emerge within each of them, a kind of independence and resilience that reassured him. He had been worried about their mental states, their potential for fracturing under the weight of their shared trauma. But he observed, with growing hope, that the shared experience had forged a powerful bond, an unbreakable chain that connected them.

The conversation flowed naturally, shifting from harrowing reminisces to light-hearted anecdotes, from tearful recollections to fits of shared laughter. They spoke of their families, their hopes and dreams, their anxieties about the future. They shared mundane details of their lives before Blackwood Cave, finding comfort in the normalcy of these shared pasts, reinforcing the shared humanity they still possessed despite the horrific events they had survived. The mundane became extraordinary in their context, a reminder of the lives they had almost lost and the beauty of a world they still wished to inhabit.

They talked about school, about college applications, about their crushes and hobbies, revealing aspects of their personalities that had been momentarily eclipsed by the intense survival instinct of the cave. These conversations brought a sense of normalcy back into their lives, allowing them to piece together the shattered remnants of their previous selves and rebuild a life moving forward. They laughed at silly memories, shared embarrassing stories from their childhoods, strengthening their bond through the intimacy of vulnerability.

As the night deepened, and the stars began to appear, they fell into a comfortable silence, punctuated by the crackling of the fire and the gentle sounds of the night. They sat huddled together, shoulder to shoulder, a silent testament to the strength of their newly forged bond. They knew the scars remained – physical and emotional – but they also knew that they were not alone in bearing them. They had each other. And in that shared vulnerability, they found a strength that transcended the individual.

The experience in Blackwood Cave had stripped away their innocence, their naiveté, replacing it with a stark awareness of life's fragility and the ever-present threat of the unknown. But it had also brought them together in a way that nothing else could have. They were no longer just a group of teenagers who dared to explore a dangerous cave; they were a tribe, bound together by the blood, sweat, tears, and shared near-death experiences.

They discussed the implications of what they had found in Blackwood Cave. They knew that the genetically engineered creatures were not simply a localized anomaly; they represented a larger, more sinister threat. The whispered conversations touched on the possibility of a vast conspiracy, of a government-sanctioned horror far greater than they could have ever imagined. This knowledge hung over them, a heavy weight, but it served only to further strengthen their resolve. The fear of the unknown was replaced by the determination to uncover the truth, to bring those responsible to justice, to prevent similar atrocities from happening again.

Kiel continued sketching, his hand moving with newfound confidence, the strokes stronger, surer. He wasn't just documenting their ordeal; he was reclaiming his narrative, rewriting his story, shifting the focus from victimhood to survival, from fear to empowerment. His art became a therapeutic process, a means of expressing the horrors he had witnessed, processing the trauma, and ultimately, transforming it into something beautiful, something powerful.

Demitra's visions became less cryptic, more focused, providing a sense of direction, of purpose. She learned to interpret the symbols and images, discerning warnings and clues, even glimpses of potential allies or adversaries. She shared her insights with her friends, carefully, cautiously, knowing the implications of what she was revealing. Their reaction was one of cautious acceptance, tempered by a growing realization that they were at the forefront of something far larger than themselves. Their survival had made them witnesses to something vast and terrifying, and they realized they had a role to play.

Sarah, finally able to acknowledge Mark's death without being consumed by grief, found a strength in his memory, transforming her sorrow into a burning desire for justice. She would not let his sacrifice be in vain. She would help bring those responsible for the atrocities in Blackwood Cave to account. Her sorrow became fuel, her grief a driving force propelling her forward, not into despair, but towards empowerment and action.

Grayson recognized the changes in his friends, the resilience that shone in their eyes, the newfound determination to fight back. He realized that their ordeal in Blackwood Cave hadn't broken them; it had forged them, tempered them, revealing a strength and unity they never knew they possessed. He was no longer simply their leader; he was their protector, their strategist, their unwavering ally in the fight ahead.

As the first rays of dawn painted the eastern sky, they stood together, silhouetted against the emerging light. The scars remained, a permanent testament to the horrors they had endured. But they were not scars of defeat. They were scars of survival. And as they looked towards the rising sun, they knew that their journey was far from over. It was just beginning. They had forged new bonds, bonds stronger than steel, bonds forged in the fires of hell, bonds that would see them through whatever lay ahead. They were ready.

The weeks that followed were a blur of therapy sessions, doctor's appointments, and the slow, painstaking process of healing. Physical wounds, thankfully, were mostly superficial – a few broken bones, lacerations that left scars, but nothing life-threatening. The psychological wounds, however, ran deeper, far deeper than any scalpel could reach. Each of them wrestled with their own demons, the memories of the gruesome campsite, the relentless chase, Mark's death, all swirling in a chaotic vortex of trauma. Yet, there was a strange sort of comfort in their shared experience, a silent understanding that transcended words. They were a unit, forged in the crucible of terror, bound by a trauma so profound it had welded them together.

Kiel's art became his sanctuary, a means of externalizing the horrors he'd witnessed. He filled sketchbooks with grotesque renderings of the creatures, their unsettling anatomy captured in detail. He moved beyond mere depiction, though, imbuing his drawings with a raw, visceral energy that conveyed not just the monstrousness of the creatures but the adrenaline-fueled terror of their escape. His art wasn't just cathartic; it was a testament to their survival, a visual record of their shared ordeal that helped to transform the experience from a nightmare into a narrative, a story they could control. He began to receive commissions, strangely, from collectors of macabre art, their fascination piqued by the unsettling realism and power of his work. The money helped, offering a practical outlet for his talent and easing the financial strain on his family.

Demitra's prophetic visions, once sporadic and terrifying, became more regular and, strangely, more manageable. They were no longer random flashes of horror but seemed to coalesce into a pattern, a narrative unfolding before her eyes. She started keeping a journal, documenting each vision, sketching the symbolic imagery, seeking patterns, connections. She discovered that her visions weren't merely glimpses of the future, but warnings, subtle clues hinting at the bigger picture – the existence of a larger conspiracy, a network extending far beyond Blackwood Cave. She learned to interpret the symbols, to decipher the language of her visions, a skill honed by necessity, fueled by the urgency to prevent future tragedies. Her new-found clarity eased her anxiety. She had a purpose, a responsibility.

Sarah's grief, while still a palpable presence in her life, gradually transformed into a steely resolve. The memory of Mark remained a wound, but a wound that was slowly knitting itself closed, leaving a strong, enduring scar. She channeled her grief into action, becoming a vocal advocate for stricter regulations concerning genetic engineering research. She started a campaign, utilizing her social media presence and newfound notoriety to raise awareness, to push for accountability. Her campaign became a beacon of hope, fueled by her loss but focused on preventing similar losses in the future. The support she received from her community, both online and offline, was surprisingly substantial, strengthening her resolve even further.

Grayson, their designated leader, quietly shed his role as the sole decision-maker. He recognized the growth and resilience within his friends, their ability to cope, their determination to understand the events at Blackwood Cave and prevent similar horrors. He transitioned from a leader into a facilitator, a support system, guiding them toward resources and helping them navigate the complex landscape of post-traumatic recovery. He focused on creating a safe space for their discussions, helping them deal with their trauma in a supportive and therapeutic way. His quiet strength provided a reassuring presence, a constant reminder of the bonds that held them together.

Their new "normal" was a delicate balance, a precarious dance between confronting their trauma and rebuilding their lives. They returned to school, albeit tentatively, their experiences casting long shadows over their academic pursuits. They still suffered from nightmares, flashbacks, bouts of intense anxiety. But they had each other. They studied together, sharing stories, offering support, leaning on each other for strength. The bond forged in Blackwood Cave remained their anchor, a solid foundation in the turbulent sea of their recovery.

The fear hadn't vanished entirely. It lingered, a low hum beneath the surface of their daily lives. They were hyper-vigilant, constantly scanning their surroundings, their senses heightened, their reflexes honed by their ordeal. They found comfort in routine, in the predictable rhythm of their days, in the simple acts of friendship, laughter, shared meals. They recreated their own rituals, like their nightly campfire sessions, transforming the fear into a shared experience, a mutual vigilance that strengthened their bonds rather than isolating them in their individual traumas.

Kiel's art began to evolve, mirroring their collective healing. His initial sketches, raw and visceral, gave way to paintings that incorporated elements of hope, resilience, and the beauty of the natural world. He used his art to represent their journey, documenting the physical and emotional scars, their healing, and their enduring camaraderie. His paintings, exhibiting in a small local gallery, received both critical acclaim and significant public attention. The renewed interest in his work brought him new opportunities and enhanced his sense of self-worth, strengthening his conviction that he had overcome his trauma.

Demitra's visions continued, leading her down an unexpected path. She started connecting with others who had experienced similar phenomena, forming an underground network of individuals with extraordinary abilities. She realized that the conspiracy was far larger and more insidious than she had initially imagined, encompassing individuals in positions of power, manipulating events from behind the scenes. This understanding strengthened her resolve to expose the truth, to prevent others from suffering the same fate.

Sarah's campaign gained momentum, attracting the attention of national media outlets. Her advocacy work reached a wider audience, and her campaign gathered support from unexpected quarters. She used her influence to advocate for legislation that would increase transparency in genetic engineering research and hold accountable those who abused the power of science. Her grief had been transformed into a force for change, a beacon of hope for others who had lost loved ones to negligence and corruption.

Grayson, in his quiet way, continued to be the steady hand that guided his friends. He helped them navigate the bureaucratic maze of insurance claims and legal proceedings, ensuring they received the care and support they needed. He was their anchor, their support system, providing the stability they needed as they rebuilt their lives and began to confront the larger conspiracy they had stumbled upon.

The setting for this new chapter in their lives was their own chosen sanctuary—a secluded cabin nestled deep within the woods, far from the city's noise and the reminders of their ordeal. It was a space where they could heal, reflect, and plan their next steps. The cabin became a symbol of their resilience, a testament to their collective strength. It was more than just a place to live; it was a haven, a refuge, a fortress built on friendship, shared trauma, and a shared determination to uncover the truth.

They knew their fight was far from over. The scars remained, both visible and invisible, a constant reminder of the horrors they had endured. But the scars were also badges of honor, symbols of their survival. They were no longer victims, but survivors, united by a shared trauma that had forged them into an unbreakable bond. They were ready for whatever lay ahead, ready to confront the darkness, ready to fight for justice, ready to face the unknown, together. Their new normal wasn't a return to innocence; it was a step toward empowerment. They had faced hell and emerged, scarred but unbroken, ready to reclaim their lives and fight for a future where such horrors could never happen again. The quiet hum of fear remained, but now it was a low, steady rhythm, a constant reminder of their shared vigil, a testament to their unbroken bond, a driving force that propelled them forward, towards the unknown future, together.

Chapter 14: Vigilance

The cabin, nestled deep within the whispering pines, offered a deceptive sense of peace. The days were long, filled with the quiet rhythm of chores – chopping wood, drawing water from the well, preparing meals over the crackling fire. But the quiet was punctuated by the sharp crack of a twig, the rustle of unseen creatures in the undergrowth, the sudden, chilling silence that descended like a shroud. Their hyper-vigilance was a constant companion, a shadow that followed them even into their sleep.

Night brought a different kind of fear. The darkness, once a comforting blanket, now held a malevolent energy, a palpable sense of being watched. The moon, a pale sentinel in the inky sky, cast long, distorted shadows that danced and writhed like the creatures they had escaped. Sleep offered little respite; their dreams were haunted by the gruesome campsite, the relentless chase, the screams of Mark. They woke frequently, startled by their own breaths or the creak of the old cabin settling. They slept in shifts, one always awake to guard the others, their senses sharpened, their reflexes honed.

Their routine became a ritual, a sacred dance between the need for normalcy and the ever-present threat. They checked the perimeter of the cabin each morning, scanning the woods for any sign of intrusion. They practiced self-defense techniques, honing their skills in hand-to-hand combat and weapon use. They studied survival skills – tracking, trapping, foraging – transforming their fear into knowledge, their vulnerability into strength.

Kiel's art had become a mirror reflecting their emotional landscape. His paintings, initially dominated by the grotesque imagery of their ordeal, gradually evolved. The darkness persisted, but it was now interwoven with threads of hope, resilience, and the enduring power of their friendship. He painted the cabin, bathed in the warm glow of firelight, a sanctuary against the encroaching darkness. He painted the forest, capturing its beauty and its menace in equal measure, acknowledging both the threat and the solace it offered. He painted portraits of his friends, capturing their strength, their scars, their shared trauma, transforming the pain into something beautiful, something enduring. His art was no longer a mere escape; it was a testament to their collective survival, their unwavering determination.

Demitra's visions continued, becoming increasingly complex and cryptic. She no longer saw mere glimpses of the future; she saw intricate webs of interconnected events, glimpses of a larger conspiracy that extended far beyond Blackwood Cave. She deciphered coded messages in her dreams, drawing intricate maps and diagrams, connecting fragmented pieces of information. Her visions were becoming a roadmap, guiding them toward a hidden truth, a network of individuals operating in the shadows, manipulating events from the highest levels of power. The more she learned, the more terrifying the reality became, but her resolve only strengthened.

Sarah's campaign continued to gain momentum. She testified before Congress, her words ringing with the authority of experience, her passion igniting a firestorm of public outrage. Her advocacy work spurred investigations, leading to the exposure of unethical practices and illegal genetic engineering experiments. The campaign demanded accountability, justice, and the closure of rogue research facilities. The weight of responsibility was immense, but she bore it with a quiet strength, fueled by her loss and her determination to prevent future tragedies. Her work was a testament to the transformative power of grief, a symbol of hope arising from the ashes of devastation.

Grayson remained the steady hand, the quiet force that held them together. He was their strategist, their negotiator, their protector. He researched ancient texts and occult lore, searching for answers to the questions that haunted them. He painstakingly pieced together fragments of information, unraveling the threads of a conspiracy that reached back centuries, a web of hidden knowledge and ancient evils. He was their shield against the darkness, their unwavering support in the face of overwhelming odds. He understood the magnitude of the danger they faced, but his unwavering belief in their collective strength kept him focused, determined, and ready to confront the future.

The vigilance was unending. They lived with a constant awareness of the unseen, the unspoken. Their senses remained heightened, their reflexes sharp, their instincts honed. They were always watching, always listening, always waiting. The fear was an intrinsic part of their lives, a constant companion that bound them together, a reminder of the horrors they had endured and the long road ahead.

Months turned into years. The scars remained – physical and psychological – but they were fading. The cabin, once a temporary refuge, had become their home. Their shared experience had transformed them, forging them into a unit, a force to be reckoned with. They were no longer the naive teenagers who had stumbled into Blackwood Cave; they were survivors, hardened by experience, united by a common purpose, driven by a shared determination to uncover the truth and prevent others from suffering their fate. They knew the fight was far from over. The ancient evil, whatever it was, remained at large. The creatures, the product of a twisted experiment, were still out there, somewhere in the darkness. The conspiracy extended far beyond the cave, reaching into the highest levels of power. But they were ready. They were watching. They were waiting. And they would not rest until justice was served and the darkness was finally extinguished. Their vigilance was eternal. Their bond, unbreakable. Their resolve, unwavering. The quiet hum of fear remained, a constant reminder, but it was no longer a source of paralysis, but a catalyst for action. The fight had just begun.

The weight of what they'd endured settled upon them like a shroud, heavy and inescapable, yet strangely unifying. The cabin, once a mere refuge, had become a testament to their shared trauma, a physical manifestation of their collective resilience. Every chipped paint on the weathered siding, every creak of the floorboards, every shadow cast by the flickering firelight, served as a tangible reminder of their ordeal. It was a shared burden, this constant awareness of the horrors they'd faced, a silent pact to never forget, to never let the memory fade. The silence within the cabin was not the peaceful quiet of a forgotten wilderness, but a tense, watchful stillness, punctuated by the occasional sigh or the rustling of papers as Grayson delved deeper into his research. The air hummed with unspoken anxieties, a collective breath held, a shared vigil against the encroaching darkness.

Kiel, despite the obvious scars that marred his arms and legs, had found a different kind of solace in his art. His canvases, once filled with the grotesque imagery of their escape from Blackwood Cave—the twisted, bioluminescent forms of the creatures, the blood-soaked ground of the campsite—now held a different narrative. The horrors remained, etched in bold strokes of charcoal and crimson, but they were now interwoven with images of strength, resilience, and unwavering friendship. He painted Demitra, her eyes reflecting a fierce intensity that belied the fragile beauty of her face, the visions dancing behind her gaze hinting at the burden she carried. He captured Sarah's unwavering determination in a series of portraits, her face etched with the grief of loss but her eyes burning with a steely resolve. And Grayson, the quiet protector, was immortalized in a charcoal sketch, his gaze distant yet watchful, a symbol of their collective vigilance. He painted the forest, not as a place of terror, but as a sanctuary, a resilient entity bearing witness to their ordeal. These weren't just paintings; they were a shared narrative, a visual chronicle of their survival, a testament to their unbreakable bond.

Demitra's visions, once fragmented and terrifying, had begun to coalesce, forming a chillingly coherent picture. The cryptic messages in her dreams had become less metaphorical, revealing a network of powerful individuals complicit in the horrors of Blackwood Cave, individuals who had used the cave as a testing ground for their grotesque experiments. Her visions were no longer fleeting glimpses of the future but detailed blueprints of the conspiracy, showing how the project had been funded, how the creatures had been engineered, and how they were planned to be deployed. The maps she drew, intricate webs of connections between seemingly unrelated events and individuals, were not merely sketches of the future, but roadmaps to expose a deeply rooted and disturbing conspiracy that stretched from the shadowy corners of clandestine research facilities to the highest echelons of power. The weight of this knowledge was immense, but Demitra carried it with a quiet strength, her visions becoming a shared responsibility, a collective burden to unravel. She would share these visions, not with trepidation, but with the determined understanding that their collective efforts were needed to unravel this terrifying truth.

Sarah, her political campaign gaining momentum, channeled her grief into action. She wasn't just fighting for justice for Mark and for the victims of the Blackwood Cave massacre; she was fighting for the future, ensuring that such horrors never repeated themselves. Her powerful testimony before Congress, laced with the raw emotion of her experience, struck a chord with the public, sparking widespread outrage and demanding accountability. Her advocacy work led to investigations, exposure of unethical practices, and the eventual dismantling of several clandestine research facilities. While her campaign aimed for legislation that would tighten regulations on genetic engineering and prohibit such unethical practices, the personal toll of fighting such a powerful, entrenched network remained immense. She faced threats, intimidation, and the constant weight of potential failure. But the shared understanding she had with her friends, a silent agreement to continue the fight, provided strength and motivation to continue her fight. It was a shared burden; not solely her responsibility, but a promise made within the sanctuary of the cabin to fight for justice, for the memory of Mark, and for the future.

Grayson, the quiet scholar, immersed himself in research, uncovering ancient texts and occult lore that hinted at the origins of the creatures, the history of Blackwood Cave, and the existence of a sinister organization that had manipulated events for centuries. His findings were unsettling, revealing the existence of an ancient evil that far predated the recent experiments, a hidden knowledge woven into the fabric of the cave itself. His late nights spent deciphering ancient texts and translating cryptic symbols were not merely acts of research; they were acts of shared responsibility, aimed at uncovering the truth and finding a way to combat the conspiracy. He was the steady hand that guided their investigation, his findings a shared asset, strengthening their resolve and guiding their actions. The knowledge he uncovered was a shared burden, to be carefully analyzed and strategically utilized in their continued fight.

Their vigilance remained unwavering. The fear was still present, a constant reminder of their ordeal, but it was no longer paralyzing. It was a catalyst, a shared driving force that fueled their resolve. Their lives were a carefully constructed balance between the ordinary and the extraordinary, the mundane tasks of maintaining their makeshift home and the extraordinary responsibility of uncovering a vast conspiracy. They shared meals, laughter, and quiet moments of reflection, but always with an undercurrent of awareness, an unspoken understanding of the ever-present danger. The cabin was a sanctuary, but it was also a base camp, a launchpad for their relentless pursuit of truth and justice.

The shared burden was not just the weight of their shared trauma, it was the weight of responsibility, the weight of knowledge, the weight of hope. They knew that the fight was far from over, that the darkness still lurked, that the conspiracy remained vast and powerful. But they were united, bound by their shared experience, strengthened by their shared grief, driven by their shared determination. They were no longer victims; they were warriors, united against the darkness, their vigilance an unbreakable bond forged in the fires of their ordeal. Their shared burden was also their shared strength. The fight had just begun, and they were ready. They were watching. They were waiting. And they would not rest.

The fire crackled, casting dancing shadows on the walls of the cabin, mirroring the restless energy that thrummed beneath the surface of their quiet vigil. Days bled into weeks, the rhythm of their lives a carefully orchestrated balance between the mundane and the extraordinary. They tended to the small garden they'd painstakingly cultivated, a splash of vibrant green against the backdrop of the unforgiving wilderness, a symbol of their own tenacious growth in the face of unimaginable horror. They shared meals, simple fare cooked over the open fire, the aroma of woodsmoke and herbs a stark contrast to the lingering scent of blood and decay that still clung to their memories. They laughed, sometimes, a brittle, fragile sound that served as a testament to their resilience, a defiant assertion against the encroaching darkness. But beneath the veneer of normalcy, a quiet intensity persisted, a shared awareness of the vast, looming threat that still cast its long shadow over their lives.

Grayson, his face etched with the fatigue of countless sleepless nights spent poring over ancient texts, presented his findings. He'd unearthed a disturbing history, a chronicle of Blackwood Cave that stretched back centuries, a history intertwined with the rise and fall of civilizations, with whispered legends of an ancient evil that predated recorded history. He spoke of rituals, sacrifices, and the deliberate cultivation of a darkness that far surpassed the genetically engineered horrors they'd encountered. The creatures they'd fought were but pawns in a much larger, more ancient game, mere manifestations of a power that resided deep within the earth, a power that had been awakened and manipulated by those who sought to control it.

His research revealed a network of hidden societies, secret orders that guarded this knowledge, manipulating events from the shadows, pulling the strings of power from behind a veil of secrecy. He spoke of symbols, of cryptic ciphers woven into the fabric of ancient languages, revealing a chilling connection between the Blackwood Cave massacre and historical events that had been dismissed as mere coincidence or folklore. The pieces of the puzzle, painstakingly assembled from fragments of forgotten texts and obscured historical accounts, painted a picture far more terrifying than anything they could have imagined. It wasn't just about a single conspiracy; it was about a centuries-old war against an ancient evil, a war that they had inadvertently stumbled into, a war they were now inextricably bound to.

Demitra's visions, initially fragmented and terrifying, had become clearer, more focused. Her dreams now provided not only glimpses into the future but a deeper understanding of the ancient evil itself, its origins, its methods, and its ultimate goals. She spoke of a cyclical pattern of destruction and rebirth, a horrifying rhythm of chaos and oblivion that seemed to dictate the fate of humanity. Her visions revealed the location of hidden repositories of knowledge, ancient artifacts imbued with power that could either destroy or protect the world. The weight of this knowledge was immense, yet Demitra bore it with a newfound strength, a quiet determination that bordered on the supernatural. Her art, initially a form of therapy, now evolved into a tool for communication, a way to translate her visions into tangible forms, to share the burden of her knowledge with her friends.

Sarah, her political campaign now a platform for exposing the truth, used her influence to push for investigations into clandestine research facilities and the shadowy organizations that funded them. She faced intense pressure, threats, and attempts to discredit her, but her determination remained unwavering. The shared understanding with her friends, the knowledge that they were all fighting the same battle, fueled her strength. She knew that the political battle was only one front in a much larger war, but it was a crucial front, one that would determine the future of humanity's ability to combat this ancient evil. She transformed grief into action, transforming her personal tragedy into a platform for raising awareness, demanding accountability, and pushing for legislation to prevent future atrocities.

Kiel, his art evolving beyond its initial cathartic function, now served as a conduit for communicating the danger to a wider audience. His canvases, once filled with the visceral horrors of their escape, now depicted the ancient evil, the hidden symbols, the intricate network of those who sought to control it. His work became a visual testament to the conspiracy, a warning to the world. He used his art to transcend language barriers, to communicate the urgent need for vigilance, to awaken a sleeping world to the impending threat. His art was not just a personal journey of healing but a shared responsibility, a warning cry echoing across the world.

Their collective efforts resulted in the formation of a covert task force, a small, highly skilled group dedicated to uncovering the truth and combating the ancient evil. They shared their knowledge, combining their individual strengths to create a formidable force. Grayson's research, Demitra's visions, Sarah's political influence, and Kiel's artistic communication all played crucial roles in their mission. They faced constant threats, near-misses, and setbacks, but their bond remained unbreakable, their resolve unshaken.

Their greatest contribution, however, wasn't in simply battling the immediate threat but in preparing for the future. They created a hidden archive, a repository of their knowledge, a testament to their ordeal and a warning for future generations. This archive, secured deep within the wilderness, contained all of their findings – Grayson's research, Demitra's visions, Sarah's political documentation, and Kiel's art. It served not only as a record of their struggle but as a blueprint for future generations to understand the ancient evil and how to potentially fight against it. They documented their discoveries, ensuring that the knowledge they had so painfully acquired would not be lost. They developed a system of coded messages, intricate symbols, and hidden clues that would allow future generations to access the archive, passing the torch of vigilance to others.

The passing of the torch wasn't a symbolic gesture; it was a vital necessity, a desperate gamble against oblivion. They knew that the fight against the ancient evil was far from over.

The darkness remained, a persistent, insidious threat, but they would not be defeated. They had faced the worst and survived, and in their survival, they had found not only resilience but a sacred duty to protect the future. They knew the struggle was a marathon, not a sprint; a legacy, not a momentary victory. Their legacy would be vigilance, a constant watch, a shared responsibility to ensure that the ancient evil remained dormant, that its horrors would not be unleashed again upon the world. The fire in the cabin burned brightly, a beacon against the encroaching night, a symbol of their unwavering determination to protect the world, not just for themselves, but for all who would come after them. The watch continued, ever vigilant, ever watchful, ever prepared. The torch had been passed. The fight was far from over.

The cabin, nestled deep within the protective embrace of the ancient forest, became their headquarters, a sanctuary from the prying eyes of the world, yet a strategic command center for their burgeoning operation. The quiet hum of activity within its walls belied the gravity of their mission. The air thrummed with a purposefulness born of shared trauma and a fierce determination to prevent future catastrophes. Gone were the days of raw, desperate survival; now, their focus shifted to strategic preparedness, a proactive defense against the insidious threat that lurked beneath the surface of the world.

Grayson, his gaunt face illuminated by the soft glow of a monitor displaying complex algorithms and encrypted data, continued his relentless research. He wasn't merely piecing together the past; he was building a comprehensive database of the ancient evil's weaknesses, its patterns, its methods of manipulation. He delved into forgotten languages, deciphering ancient texts that hinted at rituals and counter-rituals, exploring the subtle nuances of the symbols that marked the ancient evil's influence. He collaborated with cryptographers and linguists from around the world, building a network of specialists who shared his relentless pursuit of knowledge. He established a secure server farm, cloaked in multiple layers of encryption, protecting their findings from prying eyes and potential threats. The data was backed up in multiple undisclosed locations, a safeguard against sabotage or destruction. He wasn't just studying history; he was building a strategic playbook for future conflict.

Demitra's visions, once a source of terror, had become a roadmap to understanding the ancient evil's capabilities. Her dreams, recorded and analyzed, revealed not only its strategic plans but also its vulnerabilities. She learned to control the flow of her visions, to focus them, to extract vital information that could be used to inform their strategies. She worked with neuroscientists and psychologists, exploring the neurological basis of her abilities, pushing the boundaries of scientific understanding to harness the power of her visions for the greater good. They created a secure space within the cabin, designed to optimize the conditions for her visions, a chamber shielded from external interference, where she could safely delve into the depths of her psychic abilities. Her art, now deeply symbolic, served as a visual representation of her visions, a language accessible to others, a bridge between the unseen and the tangible.

Sarah, leveraging her political connections and newfound credibility, worked tirelessly to expose the truth to the world, one carefully orchestrated step at a time. She focused on the systematic dismantling of the shadowy organizations that funded the research into genetic engineering and the manipulation of ancient evils. Her political influence, honed by experience and tempered by grief, allowed her to navigate the treacherous world of international politics, exposing the corruption and deceit behind the seemingly innocuous facade of scientific progress. She built alliances, cultivating relationships with like-minded individuals within government agencies, leveraging her reputation to initiate investigations into clandestine activities. She established a network of informants within these organizations, working to uncover evidence that could be used to dismantle their operations and bring their perpetrators to justice. She knew the fight was a marathon, not a sprint, and her political strategy was designed for long-term success.

Kiel, his artistry transformed from a cathartic outlet into a powerful instrument of public awareness, created a series of artworks that subtly revealed the truth, seeding the world with visual clues and hidden messages. He worked with art historians and cultural influencers, positioning his work in influential galleries and museums, creating a subliminal campaign that informed the public without overtly revealing their secret knowledge. He established a global network of artists who mirrored his style, creating a visual language that subtly alluded to the larger threat, weaving a tapestry of interconnected images that only those in the know would fully comprehend. His artwork became a silent, yet powerful, warning to the world. His art was no longer just a reflection of his personal trauma, but a strategic tool in their war against the ancient evil.

Their collective efforts culminated in the creation of a global network of vigilance, a network of hidden cells spread across the world, each comprised of individuals from various walks of life – scientists, artists, politicians, and ordinary citizens – all bound by their shared knowledge and their commitment to protecting humanity. They established secure communication channels, developing a complex system of codes and encrypted messages to safeguard their information. They created training programs, preparing individuals for potential future confrontations, honing their combat skills, and equipping them with the knowledge they needed to face the ancient evil. They built a vast network of hidden caches of supplies and weaponry, strategically positioned across the globe, ensuring that they had the resources to confront any threat, no matter where it might emerge.

They didn't merely react; they prepared. They anticipated, they strategized, they planned for every conceivable scenario. They researched potential weaknesses of the creatures, devising countermeasures that were based on Grayson's intricate understanding of the ancient evil's weaknesses. They planned for different types of attacks, developing contingency plans that accounted for various forms of conflict. They established communication protocols, ensuring that they could coordinate their actions effectively, even under duress. They simulated potential scenarios, developing their teamwork and strategy in controlled environments before confronting a real threat. They didn't want to merely survive; they wanted to prevail. They wanted to protect humanity from the ancient evil, and to ensure its dormancy for generations to come. The fire in their cabin burned steadily, not just a source of warmth, but a symbol of their unwavering commitment – a beacon against the encroaching darkness, a testament to their preparedness, a promise of vigilance for the future. The watch continued. The fight had only just begun.

The months that followed were a blur of shadowed figures, hushed conversations, and the constant, gnawing dread that clung to them like a shroud. The vibrant hues of their youthful lives had been leached away, replaced by a muted palette of exhaustion, grief, and a chilling, ever-present awareness of the lurking danger. Blackwood Cave had stolen a piece of each of them, leaving behind gaping wounds that no amount of time could fully heal. Their laughter was now a distant memory, replaced by the strained silences that stretched between them, punctuated only by the occasional, involuntary shudder.

The cabin, though a sanctuary, had become a somber testament to their shared ordeal. The walls, once alive with the boisterous energy of teenage life, now echoed with the ghosts of their past. Each creak of the floorboards, each rustle of leaves outside, sent a jolt of adrenaline through their bodies, reminding them of their vulnerability. Sleep became a luxury, a brief respite from the nightmares that haunted their waking hours. The constant vigilance, the unspoken understanding that the threat remained, hung heavy in the air.

Grayson, his eyes perpetually shadowed with fatigue, continued his relentless research, his fingers flying across the keyboard, deciphering cryptic symbols, analyzing genetic sequences, piecing together the fragments of an ancient, terrifying puzzle. The weight of the world rested upon his shoulders, the responsibility of understanding and countering the ancient evil pressing down on him with crushing intensity. He poured over satellite imagery, searching for anomalies, for patterns that might betray the presence of the creatures, their breeding grounds, or their methods of travel. He worked in shifts, fueled by caffeine and the sheer force of his determination, rarely allowing himself to sleep more than a few hours at a time. He was driven by a fear not of failure, but of success coming too late, of the unspeakable horrors that might befall the world if his efforts fell short.

Demitra's visions were less frequent, but no less terrifying. They arrived in fragmented bursts, glimpses of horrifying landscapes, of grotesque creatures contorting themselves in unnatural ways, of clandestine meetings in shadows, and whispers of unspeakable plans. The vivid images, once overwhelming, were now distilled into raw data points, pieces of a larger, disturbing puzzle. The visions felt like scars, permanently etched onto her mind, but she learned to control them, to sift through the chaos and identify the critical information that Grayson and the others needed. The constant strain on her mind was physically exhausting, and yet, she held fast, knowing that her gift – a cruel twist of fate – was now their greatest weapon. Her art became a form of therapy, a visual journal of her torment and her strength.

Sarah, navigating the treacherous currents of international politics, had become a phantom, a whisper in the corridors of power. She moved with a quiet determination, her every move carefully calculated, her words carefully chosen. She worked to discredit those who sought to exploit the creatures, to expose the funding networks and the shadowy organizations that sought to profit from the ancient evil's power. The fight was long and arduous, requiring patience and persistence in equal measure. She had become acutely aware of the constant surveillance, the subtle threats, the veiled attempts to silence her. But fear, which once paralyzed her, had been replaced by a steely resolve, fueled by the memory of her fallen friends and the weight of responsibility to expose the truth. She knew she had to succeed; for their memories, for the world.

Kiel's art evolved. His paintings no longer reflected a raw emotional response to trauma, but carried a subliminal message. He used coded symbols, hidden within the vibrant colors and surreal landscapes, messages only those initiated into their circle could decipher. He turned his art into a potent weapon against the ancient evil; a silent warning, subtly placed in galleries and museums around the world, an infiltration of the established art scene – a clever yet dangerous subterfuge. The risk was immense, as the identification of his style could bring immediate and devastating consequences. But the responsibility, the necessity of his action, far outweighed his fear. He knew that his art was more than just a creative expression – it was a crucial part of their defense, an alert system for the few who were awake to the threat.

Their network of silent guardians expanded, slowly, deliberately, drawing in individuals who shared their secret knowledge, individuals from every corner of the globe. Scientists, analysts, linguists, hackers, politicians – people from all walks of life – became part of this hidden, global community. They met in coded locations, communicated through encrypted channels, their every move carefully calculated. They lived in the shadows, perpetually vigilant, their world divided between the deceptive normalcy of their everyday lives and the grim reality of the ancient evil's continued threat.

The training was brutal. Each member honed their skills, mastering hand-to-hand combat, weapons proficiency, survival techniques. They were not simply observers; they were preparing for a war, a silent, strategic campaign that might erupt at any moment. The knowledge they held was a burden, a heavy weight of responsibility. Every moment was steeped in an undercurrent of anxiety, the ever-present fear that they were being watched, that their secrets would be discovered.

The atmosphere within their small group was often tense, laden with unspoken anxieties and the ever-present shadow of the past. The shared trauma bound them together but also created a chasm of unspoken grief that threatened to fracture their alliance. Their conversations were punctuated by silences, an unspoken understanding of the horrors they had faced, a mutual agreement to avoid revisiting the psychological wounds inflicted by their experience. They had lived through hell and had brought back memories too dark and gruesome to ever fully share, but they knew their shared experience gave them a unique bond.

Their strategy was more than just reacting to potential threats; it was anticipating, analyzing, planning for every possibility. Their efforts were both defensive and offensive. They created a system of early warning signs, utilizing satellite imagery, seismic sensors, and advanced AI to detect the presence of the creatures before they could launch an attack. They developed countermeasures to neutralize the creatures, drawing upon Grayson's research and Demitra's visions. Their preparation was exhaustive, obsessive even, a relentless pursuit of knowledge and preparedness that allowed them to sleep only through sheer exhaustion.

The watch continued, relentless and unwavering. The world lived on, oblivious to the looming darkness, its citizens unconcerned about the silent guardians who kept vigil, prepared to face the horrors that lurked just beneath the surface of their everyday lives. The fight for humanity's survival was far from over, a war waged in shadows, fought with determination, dedication and a profound sense of dread. The silence, more than any words, served as a constant, sober reminder of the immense task that lay ahead. The vigilance, the constant, unrelenting watch, was the only thing that stood between them and utter annihilation. And so, they waited, armed and prepared for the inevitable return of the ancient evil. The shadows stretched, the silence held, and the watch continued.

Chapter 15: Epilogue

The old farmhouse stood silent, nestled amongst rolling hills that shimmered under the summer sun. Years had passed since the ordeal in Blackwood Cave, years that had etched themselves onto the faces of its inhabitants, leaving behind a tapestry of quiet resilience and lingering scars. The vibrant laughter of carefree youth had been replaced by a subdued hum of activity, the sounds of lives carefully rebuilt, yet still tinged with the echoes of past trauma.

Grayson, his once perpetually shadowed eyes now holding a glimmer of weary acceptance, had traded the relentless pursuit of scientific answers for the quiet rhythm of rural life. His research continued, of course, but it was a more measured affair, conducted in the hushed solitude of a converted barn, a sanctuary shielded from the intrusive gaze of the world. The frantic energy that had once consumed him was now channeled into the cultivation of his small vegetable garden, a soothing counterpoint to the turmoil that still lived within him. The scent of soil, the gentle rhythm of nature, served as a balm to the raw wounds of his memories. He still kept in contact with the others, a subtle network of shared vigilance, but the weight of the world no longer rested solely on his shoulders. He had learned to share the burden, to accept the fragile balance between his need to understand and the necessity to preserve his own sanity. He found solace in the quiet evenings spent tending to his bees, their industrious hum a soothing counterpoint to the silent screams of his memories.

Demitra, her artistic genius now tempered with a profound sense of loss, continued to create, but her canvases had shifted from the surreal landscapes of her nightmares to more introspective, almost abstract pieces. The vibrant hues of her earlier works had faded, replaced by a more muted palette of browns, greys, and muted blues, mirroring the landscape of her emotions. Her visions had lessened, but the images still clung to the edges of her consciousness, a phantom echo of the horrors she'd witnessed. Instead of unleashing the terrifying images onto her canvases, she now used intricate, almost microscopic detail to express the fragility of life, the delicate balance between chaos and order. She found a strange peace in the intricate process, the controlled precision a welcome contrast to the uncontrolled surges of her visions. Her art remained a form of therapy, but it was a more controlled, more personal expression, a testament to her journey from victim to survivor. She started to teach art to underprivileged children, a way to express her own healing while providing a creative outlet for others.

Sarah, once a phantom flitting through the corridors of power, had stepped back from the forefront of international politics. She wasn't entirely out of the game; rather, she operated in the background, her influence more subtle, more pervasive. She had transitioned to philanthropic work, focusing on organizations dedicated to promoting transparency and accountability within government structures, ensuring that the mistakes of the past would not be repeated. Her work was less overtly political, more focused on long-term systemic change; a careful, deliberate dismantling of the networks that had facilitated the horrors they had faced. The quiet determination that had driven her through the darkness now manifested as a tireless commitment to creating lasting positive change. Her presence remained a calming force within the small group, her wisdom and strategic thinking often tempering the more impulsive reactions of her friends.

Kiel's art had evolved significantly. The surreal imagery had been replaced with a more classical style; his focus now on capturing the beauty of the natural world, subtly incorporating symbols and coded messages within his work. He'd achieved recognition within the art world, his pieces commanding considerable prices, but only a select few understood the deeper meaning embedded within his vibrant landscapes. His art remained a weapon, a silent alarm, but it was a far more subtle one, integrated within the accepted norms of artistic expression. He'd established a foundation that supported emerging artists, providing a platform for others who might unknowingly share his unique perspective. This, he believed, was a far more effective way to spread awareness of the potential dangers, subtly awakening others to the possibilities of a hidden reality.

The cabin, once a testament to their shared ordeal, was now a peaceful haven, a symbol of their resilience. The weight of their collective past still permeated the walls, but it was a weight they carried together, a shared burden that forged a bond stronger than any trauma could break. The laughter was still quiet, the silences still heavy, but there was a new understanding within their quiet communion, a silent acknowledgment of their shared journey through the darkness. Their shared experiences forged an unbreakable bond, a silent understanding that transcended words. They were family, bound not by blood, but by the fires of a shared trauma, and the shared determination to prevent the horrors they had endured from repeating themselves.

They met periodically, not in clandestine locations shrouded in shadow, but in places that celebrated the beauty of nature; quiet mountain trails, secluded beaches, or amidst the towering redwoods. Their discussions were measured, their anxieties less about the immediate threat and more about the long-term implications of their experiences. They talked about their lives, their families, their future, always conscious of the lingering shadow of what they'd survived, but no longer consumed by its power. The shadows remained, of course, reminders of the ancient evil that still lurked beneath the surface, but they no longer held the power to paralyze them.

The years had mellowed the harsh edges of their trauma, allowing space for healing, for reflection, for the quiet acceptance of what had passed. The world continued to spin, oblivious to the silent vigil they kept, the silent protectors who stood guard against the darkness that had once consumed them. Their quiet lives were a testament to their resilience, a quiet declaration of defiance against the ancient evil that sought to dominate their existence. Their peaceful existence was a calculated risk, a conscious decision to balance vigilance with the pursuit of a normal life. They recognized the ever-present threat but chose to refuse it the power to dictate their lives.

The sun set over the rolling hills, casting long shadows across the landscape. The crickets chirped their nightly serenade, a peaceful counterpoint to the inner turmoil that still lingered within them. But the serenity was a hard-won peace, a product of years of vigilance, of shared sacrifice, and a profound understanding of the fragile nature of safety. They had stared into the abyss, faced unspeakable horrors, and emerged bearing the scars of their battles, but not broken. Their lives were a quiet testament to the enduring strength of the human spirit, a silent promise that even in the darkest of times, hope, however fragile, can endure. The watch continued, but now it was a more peaceful vigil, a quiet determination to ensure that the ancient evil would never again plunge the world into the darkness they had known. The silence was no longer a constant reminder of dread, but a testament to their resilience, a quiet declaration that even the deepest darkness can be overcome. The world slumbered, unaware, but the silent guardians remained, ready, watching, waiting.

The rhythmic tick-tock of the grandfather clock in the hallway was the only sound that punctuated the stillness of Grayson's farmhouse. He sat by the window, a half-finished cup of tea cooling beside him, his gaze lost in the twilight hues painting the sky. The tranquility was deceptive; a thin veneer over the persistent unease that had become a permanent resident in his soul. The scars on his arm, barely visible beneath the long sleeves of his shirt, were a constant reminder of Blackwood Cave, a physical manifestation of the horrors he'd witnessed. He traced the faint lines with a fingertip, the ghostly touch a phantom echo of the pain. The physical wounds had healed, but the psychological ones remained, deep and festering.

Sleep offered little respite. Nightmares, vivid and visceral, dragged him back into the suffocating darkness of the cave, the chilling shriek of the creatures echoing in his ears, the slick, cold grip of fear constricting his chest. He'd learned to manage them, to recognize the signs of an impending episode, to employ the breathing techniques he'd learned from a therapist, but the underlying anxiety never truly abated. It was a constant hum beneath the surface of his daily existence, a low-level thrumming that vibrated in his bones.

Demitra's art, though a testament to her healing, still bore the imprint of her trauma. The muted palette, the detail — these weren't just artistic choices; they were reflections of her inner turmoil. She had found a new form of expression, a way to channel her fears into something beautiful, but the underlying fear remained. The visions, though less frequent, still haunted her, fleeting glimpses of twisted forms and shadowed figures lurking in the periphery of her vision. They came unbidden, sudden and jarring intrusions into her reality, shattering the fragile peace she'd managed to build. She learned to manage them, to create rituals and practices that grounded her in the present, but she never truly escaped their presence.

Sarah, despite her outward calm, carried a burden of guilt. The knowledge of the cover-up, the deliberate obfuscation of the truth, weighed heavily on her conscience. She'd dedicated her life to transparency and accountability, but the lingering shadow of her complicity in the initial deception continued to haunt her. She'd made amends, she'd attempted to right the wrongs, but the weight of responsibility still pressed upon her, a subtle but persistent pressure. She spent sleepless nights wrestling with ethical dilemmas, replaying the events of the past, searching for a way to fully atone for her involvement.

Kiel's success in the art world was a façade, a carefully constructed mask concealing the depth of his emotional scars. His paintings, ostensibly beautiful depictions of nature, were actually cryptic messages, warnings woven into the fabric of his work. Only a select few understood the coded imagery, the subtle symbolism that hinted at the terrifying truth of Blackwood Cave and the continuing threat of the creatures. He knew the danger remained, that the world was oblivious to the peril lurking beneath the surface, and he felt a responsibility to warn others, to subtly awaken them to the reality he'd witnessed. The success brought him little joy; instead, it fueled his sense of urgency, his conviction that he must continue his clandestine campaign.

Their periodic meetings, once a necessity for mutual support and strategic planning, had evolved into something more akin to a sacred ritual. They met not to strategize against an immediate threat, but to acknowledge the ever-present danger, to share their anxieties, and to reassure each other that they weren't alone in their struggle. Their conversations were a carefully orchestrated dance between normalcy and acknowledgment of the ever-present threat. They spoke of mundane things – their families, their work, their dreams – but beneath the surface of their casual conversations flowed a silent current of shared vigilance, a tacit understanding that their lives would forever be intertwined with the chilling legacy of Blackwood Cave.

The silence that enveloped them during those meetings was profound. It wasn't the silence of comfort, but rather a shared understanding of a world unseen, a reality hidden from the rest of humanity. Each silence held a weight, a silent acknowledgment of the terrifying knowledge they shared, a silent vow to protect themselves, and each other, from the darkness they knew lurked in the shadows.

The farmhouse, the converted barn, Demitra's studio, Kiel's gallery, Sarah's quiet office — each location became a sanctuary, a carefully constructed fortress against the encroaching darkness. Yet, despite their efforts to build a semblance of normalcy, the constant awareness of the unseen menace clung to them like a shadow, an insidious reminder of the horrors they had survived. The sun might shine brightly, the birds might sing their cheerful melodies, but the ever-present threat cast a long, chilling pall over their existence.

The years had brought resilience, but not immunity. The fear remained, a subtle but constant companion, a gnawing anxiety that never truly subsided. It was a testament to their courage, their perseverance, that they had managed to forge a life amidst the shadow of their trauma, but it was a hard-won victory, constantly fought and never fully achieved. The battle wasn't over; it was a constant state of vigilance, a perpetual state of preparedness, an acceptance that the world they knew was fragile, that darkness lurked beneath the surface, and that they were the silent sentinels, ever watchful, ever prepared. The shadows continued to dance in the corners of their eyes, but their steps never faltered. They lived, they loved, they healed, all the while knowing that the nightmare of Blackwood Cave was only a heartbeat away, lurking just beneath the surface of their seemingly peaceful existence. The fight was far from over. The watch continued.

The years marched on, each one a testament to their resilience, a testament to the unbreakable bond forged in the crucible of Blackwood Cave. The farmhouse, once a refuge from the immediate horror, became a symbol of their enduring friendship, a silent testament to their shared trauma and unwavering commitment to protect others. Grayson, his hands calloused from years of tending the sprawling garden that now surrounded the house, found solace in the quiet rhythm of nature's cycle. The vibrant colors of the flowers, a riot of life against the backdrop of the ever-present threat, were a counterpoint to the darkness that continued to haunt his dreams. The nightmares, though still present, had lessened in intensity, their icy grip less constricting, the screams more distant echoes. He still carried the scars, both physical and emotional, but they were no longer a source of crippling fear. They were battle wounds, reminders of a fight survived, a testament to their collective strength.

Demitra's art evolved, becoming less a reflection of her trauma and more a celebration of survival. Her canvases burst with color, vibrant and bold, her brushstrokes imbued with a newfound confidence. The muted palette had given way to a riot of hues, each one a vibrant expression of life's resilience. The visions still flickered at the edges of her perception, but she met them not with fear, but with a determined acceptance. She had learned to weave them into her art, transforming the haunting images into powerful statements of defiance, converting the shadows into light. The detail remained, a testament to her unwavering dedication, but now it served to accentuate the beauty of life's tenacious hold.

Sarah, having finally confronted the weight of her guilt, had found a new path. She channeled her energy into advocacy, using her position to shine a light on government cover-ups and corporate negligence. She dedicated her life to ensuring that no one else would have to suffer in silence, that the truth, no matter how dark, would always eventually see the light of day. The relentless pursuit of justice became her penance, her way of atoning for her past mistakes. The sleepless nights remained, but they were now filled not with self-recrimination but with a burning determination to right the wrongs that she had witnessed firsthand. The weight on her conscience hadn't lifted completely, but it was no longer crushing; it was a driving force.

Kiel, his success in the art world continuing to soar, used his influence to subtly spread awareness of the dangers lurking just beneath the surface of society. His coded messages, once hidden within his paintings, became more overt, his art taking on a new layer of meaning – a silent warning embedded within the beauty. His gallery became a gathering place, not just for art enthusiasts, but for those who sensed a truth beyond the ordinary, for those who felt the subtle tremor beneath their feet. He found a way to use his art to empower others, to help them become aware of the subtle signs of the unseen, to teach them how to recognize the whispers of the unknown. The success he attained no longer felt empty; it was a tool, a weapon against the darkness.

Their meetings, once shrouded in secrecy, became less about strategic planning and more about shared reminiscence and mutual support. They still held the underlying awareness of the ongoing threat, the knowledge that the creatures of Blackwood Cave remained at large, but the discussions now focused on the more human aspects of their shared experience. They spoke of family, of love, of the lives they had built despite the trauma they had endured. Their bond had become stronger, deeper, forged not just by shared fear but by shared resilience, by shared hope. The silence between them was no longer fraught with unspoken terror, but with a profound understanding, a shared comfort in the knowledge that they were not alone.

Their individual lives flourished, but their collective vigilance never waned. They remained ever watchful, alert to the slightest anomaly, to any hint of the unseen presence that had once so nearly consumed them. They had become a silent network, a brotherhood, a sisterhood, bound not by blood but by shared experience, a testament to the strength of the human spirit in the face of unimaginable horror. Their lives were a complex tapestry woven from threads of trauma and triumph, a story of survival and redemption against the odds.

The farmhouse, transformed into a haven of warmth and laughter, still stood as a testament to their enduring bond, a beacon of hope in the darkness. The laughter of children echoed through its halls, a sweet melody that countered the haunting whispers of the past. The scent of freshly baked bread filled the air, a comforting aroma that chased away the lingering chill. The garden, once a symbol of Grayson's quiet contemplation, now overflowed with the joyful sounds of children playing, their carefree merriment a stark contrast to the grim memories that haunted their hearts.

Demitra's studio, once a place of quiet introspection, now buzzed with creative energy. Her paintings, vibrant and full of life, reflected her newfound peace. The shadows still danced at the edges of her vision, but they no longer held the power to diminish her spirit. She found solace in her art, using it as a medium to express the strength she had discovered within herself. Her vibrant colors and bold brushstrokes became a statement of resilience, a celebration of the human spirit's ability to overcome unimaginable trauma.

Sarah's office, once a symbol of her complicity in the cover-up, was now a bastion of transparency and accountability. She dedicated her life to ensuring that others would not suffer the same fate. Her work was a testament to her transformation, a testament to her unwavering commitment to justice and truth. The weight of her guilt had become a driving force, pushing her to tirelessly seek out and expose injustice, to hold those in power accountable for their actions.

Kiel's gallery became more than a display of his artwork; it became a community center, a place of gathering and shared support. He used his influence to promote and support artists who shared his vision – artists who used their creativity to speak truth to power, to shine a light on the unseen dangers lurking just beneath the surface. His work, a combination of beauty and warning, served as a potent reminder that the world was not always as it seemed.

Their individual lives were interwoven, their experiences forming a powerful tapestry that demonstrated the resilience of the human spirit. They were a family, bound not by blood but by a shared experience, a shared trauma that had forged an unbreakable bond. They had survived the horrors of Blackwood Cave, but they had also discovered something deeper, something more profound – the transformative power of friendship, the enduring strength of the human heart. The memory of the horrors they'd witnessed was forever etched into their souls, but it was tempered by the unwavering support and unwavering love they shared. Their resilience served as a testament to the unyielding strength of their collective spirit and their enduring bond.

The years that followed brought both joy and sorrow, love and loss, but through it all, their bond remained steadfast. They were a family, bound by a shared past, united by a common purpose – to protect each other, to protect the innocent, to ensure that the horrors of Blackwood Cave would never again be repeated. The scars remained, both visible and invisible, but they were now badges of honor, a testament to their unwavering courage and resilience. Their story was a cautionary tale, a reminder of the darkness that lurked just beneath the surface, but it was also a story of hope, a testament to the enduring strength of the human spirit, and the unbreakable bonds of friendship forged in the face of unimaginable terror. The shadows might still dance in the corners of their eyes, but the light of their friendship shone brighter than ever. Their watch continued, but now, it was a vigil of hope, a vigil of resilience, a vigil of love. Their bond, forged in darkness, would endure.

The whispers of Blackwood Cave, however, refused to be silenced. They were a persistent hum beneath the surface of their lives, a low thrumming that resonated in the quiet moments, in the stillness of the night. It wasn't a constant roar, but a subtle undercurrent, a disquieting presence that reminded them of the fragility of their existence, the ever-present shadow of what they had witnessed. Grayson, tending his garden, would sometimes pause, his trowel suspended mid-air, as a cold wind, seemingly originating from nowhere, would rustle the leaves, carrying with it a faint, metallic scent that he knew all too well – the lingering aroma of blood and decay from the cave's depths.

Demitra, amidst the vibrant colors of her studio, would occasionally catch a glimpse of movement in her peripheral vision, a fleeting shadow that vanished as quickly as it appeared. The details, sharp and horrifying, would flash across her mind – the grotesque mutations, the glistening fangs, the hollow, unseeing eyes. These visions, once paralyzing, were now integrated into her art, used as a source of inspiration, a catalyst for her creativity. But they remained a constant reminder of the darkness that continued to exist, hidden just beyond the veil of normalcy.

Sarah, in her relentless pursuit of justice, found herself increasingly drawn to cases that mirrored the horrors of Blackwood Cave – cases involving suppressed research, corporate malfeasance, and government cover-ups that echoed the systematic negligence she had witnessed firsthand. She sensed a pattern, a hidden network of power, pulling the strings from the shadows, orchestrating events that seemed coincidental but were, in reality, carefully orchestrated. The whispers of the cave had become a siren's call, guiding her toward a larger, more insidious truth.

Kiel, surrounded by the beauty and success of his art, felt the weight of responsibility increasingly heavy. His art became a vehicle for warning, a subtle call to action, an attempt to awaken others to the unseen dangers lurking in plain sight. He noticed that certain art collectors, the wealthy and powerful, seemed to gravitate to his work, their interest extending beyond mere aesthetic appreciation. He sensed their curiosity hinted at more than just a passion for art. Their eyes held a knowing glint, a recognition that transcended the superficial. He suspected these individuals were more than mere patrons; they were players in a game far larger and more dangerous than he could have ever imagined. He continued to use his art as a means of communication, weaving subtle warnings, cryptic messages into his canvases, leaving breadcrumbs for others who were attuned to the whispers of Blackwood Cave.

The bond between them, however, remained their strongest weapon. Their shared trauma, instead of isolating them, had forged an unbreakable link, a deep understanding that transcended words. They met regularly, not to relive the horrors, but to strategize, to share information, to support each other in the face of an unseen enemy. They knew, instinctively, that they were being watched, that the events of Blackwood Cave were not an isolated incident. The whispers were not just a reminder of the past; they were a warning about the future.

One evening, during one of their quiet gatherings at the farmhouse, Grayson noticed a subtle change in the air. The usual comforting aroma of freshly baked bread was overwhelmed by a faint, metallic tang, the same unsettling scent that had haunted him since the cave. Demitra, her usually vibrant energy subdued, fell silent, her eyes fixed on a spot beyond the window, where the shadows seemed to writhe and twist. Sarah, her face pale, revealed a disturbing discovery – a pattern of similar incidents, similar cover-ups, reaching back decades, all connected to a single, shadowy organization. Kiel, his usually calm demeanor shaken, presented a chilling piece of evidence – a coded message hidden within a recent acquisition, a symbol that mirrored the markings he had witnessed within Blackwood Cave.

The pieces began to fall into place, revealing a terrifying truth. The creatures they had encountered in Blackwood Cave were not an anomaly; they were a product of a clandestine program, a dark experiment gone horribly wrong. The organization responsible was not merely negligent; they were actively working to conceal their actions, suppressing any information that could expose their horrifying creation. The whispers of Blackwood Cave were not just a lingering memory; they were an ongoing threat, a silent alarm signaling a much larger, more sinister plot.

Their peaceful lives, once rebuilt from the ashes of their trauma, were now threatened once more. The comfortable façade of normalcy crumbled, revealing a terrifying reality — they were not merely survivors; they were targets. The organization responsible for the creatures of Blackwood Cave was aware of their survival, and they were coming for them. The whispers had evolved from haunting reminders into a dire warning, a prelude to a new, more terrifying chapter in their lives. Their vigilance would need to be sharper, their resolve stronger. The friends, forged in the crucible of Blackwood Cave, were about to face their greatest challenge yet. Their shared trauma had created a bond stronger than any genetic manipulation, a shared determination to fight against the very darkness that had nearly consumed them.

The fight for survival had begun anew, not within the claustrophobic confines of the cave, but within the seemingly safe spaces of their ordinary lives. The whispers served as a constant reminder of the ever-present threat, a subtle pressure, a constant feeling of unease, like the low hum of an unseen machine. The shadows danced at the edges of their vision, and the scent of blood and decay lingered, a haunting testament to their past, a chilling prophecy of their future. Their tranquil havens became battlegrounds, their lives once again intertwined, not just through friendship but through shared danger, a relentless, unseen enemy that sought to erase them from existence. Their past had prepared them for this, but the future held a new level of terror, far more pervasive, far more insidious, than the horrors of Blackwood Cave. The fight wasn't just for survival anymore; it was for the soul of humanity itself. The whispers of Blackwood Cave had become a clarion call to action, a warning to the world. The battle had begun. The fight for humanity had begun.

The years that followed saw a fragile peace settle over the survivors. The wounds, both physical and emotional, healed, leaving behind a tapestry of scars – a testament to their ordeal. Grayson's garden flourished, a vibrant counterpoint to the darkness they had faced, yet the metallic tang of blood occasionally lingered in the air, a phantom scent that stirred unsettling memories. Demitra's art, once a raw expression of trauma, evolved, becoming a powerful blend of beauty and terror, a stark warning disguised as breathtaking artistry. Her canvases pulsed with a hidden energy, capturing not just the grotesque forms they'd encountered but the chilling intelligence behind them. Sarah, despite the lingering trauma, thrived in her career, becoming a formidable force in uncovering corporate conspiracies and government cover-ups, her relentless pursuit of justice fueled by the injustice she'd witnessed in Blackwood Cave. Kiel, his fame growing, used his art as a subtle form of activism, weaving coded messages into his work, alerting those who were perceptive enough to recognize the warnings he subtly embedded.

Their shared experience, however, did not leave them unchanged. The bond forged in the crucible of terror proved unbreakable, their meetings a ritualistic exchange of information, a silent acknowledgment of the lurking threat. They trained diligently, honing their physical and mental capabilities, preparing for the inevitable return of the darkness they had barely escaped. They knew, with a chilling certainty, that their victory in Blackwood Cave was not the end, but a temporary reprieve.

The passage of time, however, brought with it a new generation, born into a world seemingly untouched by the horrors they had witnessed. Children played in the sun-drenched meadows, oblivious to the shadows that danced at the edges of their innocent games. These children were the inheritors of the world, a world that the survivors had fought so desperately to protect. But the threat, as the survivors knew too well, was not easily extinguished. It was a persistent, adaptable entity, capable of evolving, adapting, and striking when least expected.

The survivors, aware of this cyclical nature of the threat, understood that they could not simply protect themselves. They had to prepare the next generation, to instill in them the vigilance and knowledge that would allow them to survive if – or rather, when – the darkness returned. This task was fraught with peril. How could they explain the horrors they had experienced to those who only knew peace? How could they instill the fear necessary to survive without crippling their spirits?

Their approach was subtle, almost clandestine. They began by sharing fragmented stories, weaving cautionary tales into bedtime stories, using allegories and metaphors to convey the underlying dangers without overwhelming the young minds. Kiel painted vivid landscapes, incorporating hidden symbols and unsettling imagery that would subtly pique their curiosity and alertness. Demitra taught art classes, using the children's own creativity as a vehicle to explore themes of resilience and the strength found in unity. Grayson introduced the children to nature, subtly illustrating the dangers of hidden predators and the importance of careful observation. Sarah, in her spare time, taught classes on critical thinking and independent investigation, encouraging them to question authority and uncover hidden truths.

Their efforts were not without their challenges. The children, initially intrigued by their stories, gradually developed a healthy respect for the unexplored and the unknown. They learned to observe their surroundings with an acute awareness, sensing the subtle anomalies and disturbances that hinted at something sinister lurking just beyond the ordinary. The survivors watched with a mixture of pride and trepidation as these children, now equipped with a heightened sense of awareness and a deeper understanding of the hidden threats, began to mimic their vigilance.

One day, a group of teenagers, emulating the youthful recklessness of the survivors, decided to explore a series of abandoned tunnels, a network of forgotten passages that ran beneath their town. These tunnels, though unknown to the general population, bore a chilling resemblance to Blackwood Cave – a claustrophobic labyrinth of darkness, echoing with the whispers of history. These teenagers, unlike their parents' generation, knew the legends. The hushed warnings passed down through subtle stories. They had, unconsciously, absorbed the knowledge the survivors had imparted, and were instinctively wary of what lay hidden beneath their feet.

Armed with flashlights and basic survival gear, these youngsters ventured into the darkness, their youthful bravado tempered by a cautious awareness. Their descent was slow and deliberate, their movements precise, their senses heightened, guided by the ancestral memory of the horrors that dwelled in the darkness. They encountered unsettling signs: strange symbols carved into the walls, disturbing graffiti, the faint scent of decay, the unnerving silence punctuated only by their own breathing and the echoing drip of water.

Their exploration revealed a startling discovery. Deep within the tunnels, they stumbled upon a hidden laboratory, a relic of a clandestine operation, the echoes of Blackwood Cave's horrific secrets. The laboratory, long abandoned, bore evidence of experiments similar to the ones conducted in Blackwood Cave. Genetic material, strange equipment, and fragmented research papers painted a grim picture – a chilling testament to a continuing threat, a renewed attempt to create the same horrors that had nearly destroyed the previous generation. They found no living creatures, but the evidence of the project's failure hinted that such an experiment would likely be repeated at a later date.

The teenagers, having absorbed the lessons of the survivors, did not panic. They carefully documented their findings, securing evidence, photographing anomalies, and making detailed notes. They understood that their discovery was not merely a historical curiosity; it was a warning, a harbinger of future peril. Unlike the survivors before them, who had stumbled into the horrors unprepared, this new generation was equipped with the knowledge and vigilance needed to anticipate, understand, and confront the threat.

Upon returning, they immediately contacted the survivors, presenting their findings with a chilling calm. The survivors, though initially apprehensive about the recurrence of the horrors, were impressed by the teenagers' preparation and astute observations. The new generation had inherited not only the knowledge of the past but also the unwavering determination to protect their future, a cycle of vigilance and courage that extended beyond the events of Blackwood Cave. The whispers persisted, but now, the echoes were met with a more resolute silence, a collective vow to defend the innocence of their children against the horrors that threatened to consume them again. The fight for humanity had not ended. It had merely taken on a new form – a quieter, more persistent vigilance against the whispers of the darkness. The future was uncertain, yet, with each passing year, their resolve only hardened, their grip on the knowledge more certain. This, the survivors realized, was the true legacy of Blackwood Cave: a generational commitment to the preservation of humanity.

Acknowledgments

My thanks go to the countless readers whose passion for the horror genre inspires me to push creative boundaries. Your feedback and enthusiasm fuel my writing. Finally, I offer my heartfelt appreciation to my family and friends for their patience and understanding during the demanding process of writing this book. Their unwavering support has been, and always is, my greatest strength.

Compact list of Definitions

Blackwood Cave: The fictional cave system serving as the primary setting of the novel, known for its history of disappearances and unexplained phenomena.

GMOs (Genetically Modified Organisms): In this context, refers to the monstrous, artificially created creatures inhabiting Blackwood Cave.

Project Chimera: A fictional clandestine government project responsible for the creation of the GMOs. Details are revealed throughout the narrative.

The Whispers: A recurring motif describing the subtle, unsettling sounds and sensations that precede the appearance of the creatures.

Disclaimer

While this novel is a work of fiction, the themes explored – namely the dangers of unchecked scientific ambition and the resilience of the human spirit – draw inspiration from various sources.